D0520654

THE BOOK OF SKAITH

THE BOOK OF SKAITH:

The Adventures of Eric John Stark

THE GINGER STAR
THE HOUNDS OF SKAITH
THE REAVERS OF SKAITH

by LEIGH BRACKETT

NELSON DOUBLEDAY, INC. Garden City, New York

Published by arrangement with Ballantine Books
A Division of Random House
201 East 50 Street
New York, New York 10022

Printed in the United States of America

CONTENTS

THE GINGER STAR 1

THE HOUNDS OF SKAITH 145

THE REAVERS OF SKAITH 301

Guide to Characters and Locale 461

THE BOOK OF SKAITH

The Ginger Star

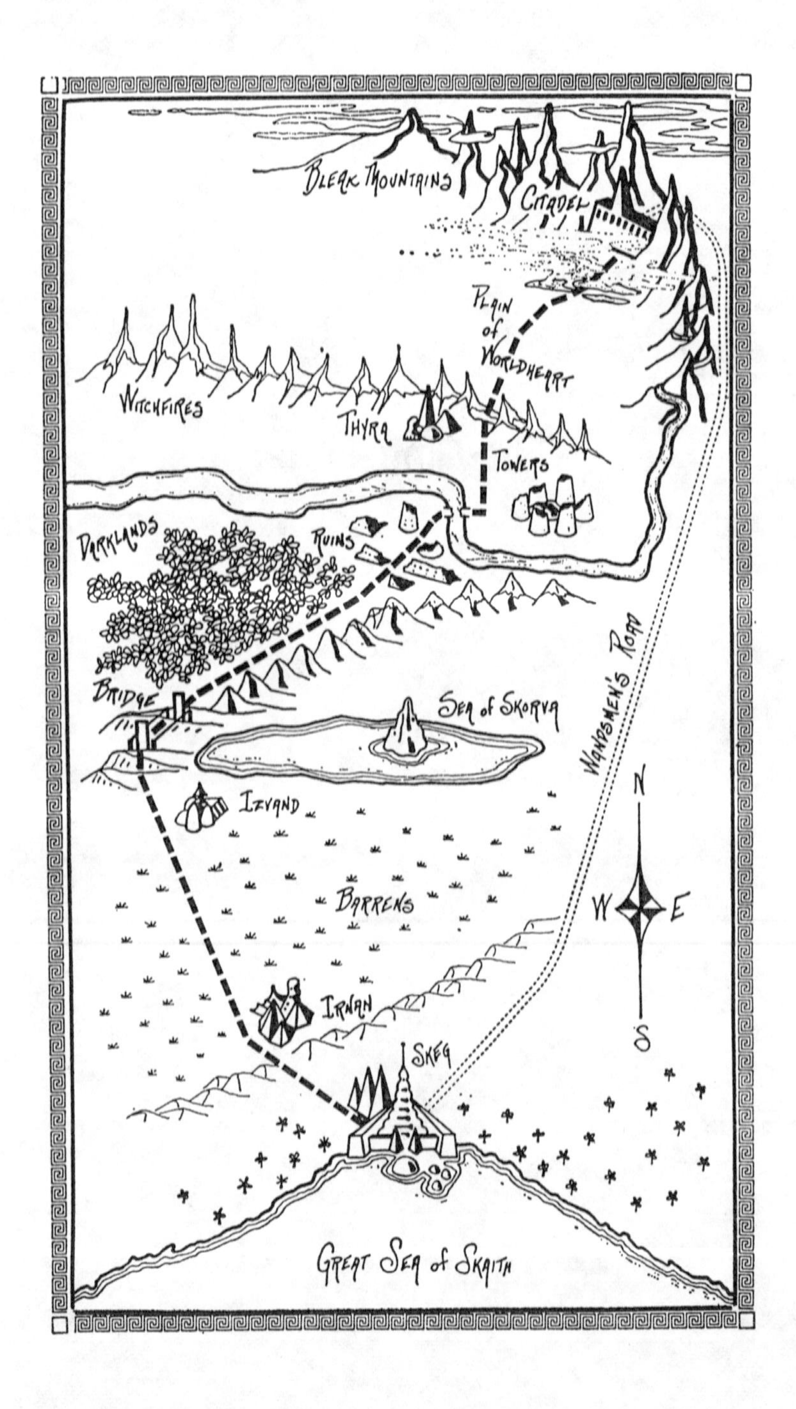
BLEAK MOUNTAINS
CITADEL
PLAIN of WORLDHEART
WITCHFIRES
THYRA
TOWERS
DARKLANDS
RUINS
BRIDGE
SEA of SKORVA
WANDSMEN'S ROAD
IZVAND
BARRENS
N
W
E
S
IRNAN
SKEG
GREAT SEA of SKAITH

1

STARK GOT his final view of Pax from the tender, going out to the spaceport moon, and that was the best view he had had of it. Pax is the chief habitable planet of Vega. It is also a city, and the proud boast of that hopefully and precariously christened world is that not one single grain of corn grows upon it, nor is one single useful item manufactured.

The city soars up into the sky. It spreads out over every landmass and swallows up small seas. It burrows underground, level upon level. Large areas of it are especially conditioned and equipped for non-humans. Everything comes into it from the outside. All supplies are shipped to the lunar docks and brought on down by freight tenders. Nothing lives on Pax but bureaucrats, diplomats, and computers.

Pax is the administrative center of the Galactic Union, a democratic federation of star-worlds flung across half the Milky Way and including, very incidentally, the worlds of little Sol. In this place the millions of problems besetting billions of people inhabiting thousands of diverse planets are reduced to tidy and easily manageable abstractions on tapes, cards, and endless sheets of paper.

A paper world, Stark thought, full of paper people.

Simon Ashton was not made of paper. Time, and accomplishments in planetary administration, had promoted him to a comfortable office at the Ministry of Planetary Affairs and a comfortable apartment in a mile-high building which he need not ever leave, if he did not wish to, except to take one of the moving walkways to work. Still, like many of his colleagues in that Ministry, Ashton had never lost his rawhide, taut-wire energy. He often went into the field, knowing that the problems of actual beings in actual places could not be solved merely by the regurgitation of data from a bank of clacking machines.

He had gone once too often into the field. He had not come back.

Stark received that information on one of the unlicked worlds outside the Union, where life was a little more relaxed for people like himself. He was, as the old phrase had it, a wolf's-head—a totally masterless man in a society where everyone respectable *belonged* to something. He bestowed his allegiance only where he chose, usually for pay. He was a mercenary by trade, and there were enough little wars going on both in and out of the Union, enough remote peoples calling on him for the use of his talents, so that he was able to make a reasonable living doing what he did best.

Fighting.

He had begun fighting almost before he could stand. Born in a mining colony in Mercury's Twilight Belt, he had fought to live on a planet that did not encourage life; his parents were dead, his foster-parents a tribe of sub-human aboriginals clawing a precarious existence out of the sun-stricken valleys. He had fought, without success, the men who slaughtered those foster-parents and put him in a cage, a snarling curiosity. Later on, he had fought for a different kind of survival, the survival of himself as a man.

He would never have got past square one without Simon Ashton.

He could remember vividly the heat, the raw pain of loss, the confinement of the bars, the men who laughed and tormented him. Then Ashton came, Ashton the wielder of authority, the savior, and that was the beginning of the life of Eric John Stark, as distinguished from N'Chaka, the Man-Without-a-Tribe.

Now twice-orphaned, Eric/N'Chaka gradually accepted Ashton as his father-in-being. More than that, he accepted Ashton as his friend. The years of his growing-up were associated almost solely with Ashton because they had been much alone in the frontier stations to which Ashton was sent. Ashton's kindness, his counsel, his patience, his strength and his affection were stamped indelibly on the fibers of Stark's being. He had gotten even his name through Ashton, who had searched the records of Mercury Metals and Mining to track down his parents.

And now Simon Ashton was missing, disappeared, on the world of a ginger star somewhere at the back of beyond, out in the Orion Spur. A newly discovered, newly opened world called Skaith that hardly anyone had ever heard of, except at Galactic Center. Skaith was not a member of the Union but there had been a consulate. Someone had called to the Union for help, and Ashton was the man who went to see about it.

Ashton had, perhaps, exceeded his authority. Even so, his superiors had done their best. But the local powers closed the consulate and refused entrance to officers of the Union. All attempts to discover Ashton's whereabouts, or the reason for his disappearance, had ended at a blank wall.

Stark caught the first available ship outbound for Galactic Center and Pax. Looking for Ashton had become his personal business.

The weeks he had spent at Pax had been neither pleasant nor easy. He had had to do a great deal of talking and convincing and, after that, much learning. He was glad to be leaving, impatient to get on with the job.

The world-city dropped behind him, and he breathed more freely. Presently the enormous intricacies of the lunar spaceport engulfed him, sorted him, tagged him and eventually spewed him into the bowels of a trim little cargo liner which took him about a third of the way to his destination. Three more changes were scheduled after that, progressively downward, into a rickety old tramp—the only sort of ship that served Skaith.

He endured the voyage, continuing by means of tapes the education into things Skaithian he had begun at Pax. He was not popular among his fellow travelers. His cabin mate complained that he twitched and growled in his sleep like an animal, and there was something in the gaze of his pale eyes that disconcerted them. They called him "the wild man" behind his back and ceased trying to lure him into games, the discussions of schemes for turning a quick profit, or personal reminiscences.

The tramp trader made several planet falls along the way. But eventually it creaked and rattled out of FTL drive within sight of a solar system lost in the wilderness of Orion Spur.

It was the fourth month, by Galactic Arbitrary Time, after Ashton's disappearance.

Stark destroyed his tapes and collected his few belongings. The rickety trader settled down on the rickety starport at Skeg, the only one on the planet, and discharged its passengers.

Stark was the first man off the ship.

His papers gave his right name, which meant nothing here, but they did not mention Pax as a point of origin for his flight. They said that he was an Earthman, which he was in a way, and a dealer in rarities, which he was not. At the barrier shed a couple of surly men confiscated his purely defensive stunner—he could have it back, they said, when he left—and searched him and his meager luggage for other weapons. He was then given a terse lecture, in bad Universal, on the rules and regulations governing life in Skeg and was sent on his way with the parting information that all roads out of Skeg except the one leading to the starport were closed to off-worlders. He was not under any circumstances to leave the city.

He rode the ten miles in a jolting cart, past plantations of tropical fruits, waterlogged paddies where some form of grain was growing lushly, and patches of jungle. Gradually the smell of mud and vegetation was overlaid by a smell of sea water, salty and stagnant. Stark did not like it much.

When the cart topped a low line of jungled hills, he found that he did not much like the look of the sea, either. Skaith had no moon, so there were no tides to stir it, and there was a milky, greasy sheen to the surface. Skaith's old ginger-colored sun was going down in a senile fury of crimson and molten brass, laying streaks of unhealthy brilliance across the water. The sea seemed a perfect habitat for the creatures who were said to live in it.

Beside the sea, on the bank of a river, was Skeg. The river had grown thin with age, too weak to do more than trickle through a narrow passage where the silt of centuries had all but closed its mouth. A ruined fortress-tower was set on low cliffs to guard a vanished harbor. But the city itself looked lively enough, with lamps and torches glowing out as the sun sank.

Presently, Stark saw the first of the Three Ladies, magnificent starclusters—the ornament of Skaith's night skies—that made it impossible to come by a decent darkness. He glowered at the Lady, admiring her beauty but thinking that she and her sisters could make things very difficult for him.

As though the situation would not be difficult enough.

The cart eventually came clumping into the town. Skeg was one great open market where almost anything could be bought or sold, and the streets were busy. Shops and stalls were brightly lighted. Vendors with barrows cried their wares. People from all over the Fertile Belt—tall, leather-clad warrior-burghers from the outlying city-states as well as the small silken folk of the tropics—mingled with the off-worlders who came to traffic, exchanging precious foreign items like iron pigs for drugs, or artifacts looted from Skaith's plentiful supply of ruins.

And of course there were the Farers. Everywhere. A conglomerate of all the races, dressed or undressed in every imaginable fashion, trooping about, lying about, doing whatever happened to occur to them at the moment; the careless itinerant children of the Lords Protector, who neither toiled nor spun, but blew lightly with the winds of the world. Stark noticed some off-worlders among them, drifters who had found the good life here in the warm twilight of a planet where everything went and where, if you belonged to the right groups, everything was free.

Stark paid off his driver and found lodgings at an inn catering to off-worlders. The room was small but reasonably clean, and the food, when he sampled it, not at all bad.

In any case, he was not interested in comfort. He was interested in Ashton.

When he had eaten, he approached the landlord in the common-room of the inn, which was built in the breezy tropical style of Skeg, being mostly windows with reed curtains that rolled down to shut out the rain. It was not raining now, and the sea wind blew through, heavy and damp.

"How do I find the Galactic Union consulate?"

The landlord stared at him. He was a dark purple in color, with a face of stone and startlingly light, very cold gray eyes.

"The consulate? Didn't you know?"

"Know what?" asked Stark, looking suitably blank.

"There isn't one. Not any more."

"But I was told—"

"The Farers wrecked it, not quite four months ago. Sent the consul and his staff packing. They—"

"The Farers?"

"Surely you were told about them at the starport. All that human garbage littering up the streets."

"Oh, yes," said Stark. "I was just surprised. They seem—well, too indolent."

"All they need is the word," said the landlord sourly. "When the Wandsmen say go, they go."

Stark nodded. "I was warned about the Wandsmen, too. Pain of death and all that. They seem to be very important men on Skaith."

"They do the dirty work for the Lords Protector. The Chief Wandsman of Skeg, the almighty Gelmar, led the Farers. He told the consul to get gone and stay gone, they wanted no more outside interference. In fact, for a while it seemed they might kick us all out and close the starport. They didn't, quite. Needed the imports too badly. But they treat us like criminals."

"I got the feeling that foreigners weren't popular," Stark said. "What was the row about?"

The landlord shook his head. "Some damned official busybody from Pax. It's a fairly open secret that he was here to arrange emigration from one of the city-states. More fool he."

"Oh? What happened to him?"

"Who knows? Except the Wandsmen." The cold eyes regarded Stark suspiciously. "Got a particular interest?"

"Hardly."

"Then drop the subject. We've had trouble enough already. What did you want with the consulate, anyway?"

"Some routine business about travel papers. It'll have to wait till my next port of call."

He bade the landlord good night and walked out.

Some damned busybody from Pax.

Ashton.

And only the Wandsmen knew what had happened to him.

Stark had made that assumption himself, some time ago, so he was not downcast. He had not expected to walk into Skeg and find signs posted to tell him his way.

He walked through the crowded streets, a dark man in a dark tunic—a big man, powerfully muscled, who carried himself as lightly and easily as a dancer. He was in no hurry. He let the city flow around him, absorbing it through all the senses, including one that civilized men have largely lost. But he was not civilized. He was aware of the lights, the colors, the mingled smells, the strange musics made by unnameable instruments and alien voices, the bright banners that hung above the sin-shops, the movements of people; underneath it all he sensed a rich, ripe stink of decay. Skaith was dying, of course, but it did not seem to him to be dying well.

He could see no reason to delay sticking his head into the noose, and so presently he entered a tavern and began his work.

He went about it most discreetly. He had spent what felt like an eternity at Pax, going with cold bitter patience through all the existing information on Skaith—learning the language, learning as much as was known about the people and their customs, talking to the ex-consul in an effort to learn more. It was already, of course, too late to save Ashton—had been too late from the moment he disappeared—if the Wandsmen had decided he should die. Two possibilities remained: rescue or revenge. For either one, Stark needed all the knowledge he could get.

It was not extensive. Contact with Skaith had only occurred a dozen or so years ago, and the consulate was not established until five years later. Much was known about Skeg and the adjacent country. Something was known about the city-states. Very little was known about the lands beyond the Fertile Belt, where most of the population of Skaith was now gathered. He had heard tall tales about the Barrens and the People of the Barrens, and perhaps some of them were true, and perhaps not.

Nothing was known about the Lords Protector, in the sense that no one knew exactly what they looked like or exactly where they dwelt—no one except the Wandsmen, who kept this knowledge as a high and holy secret. The beliefs of various sects and cults only confused matters. The consul's report had said:

"The Lords Protector, reputed to be 'undying and unchanging,' were apparently established long ago by the then ruling powers, as a sort of super-benevolence. The Great Migrations were beginning, the civilizations of the north were breaking up as the people moved away from the increasing cold, and there was certain to be a time of chaos with various groups competing for new lands. Then and later, when some stability was re-established, the Lords Protector were to prevent too great a trampling of the weak by the strong. Their law was simple: to succor the weak, to feed the hungry, to shelter the homeless, to strive always toward the greatest good of the greatest number.

"It appears that through the centuries this law has been carried far beyond its original intent. The Farers and the many smaller non-productive fragments of this thoroughly fragmented culture are now the greater number, with the result that the Wandsmen, in the name of the Lords Protector, hold a third or more of the population in virtual slavery to supply the rest.

"It is quite obvious to me that when the Wandsmen learned of the intention of the Irnanese to emigrate, they took immediate and violent action to prevent it. If Irnan were to accomplish this removal, other communities would surely follow, leaving the Wandsmen and their charges in a sad state. Ashton's disappearance and the forcible closing of the consulate came as a shock to us, but hardly a surprise."

A great deal was known about the Wandsmen.

What Stark wanted to do was seek out Gelmar and tear him slowly and painfully into small bits until he told what he had done to Ashton. This was not possible because of the Farers, the devoted, perpetual, ever-ready, instant mob. So he set himself out as bait.

For two days he walked quietly in the streets and sat quietly in the taverns and talked quietly to anyone who would listen, asking questions, occasionally letting slip the name *Irnan*.

On the evening of the second day the bait was taken.

2

He was in the principal street of Skeg, in the main market square, watching a troupe of acrobats performing indifferent stunts with a minimum of skill, when someone came and stood close to him, very close, warm and breathing.

He looked down. It was a girl—he had known that, of course, from the touch—a Farer, stark naked except for body-paint laid on in fanciful loops and spirals and her hair, which hung over her shoulders like a cloak. She looked up at Stark and smiled.

"My name is Baya," she said. It meant Graceful, and she was. "Come with me."

"Sorry. I'm not in the market."

She continued to smile. "Love can come later, if you wish. Or not, as you wish. But I can tell you something about the man Ashton, who took the road to Irnan."

He said sharply, "What do you know about that?"

"I am a Farer. We know many things."

"Very well, then. Tell me about Ashton."

"Not here. Too many eyes and ears, and that is a forbidden subject."

"Then why are you willing to talk?"

Her eyes and her warm mouth told him why she was willing. "Besides, I don't care for rules, any rules. You know the old fortress? Go there, now. I'll follow."

Stark hesitated, frowning, suspicious.

She yawned and said, "It's up to you."

She drifted away into the crowd. Stark stood a moment, then began to walk casually along the street, toward the lower end where it narrowed into a quiet lane and came at last to the river.

A bridge had been here once, but now there was only a ford paved with stones. A man dressed in a yellow robe picked his way across it, his skirts tucked up and his wet thighs flashing. Half a dozen men and women followed him in a body, holding each other's hands. Stark turned onto the broken pavement of the embankment.

The fortress was ahead, with the sea lapping the cliffs below it. The ginger star was setting in the same lurid manner as before; gaudy sunsets seemed the normal thing here. The tideless water gleamed, gradually taking on a sheen of pearl. Things swirled and splashed in it, and a strange, far-off sound of hooting voices made Stark shiver. The consul had dutifully written down what had been told to him about the Children of the Sea-Our-Mother, but he obviously had not believed it. Stark kept an open mind.

Even a stupid animal would have known it was heading into a trap, and Stark was not stupid. The ancient walls of the fortress towered beside him, still with the stillness of idle centuries, gaping doors and window-places dark and empty. He could hear nothing, see nothing that was threatening, yet the nerves rippled under the skin of his back. He leaned against the stones and waited, tasting the wet rankness of the air.

The girl came, padding on little bare feet. And there was someone with her, a tall man who wore a rich tunic of somber red and carried a wand of office. A man with a high, proud, calm face, a man of power who had never known fear.

"I am Gelmar," he said, "Chief Wandsman of Skeg."

Stark nodded. There did not seem to be anyone near but these two.

"Your name is Eric John Stark," said Gelmar. "An Earthman, like Ashton."

"Yes."

"What are you to Ashton?"

"Friend. Foster-son. I owe him my life." Stark stepped forward. "I want to know what happened to him."

"And perhaps I'll tell you," said Gelmar easily. "But first you must tell me who sent you."

"No one. When I heard that Ashton was missing, I came."

"You speak our language. You know about Irnan. You must have been at Galactic Center, to learn these things."

"I went there to learn."

"And then you came to Skaith because of your love for Ashton."

"Yes."

"I don't think I believe you, Earthman. I think you were sent to make more mischief here."

In the reddening dusk Stark saw that they were looking at him in a very odd way, and when Gelmar spoke again his tone had changed subtly, as though the seemingly innocent questions had a secret importance.

"Who is your master? Ashton? The Ministry?"

Stark said, "I have no master." His breathing now was shallow, his ears stretched for little sounds.

"A wolf's-head," said Gelmar softly. "Where is your home?"

"I have none."

"A landless man." This was beginning to have a ritual sound. "Who are your people?"

"I have none. I was not born on Earth. My other name is N'Chaka, Man-Without-a-Tribe."

Baya sighed, a little sharp sound. "Let me ask him," she said. Her eyes were very bright, catching the afterglow. "A wolf's-head, a landless man, a man without a tribe." She reached out and touched Stark with a small hand, and the fingers were cold as ice. "Will you join with me and be a Farer? Then you will have one master, love. And one home, Skaith. And one people. Us."

Stark said, "No."

She drew back from him, and her eyes seemed to grow brighter with some light of their own.

She said to Gelmar, "He *is* the Dark Man of the prophecy."

Astonished, Stark said, "What prophecy?"

"That is something they could not tell you at Pax," said Gelmar. "The prophecy was not made until after the consul had gone. But we have been waiting for you."

The girl gave a sudden cry, and then Stark heard the sounds he had been expecting.

They came from both sides, around the fortress, perhaps twenty of them, male and female, leaping grotesques of all shapes and sizes. Careless garments flapped. Hands brandished sticks and stones. Some were chanting, "Kill, kill!"

Stark said, "I thought it was forbidden to kill at Skeg."

Gelmar smiled. "Not when I order it."

Baya drew a long pin like a stiletto from the darkness of her hair.

Stark stood, in the second or two that remained to him, looking this way and that like one desperate to find a way of escape. Gelmar moved away toward the edge of the cliff, giving his Farers free room as the stones began to fly.

Out over the water, the hooting voices called and chuckled.

Stark sprang like a wild beast for Gelmar and bore him into the sea.

They sank down to a slimy bottom, and it was instantly apparent that Gelmar could not swim. Small wonder, Stark thought, and held him down relentlessly until his struggles weakened. Then he brought him to the surface and let him breathe. Gelmar stared at him in such shocked amazement that Stark laughed. Upon the cliff the Farers stood, stunned, in a ragged line.

"The Children of the Sea-Our-Mother," Stark said. "I am told they eat men."

"They do," said Gelmar, strangling. "You must be . . . insane . . ."

"What have I to lose?" said Stark, and pushed him under. When he let him up again the last of Gelmar's arrogance was gone, lost in a paroxysm of retching.

The hooting voices had come closer, and there was a new note in them of alert interest, as when hounds pick up a scent.

"Two questions," said Stark. "Is Ashton alive?" Gelmar choked and gagged, and Stark shook him. "Do you want the Children to share you? Answer me!"

Feebly, Gelmar answered. "Yes. Yes. He's alive."

"Do you lie, Wandsman? Shall I drown you?"

"No! Lords Protector . . . wanted him . . . alive. To question. We took him . . . on the road to Irnan."

"Where is he?"

"North. Citadel . . . Lords Protector . . . at Worldheart."

The Farers had begun wailing, a collection of banshees. They were forming a human chain down the cliff, reaching out their hands to succor Gelmar. The first of the Three Ladies silvered sky and sea. There was a great and savage joy in Stark's belly.

"Good. Then I will ask a third question. What prophecy?"

"Gerrith . . . wise woman of Irnan." Gelmar was finding his tongue as the seaward sounds came nearer. "She prophesied . . . an off-worlder would come . . . destroy the Lords Protector . . . because of Ashton." The eyes, no longer so proud and calm, yearned toward the cliff.

"Ah," said Stark. "Did she now? And perhaps she was right."

He thrust Gelmar from him, toward the reaching hands, but did not wait to see whether or not he made it. Across the warm and somehow unclean water there were flashes of white in the clusterlight, like many swimmers tossing spray.

Stark kicked off his sandals, put his head down, and made for the opposite shore.

The rush of his own passage blotted out all other noises, yet he knew they were gaining on him. He managed to lengthen his stroke just a fraction more. Then he began to feel the vibrations, a sort of booming in the water as something displaced it with rhythmic blows. He was aware of a body, immensely strong, impossibly swift, pulling ahead of him.

Instead of turning and fleeing blindly, as he was expected to, Stark swerved to the attack.

3

ALMOST AT ONCE, Stark realized that he had made a mistake. Quite possibly, his last one.

He had the advantage of surprise, but that was short-lived. In the matter of strength and reflexes he was as near animal as a man can reasonably be, but the creature he fought with was in its own element. Stark grappled with it and it shot upward from the water like a tarpon, breaking his grip. He saw it briefly above him in the cluster-light, outstretched arms shaking diamond drops, body girdled with foam. It looked down at him, laughing, and its eyes were like pearls. Then it was gone in a curving arc that drove it beneath the surface. Its form was manlike, except that there seemed to be webs of skin in odd places, and the head was earless.

And it was somewhere beneath him now, out of sight.

Stark rolled and dived.

The thing circled him round, flashed over him, and again was gone. It was having fun.

Stark came back to the surface. Farther out, the splashing had ceased. He could see heads bobbing about, and hear those hateful voices hooting and ha-haing. For the moment the pack seemed to be standing off, allowing their leader to play out his game.

Stark could see nothing between himself and the shore. He set off toward it again, swimming like one in a panic.

For a little while nothing happened, and the shore was so tantalizingly close that he almost thought he might make it. Then a powerful hand closed on his ankle and drew him smoothly under.

Now he had to hurry.

Recklessly expending strength because there was nothing to save it for, he bent his knees, doubling his body against the thrust of the water that wanted to keep it stretched. He grasped his own ankle, found the odd hand that did not belong there, and shifted his grip to the alien wrist. And all the time he and the sea-thing were plunging deeper, the milky light growing dimmer.

The arm was long and furred, and powerful muscles were imbedded in a layer of fat. Stark's grip kept slipping, and he knew that if he lost it he was finished. He had been over-breathing while he swam, storing up oxygen; but he was using it at a great rate, and his heart was already hammering. His fingers clawed and tore, moving convulsively toward the point of leverage.

The smooth descent stopped. The creature turned its head and Stark saw the blurred face, eyes filmed and staring, bubbles trickling from a vestigial nose. The free arm that had been oaring them downward now swung over, not toward his hands but toward the back of his neck. The game was over.

Stark sunk his head between his shoulders. Talons ripped at the wet ridges of muscle. His own hand found a grip in a web of skin backing the creature's armpit. He straightened his body with a violent thrust and his ankle came free. He pulled himself under the creature's arm.

This Child of the Sea had also made a mistake. It had underestimated its victim. The humans who came its way, capsized fishermen or ritual offerings provided by the landbound worshippers of the Sea-Our-Mother, were easy prey. These poor souls knew they were doomed. Stark wasn't sure, and he had the thought of Ashton and the prophecy to bolster him. He managed to clamp his arms around the sinewy neck from behind, to lock his legs around the incredibly powerful body.

Then he hung on.

That in itself was a nightmare. The creature rolled and sounded, fighting to shake him off. It was like riding an angry whale, and Stark was dying, dying, tightening his hold in a blind red rage, determined not to die first.

When the sodden cracking of the neckbones came at last, he could hardly believe it.

He let go. The body fell away from him, dribbling dark bubbles from nose and mouth where the trapped breath vented. Stark went like an arrow for the surface.

Instinct made him break quietly. He hung there, savoring the deliciousness of fresh air in his lungs, trying not to sob audibly as he gulped it in. He could not at first remember why being absolutely quiet was imperative. Then, as the ringing darkness in his mind began to clear, he could hear again the laughing, hooting voices of the pack, waiting for their leader to bring them meat. And he knew that he dared not rest for long.

The battle had carried him beyond the narrow boat-channel, which was as well because he could not in any case go back to Skeg. The group on the cliff, like the Children, were still waiting. He could see them only as a dark blob in the distance, and he was sure they could not see him at all. With any luck, they might think he had perished in the sea.

With any luck. Stark smiled cynically. Not that he did not believe in luck. Rather, he had found it to be an uncertain ally.

With infinite caution, Stark swam the short distance to the shore and crawled out on dry land. There were ruins on the river bank here, a tangle of old walls long abandoned and overgrown with vines.

They made excellent cover. Stark went in among them and then sat down, leaning his back against warm stone. Every joint and muscle was a separate anguish, bruised, strained, and clamoring.

A voice said, "Did you kill the thing?"

Stark looked up. A man stood in a gap in the wall, on the landward side. He had made no sound in coming there; it was as though he had been waiting for Stark's arrival and had only to move a handsbreadth. He wore a robe, and though the cluster-light altered colors, Stark was sure the robe was yellow.

"You're the man I saw at the ford."

"Yes. Gelmar and the girl came after you, and then a gang of Farers. The Farers threw stones at us and told us to go away. So we crossed back. I left my people and came down here to see what happened." He repeated, "Did you kill the thing?"

"I did."

"Then you'd better come away. They're not entirely seabound, you know. They'll be swarming here in a few minutes, hunting you." He added, "By the way, my name is Yarrod."

"Eric John Stark." He rose, suddenly aware that seaward the voices of the Children had fallen silent. Too much time had passed; they would know by now that something had gone wrong.

Yarrod set off through the ruins, and Stark followed until they had come what he thought to be a safe distance from the bar. Then he set his hand on Yarrod's shoulder and halted him.

"What have you to do with me, Yarrod?"

"I don't know yet." He studied Stark in the cluster-light. He was a tall man, wide in the shoulder, bony and muscular. Stark guessed that he was a warrior by trade, masquerading for some reason as something else. "Perhaps I'm curious to know why Gelmar would want to kill an off-worlder in a place where killing is forbidden even to the Farers."

From the sea there came a wild howling of grief and rage that set Stark's hackles bristling.

"Hear that?" said Yarrod. "They've found the body. Now Gelmar will know that you killed the thing, and he'll wonder whether or not you died also. He's bound to try and find out. Would you like to be hunted through these ruins by the Farers, or will you trust me to give you safe hiding?"

"I seem not to have much choice," said Stark, and shrugged. But he went warily behind Yarrod.

The tone of the howling changed as some of the creatures, from the distant sounds, began to clamber out onto the bar.

"What are they? Beast or human?"

"Both. A thousand or two years ago some people got the idea that the only salvation was for man to return to the Sea-Our-Mother, from whose womb we came. And they did it. They had their genes altered by some method that was still known then, to speed up the adaptation. And there they are, losing more of their humanness with every generation, and happier than we."

He increased his pace, and Stark matched it; the savage howling grew fainter in his ears. The consul might doubt the story that was told about the Children of the Sea; Stark did not. Not any more.

As though reading his thoughts, Yarrod chuckled. "Skaith is full of surprises. You've another one just ahead."

High on the bank above the ford of the river there was part of a barrel arch, intact overhead, open at both ends, which in that gentle climate scarcely mattered. Drooping vines acted as curtains. There was a fire burning inside, and the half dozen men and women Stark had seen before with Yarrod sat by it in a close group, heads together, arms intertwined. They neither moved nor looked up as Stark and Yarrod entered.

"Pretty good, aren't they?" said Yarrod. "Or do you know?"

Stark clawed back through his mental file on Skaith. "They're pretending to be a pod. And you're supposed to be a pod-master."

A pod, according to the file, was a collection of people so thoroughly sensitized by a species of group therapy that they no longer existed as individuals but only as interdependent parts of a single organism. The pod-master trained them, and then kept them fed and washed and combed until such time as the hour arrived for Total Fulfillment. That was when one of the components died and the whole organism went, finding escape at last. The average life of a pod was four years. Then the pod-master started over again with another group.

"Pod-masters can go anywhere," said Yarrod. "They're almost as holy as the Wandsmen." He turned to the group. "All right, friends, you may breathe again, but not for long. Gelmar and his rabble will be coming soon, looking for our guest. Breca, go keep watch on the ford, will you?"

The group broke up. A tall woman, evidently Breca, went past them, giving Stark a strangely penetrating look, and then vanished without a sound through the vines. Stark studied the faces of the remaining five in the firelight. They were strong faces, alert and wary, intensely curious, as though he might mean something to them.

One of the five, a big man with a contentious air and a jealous eye, whom Stark disliked on sight, asked Yarrod, "What was all that howling from the bar?"

Yarrod nodded at Stark. "He has killed a Child of the Sea."

"And lived?" He sounded incredulous.

"I saw it," said Yarrod curtly. "Now tell us, Stark. Why did Gelmar set the Farers on you?"

"Partly because I had been asking about Ashton. And partly because of a prophecy."

Now they sighed sharply, as the Farer girl had.

"What prophecy?"

"Someone called Gerrith, the wise woman of Irnan, prophesied that an off-worlder would come and destroy the Lords Protector because of Ashton." He looked at them shrewdly. "But you know all about that, don't you?"

"We're all from Irnan," said Yarrod. "We waited and waited, but Ashton never came, and then Gerrith made her prophecy and the Wandsmen killed her. What was Ashton to you?"

"What is a father to a son, a brother to a brother?" Stark moved, easing the pains of his body, but there was no ease for the deeper pain, and they saw that and were disturbed. Stark's eyes held a lambent light.

"You people of Irnan decided to leave this planet, which I can readily understand. You applied through the GU consul at Skeg, keeping the matter very confidential, for help. The Ministry of Planetary Affairs agreed to find you a suitable place on another world and to supply the ships for your emigration. Ashton came to Skaith from the Ministry to discuss this with your leaders and make the final arrangements. As someone said, more fool he—because the whole thing had stopped being confidential. Who talked?"

"None of us," said Yarrod. "Perhaps someone at the consulate. Perhaps Ashton was clumsy."

"Gelmar took him on the Irnan road."

"Did Gelmar tell you that?"

"I don't think he meant to. He had other plans for me, and the information would have been breath wasted. So I took him with me into the sea and gave him a choice."

Yarrod groaned. "You took him into the sea. Don't you know that it is forbidden, absolutely forbidden on pain of death, to lay hands upon or interfere with a Wandsman in any way?"

"I was already under pain of death, and it seemed to me that in any case Gelmar needed a lesson in manners."

They stared at him. Then one of them laughed, and then they all laughed except the big man with the jealous eye who only showed his teeth. Yarrod said, "You may be the Dark Man at that."

The curtain of vines rustled faintly as Breca returned.

"There are people," she said, "coming to the ford. About twenty of them, and in a hurry."

4

IMMEDIATELY the group fell silent. Yarrod began making swift gestures. "In here," he said in Stark's ear, and motioned to a fissure in the stonework at one side, barely large enough to accept a body the size of Stark's and of no size at all to permit any motion, offensive or defensive.

"Make up your mind," said Yarrod. "In a moment more we'll have to give you up to save ourselves."

Stark accepted the inevitable and slid himself into the crevice. The aperture was closed within seconds by the meager possessions of the Irnanese—leather bottles, sacks of meal and dried meat for the journey, a spare shift apiece—and by the pod itself, as the Irnanese formed their tight group beside the heap of dunnage. Stark had some difficulty breathing and he could not see anything, but he had been in worse places.

Provided the Irnanese did not sell him out. But he could not do much about that. He settled himself to endure.

From outside the vault he could hear no more than a muddy crowd sound. Then Gelmar entered the vault, and Stark could hear him quite clearly speaking to Yarrod.

"May your people have peace and quick Fulfillment, Master. I am Gelmar of Skeg."

Courtesy required that Yarrod should now identify himself in turn. He did so, giving a totally false name and place of origin and ending with a gravely unctuous, "What may I do for you, my son?"

"Has anyone passed this way? A man, an off-worlder, fresh from the sea, perhaps hurt?"

"No," said Yarrod, his voice steady and unconcerned. "I've seen no one. Besides, who escapes from the sea? I've heard the Children hunting within the hour."

"Perhaps the Master is lying," said a girl's voice spitefully, and Stark knew it well. "He was at the ford. He saw us."

"And your people threw stones at us," said Yarrod, sternly reproachful. "My pod became frightened, and it has cost me much effort to calm it. Even a Farer should have more respect."

"One must forgive them," said Gelmar. "They are the children of the Lords Protector. Do you lack for anything? Food? Wine?"

"There is enough. Perhaps tomorrow I shall come to Skeg and ask."

"It will be given gladly."

There were some parting formalities. Gelmar and the girl apparently left the vault, and in a moment Stark could hear whoops and cries as the Farers went haring away through the ruins.

Looking for me, Stark thought, and he was glad of his close crevice. A sorry rabble they were; but one against twenty, and the one unarmed, made for unpleasant odds.

For a time nothing happened except that Yarrod began to lead his pod in a kind of litany, a murmurous chant that almost put Stark to sleep. These people must have practiced well. There had to be a powerful reason to make them do it, and he thought he knew what it was.

The chanting faded gently to a small contented humming, and then Stark heard voices and sounds outside, returning.

Yarrod's voice came clearly. "You didn't find him?"

Rather distantly, Gelmar answered, "There was no sign. But the Children have been on the bar."

"No doubt they have already shared him, then."

"No doubt. Still, if you should see him . . . The man is a lawbreaker and dangerous. He laid hands on me and, being an off-worlder, he might not respect your robe."

"I have no fear, my son," said Yarrod, laying it on just a bit too much, Stark thought. "What do we all wish for but Fulfillment?"

"True," said Gelmar. "Good night, Master."

"Good night. And please to take your unruly flock with you. Each time the tranquillity of my pod is disturbed, the day of release is that much delayed."

Gelmar made some answer, and then there were more sounds, of people going away.

After what seemed a very long wait, Yarrod lifted aside the bundles. "Keep your voice down," he cautioned. "I think Gelmar left a few behind him. It's like trying to count vermin so I can't be sure, but I didn't see the girl."

Stark stood up and stretched. The pod had broken up again, and the woman Breca was missing, presumably on watch.

"Now then," said Yarrod brusquely, "we have a decision to make."

They all considered Stark.

"You believe that he is the Dark Man?" This was the big Irnanese who had spoken before with doubt.

"I think it likely. Gelmar appeared certain."

"But suppose he is not the Dark Man. Suppose we rush back to Irnan only to learn that. Then all our work is wasted and our mission is thrown away for nothing."

There were mutters of assent.

"That's possible, Halk. What do you suggest?"

"That we let him get to Irnan by himself. If he is truly the Dark Man, he'll make it."

"I don't particularly want to go to Irnan," said Stark, with a certain dangerous cheerfulness. "Ashton's not there."

"And well we know that," said Yarrod. "Where is he?"

"The Citadel of the Lords Protector, at Worldheart, wherever that is."

"North, in any case," said Yarrod. "And in any case, you must go to Irnan."

"Why?"

"So that Gerrith, the daughter of Gerrith, may say if you are truly the Dark Man of the prophecy."

"Oh. Gerrith had a daughter."

"All wise women have daughters if they can possibly manage it. Otherwise the precious genes are lost. And you see, Stark, we must know, or we cannot follow you. And without us and our help, you'll find it hard to do what you've come for."

"He'll find it hard anyway," said Halk, "but he might as well co-operate." He smiled at Stark. "You can't get away from Skaith now. Not through the starport. And there is no other way."

"I know that. Since I have no wish to leave, it scarcely matters, does it?" Stark turned to Yarrod. "Perhaps I can solve the immediate problem. Obviously you couldn't have come here to rescue me, so you must have had another reason. What was it?"

Yarrod fairly snarled. "We of Irnan are no longer allowed to travel without a special permit from the Wandsmen, and we didn't think they'd give us one for this journey. That's why we're flapping about in this silly disguise, so that we could come to Skeg and perhaps find out what the Galactic Union intends to do about us, if anything. I don't suppose they told you that at Pax? They seem to have told you everything else."

"As a matter of fact, they did."

The whole group moved a step closer.

"What will they do? Will they send someone?"

"They have sent someone," Stark said. "Me."

There was a sort of stunned silence. Then Halk asked, "Officially?" The sneer was audible.

"No. They've tried officially to reopen contact with Skaith, and got nowhere."

"So they sent you. Who is your master, then?"

Stark took Halk's meaning and grinned. "No one. I'm a mercenary by trade. Since I was coming anyway, the Minister asked me to find out what I could about matters here and report to him—if I survived. I take no orders from him, and he takes no responsibility for me."

"Then," said Yarrod, "that is the best we can hope for?"

"Short of an invasion, yes. And the Galactic Union dislikes force. So if you want freedom you'll have to fight for it yourselves." Stark shrugged. "You must have realized that Skaith is not the most important planet in the galaxy."

"Except to us who live on it," said Yarrod. "Very well, then. We go back to Irnan. Agreed?"

Even Halk had to admit that, satisfactory or not, they had got what they came for.

"We mustn't go too quickly," said Yarrod, frowning. "That would give us away. Gelmar will expect me in Skeg tomorrow, and he'll surely keep some sort of watch on this side of the river."

Halk said, "What about Stark? We can hardly add him to the pod."

"He must go on ahead of us, tonight. He can wait at the—"

Breca came quickly through the vines, motioning for silence. "I hear them, coming this way."

"Stark—"

"Not in that hole again, thank you, though it was a good hole and welcome at the time. Did they search the roof?"

"They did." The pod began organizing itself, soundlessly and in haste.

"Then they'll likely not bother again." Stark went out through the rearward arch, letting the vines fall back quietly into place. He stood for a moment, head cocked. He could hear people moving about, some distance away. If they thought they were being stealthy they were much mistaken. The beautiful sky glowed with its islands of milky fire. In the cluster-light, Stark studied the broken masonry of the vault and then began to climb.

5

The top of the vault offered reasonable cover, with crumbling bits of wall still standing above the edges. Stark was not so much concerned now, since the main body of Farers had gone, but it would be wiser to avoid being seen.

He had no more than settled himself when Baya and two others came in view. Gelmar might have left them behind on purpose, after the search had failed, in the hope of catching somebody off guard. Or perhaps this scheme had been Baya's idea.

She was leading the other two, both men, who were obviously very bored and as pettish as babies. One was tall and spindly, totally naked except for body-paint that looked as if he had rolled in it. His hair and beard were full of rubbish. The other man was shorter and fatter, and that was all Stark could see of him because he was completely wrapped about with lengths of bright cloth that covered even his face. The folds were stuck full of flowers.

"Let's go back now, Baya," said the tall one, turning toward the ford. "You've seen there's no one here."

"The Dark Man died in the sea," said the shorter one, his voice squeaking impatiently through his veils. "The Children shared him. How could it be otherwise?"

Baya lifted her shoulders as though a breath of cold air had touched her. She shook her head.

"I spoke to him," she said. "I touched him. There was something about him. Strength, a terrible strength. He killed a Child of the Sea, remember?"

"You're being silly," said the short one, and hopped up and down like a rabbit. "Girl-silly. You saw his muscles, and you want him to be alive. You're sorry he didn't love you before he died."

"Hold your tongue," said Baya. "Maybe he's dead, and maybe he isn't, and if he isn't, someone is hiding him. Stop whining and look around."

"But we've already searched—"

The rubbishy one sighed. "We'd better do as she says, I suppose. You know what a terrible temper she has."

They wandered off, out of Stark's sight but not out of his hearing. Baya continued to stand where she was, frowning at the flickerings of firelight that shone from the vault. Then she sauntered over, her insolent body agleam in the light of the Three Ladies. Stark lost sight of her, too, since she was directly beneath him, but he could hear the vines rustle as she swept them aside.

"Master . . ."

Yarrod's angry voice sounded from the vault. "You have no business here. Get out."

"But, Master, I'm only curious," said Baya. "I might even want to join a pod myself one day, when I'm tired of being a Farer. Tell me about them, Master. Is it true that they forget about everything, even love?"

The vines swished as she entered the vault and let them fall behind her.

The voices from within were now too muffled for Stark to understand the words. In a very few minutes a squeal of pain came from Baya, and the vines thrashed wildly as she and Yarrod came through them. Yarrod had his hand wound cruelly in her hair, and he marched her, crying and struggling, away from the vault. He took her to the river bank and pushed her in.

"You've done enough mischief for one day," he said. "If you come near my pod again, I'll make you regret it." And he spat, and added, "Farer trash! I have no need of you."

He left her and strode back to the vault. She stood in the shallow water of the ford and shook her fists at him, screaming.

"You live on the bounty of the Lords Protector just the same as we do! What makes you so much better, you—" She poured out obscenities, then choked on her own rage and ended up coughing.

There was a sudden delighted outcry from among the ruins where her two companions were poking around. She came up the bank.

"Have you found him?"

"We found love-weed! Love-weed!" The two Farers reappeared, waving handsful of something they had grubbed up, chewing greedily. The tall one held some out to Baya.

"Here. Forget the dead man. Let us love and enjoy."

"No. I don't feel like loving now." She turned away, toward the vault. "I feel like hating. Pod-masters are supposed to be holy men. This one is too full of hate."

"Perhaps it's because we threw stones," said the short one, cramming his mouth full.

"Who cares?" said the tall one, and grabbed Baya by the shoulder. "Eat this, and you'll feel like loving." He pushed some of the weed by main force into Baya's mouth.

She spat it out. "No! I must talk to Gelmar. I think there's something—"

"Later," said the Farer. "Later." He laughed, and the short one laughed, and they shoved Baya back and forth between them. The struggle seemed to pleasure them, and hasten the action of the drug. Baya pulled the bodkin from her hair. She slashed the naked one once, not deeply, and they laughed some more and took the bodkin away from her. Then they worried her down to the ground and began beating her.

The roof of the vault was not high. Stark came down off it in one jump. The Farers neither heard nor saw him. They were far too busy, and Baya was screaming at the top of her lungs. Stark hit the tall one a chopping blow at the base of the skull and he fell, and the shorter one followed him without a groan, strewing the last of his flowers. Stark heaved the bodies aside. Baya looked up at him, her eye wide and dazed. She said something, perhaps his name. He could not be sure. He found the nerve-center in the side of her neck and pressed it; she was quiet.

He saw that Yarrod had come out and was standing over him, looking like thunder.

"That was ill-done," said Yarrod. "You fool, who cares what happens to a Farer?"

"You're the fool," said Stark. "You gave yourself away. She was going to tell Gelmar that the pod-master was a fraud." He lifted the girl smoothly to his shoulder and stood up.

"She saw you, I suppose."

"I think so."

"And these?"

The two men had begun to snore heavily. They smelled of a sweet-sour pungency. Their mouths were open and smiling.

"No," said Stark. "But they heard Baya. About you, I mean. They may remember."

"All right," said Yarrod, still angry. "I suppose it makes no difference who's to blame. The only choice we have now is to run, and run fast."

He looked across the river to the lights of Skeg and then went stamping back to the vault.

Within minutes they were on their way, through the sprawling ruins and into the jungle. The Three Ladies smiled serenely. The warm air was moist, heavy with the smells of night-flowering creepers, mud, and decay. Nameless things scuttled and clicked, bickering in tiny voices round their feet. Stark adjusted Baya's light weight more comfortably across his shoulders.

"The roads are closed to off-worlders," he said. "I suppose you've thought of that."

"You don't imagine we came here by the road, do you?" Yarrod said. "We got out of Irnan by pretending to be a hunting party. We left our mounts and all our proper gear at a place on the other side of the hills and walked in, by a jungle path." He squinted at the sky. "We can be there by tomorrow noon, if we kill ourselves."

"There's a chance, isn't there," said Stark, "that Gelmar will think you've moved your people out because of the disturbance? And that Baya simply ran off? She stabbed one of her friends, you know, and her knife is still there."

"Of course there's a chance. He can't be sure of anything, can he? He can't even be sure whether you're dead or alive. So if you were Gelmar, what would you do?"

"I'd send word along to be on watch, especially to Irnan." And he cursed the name of Gerrith, wishing that she had kept her mouth shut.

"She got her death by it," said Yarrod curtly. "That should be punishment enough."

"It's my death that I'm like to get by it that worries me," said Stark. "If I'd known about the damned prophecy, I'd have laid my plans differently."

"Well," said Halk, smiling his fleeting smile at Stark, "if it's a true prophecy, and you are a fated man, you have nothing to fear, have you?"

"The man who doesn't fear, doesn't live long. I fear everything." He patted Baya's bare thigh. "Even this."

"In that, you're well-advised. You'd do best to kill it."

"We'll see," said Stark. "No need to hurry."

They moved on, following a little still green star that Yarrod called the Lamp of the North.

"If Gelmar does send word to Irnan, he'll do it in the usual manner, by messenger, by the roads. Barring accident, we should be well ahead."

"If," said Halk, "the Dark Man and his baggage don't slow us down."

Stark showed the edges of his teeth. "Halk," he said, "I have a feeling that you and I are not going to be the best of friends."

"Bear with him, Stark," said Yarrod. "He's a fighter, and we need swords more than we need sweet tempers."

That at least was true. Stark saved his breath for walking. And there was plenty of that for all of them.

6

It was daybreak and they had stopped to rest, high on the shoulder of a jungle hill. The dreaming sea lay far behind them, all its deadliness hidden by distance and morning mists that took fantastic colors from the rising of the ginger star. The Irnanese faced eastward and each one poured a small libation. Even Baya bowed her head.

"Hail, Old Sun, we thank you for this day," they muttered, and sounded as though they meant it. Then Halk, as usual, spoiled the effect. He turned defiantly to Stark.

"We were not always paupers, hoarding our little daylight, grudging every scrap of metal so that we can still have a knife to cut our meat. There were ships on that sea. There were machines that flew in the air, and all manner of things that are only legend now. Skaith was a rich world once, as rich as any."

"It lived too long," said Yarrod. "It's senile and mad, growing madder with every generation. Come and eat."

They sat down and began sharing meager rations of food and sour wine. When it was Baya's turn they passed her by.

Stark asked, "Is there none for the girl?"

"We've been feeding her and the likes of her all our lives," said Breca. "She can do without."

"Besides," said Halk, "we didn't ask her to come."

Stark divided his own ration and gave her half. She took it and ate it quickly, saying nothing. She had been docile enough since she regained consciousness, going on her own feet with only a small amount of whimpering, Stark leading her like a puppy with a halter round her neck. He knew she was afraid, surrounded by people who made no secret of their hatred and with no protective Wandsman at hand to whip them into line. Her eyes were large and hollow and her body-paint was a sorry mess, all sweated and smeared.

"The old civilizations," said Yarrod, around a flap of tough bread, "for all their technology, never achieved space-flight. I suppose they were busy with more important things. So there was no escape, for them or for us. No hope of escape. And then suddenly there was talk that starships had landed, talk about a Galactic Union and about other worlds; you see what that did to us when we knew it was true. There was hope. We could escape."

Stark nodded. "I can see also why the Wandsmen would be unhappy about the idea. If the providers start leaving, their whole system collapses."

Halk leaned toward Baya. "And it will collapse. And what will you do then, little Farer girl? Eh?"

She shrank away from him, but he kept on at her until he brought her deep anger flaring up.

"It'll never happen," she snarled at him. "The Protectors won't let it. They'll hunt you all down and kill you." She looked hatefully at

Stark. "Off-worlders have no business here, making trouble. They should never have been allowed to come."

"But they did come," said Stark, "and things will never be the same again." He smiled at Baya. "If I were you I'd start thinking about learning to scratch for myself. And of course, you could always emigrate."

"Emigrate," said Halk. "Ha! Then she would have to do more than just love and enjoy."

"Skaith is dying," said Baya. "What else is there to do?"

Stark shook his head. "Skaith will last out your lifetime, and one or two more. So that's not much of a reason."

She cursed him and began to cry furiously. "You're wicked, you're all wicked, you'll all die just like that woman Gerrith. The Lords Protector will punish you. They defend the weak, they feed the hungry, they shelter the—"

"You can keep that," said Halk, and he cuffed her. She shut up, but her eyes still smoldered. Halk lifted his hand again.

"Let her be," said Stark. "She didn't invent the system." He turned to Yarrod. "If Irnan is as closely watched as you say, how shall I get in and out of the city without being seen?"

"You won't have to. The wise woman's grotto is in the foothills, at the head of the valley."

"Don't they watch her, too?"

"Like hawks." And he added grimly, "We can handle that."

Halk was still looking at Baya, full of malice. "What will you do with her?"

"Turn her loose, when her tongue can do us no harm."

"When will that be? No, give her to me, Dark Man. I'll see to it that she's harmless."

"No."

"Why the tender care for her life? She was ready enough to help take yours."

"She has reason to hate and fear me." Stark looked at Baya's tear-stained face and smiled again. "Besides, she was acting only from the noblest motives."

"Hell," said Yarrod, "who isn't?"

When they had eaten they started on again, pushing themselves almost to the limit of endurance, which meant far past Baya's limit. Stark carried her part of the time, staggering a little with weariness himself and fully conscious of every ache bequeathed to him by the late Child of the Sea. They climbed, and the ginger star climbed above them. About midmorning they crossed the ridge and began going down, which was easier at first and then harder as the grade became steeper. The dim path switched back and forth across the face of the slope, but in many places Yarrod led them straight down in order to save time.

They did not quite kill themselves. They did not quite reach the place they were heading for by noon, either. Stark judged that Old Sun was at least an hour past his zenith when Yarrod at last signaled a halt.

They were in a dense grove of trees, with pale trunks all grooved and ridged and dark foliage high above that shut out the sky. Moving cautiously, Yarrod started on again. Halk went with him. Stark handed Baya's leash to Breca and joined them. The Irnanese were expert woodsmen, he noticed, and yet his ears winced at the noise they made. When they reached the edge of the grove they became even more careful, peering out from behind the trees.

Stark saw a broad sunny meadow. There was a ruined tower some distance along it that might once have been a mill or part of a fortified dwelling. Two men in bright tunics and leather jerkins sat in the doorway of the tower, relaxed and at ease, their weapons leaned beside them. It was too far away to see their faces. Scattered about between the grove and the tower, a dozen or so big shaggy rusty-brown animals fed contentedly on lush grass. There were no sounds except the natural ones; breezes rustling overhead, animals cropping.

Yarrod was satisfied. He had expected no less. He turned to call the others on.

And Stark caught his shoulder in a grip of iron. "Wait!"

Where a moment ago there had been no sounds, now all at once there were a multitude.

"Men. There. And there—"

It was plain for all to hear—the creak of sandal-leather, the clink of metal, the swift stealthy motion.

"All around us, closing in—"

Yarrod shouted. The Irnanese, aware that they were in a trap, began to run. Baya stumbled and fell, or perhaps deliberately lay down. At any rate, they left her. Voices called out with peremptory orders to halt. There was a loud trampling of feet. The Irnanese fled across the meadow, toward the tower where their weapons were.

Arrows flew, whickering in the bright air. Two Irnanese fell, and only one got up again. They dodged in and out among the grazing animals that snorted and lumbered aside. Then Stark saw that the men in the doorway had not moved, and he knew they were dead.

The meadow was wide, wide and naked in the sunlight, and now a flight of arrows came from the tower and stuck quivering in the ground around them.

Yarrod stopped. He looked from side to side, but there was no hiding place, no hope. Men were coming out of the grove behind them, arrows nocked. More men came out of the tower, kicking the bodies aside. A small rufous man led them. He wore a dark red tunic and carried no weapon but his wand of office. Halk said one word, a name, and he said it like a curse.

"Mordach!"

Stark had made his own decision. Those arrows were long and sharp, and he was sure that he could not outrun them. So he, too, stood and waited, having no wish to die in this meaningless place under the ginger star.

"Who is Mordach?" he asked.

"Chief Wandsman of Irnan," said Yarrod, his voice breaking with rage and despair. "Someone talked; someone betrayed us."

The men formed a wall around them, and Mordach came through that wall to stand smiling up at the tall Irnanese.

"The hunting party," he said. "In strange attire, and without weapons. Yet I see that you did find game of a sort." His gaze fastened on Stark, and Stark thought that perhaps he ought to have chanced the arrows after all.

"An off-worlder," said Mordach, "where off-worlders are forbidden to be. And traveling with a company of lawbreakers. Was this what you went to find? Someone who could pretend to fulfill your prophecy?"

"Perhaps he does fulfill it, Mordach," said Halk wickedly. "Gelmar thought so. He tried to kill him, and could not."

Thank you, friend, thought Stark, and felt his guts tighten in anticipation.

Two men came up supporting Baya between them. "We found her in the grove. She doesn't look to be one of them."

"I'm a Farer," said Baya, and went on her knees to Mordach. "In the name of the Lords Protector—" She held out the end of the halter and shook it. "He took me by force, away from Skeg."

"He?"

"That man. The off-worlder. Eric John Stark."

"Why?"

"Because he lived when he ought to have died." She looked up at Stark, trembling with malevolence. "He escaped from us, into the sea. You know what that means, but he lived. He killed a Child of the Sea, and lived. And I saw him." If she had had strength and breath left she would have screamed, "He is the Dark Man of the prophecy! Kill him! Kill him now!"

"There," said Mordach absently, and caressed her tangled hair. He considered Stark, his eyes hooded and cold. "So. And perhaps even Gelmar could be mistaken. Either way—"

"Kill him," Baya whimpered. "Please. Now."

"Killing is a solemn matter," Mordach said, "and salutary. It ought not to be wasted." He motioned to some of his men. "Bind them. Securely, very securely, and especially the off-worlder." He lifted Baya to her feet. "Come, child, you're safe now."

"Mordach," said Yarrod. "Who betrayed us?"

"You did," said Mordach. "Yourselves. All your preparations took time and effort, and some of them were observed. You and Halk are known to be among the most active of the Emigration Party; the others were known to be associates. When you all went off together to hunt, we were curious to know what the quarry might be. So we followed. After we came here to the tower, we only had to wait." His gaze wandered again to Stark. "You were bringing him back to Gerrith's daughter, weren't you?"

Yarrod did not answer, but Mordach nodded. "Of course you were. And of course they must meet, and I promise you they shall—openly, where all can see."

He went off with Baya, who looked back once over her shoulder as the men-at-arms moved in with leather thongs and began to bind the captives. They were neither rough nor gentle, merely very efficient. They were of a type Stark had not seen before, having lint-white hair and sharply slanted cheekbones and slitted yellow eyes that gave them the look of wolves. They were certainly not Farers.

"Farers are only a mob, for trampling and tearing," Yarrod said. "Wandsmen in the city-states like to have a small force of mercenaries for the serious work, and they recruit them along the Border. These are from Izvand, in the Inner Barrens." His head hung down in shame and misery, but he lifted it fiercely when one of the mercenaries brought a halter for his neck, so that he might take the rope easily and with a semblance of pride. "I'm sorry," he said, and would not meet Stark's eye.

And now it was Stark's turn to wear a halter round his own neck, and to walk behind in the dust while Baya rode.

So at length the Dark Man came to Irnan.

7

IT WAS a gray city, walled in stone and set on a height roughly in the center of a broad valley that was green with spring. Mordach and his prisoners and his mercenaries had journeyed a long way north, and a long way up over rainy mountains, and they had left the tropical summer far behind. All around Irnan were tilled fields and pastures and orchards in blossom, a froth of pink and white oddly tarnished by the light of the ginger star.

A road led to the city. There was much traffic on it: farm carts, people going to and from their work in the fields or driving beasts before them, traders and long strings of pack-animals jingling with bells, a troop of mountebanks, a caravan of traveling whores of both sexes with bright banners advertising their wares, and the motley assortment of wanderers that seemed to be omnipresent on Skaith. Mordach's party went down the middle of the road, four men-at-arms riding in front and clashing short stabbing spears rhythmically against their shields. A clear way was made for them, and behind them the people stood along the roadside ditches and stared and pointed and whispered, and then began to follow.

Two Wandsmen, in green tunics that indicated their lesser rank, came out of the gate to meet Mordach, with a rabble of Farers at their heels. And within minutes, the word was running ahead like wildfire.

"The Dark Man! They've taken the Dark Man! They've taken the traitors!"

More Wandsmen appeared as though from between the paving stones. A crowd gathered, clotting round Mordach's party like swarming bees. The mercenaries drew their ranks tighter, until their mounts all but trod upon the captives, and their spears pointed outward, forming a barrier against the press of bodies.

"Keep up, keep up," said the captain of the Izvandians. "If you fall, we can't help you."

They passed beneath the arch of the great gate. Stark saw that the stone was stained and weathered, the carvings grown dim with time. A winged creature with a sword in its claws crouched on the capstone, fierce jaws open to bite the world. The valves of the gate were very strong, sheathed in cured hides almost as hard as metal. There was a passage through the thickness of the wall, a sort of dark tunnel where every sound was caught and compressed and the din of voices was stunning. Then they were in the square beyond and forcing their way between market stalls, toward a central platform built stoutly of wood and higher than the jostling heads of the mob. Some of the mercenaries stood guard while others dismounted and hurried the captives up a flight of steps. Stark guessed that the square was the only open space of any size within the walls and that the platform was used for all public occasions such as executions and other edifying entertainments.

There were standing posts, permanently placed and black with use. Within moments Stark and Yarrod and the others were bound to them. The mercenaries took up stations at the edges of the platform, facing outward. The two Wandsmen in green went away; apparently Mordach had sent them on some errand. Mordach himself addressed the crowd. Much of what he said was drowned in an animal howling, but there was little doubt about the burden of his speech. Irnan had sinned, and those who were guilty were about to pay.

Stark flexed himself against the hide ropes. They cut his flesh but did not give. The post was firm as a tree. He leaned back against it, easing himself as much as possible, and looked at this place where presumably he was about to die.

"What do you think now, Dark Man?" asked Halk. He was bound to the post on Stark's left, Yarrod on his right.

"I think," said Stark, "that we'll soon know whether Gerrith had the true sight."

And once more he cursed the name of Gerrith, but this time he kept it to himself.

The crowd was still growing. People came until it seemed that the space could not hold any more, and still they came. Around the inner sides of the square there were buildings of stone, narrow and high, shouldering together, slate roofs peaked and shining in the sun. The upper windows were filled with people looking down. After a while folk were straddling the rooftrees and perching on the gutters, and the tops of the outer walls were packed.

Two distinct elements were in the crowd, and they seemed not to mingle. Foremost round the platform, doing all the screaming, were the Farers and the other flotsam. Beyond them, and quite quiet, were the people of Irnan.

"Any hope from them?" asked Stark.

Yarrod tried to shrug. "Not all of them are with us. Our people have lived in this place a long time, and the roots go deep. And Skaith, with all its faults, is the only world we know. Some folk find the idea of leaving it frightening to the point of blasphemy, and they won't lift a hand to help us. About the others, I'm not making any bets."

Mordach was urging the mob to be patient; more things were to come. Still they pushed and clamored for blood. A band of women forced their way to the steps and began to climb. They wore black bags over their heads, covering their faces. Otherwise they were naked and their skin was like tree-bark from long exposure.

"Give us the Dark Man, Mordach!" they cried. "Let us take him to the mountain top and feed his strength to Old Sun!"

Mordach held up his staff to halt them. He spoke to them gently, and Stark asked, "What are they?"

"They live wild in the mountains. Once in a while, when they get hungry, they come in. They worship the sun, and any man they can manage to capture they sacrifice. They believe that they alone keep Old Sun alive." Halk laughed. "Look at the greedy beasts! They'd like to have all of us."

Arms like gnarled branches reached and clawed.

"They will die, little sisters," said Mordach. "They will all feed Old Sun, and you shall watch and sing the Hymn of Life."

Gently he urged them back, and reluctantly they returned to the crowd. All at once Stark heard a shouting and a turmoil about the doors of one of the buildings overlooking the square, and a procession moved out from it with the green Wandsmen leading and a fringe of Farers flapping at the sides and rear. At the center, Stark made out a dozen or so men and women in sober gowns, with chains of office round their necks. They walked in an odd manner, and as they came closer he could see that they were bound in such a way as forced them to bend forward and shuffle like penitents.

A low deep groan came from the people of Irnan, and Yarrod said between his teeth, "Our chiefs and elders."

Stark thought he saw the beginning of movement among the Irnanese, and he hoped they would rush the crowd and rescue their leaders by force, starting a general revolt. The movement rippled and died. The procession came to the steps and climbed haltingly while the mob jeered. The elders were herded onto the platform and made to stand, and Mordach pointed his staff at them in a gesture of wrath and accusation.

"You have done wickedness," he cried, in a voice that rang across the square. "Now you shall do penance!"

The crowd screamed. They threw things. The citizens of Irnan stirred uneasily. They muttered, but still they did not move.

"They're afraid," Yarrod said. "The Wandsmen have packed the town with Farers, as you see. One word, and they'll start tearing Irnan apart stone by stone."

"Still, the Irnanese outnumber them."

"Our party does not. And the Wandsmen have hostages." He nodded his red head at the men and women standing bent in the sun.

There was a smell in the air now. The hot, close, frightening smell of mob; mob excited, hungry, dreaming blood and death. The primitive in Stark knew that sweaty acridity all too well. The ropes cut him; the post was hard against his back. The ginger star burned him with brassy light and his own sweat ran down.

Someone shouted, "Where is the wise woman?"

Other voices took up the cry, howled it back and forth between the gray walls.

"Where is the wise woman? Where is Gerrith?"

Mordach calmed them. "She has been sent for. She will be with us soon."

Yarrod cursed Mordach. "Do you plan to murder her as you did her mother?"

Mordach only smiled and said, "Wait."

They waited. The crowd became increasingly restless. Roving bands began looting the market stalls, scattering food and produce, smashing the stalls themselves to make clubs. Wine and drugs passed freely. Stark wondered how much longer Mordach could hold them.

Then the cry went up from the gate. "The wise woman! Gerrith is coming!"

An expectant quiet settled over the square. The hundreds of heads turned, and it seemed as though the Irnanese all drew one deep breath and held it.

Men-at-arms appeared, clearing a way through the press. Behind them came a cart, a farm cart soiled and reeking with the work of the fields, and after that more men-at-arms bringing up the rear.

Inside the cart were two Wandsmen, each one clinging with one hand to the jolting stakes and holding with the other the tall figure of a woman who stood between them.

8

She was dressed all in black, in a great veil that enveloped her from head to heels, a single shroud-like garment that concealed her face and all else beside her height. Set upon her head and circling the veil was a diadem the color of old ivory.

"The Robe and Crown of Fate," said Yarrod, and the folk of Irnan let out that held breath in a savage wail of protest.

The mob drowned it in their own blood-cry.

Men-at-arms and farm cart crossed the square, halted at the platform steps. The woman was made to leave the cart and climb. The diadem appeared first above the level of the floor. It looked very frail and old, and its ornament was a circle of little grinning skulls. Then there was the sway of dark draperies, and Gerrith, the wise woman of Irnan, stood before Mordach with the Wandsmen on either side.

Because of the veil Stark could not be sure, but he thought that Gerrith was looking past Mordach, straight at him.

Yet she spoke to Mordach, and her voice was clear and sweet and ringing, without a hint of fear.

"This was not well done, Mordach."

"No?" he said. "Let us see." He turned from her, speaking over the heads of his Farers to the people of Irnan. His voice carried to the walls. "You of Irnan! Watch now, and learn!"

He turned again to Gerrith and pointed his wand at Stark. "What do you see there, daughter of Gerrith?"

"I see the Dark Man."

"The Dark Man of your mother's prophecy?"

"Yes."

Well, thought Stark, and what else could she say?

"The Dark Man, bound and helpless, waiting for death." Mordach laughed. He laughed often, as though he found these human lapses from reason genuinely amusing. "He will destroy nothing. Do you recant, woman? Do you admit the lie?"

"No."

"Then you are no wiser than your mother, and your sight is no more true. Do you hear out there, you of Irnan?" Again his words carried far, and where they did not reach other tongues took them up and passed them on, whispering like surf against the walls, up to the windows and the rooftops. "Your prophecy is false, your wise woman a liar, your Dark Man a sham!"

In one swift motion he ripped crown and veil from Gerrith.

Astonishment, surprise, shock, outrage! Stark could hear the sounds beyond the delighted screaming of the mob. Halk, Yarrod, and the other Irnanese on the platform made instinctive, futile movements toward the killing of Mordach.

Only Gerrith stood tall and calm, as though she had expected this. As indeed she must have done, thought Stark, unless the wise women of Irnan habitually went naked beneath the ceremonial veil. And naked she was, all warm bronze with the sunlight on her and a thick braid of bronzy hair hanging down her back. Her body was strong and straight and proud, not flinching before the lewdness of the crowd. Nudity was commonplace on Skaith and hardly to be noticed, but this was different. This act was a stripping of more than the mere body. Mordach was attempting to strip her soul.

He tossed the black veil out to the mob and let them tear it. The diadem he smashed beneath his feet and kicked the old yellowed fragments contemptuously away.

"There are your robe and crown," he said. "We will have no more wise women at Irnan."

This, too, she had expected. But her eyes held a cold and terrible light.

"And you will have no more Irnan to rob, Mordach." She spoke with the tongue of prophecy, and it made Stark shiver with its finality. "The Crown has come with us from the old Irnan, all through the Great Wandering and the centuries of rebuilding. Now you have destroyed it, and the history of Irnan is finished."

Mordach shrugged and said, "Bind her."

But before the men-at-arms could reach her she turned and raised her arms and cried out in that wonderful ringing voice.

"Irnan is finished. You must go and build a new city, on a new world."

Then she submitted herself to the binding, and Mordach said, "Do not go at once, people of Irnan! Stay a while and watch the Dark Man die."

A roar of laughter swept the crowd. "Yes, stay!" they jeered. "Don't leave us now. At least wait for the ships to come."

Yarrod, bound to his post, threw back his head and screamed a harsh wild scream.

"Rise up, you dogs! Rise up and tear them! Where are your guts, your pride, your manhood—"

The madness was on him, the madness that makes dead men and heroes. Mordach lifted his hand. One of the Izvandians stepped up and quite impersonally thrust his short spear into Yarrod's breast. A clean and merciful stroke, Stark noticed, though he was sure Mordach would have preferred something more lingering. Yarrod fell silent and sagged against the post.

"Cut him down," said Mordach. "Throw his body to the crowd."

The tree-bark women commenced a shrill chanting, raising their arms to the sun.

Yarrod's red head, cometlike, marked his passage. Stark preferred not to watch what happened after that, though he could not shut out the sounds. He lifted his gaze to the walls of Irnan, the windows and the rooftops, peripherally aware that Gerrith was brought and bound to the post that Yarrod had just quitted.

Amazingly, at his other side, Halk had begun to weep.

Mordach and the other Wandsmen stood benignly watching the flock, talking among themselves, planning the next act, the dramatic climax of their lecture on the folly of rebellion. In the background, many of the Irnanese were going. They had their cloaks pulled over their heads, as though they could not bear any more. They melted away into the narrow streets around the square.

Gerrith was speaking. "So they leave us," she said. Stark turned his attention to her. She was looking at him. Her eyes were a warm gold-bronze in color—very honest eyes, sorrowful but calm.

"It seems that Mordach is right, that Gerrith's prophecy was born of her own desires and not the true sight. So you will die for nothing and that is a great pity." She shook her head. The bronze braid had fallen forward over her shoulder and the shining end of it moved between her breasts. "A great pity." She studied him, his size and strength, the structure of his facial bones, the shape of his mouth, the expression of his eyes. She seemed full of regret and compassion. "I'm sorry. Why did you come here?"

"Looking for Ashton."

She seemed astounded. "But—"

"But that's what Gerrith said, isn't it? So perhaps, after all—"

She would have spoken again but he cautioned her to silence. The Wandsmen were still talking. The men-at-arms had returned to their positions, looking disdainfully at the mob that growled and howled and bestially tore. Stark glanced again at the windows.

Perhaps he was imagining—

The windows were no longer crowded with watchers. They were empty, and shutters were being pulled to but not closed, as though to hide what went on in the rooms behind them and yet leave a view of the square. There were still people on the roofs but not so many, and there seemed to be movement of a furtive sort behind turrets and chimney-stacks. Stark took a deep breath and allowed himself a very small bit of hope.

The thing was to be ready if it happened.

Mordach came and stood before him. "Well," he said, "and how shall the Dark Man die? Shall I give him to the Little Sisters of the Sun? Shall I let my Farers play with him? Or shall I have him flayed?" The tip of his wand traced lines on Stark's skin. "Slowly, of course. A strip at a time. Yes. And whom shall we call to flay our Dark Man? The Izvandians? No, this is not their affair." He looked at the Irnanese elders standing bowed in their shackles. "It is *their* affair. *They* planned to desert us, to deny their duty to their fellow men. *They* fell into the error of selfishness and greed. The Dark Man is their symbol. *They* shall flay him!"

The crowd was overjoyed.

Mordach took a dagger from his belt and thrust it into the hand of a graybeard, who stared back at him with loathing and dropped it.

Mordach smiled. "I haven't given the alternative, old man. The choice is simple. A strip of his skin, or your life."

"Then," said the graybeard, "I must die."

"As you wish," said Mordach. He turned toward the nearest man-at-arms, one hand uplifted, his mouth open to speak.

Stark heard the ripping thud of the arrow into flesh, saw the feathered butt rise out of Mordach's breast as though it had suddenly blossomed there. Mordach drew in one shocked breath, a kind of inverted scream. He looked up and saw all the shuttered windows opening and the men with bows standing in them, and the shafts beginning to pour down like hissing rain, and then he went to his knees and watched his Izvandians and his green Wandsmen drop; and he turned his face to Stark and the wise woman with the beginning of a horrible doubt. Stark was glad that Mordach had that to take with him into the dark.

The graybeard had been a warrior in his time. He touched Mordach's body with his foot and said fiercely, "Perhaps there's hope for us after all."

More archers appeared, on the walls, on the roofs. They were shooting into the mob now. There was a great squalling and shrieking, a surge of panic this way and that as the entertainment ceased to be fun.

Stark saw a body of mercenaries come in from the gate. At the same time, from the side streets, the citizens of Irnan began to stream into the square, armed with anything they could get their hands on. Among them was one group, well armed and keeping close order. These men cut their way through the pack with ruthless efficiency, heading for the platform. They gained it. A few of them stayed to hold the steps. The others hustled the elders down and cut the captives loose. Stark and the survivors of Yarrod's band caught up weapons from the dead Izvandians. They went down the steps and closed ranks around Gerrith and the elders. They started to fight their way back into the streets.

Some of the Farers, crazy with drugs and fanatic hatred, rushed the group, careless of the swords. The Irnanese cried, "Yarrod! Yarrod!" They killed their way across the square to the rhythm of their savage, bitter chant.

They passed into a narrow street between buildings of gray stone that had grown up during the centuries and then grown together overhead, so that in some places the street was more like a tunnel. It was quiet here. They hurried on, as rapidly as the elders could move, and presently entered a doorway. Beyond it was a hall of some size, hung with banners and furnished with one great table and a row of massive chairs. Some people were gathered there. Immediately they took the elders and helped them to the chairs, and one man shouted,

"Armorer! Come here and get these shackles off!"

Someone had brought a cloak to Gerrith and covered her. She was standing beside Stark. She turned to him with a fey look and said,

"Now, indeed, I believe."

9

HALK SPOKE. His eyes were red with rage and weeping but his mouth smiled, all teeth and vengefulness.

"They don't need us here, Dark Man. Are you coming?"

Gerrith nodded. "Go if you will, Stark. Your bane is not in Irnan."

He wondered if she knew of another place where it would be.

He went back into the streets with Halk. Little bands of citizens were hunting Farers down like rabbits in the twists and turns of the narrow ways. Obviously the Irnanese had matters firmly in hand. In the square, archers were taking up new positions around the gate, where scores of Farers were shrieking and trampling one another, fighting to get out and away. Stark saw no sign of the Izvandians. With their paymaster dead, he guessed they had simply retired into their barracks and let the battle go on without them. The tree-bark women had taken refuge underneath the platform, more to escape the crush, apparently, than because they were afraid. They were chanting ecstatically, busy with the task of feeding Old Sun. The ginger star was feasting well today.

There was really not much left to do. A few last pockets of resistance, some mopping up of strays, but the fight was won, had been won, really, with that first flight of arrows. Mordach's body still lay on the platform. The little man had pushed too hard. Even the folk whom Yarrod had said would not lift a hand to save them had lifted both hands to save their elders and their wise woman and to cleanse themselves of the shame Mordach had put upon them.

Stark let Halk go on alone to exact more payment for Yarrod. He couldn't see that he was needed anywhere, so he put up his sword and climbed to the platform. Among the sprawled bodies he found the fragments of old ivory where Mordach had trampled the crown. Only one of the little skulls was still intact, grinning as though it could taste the blood that speckled it. He picked it up and went down the steps again, with the voices of the tree-bark women shrill in his ears. He hoped that he would never meet a pack of them baying on their own mountain-tops. He found his way through the streets, back to the council hall.

There was a bustle of messengers, people coming and going, a feeling of urgency. Stark did not see Gerrith, so he put the small skull away in the rags of his tunic. He was standing wondering what to do next when a man came up to him and said,

"Jerann asks that you come with me."

"Jerann?"

The man indicated Graybeard. "The chief of our Council. I am to see that you have everything you need."

Stark thanked the man and followed him along a corridor and up a winding stair to another corridor and into a chamber with narrow windows set in the thickness of the stone walls. A fire burned on the hearth. There was a bed, a chest, a settle, all heavy and well made, and a rug of coarse wool on the floor. Opening off the chamber was a bathroom with a little stone bath reached by three steps. Serving men waited with pails of steaming water and rough towels. Gratefully Stark consigned himself to their care.

An hour later, washed and shaved and dressed in a clean tunic, he was finishing the last of a solid meal when the man came again and said that Jerann required him in the council hall.

Freed of his shackles, Jerann was tall, erect and soldierly. He still had that look of fierce pride, but he was under no illusions.

"We are all fated men now," he said. "We can only go where our destiny leads us, and that may be to a place we would rather not see. Nevertheless, it is done. And march we shall."

He gave Stark a long, hard, measuring look. All the members of the Council were doing the same, and Stark knew what they were thinking. Why an off-worlder? Why does he bring with him this sudden stunning break from all history, all custom, all the laws under which we have endured? What has he really brought us—freedom and a new life, or death and utter destruction?

Stark had no answer for them. The prophecy said only that he would destroy the Lords Protector. It did not say what the result of that would be.

"Now, Eric John Stark, Earthman, tell us how you came to Skaith, how you came to Irnan, and why."

Stark knew perfectly well that Jerann had already heard the story, but he told it again, carefully and in detail. He told them about Ashton, and about Pax, and about how the matter of emigration stood with the Ministry of Planetary Affairs.

"I see," said Jerann. "Then it seems that we must believe in Dark Men and prophecies, and go our way in blind hope."

"What about the other city-states?" asked Stark. "They must be in much the same case as Irnan. Will they rise to help you?"

"I don't know. We'll do what we can to persuade them, naturally. But I think most of them will wait and see."

"Wait and see what?"

"If the prophecy is true." Jerann turned to an aide. "Have the Izvandian brought to me." The man hurried away, and Jerann said to Stark, "We must all know that, as soon as possible."

There was a wait, an awkwardness, a vacuum of uneasy silence within the encompassing sounds of triumph from outside in the streets. The members of the Council were tired and showing strain. The enormity of the commitment that Irnan had made this day must be weighing on them very heavily.

A knot of people came in, clustered round one tall lint-haired warrior. Stark noticed the gold ornaments on his harness, the torque and armbands. A chief, probably captain of the mercenaries. He was marched up the hall to where the Council sat, and he stood facing Jerann without emotion.

Jerann said coldly, "Greetings, Kazimni."

The Izvandian said, "I see you, Jerann."

Jerann took up a small heavy sack from the table. "This is the gold which is owed to you."

"To my dead as well? There are families."

"To your dead as well." He weighed the sack in his hand. "And there is in addition half as much again."

"If you wish to bribe us to leave Irnan," said Kazimni contemptuously, "keep your gold. We have no further business here."

Jerann shook his head. "No bribe. Payment for services."

Kazimni cocked one pale insolent eyebrow. "Oh?"

"Some of our people are going into the Barrens. A small party. We want you to escort them as far as Izvand."

Kazimni did not bother to ask why a party of Irnanese were going into the Barrens. It was no concern of his.

"Very well," he said. "Give us leave to bury our dead and make ready for the journey. We'll go when Old Sun rises." And he added, "With our arms."

"With your arms," said Jerann. He gave Kazimni the gold and said to the Irnanese escort, "You heard. Let them bury their dead, and give them what they need of supplies."

"Better to give them the sword," muttered one of the Irnanese. But they took Kazimni away obediently enough.

Stark asked, "Why Izvand?"

"Because it is that much closer to the Citadel. And for that distance you will have the protection of an escort. From there you must make your own arrangements, and I warn you—do not underestimate the dangers."

"Where exactly is this Citadel? Where is Worldheart?"

"I can tell you where tradition puts them. The fact you will learn for yourself."

"The Wandsmen know."

"Yes. But none are left alive in Irnan to tell us."

So that was no help. "Where is Gerrith?"

"She returned to her own place."

"Is that safe? The countryside must be full of wandering Farers."

"She's well guarded," Jerann said. "You'll see her in the morning. Go now and rest. It's a long road you've come, and a longer one you'll be taking tomorrow."

All night, in the intervals of sleep, Stark could hear the restless voices of the city, where preparations were being made for war. The revolt was well begun. But it was only a beginning, and it seemed a large order to turn an entire planet upside down just so two men, and off-worlders at that, could escape from it. Still, that order had been handed to him with no solicitation on his part, and at this moment he could see no other way out.

Well, he thought, that was for the future, and it was Gerrith's job to look ahead, not his. He would leave it to her. He slept, and in the dark morning he rose and dressed and was waiting patiently when a man came to waken him.

Jerann was below in the council hall. Stark thought that he had been there all night. Halk was there too, and Breca and two others of Yarrod's party.

"I am sorry," the old man said, "that Irnan cannot spare you the men you ought to have. We need them here."

Halk said, "We'll have to rely on being quick and hard to see. But with the Dark Man to lead us, how can we fail?"

Stark, who would just as soon have gone alone, said nothing. Food was brought, and strong bitter beer. When they had eaten, Jerann rose and said,

"It is time. I'll ride with you as far as the wise woman's grotto."

The square was eerily quiet in the chill first light of dawn. Some of the bodies had been taken away. Others were piled stiffly together, awaiting the carts. The tree-bark women had gone. Sentries manned the wall and the guard-towers by the gate.

The Izvandians, about sixty of them, were already mounted, men and animals alike blowing steam in the cold air. Beasts had been brought for Stark and his party. They mounted and fell in behind the troop, where Kazimni rode by and gave them a curt greeting.

Old Sun came up. The gates creaked open. The cavalcade moved out.

The road, so crowded and noisy the day before, was deserted except for the occasional dead. Some of the Farers had not run fast enough. Morning mist rose thick and white from the fields, and there was a fresh clean smell of growing things. Stark breathed deeply.

He became aware that Jerann was watching him. "You're glad to leave the city. You don't like being within walls."

Stark laughed. "I didn't realize it was so apparent."

"I am not acquainted with Earthmen," said Jerann courteously. "Are they all like you?"

"They find me quite as strange as you do." His eyes held a cruel gleam of amusement. "Perhaps even stranger."

The old man nodded. "Gerrith said—"

"A wolf's-head, a landless man, a man without a tribe. I was raised by animals, Jerann. That is why I seem like one." He lifted his head, looking northward. "Earthmen killed them all. They would have killed me too, except for Ashton."

Jerann glanced at Stark's face and shivered slightly. He did not speak again until, at the upper end of the valley, they reached the wise woman's grotto.

10

ONLY Stark and Jerann turned aside. The cavalcade went on, moving at a steady walking pace that covered a surprising amount of ground without tiring the animals. Stark could catch up with them easily. He slid off the soft, wooly-haired hide of the saddle-pad and followed Jerann up a steep path that wound through a dark overhanging wood. Finally they came to a hillside where the naked rock jutted out, forming rough pillars on either side of a cave. A party of men on guard there rose from around their fire and spoke to Jerann. The wise woman was within, and safe.

Inside the cave mouth was an antechamber, where Stark supposed that folk must wait to hear the oracle. At the far end were heavy curtains of some purple stuff that looked as if it had done duty for many Gerriths, and there were solemn designs embroidered in black. All in all, not a cheerful room. And cold, with the dusty tomb-smell of places shut away forever from the sun.

A tall old woman parted the curtains and signed to them to enter. She wore a long gray gown and her face was all bony sternness. She looked at Stark as though she would tear him with her sharp gaze, rip away his flesh and see what was beneath it.

"My old mistress died because of you," she said. "I hope it was not for nothing."

"So do I," said Stark, and stepped past her into the inner room.

This was somewhat better. There were rugs and hangings to soften the stone, pierced lamps for light and a brazier for warmth. But it was still a cave, and Gerrith looked out of place in it with her youth and her golden coloring. She was made for sunlight.

She sat in a massive chair behind a massive table. A wide, shallow bowl of silver stood on the table, filled with clear water.

"The Water of Vision," she said, and shook her head. "It has given me nothing." There were shadows around her eyes and her face was drawn, as though she had sat there all night. "I never had my mother's gift. I never wanted it, though she told me it would come in its own time, whether I wanted it or not. My own gift is small and not to be ordered. It's worse than having none at all. Always before I was able to use the Crown, and I think something of my mother and all the other Gerriths down through the centuries—the name is a tradition with us, Stark—lived on in it and could speak through it. Now there is no Crown and, as Mordach said, no wise woman in Irnan."

Stark took from his girdle an object wrapped in a bit of cloth and handed it to her.

"This is all that was left."

She opened the wrapping. The little yellow skull grinned up at her. Her face changed. "It is enough," she said. She leaned over the bowl, holding the skull between her hands. The water rippled as though in a sudden wind, and then was still.

Stark and Jerann waited, silent. And it seemed to Stark that the clear water turned red and thick and that shapes moved in it, shapes that brought the hackles prickling up at the back of his neck and stirred a small sound in his throat.

Gerrith looked up at him, startled. "You saw?"

"Not really." The water was clear again. "What were they?"

"Whatever they are, they stand between you and the Citadel." She stood up. "And I must go with you."

Jerann said, "But Lady! You can't leave Irnan now . . ."

"My work in Irnan is finished. I told you that. Now the Water of Vision has shown me where my path lies."

"Has it shown you what the end of that path will be?"

"No. You must find your own strength and your own faith, Jerann." She smiled at him, with genuine affection. "You've never lacked for either. Go back to your people, and if you have time now and again, pray for us."

She turned suddenly and laughed at Stark. "Not so downcast, Dark Man. I'll not burden you with bowls and braziers and tripods. Only this." She placed the little skull in a pouch at her girdle. "And I can ride and shoot as well as any." She called to the old woman and disappeared through the hangings into some inner chamber.

Jerann looked at Stark. There did not seem to be anything to say. They nodded to each other and Jerann left. Stark waited, scowling at the placid water in the silver bowl and cursing wise women. Whatever it was he had glimpsed there, he would as soon not have seen until the time came.

In a short time Gerrith returned, wearing tunic and riding cloak.

She and Stark went together out of the cave and down the steep path, and the old woman stood in the cave entrance and watched them with eyes like cold steel daggers. Stark was glad when the trees hid them from her sight. At the foot of the path a gnarled old man had brought Gerrith's mount, with a sack of provisions tied to the saddle pad. She thanked him and bade him goodbye, and they rode away.

They came up with the party around noon, when Old Sun threw rusty shadows under the bellies of the beasts. Halk shrugged when he saw Gerrith.

"We shall have all the bogles on our side now," he said, and his mouth twisted in what might pass for a smile. "At least we see that the wise woman has enough faith in her mother's prophecy to put herself in danger."

They moved steadily toward the Barrens, following the Lamp of the North.

At first the road ran between mountains. There were peel-towers on the ridges, falling down, and ruins of fortified villages stuck to the cliffs like wasps' nests. But the mountains were still inhabited. For three days a band of very shaggy people followed them, going along their own secret trails parallel to the road. They carried crude weapons and ran with a curious loping stride, bent forward from the waist.

"One of the Wild Bands," Gerrith said. "They have no law at all except that of blind survival. They even come as far as Irnan sometimes. The Wandsmen hate them because they kill Wandsmen and Farers as readily as they kill us."

The Izvandian escort was too strong to be attacked, and there were no stragglers. At night, beyond the meager fires, Stark could hear stealthy rustlings, and several times the Izvandian sentries loosed arrows at things creeping toward the picket lines. They killed one of the intruders and Stark looked at the body in the light of morning. His nose wrinkled. "Why do they want to survive?" he wondered.

Halk said, "The vermin are leaving it. Stand back."

They left the heap of bones unburied on the stony ground.

The mountains dwindled away into hills covered with a dark, stunted scrub. Beyond them the land flattened out to the horizon, a treeless immensity of white and gray-green, a spongy mossiness flecked with a million icy ponds. The wind blew, sometimes hard, sometimes harder. Old Sun grew more feeble by the day. The Irnanese were stoical, riding the cold hours uncomplaining, wrapped in frosty cloaks. The Izvandians were comfortable and gay. This was their own, their native land.

Stark rode often beside Kazimni.

"In the days when Old Sun was young," Kazimni would say, and spin out one of the thousand or so legends he seemed to have at his fingertips, all of warmth and richness and the fatness of the land. The men of those days had been giants, the women beautiful and willing beyond belief. Warriors had magic weapons that killed from afar; fishermen had magic boats that sailed the skies. "Now it is as you see it," he would finish. "But we survive. We are strong. We are happy."

"Good," said Stark on one occasion. "I congratulate you. And where is this place they call Worldheart?"

Kazimni shrugged. "North."

"That's all you know?"

"Yes. If it exists at all."

"You sound as if you don't believe in the Lords Protector."

Kazimni's wolf-face expressed aristocratic scorn. "We do not require them. It makes little difference whether we believe in them or not."

"Yet you sell your swords to the Wandsmen."

"Gold is gold, and the Wandsmen have more of it than most. We do not have to like them, or follow their religion. We're free men. All the People of the Barrens are free. Not all of us are good. Some do business with the Wandsmen, some do not. Some trade with the city-states; some trade with each other; some do not trade at all but live by rapine. Some are mad. Quite mad. But free. There are no Farers here, and we can defend ourselves. The Wandsmen have found poor pickings among us. They let us alone."

"I see," said Stark, and rode for a time in silence. "Something lives in that place by Worldheart," he said at last. "Something not human, and yet not quite animal."

Kazimni gave a sidelong glance out of his tilted yellow eyes. "How do you know that?"

"Perhaps the wind whispered it to me."

"Or perhaps the wise woman."

"What are they, Kazimni?"

"We're great talkers here in the Barrens. Great tellers of tales. We fill the winter nights with talk. When our throats go dry with it we wet them with more khamm and talk again."

"What are they?"

"The Harsenyi nomads bring us tales, and so do the darkland traders. Sometimes they winter with us at Izvand, and those are good winters." He paused. "I have heard stories of Northhounds."

Stark repeated the name. "Northhounds." It had a solemn ring to it.

"I can't tell you if the stories are true. Men lie without meaning to. They talk as if they had been part of a thing that happened to someone they never knew and only heard of by sixth remove. Northhounds are a sort of demon to the Harsenyi, and to some of the traders. Monsters that appear out of the snow-mist and do terrible things. It is said that the Lords Protector created them long ago, to guard their Citadel. It is said that they still guard it, and woe take any wanderer who stumbles into their domain."

Hairs prickled briefly at the back of Stark's neck, just at the memory of those shapes he had seen in the Water of Vision. "I think you can believe in Northhounds, Kazimni." He changed the subject. "Is that why your people are content with life in the Barrens—because they are free?"

"Is it not enough?" Kazimni jerked his chin contemptuously toward the Irnanese. "If we lived soft, as they do, we too would be slaves, as they are."

Stark could understand that. "You must have known what brought on the trouble at Irnan."

"Yes. Good trouble. As soon as we've rested and seen our wives, we'll be back on the Border. There'll be need of fighting men."

"No doubt. But how would your people feel about emigrating?"

"To another world?" Kazimni shook his head. "The land shapes us. We are what we are because of it. If we were in another place, we would be another people. No. Old Sun will last us yet a while. And life in the Barrens is not so bad. You will see that when we come to Izvand."

The road looped and wound among the frozen ponds. There were other travelers on it, though not as many as in the Fertile Belt. They were of a different breed, darker and grimmer than the flotsam of the southern roads. There was a good deal of trade back and forth across the border; drovers with herds for the markets of Izvand and Komrey, merchants with wagon-loads of grain and wool, strings of pack-animals carrying manufactured goods from the southern workshops, long lines of great creaking wains hauling timber from some far place in the mountains. Coming the other way were caravans bringing furs and salt and dried fish. All traveled in groups, well armed, each lot keeping to itself. There were inns and rest-houses along the way but Kazimni avoided them, preferring to camp in the open. "Thieves and robbers," he said of the inn-keepers. And of the accommodations, "They stink."

The Izvandians moved rapidly, passing everything else on the road. And yet sometimes Stark felt as though that movement was only an illusion and they were trapped forever in the unchanging landscape.

Gerrith felt his impatience. "I share it," she told him. "For you, one man. For me, a people. Yet things must go at their own pace."

"Does your gift tell you that?"

She smiled at him. It was night, with the Three Ladies shining through gaps in scudding cloud-wrack. They were in an unfamiliar quarter of the sky now, but still beautiful. Old friends. Stark had grown quite fond of them. Nearer at hand, the light of a little fire flared and flickered across Gerrith's face.

"Something tells me. Everything is in train now, and the end has already been written. We have only to meet it."

Stark grunted, unconvinced. The beasts, huddled together with their tails to the wind, munched at heaps of moss piled up for them. The Izvandians laughed and chattered around their fires. The Irnanese were wrapped bundles, suffering in silence.

Gerrith said, "Why do you love this man Ashton so deeply?"

"But you know that. He saved my life."

"And so you cross the stars to risk losing it on a world you never heard of before? To go through all this when you know that he may already be dead? It's not enough, Stark. Will you tell me?"

"Tell you what?"

"Who you are. What you are. A lesser gift even than mine could sense that you're different. Inside, I mean. There's a stillness, something I can't touch. Tell me about you and Ashton."

So he told her, of his childhood on a cruel planet far too close to its sun, where the heat killed by day and the frost by night, where the sky thundered and the rocks split, where the ground shook and the mountains fell down.

"I was born there. We were part of a mining colony. A quake and a great fall of rock killed everyone but me. I'd have died too, but the People took me in. They were the aborigines. They weren't human, not quite. They still had their hairy pelts, and they didn't talk much, a few clicks and grunts, cries for hunting and warning and calling-together. They shared all they had with me."

Heat and cold and hunger. Those were the most of it. But their hairy bodies warmed his small nakedness in the bitter night, and their hard hands fed him. They taught him love, and patience, how to hunt the great rock-lizard, how to suffer, how to survive. He remembered their faces, wrinkled, snouted, toothed. Beautiful faces to him, beautiful and wise with the wisdom of first beginnings. His people. Always his people, his only people. And yet they had named him Man-Without-a-Tribe.

"More Earthmen came, in time," Stark said. "They needed the food and water the People were using, so they killed them. They were only animals. Me they put in a cage and kept for a curiosity. They poked sticks between the bars to make me snap and snarl at them. They were going to kill me too, when the novelty wore off. Then Ashton came."

Ashton the administrator, armed with the lightnings of authority. Stark smiled wryly.

"To me he was just another flat-faced enemy, something to be hated and killed. I'd lost all my human origins, of course, and the humans I'd met had given me little cause to love them. Ashton took me, all the same. I couldn't have been a very pleasant charge, but he had the patience of mountains. He tamed me. He taught me house manners, and how to speak in words, and most of all he taught me that while there are bad men, there are also good ones. Yes, he did give me much more than just my life."

"I understand now," Gerrith said, and he thought she did, truly, as well as anyone could. She stirred the fire and sighed. "I'm sorry I can't tell you whether your friend is still alive."

"We'll know that soon enough," Stark said, and lay down on the cold ground and slept.

And dreamed.

He was following Old One up a cliff, angry because his feet did not have long clever toes, fiercely determined to make up for his deformity by climbing twice as hard and twice as high. The sun burned terribly on his naked back. The rock scorched him. Black peaks pierced the sky on all sides.

Old One slid without sound into a crevice, making the imperative sign. The boy N'Chaka crept in beside him. Old One pointed with his throwing-stick. High above them on a ledge, its huge jaws open in sensuous languor, a rock-lizard slept half-lidded in the sun.

With infinite care, moving one muscle at a time, his belly tight with emptiness and hope, the boy began again to follow Old One up the cliff—

He did not like the dream. It saddened him even in sleep, so that he started awake in order to escape it. He sat a long time by the dying fire, listening to the lonely sounds of the night. When he slept again it was without memories.

Next day, in the afternoon, they saw the roofs of a stockaded town by the shore of a frozen sea. With pride and affection, Kazimni said, "There is Izvand."

11

It was a sturdy town, solidly built of timber brought from the mountains, with steep roofs to shed the snow. Izvand was the trade center for this part of the Inner Barrens, so that there was a constant coming and going of wagons and pack trains. Traffic churned the narrow streets by day, and at night the mud froze into ankle-breaking chaos. In the summer, Kazimni said, fishing was the business of many Izvandians, and as soon as the ice went out of the harbor the high-prowed boats would be hauled from their winter sheds.

"Not a bad life," he said. "Not bad at all. Plenty of food and fighting. Why don't you stay with us, Stark?"

Stark shook his head, and Kazimni shrugged. "Very well. This is the season for the darkland traders to start moving north. I'll see if I can arrange something. Meantime, I know a good inn."

The inn had a creaking sign, much weathered, depicting some large and improbable fish with horns. There were stabling and fodder for the beasts, and rooms for the people. These were small and cold, sleeping four apiece in two close-beds, and they had lacked soap and water for a long time. The common-room steamed with warmth and sweat and the not-unappetizing odor of fish soup. It was good to be warm again, to eat hot food and drink khamm, which was like sweet white lightning. Stark enjoyed these simple pleasures without guilt.

When he saw that the others were all finished he stood up, and Halk said, "Where are you going?"

"I have a mind to see the town."

"Don't you think we had better be planning what we're going to do next?" He had drunk quite a bit of khamm.

"A little more information might help us decide," said Stark mildly. "In any case, we'll need warmer clothing and more provisions."

Without noticeable enthusiasm, the Irnanese rose and fetched their cloaks and followed him into the chilly street.

Halk. Breca, who was Halk's shield-mate. Gerrith. Atril and Wake, the brothers, two of Yarrod's picked men. Stark could not have asked for better. Yet they six were a small handful against the North. Not for the first time Stark considered slipping away from them to finish his journey alone and unencumbered.

He was surprised to hear Gerrith say softly, "No. Me at least you must have with you. Perhaps the others as well, I don't know. But if you go alone, you will fail."

"Your gift?" asked Stark, and she nodded.

"My gift. On that score it is quite clear."

The market was roofed against snow. Doors at the entrances shut out most of the cold wind. Smoky lamps and braziers burned. Merchants sat amid their wares, and Stark noticed that few of them were of Izvand. The pale-haired warriors apparently scorned such occupation.

The market was busy. The party from Irnan wandered with the crowd, buying furs and boots and sacks of the sweet, fatty journey-cake they make in Izvand against the cold. After a while Stark found what he was looking for, the street of the chart-makers.

It was a small street, lined with alcoves where men sat hunched over their drawing tables, surrounded on three sides by honeycomb shelves stuffed with rolls of parchment. Stark went from shop to shop, emerging at last with an armload of maps.

They went back to the inn. Stark found a relatively quiet table in a corner of the common-room and spread out his purchases.

The maps were for the use of traders, and in the essentials they agreed well enough. The roads, with inns and shelter-houses marked. Modern towns like Izvand, pegs to hold the roads together where they crossed. Vestiges, here and there, of older roads leading to older cities, and most of these marked ominously with death's heads. On other matters they were vaguer. Several of them showed Worldheart, hedged about with many warnings, but each one in a different place. Others did not show it at all, merely indicating a huge area of nothing with the comforting legend *Demons.*

"Somewhere in here," said Stark, setting his hand over the blank area. "If we keep going north, sooner or later we'll find someone who knows."

"So the maps don't help much," said Halk.

"You haven't looked closely," Gerrith said. "They all show one thing, and that is that we must travel by the road as far as we can." Her fingers flicked across the wrinkled parchment. "Here we are blocked by the sea, and here by a mountain wall. Here again, where the land is low, are lakes and bogs."

"All frozen now," Halk said.

"And impassable even so. The beasts would be dead or crippled and we would be starving before a week's end."

"Besides," said Wake, who always spoke for the brothers, "there is the matter of time. Irnan may already be under attack. Even if we could make it the other way, it would take too long."

Halk looked around the table. "You're all agreed?" They were. Halk tossed back another glass of khamm. "Very well. Let us go by the road, and go fast."

"That is another point," Stark said. "Whether to travel alone, or go with some trader. A trader's company would be safer . . ."

"If you could trust the trader."

". . . but we would be held to the wagon pace."

"We didn't make this journey to be safe," said Halk.

"For once, I agree with you," Stark said. "By the road, then, and alone." The others voiced assent. Stark bent over the maps again. "I'd give much to know where the Wandsmen's road runs."

"Not on these maps," said Gerrith. "They must go up from Skeg to the east, across the desert. There would be post-houses and wells, everything to get them quickly on their way."

"And safeguards, doubtless, to make sure that no one can follow them." Stark began rolling up the parchments. "We'll leave at the fourth hour. Best get some sleep."

"Not yet a few moments," said Breca, and nodded toward the inn door.

Kazimni had just entered, in company with a lean brown man in a furred cloak who moved with the agile, hungry, questing gait of a wolverine. Kazimni saw them, and the two came toward their table.

"I'll talk," said Stark quietly. "No comment, no matter what I say."

Kazimni hailed them with great cheer. "Greetings, friends! Here is one you will be glad to meet." He introduced his companion. "Amnir of Komrey." The man in the furred cloak bowed. His eyes, gleaming like brown beryls, darted from one face to another. His mouth smiled. "Amnir trades far into the darklands. He thinks he can be of help to you."

Stark invited the men to sit and introduced his party. The merchant ordered a round of khamm for all.

"Kazimni tells me that you have an errand northward," he said, when the glasses had arrived and the ceremonial first sip was taken. "What I think of the wisdom of that errand is neither here nor there." He glanced at the heap of parchments on the table. "I see you have bought maps."

"Yes."

"You were, perhaps, thinking of going on alone?"

"Hazardous, we know," said Stark. "Nevertheless, our errand is urgent."

"Better to make haste slowly than not at all," said Amnir sententiously. "There are wicked men in the Barrens. You can't know how wicked. Six of you—and all stout fighters, I'm sure—would be as nothing against those you will meet along the road."

"What would they want with us?" Stark asked. "We have nothing worth the stealing."

"You have yourselves," said Amnir. "Your bodies. Your strength." He bowed to the ladies. "Your beauty. Men and women are sold in the Barrens, for many purposes."

Halk said, "I think anyone who tried that would find us a poor bargain."

"No doubt. But why take the risk? If you're captured, or killed resisting capture, where is your errand then?" He leaned forward over the table. Sincerity shone within him. "I trade farther into the darklands than anyone because I am able to face the dangers there not only with courage, which many others have as well, but with prudence, which many others seem to lack. I travel with fifty well-armed men. Why not share that safety?"

Stark frowned, as though pondering. Halk seemed on the point of saying something, and Breca gave him a warning glare.

"All he says is true," Kazimni said. "By Old Sun, I swear it."

"The time, though." Stark shook his head. "Alone, we can move much faster."

"For a while," Amnir agreed. "And then—" He made a chopping gesture with the edge of his hand against his neck. "Besides, I'm no laggard, I can't afford to be. You'd not be losing much."

"When do you leave?"

"In the morning, before first light."

Again Stark seemed to ponder. "What price would you want?"

"No price. You'd find your own food and mounts, of course, and if we should be attacked you'd be expected to fight. That's all."

"What could be fairer?" asked Kazimni. "And look, if the pace proves to be too slow, you can always leave the wagons. Is that not so, Amnir?"

Amnir laughed. "I'd not be the one to stop them."

Stark looked across at Gerrith. "What does the wise woman say?"

"That we should do what the Dark Man thinks best."

"Well," said Stark, "if it's true that we can go our own way if we choose to later on—"

"Of course. Of course!"

"Then I think we ought to go with Amnir in the morning."

They struck hands on it. They drank more khamm. They arranged final details, and the two men left. Stark gathered his maps and led his party upstairs. They crowded into one of the small rooms.

"Now what does the wise woman say?" asked Stark.

"That Amnir of Komrey means us no good."

"It needs no wise woman to see that," said Halk. "The man smells of treachery. Yet the Dark Man has agreed to go with him."

"The Dark Man is not above telling lies when he thinks they're called for." Stark looked round at them. "We'll not wait for the fourth hour. As soon as the inn is quiet, we go. You can do your sleeping in the saddle."

In the star-blazing midnight, they rode out of Izvand. The cold ribbon of road stretched north toward the darklands, and they had it all to themselves. They made the most of it. Halk seemed to be consumed with a passion for haste, and Stark was in no mood to dispute him. He, too, wanted to leave Amnir as far behind as possible.

The land had begun its long slope upward to the ice-locked ranges of the north, and from the higher places Stark could keep a watchful eye on the backtrail. He could also sniff the wind and listen to the silence and feel the vast secret land that encircled him.

It was not a good land. The primitive in him sensed evil there like a sickness. It wanted to turn tail and go shivering and howling back to the smoky warmth of Izvand and the safety of walls. The reasoning man in him agreed, but kept moving forward nevertheless.

Clouds hid the Three Ladies. Snow began falling. Stark disliked the inability to see clearly; anything might come upon them out of those pale drifting clouds. The party rode more slowly, keeping close together.

They came upon an inn, crouched over a crossroads. It had a tall roof like a wizard's hat, and one slitted yellow eye. Stark considered stopping there and instantly decided against it. By common consent they left the road and made a wide circle round the inn, walking the beasts carefully so as to make no sound.

Daylight was slow in coming, and when Old Sun did show himself at last it was only as a smear of ginger-colored light behind a blur of snowflakes.

It was in that strange brassy glow that they came to the bridge.

12

The bridge, the rocky gorge it spanned, and the village that existed solely to administer to and extort for the bridge, were clearly marked on all the maps. There was apparently no way around that did not take at least a week, even without snow, and the toll seemed reasonable. Stark loosened his sword in its scabbard and dug some coins from the leather bag that hung about his neck underneath the bulky furs. The Irnanese checked their own weapons.

In close order, they trotted themselves and their pack animals toward the toll-house, a squat blocky structure commanding the southern end of the bridge. An identical structure was at the northern end. Each building contained a winch that raised or lowered a portion of the bridge floor, so that no one could force his way through without paying. You might take one toll-house but never both, and a part of the bridge would always be unreachably open. The drop below it was unpleasant, several hundred feet down past jagged boulders rimed with snow and frozen spray to a vicious little river that drained some glacier slope higher up. The village was built on the southern side, against the face of a low cliff, strongly fortified. Stark guessed that the convenience of the bridge outweighed the nuisance factor, and so generations of merchants had let it survive.

Three men came out of the building. Short, broad and ugly troll-like men, with many furs and too-wide smiles. They smelled.

"How much?" asked Stark.

"For how large a party?" Small eyes probed the snowfall behind them. "How many beasts? How many wagons? The bridge floor suffers. Lumber is costly. Planks must be replaced. This is heavy labor, and our children starve to pay for the wood."

"No wagons," said Stark. "A dozen beasts. What you see."

Three faces stared in disbelief. "Six persons, traveling alone?"

Again Stark asked, "How much?"

"Ah. Um," said the chief of the three men, suddenly animated. "For so small a party, a small price." He named it. Stark leaned down and counted the coins into his grimy palm. It seemed, indeed, too small a price. The men departed chattering into the toll-house. They had some way of signaling to the other side of the gorge, and presently both sections of the bridge went creaking down into position.

Stark and the Irnanese rode onto the bridge.

The signaling was very effective, because before they could reach the other side the northern section of the bridge shot upward again, leaving a large cold gap to death.

"All right, then," said Stark wearily, "we fight."

They turned, with the intention of bolting back off the bridge, but a flight of arrows came from slits in the toll-house wall and thumped into the planking in front of them.

"Stand where you are!" a voice shouted. "Lay down your weapons."

A whole band of trolls, furred and armed, came waddling at speed from the village. Stark looked at the nasty little slits in the wall, where more arrow-tips were visible. "I think we're fairly caught," he said. "Shall we live a little longer, or die now?"

"Live," said Gerrith.

They laid their weapons down and stood where they were. The villagers swarmed onto the bridge and took them, dragging them out of the saddle, pushing, pummelling, laughing. The beasts were led off and tethered to a rack by the toll-house. The bridge-keeper and his friends came out.

"Six persons traveling alone!" said the bridge-keeper, and lifted his hands to the brassy glow in the south. "Old Sun, we thank you for sending us fools." He turned and pawed at Stark's garments, searching for the purse.

Stark resisted a strong impulse to tear the man's throat out with his teeth. Halk, who was being similarly handled, got his hands free and fought. He was immediately clubbed down.

"Don't damage him," said the bridge-keeper. "All that muscle is worth its weight in iron." He found the purse and slashed the thong that held it, then prodded at Stark's chest with his dirty fingers. "This one, too—all strong big men, the four of them. Good, good! And the women—" He cackled, skipping on his thick feet. "Maybe we'll keep them here for a while, eh? Until we're tired, eh? Look at them, lads, and their damned long legs—"

Gerrith said, "I was wrong. It would have been better to die."

And Stark answered, "Listen."

It was difficult to hear anything over the chattering of the villagers, and her ears were not as keen as his. But as the sounds swept nearer she heard, and then everybody heard; the rush of hoofbeats, the jingle of harness, the clash of arms. Riders appeared out of the falling snow. They came in strength, they came like the wind, their lances were sharp, and Amnir of Komrey was at their head.

The villagers turned and ran.

"Oh, no," said Amnir, and the riders herded them back, jabbing them painfully so that they leapt and screamed. The bridge-keeper stood stock still with Stark's purse in his hand.

"You have broken the covenant," Amnir said. "The covenant by which we let you live, which is that once a man has paid fair toll for his passage across your bridge, he shall pass without let or hindrance."

"But," said the bridge-keeper, "six persons alone—such fools are doomed in any case. Could I spurn the gift of Old Sun? It is seldom enough that he sends us one."

Amnir's hard eyes looked down upon him. Amnir's lance-tip

pricked his throat. "That which is in your hand. Does it belong to you?"

The man shook his head. He let the purse drop with a small heavy clink at his feet.

"What shall I do," asked Amnir, "with you and your people?"

"Lord," said the bridge-keeper, "I'm a poor man. My back is broken from the labor of the bridge. My children starve."

"Your children," said Amnir, "are as fat as hogs and twice as dirty. As for your back, it's fit enough for thieving."

The bridge-keeper spread his hands. "Lord, I'm greedy. I saw a chance for profit and I took it. Any man would do the same."

"Well," said Amnir, "and that is true. Or nearly so."

"You can slay us, of course," said the bridge-keeper, "but then who will do our work? Think of the time it will cost you. Think of the wealth you will lose." He shuddered. "Think of the Gray Feeders. Perhaps even you, lord, might make your end upon their hooks."

"It does not become you, at this time, to threaten me," said Amnir, and thrust a little harder with his lance.

The bridge-keeper sighed. Two large tears formed and rolled down his cheeks. "Lord, I am in your hands," he said, and wilted inside his furs.

"Hm," said Amnir. "If I spare you, will you keep the covenant?"

"Forever!"

"Which means until the next time you think you can safely break it." He turned in the saddle and shouted. "Back to your sties, filthy ones! Go!"

The villagers fled. The bridge-keeper wept and tried to embrace Amnir's off-side knee.

"Free passage, lord! For you, no toll."

"I'm touched," said Amnir. "And pray remove your dirty paws." The bridge-keeper scuttled, bowing himself backward, into the toll-house. Amnir dismounted and came to Stark and his party. Halk, bloodied and furious, had been helped to his feet.

"I warned you," said Amnir. "Did I not warn you?"

"You did." Stark looked past him at the riders, seeing how they had moved quietly to form a half-circle of lances that pinned the unarmed Irnanese against the end of the open bridge. "You must have ridden hard to overtake us."

"Very hard. You ought to have waited, Stark. You ought to have gone with my wagons. What was the matter? Didn't you trust me?"

Stark said, "No."

"You were wise," said Amnir, and smiled. He motioned to his men. "Take them."

13

The Three Ladies were remote, withdrawn, scarcely showing their faces. The Lamp of the North, like a burning emerald, dominated the sky. The short days of the darklands were little brighter than the nights. Old Sun's dull gleaming stained the sky rather than brightened it. The white snow turned the color of rust, and the vast plain, strewn with the wrecks of abandoned cities, tilted upward to a distant wall of mountains all dabbled in the same red-ochre. The line of great wagons creaked and crawled across this unreal landscape, sixteen of them with canvas tops booming in the wind. From long before sunrise until long after dark the wagons moved, and when they halted they made their own fort, with the beasts and the people inside.

Stark and the Irnanese rode their own mounts and were fed from the rations they had bought at Izvand. Amnir was delighted that their transportation was costing him nothing. Each mount was led by an armed rider. The captives had their fur-gloved hands bound and their fur-booted ankles tied together with a thong under the animal's belly. The bonds were arranged expertly to hold without impeding circulation, so that the extremities should not freeze.

Uncomfortable as this was, it was an improvement over the first days, when Amnir kept them close in the wagons, away from curious eyes. Other parties of armed merchants were on the roads, and Amnir had business at two or three centers where itinerant traders like the Harsenyi nomads brought their wares. These places were like blockhouses, with crude shelters around them where travelers might find some respite from snow and wind. Amnir stayed away from the shelters. He seemed to have no friends among the darkland traders.

His men did not mingle with men of other wagon trains, but remained aloof and perpetually on guard.

At the last of the centers there was an altercation with some wild-looking people bringing in a string of little shaggy beasts loaded with bundles. These people called Amnir unpleasant names in a barbarous dialect. They threw stones and clots of ice. Amnir's men stood ready but no real attack developed and the wild ones withdrew once they had worked off their bad tempers.

Amnir was not disturbed. "I took a large portion of their trade away from them," he said. "It was necessary to kill some of them. Let them yabble at me, if it gives them pleasure."

After that they left the marked roads and went off into this enormous emptiness, where the wagons followed a dim and ancient track that was only apparent when it went through some cut or over a causeway that showed an engineering skill long lost on Skaith.

"An old road," said Amnir. "Once, when Old Sun was young, all this land was rich and there were great cities. This road served them. Folk didn't ride on beasts in those days, or drive clumsy wagons. They had machines, bright shining things as swift as the wind. Or if they wanted to they could take wing and rush through the sky like shooting stars. Now we plod, as you see, across the cold corpse of our world."

But a note of pride was in his voice when he said it. *We are men, we survive, we are not defeated.*

"For what purpose," asked Stark, "do we plod?"

Amnir had refused to tell them what he intended doing with them. It was obvious from the pleased speculative looks he gave them that he had large plans. Whatever they might be, Kazimni had certainly had a part in making them and would share in the profits. Stark bore Kazimni no ill-will for that. He had done his task honorably, getting the party safely to Izvand. Nothing had been said about getting them safely out again.

Knowing perfectly well what Stark wanted, Amnir smiled and evaded.

"Trade," he said. "Wealth. I told you that I trade farther into the darklands than others, and this is the way of it. Metal ingots kept appearing in the market-places of Komrey and Izvand, ingots unlike any I had seen before. Ingots of a superior quality, stamped with a hammer mark. My centers of greed are highly developed. They began to deliver certain juices which stimulate curiosity and the ability to scent profit. I traced these ingots back through a long and complicated chain of trade carried on by such as you saw back there with their bundles. Men died in that tracing, but I found the source."

He was riding, as he often did, beside Stark, whiling away the long cold hours with talk.

"These people of the ingots love me. They look upon me as their benefactor. Formerly they were at the mercy of many things: accident, loss, theft, stupidity, the haphazards of going through many hands. Now that I give them direct and honest trade, they have become so rich and fat that they no longer have to eat each other. Of course, because of this, their population is growing, and one day some of them will have to leave Thyra and find another city."

"Thyra," said Stark. "A city. One of those marked with a death's head?"

"Yes," said Amnir. He smiled.

"But they no longer have to eat each other."

"No," said Amnir, and smiled the wider. "Pray that we reach it, Earthman. There is worse between." And he added fiercely, "No great profit is made without risk."

Stark kept a watchful eye on the landscape. As they went farther on he was sure that he saw, in the rusty gloom, pale things slipping furtively behind hillocks and into ravines. They were distant. They were silent. Perhaps they were only shadows. In this light, vision became confused. In the moonless mornings and afternoons, one could be sure of nothing. Still, he watched.

In those moonless hours, Amnir would now and again stare up at the stars, as though for the first time in his life he was thinking of them as suns with families of planets, other worlds with other people and other ways. He seemed not entirely happy with the thought, and he blamed Stark for having brought it home to him.

"Skeg was a long way off. We had heard about the ships, and the strangers, but we thought little of it. We never quite believed. It was too large a thought, too strange. We had enough to think about without that. Eating. Drinking. Begetting children. I have six sons, did you know that? And daughters as well. I have wives. I have family matters. I have property. Many people depend upon me for their livelihood. I have matters of trade to consider, to judge and act upon. These things take up my days, my years, my life. They are quite sufficient.

"Like the Izvandians, we of Komrey are descended from folk who came originally from the high north, who did not wish to go farther south than was necessary to sustain our way of life. We remained in the Barrens by choice. We consider the people of the city-states, like the Irnanese, to be soft and corrupt." He glared at the stars as though he hated them. "One is born on a world. It may not be perfect, but it's the world one knows, the only world. One adjusts, one survives. Then suddenly it appears that there is no need to struggle because one has a choice of many worlds. It's confusing. It shakes the whole foundation of life. Why do we need it?"

"It isn't a question of whether or not you need it," said Stark. "It's there. You can use it or not, as you please."

"But it makes everything so pointless! Take the Thyrans. I've heard all their ballads, *The Long Wandering, The Destruction of the Red Hunters, The Coming of Strayer*—he's the folk-hero who is supposed to have taught them how to work metal, though I suspect there were many Strayers—*The Conquest of the Mountain*, and so on. The long dark years, the courage, the dying and the pain, and finally the triumph. And now we see that if they had only known it, they could have run away to a better world and avoided all that." Amnir shook his head. "I don't like it. I believe in a man staying by what he knows."

Stark refused to argue this. And then Amnir's curiosity would betray him and he would ask how it was on other worlds, how the people ate and dressed and traded and made love, and if they really were *people*. Stark took a wicked pleasure in answering, unstitching Amnir's self-assurance, opening up the wide heavens to show him a thousand places where Amnir-out-of-context would not exist.

Amnir had a way of setting his jaw. "I don't care. I am myself, I've fought my fight and made my place. I ask for nothing better."

Stark played the tempter. "But it makes you a little dissatisfied, doesn't it? You're a greedy man. Do you see the great ships coming and going between the suns, bearing cargoes you haven't got a name for, worth more money than your small horizon can hold? You could have a ship of your own, Amnir, just for the asking."

"If I set you free. If you succeed. If, if. The odds are too long. Besides—I am a greedy man, yes, but a wise greedy man. I know my small horizon. It fits me. The stars do not."

As a matter of policy, Amnir kept his captives apart. There was less likelihood of mischief, and he knew that the thought of escape was always in their minds. Stark could see the others, hooded and wrapped in furs like himself, riding their led beasts, but he had no chance to talk to them. He wondered what Gerrith would be thinking now about the prophecy.

Halk made one desperate, ill-considered attempt at breaking away, and after that he was confined to one of the wagons. At night they were all put inside. Stark was bound to the wagon frame in such a way that he could not bring his hands together nor get at the tough thong with his teeth. Each time they bound him he tested the bonds to see if they had been careless. When he found they had not, he lay on the bales of goods that formed his bed and slept, with the iron patience of a wild thing. He had not forgotten Ashton. He had not forgotten anything. He was simply waiting. And every day brought him closer to where he wanted to go.

He asked Amnir about the Citadel.

Amnir said, "All of you have asked me the same question. I give you all the same answer. Ask the Thyrans."

He smiled. Stark was getting bored with his everlasting smiles.

"How long have you been trading this far north?"

"If I complete it, this will be my seventh journey."

"Do you feel there's a chance you may not complete it?"

"On Skaith," said Amnir, for once not smiling, "there is always that chance."

The ruins became more extensive. In places they were no more than shapeless hummocks of ice and snow. In others there were stumps of towers still standing, and great mazes of walls and pits. Several sorts of creatures laired in the hollow places. They seemed to live by hunting each other, and the more aggressive ones came howling and prowling around the wagons at night to put the beasts in an uproar.

Twice the wagons were attacked in force, and by day. It seemed that the squat ferocious shapes emerged from the ground itself, rushing forward in the rusty twilight, hurling themselves at anything that lived, all teeth and talons and wild harsh screamings. They impaled themselves on lances, spitted themselves on swords, and their fellows tore them to bits and devoured them while still they screamed. The armed men drove them off, but in each case not before some of the beasts had been pulled down in harness by swarming bodies and reduced to stripped bones in a matter of minutes. The creatures did not stop eating even long enough to die. The worst thing about it to Stark was that the overpowering stench of them was undeniably human.

As they passed these danger points in the ruins, the shadows that slipped and slid along the edges of vision disappeared, only to reappear farther on.

It was obvious that Amnir had been aware of them, too, and that he was worried.

"You know who they are?"

"They call themselves the People of the Towers. The Thyrans say they're great magicians. The Gray Maggots, they call them, and will have nothing to do with them. I've always paid them a generous tribute for passage through their city, and we've had no trouble. But they've never done this before, this spying and following. I don't understand it."

"How soon do we reach their city?"

"Tomorrow," said Amnir, and his hand tightened on his sword hilt.

In the dark morning-time, under the green star, they crossed a river on the ice, beside the piers of a vanished bridge. On the other side of the river a cluster of towers reared against the sky, jagged and broken in outline. They were perfectly silent, except for the wind. But they showed lights.

The road ran straight to the towers. Stark looked at them with immense distaste. Ice glazed them. Snow choked their crevices, frosted their shattered edges. It was somehow indecent that there should be lights within those walls.

Amnir rode along the line of wagons. "Close up there. Close up. Smartly now! Let them see your weapons. On your guard, watch my lance point, and keep moving."

The broken towers were grouped around an open circle, which had a huge lump of something in the middle that might once have been a monument to civic pride. Three figures stood beside the monument. They were gaunt, tuck-bellied, long-armed, slightly stooped. They wore tight-fitting garments of an indeterminate gray color, hoods covering narrow heads. Their faces were masked against the wind. The masks were worked in darker threads with what appeared to be symbols of rank. The three stood immobile, alone, and the ragged doorways of the buildings gaped darkly on either hand.

Stark's nostrils twitched. A smell of living came to him from those doorways—a dry subtle taint of close-packed bodies, of smoke and penned animals, of dung and wool and unnameable foods. He was riding in his usual place beside the third wagon in line. Gerrith was behind him, beside the fourth; the other captives strung out behind her, except for Halk, who was still confined. Stark tugged nervously at his bonds, and the armed man who led his beast thumped him with his lance butt and bade him be still.

The noise of the wagons rolled against the silence. Amnir rode aside, toward the three gray figures. Men came after him bearing sacks and bales and rolls of cloth.

Amnir halted and raised his hand. The hand held a lance, point upward.

"May Old Sun give you light and warmth, Hargoth."

"There is neither here," said the foremost figure. Only his eyes and his mouth showed. The eyes were pale and unreadable. Above them, on the forehead of the mask, was the winged-disc sun-symbol which Stark had found to be almost universal. On the sides of the mask, covering the cheeks, were stylized grain patterns. Stark supposed the man was both chief and high priest. It was strange to find a Corn King here, where no corn had grown for centuries. The man's mouth had thin lips and very sharp teeth. His voice was high and reedy but it had a carrying quality, a note of authority.

"Here there are only my lord Darkness, and his lady Cold, and their daughter Hunger."

"I have brought you gifts," said Amnir.

And the Corn King said, "This time, you have brought us more."

The wind blew his words away. But Amnir's lance point dipped and a movement began along the line of wagons, a bristling of weapons. The man leading Stark's beast shortened up on the rein.

In a curiously flat tone Amnir said, "I don't take your meaning."

"Why should you?" said the Corn King. "You have not the Sight. But I have seen. I have seen it in the Winter Dreaming. I have seen it in the entrails of the Spring Child that we give each year to Old Sun. I have seen it in the stars. Our guide has come, the Promised One who will lead us into the far heavens, into warmth and light. He is with you now." A long slender arm shot out and pointed straight at Stark. "Give him to us."

"I do not understand you," Amnir said. "I have only captives from the south, to be sold as slaves to the Thyrans."

The lance point dipped lower. The pace of the wagons quickened.

"You lie," said the Corn King. "You will sell them to the Citadel. Word has come from the high north, both truth and lies, and we know the difference. There are strangers on Skaith, and the star-roads are open. We have waited through the long night, and now it is morning."

As though in answer, the first sullen glimmer of dawn stained the eastern sky.

"Give us our guide now. Only death waits for him in the high north."

Stark shouted, "What word have you of strangers?"

The armed man clouted him hard across the head with the lance butt. Amnir voiced a shrill cry, reining his beast around, and the wagons began to move, faster and faster, the teams slipping and scrabbling on the frosty ground.

14

Bound so that he could neither fight nor fall, half unconscious from the blow, Stark saw the encircling walls and dark doorways rush past him in a ringing haze. He wanted the people inside those doorways to come out and attack, to set him free, but they did not. And the Corn King with his attendants remained motionless beside the monument. In a few moments the whole clattering, jouncing caravan of wagons and armed men was clear of the circle and racing along between lesser ruins, lightless and deserted. By the time Old Sun had dragged himself above the horizon they were in open country, and unpursued.

Amnir halted the train to rest the beasts and restore order along the line. Stark managed to twist himself around far enough to see that Gerrith was all right. Her face was white, her eyes large and strange.

The man-at-arms used his lance again, this time with less force, to straighten his prisoner in the saddle. Stark shook away the last of the haze from his vision and tried to ignore the throbbing in his head. Amnir was riding up to him.

There was something peculiar about the man's expression as he looked at Stark. It was plain that the encounter with the men of the Towers had shaken him.

"So," said Stark, "you meant us for the Citadel all along."

"Does that surprise you?"

"No. But the Corn King surprised me."

"The what?"

"The man you called Hargoth, the priest-king of the Towers. He knew me. He was waiting. That's why we were being watched."

"You will get little good from that," said Amnir, and turned to the man-at-arms. "See that he's put into the wagon. Now. And guarded well."

"Guarded against what?" asked Stark. "The People of the Towers? Can you guard against magicians? Or the Thyrans. Perhaps they'd prefer to sell us to the Citadel themselves, without sharing the profits. Or the Lords Protector. Suppose they see no reason to pay you the price you've been rolling under your tongue ever since Kazimni talked to you in Izvand. Suppose they send their North-hounds to hunt us all down." Stark laughed, a small unpleasant sound. "Or are you perhaps beginning, in spite of yourself, to think that there may be something in the wise woman's prophecy? If that's it, hurry, Amnir! See if you can outrun fate."

Amnir's eyelids flickered uneasily. He said something Stark could not hear, probably a curse, and rode away, kicking his beast with unnecessary viciousness.

Stark was put into the wagon and bound with even more care than usual. He lay staring up at the tilt of the rough canvas above him, hearing again the Corn King's words. *The star-roads are open. We have waited through the long night and now it is morning.*

Old Sun's pale gleaming had long since vanished from the canvas when the wagon was wheeled into place for the night. Stark lay still, feeling a curious and quite unfounded anticipation. He listened to the sounds of Amnir's men making camp. He listened to the fretting of the wind at the canvas. He listened to the beating of his own heart. And he waited.

I have seen it in the Winter Dreaming. I have seen it in the entrails of the Spring Child. Our guide has come—

The noises of the camp died away. The men had eaten and wrapped themselves for sleep, all but the sentries. There seemed to be more of them than usual, from the number of pacing feet. From time to time one of the guards looked in through the flap, making sure that the prisoner was still safely bound.

Time went by.

Perhaps I was wrong, Stark thought. Perhaps nothing at all will happen.

He had no clear idea what he was waiting for. A sudden attack, the swift rush of footsteps, shouts, cries— The watchers sent out by the Corn King had had no difficulty keeping up with the slow-moving wagons, and the People of the Towers ought to be able to come up with the train at some time during the night.

And suppose they did come; suppose they did attack. Amnir's men were disciplined and well armed. They were on guard. Could the People of the Towers overcome them? What weapons did they have? How well did they fight?

If they were truly great magicians, they would have more subtle ways of gaining their ends. But were they, truly?

He did not know. And he began at length to think that he would never know.

The cold, he thought, was more penetrating than usual. It pinched his face. He worried about frostbite and tried to burrow his nose deeper into his sleeping furs, one side at a time. The moisture of his own breath froze upon the furs, upon his flesh and hair. His lungs hurt. He grew drowsy, and he could picture himself asleep and freezing gradually into a statue with a shining glaze of ice over him like glass.

He was afraid.

He fought his bonds. He did not break free, but he generated enough heat to melt some of the frost that had gathered around him.

It froze again, and now he could *hear* the cold.

It sang. Each crystal of ice had a voice, tiny and thin.

It tinkled and crackled, faintly, sweetly, like distant music heard across hills when the wind blows.

It chimed, and the chiming spoke elfinly of sleep and peace. Peace, and an end of striving.

All living things must come to that at last.

Surrender to sleep and peace.

Stark was still fighting feebly against that temptation when the back flap of the wagon-tilt opened and a narrow person came lithely in over the tailgate. Moving swiftly, he slashed Stark's wrists and ankles free. He hauled him up, amazingly strong for all his narrowness, and forced a draught of some dark liquid down Stark's throat.

"Come," he said. "Quickly."

The face, masked in plain gray without markings, swam in the gloom, unreal. Stark pawed his way forward, and the draught he had drunk took sudden fire within him. He half climbed, half fell out of the wagon. The strong arm of the gray man steadied him.

Inside the circle of wagons the tiny hoarded fires guttered behind their windbreaks, dying. Bodies, animal and human, lay about, motionless under a shining coat of frost that shone pale in the starlight. The sentries lay where they had fallen, awkward things like dummies with uplifted arms and stiffly contracted legs.

Stark articulated one word. "Gerrith."

The gray man pointed and urged him on.

The Corn King stood on a small eminence beyond the camp. Behind him, a number of lesser priests were spaced along the line of a wide semicircle. It was as if they formed a drawn bow, with the Corn King at the tip of the arrow. They were all quite motionless, their masked faces bent upon the camp. Stark's guide took good care not to pass in front of that silent bow and arrow. He led Stark off to one side. The deadly cold relaxed its grip.

Stark said again, "Gerrith."

The gray man turned toward the camp. Two figures came stumbling from the wagons, one narrow and masked and supporting the other, clad in furs. When they came closer Stark saw a thick swinging braid of hair and knew that the fur-clad one was Gerrith.

He exhaled a breath of relief that steamed on the icy air. Then he said, "Where are the others?"

The gray man did not answer. Stark grasped him by one thin sinewy shoulder and shook him. "Where are the others?"

The Corn King's voice spoke behind him. The semicircle was broken; the work of the arrow done.

"We have no need of them," the Corn King said. "The Sun Woman I have use for. The others are worthless."

"Nevertheless," said Stark quietly, "I will have them. Now. And safe. Also, we will need arms."

Hargoth hesitated, his eyes catching a glint of starlight so the holes in his mask gleamed eerily. Then he shrugged and sent four of his people running back to the wagons.

"It will do no harm," he said, "nor any good, either. Your friends will die later on, and less kindly, that is all."

Stark looked toward the camp and at the still figures on the ground. "What did you do to them?"

"I sent the Holy Breath of the Goddess upon them." He made a sign in the air. "My Lady Cold. She will give them sleep, and the everlasting peace."

So that was the end of Amnir and his energetic greed. Stark found it difficult to feel much pity for him. The men-at-arms were doing a dangerous job for their living, but he felt little sympathy for them, either. His wrists and ankles bore the scars of their hospitality.

Hargoth indicated a long, low ridge, a fold in the plain. "My folk have made camp beyond. There is fire. We have food and drink. Come."

Stark shook his head. "Not until I see our comrades."

They stood, in the biting air, until Halk and Breca and the brothers had been brought, together with weapons borrowed from the dead. Then they followed the Corn King toward the ridge.

"There is food in those wagons," said Halk. He walked crookedly, having been bound for many days. Some of the strength had gone out of him, but he was as belligerent as ever, perhaps worse because he was conscious of his weakness. "Are you going to leave it all there for whatever beasts there are in this wilderness?"

"We do not need it," said Hargoth. "And we are not thieves. Whatever is in the wagons belongs to the Thyrans."

"Then why not us?"

"You were no part of their bargain with the trader."

Stark steadied Gerrith over a stretch of bare rock. "You said that word had come to you from the high north. Who sent that word?"

"The Wandsmen. They told us to watch for strangers coming from the south. They offered a high price for you."

"But you do not intend to take it?"

"No."

"Why not?"

"There was other news from the high north. A man not of this world has been brought to the Citadel. The Harsenyi nomads saw him with the Wandsmen in the passes of the Bleak Mountains. The Wandsmen like to hide their secrets but the Harsenyi see everything. They range over half the world, and they carry news." The Corn King glanced sidelong at Stark. "Besides, there is the Sight, and I knew who you were when my people first saw you riding beside the wagons. You are not of this world. You come from the south, and it is said that there is a place in the south where the starships land. The Harsenyi brought this word from Izvand."

"It is true," said Stark.

"Ah," said Hargoth. "I saw it clearly, in the Winter Dreaming. The ships stand like bright towers beside the sea."

They had reached the crest of the ridge. Below, somewhat sheltered from the wind, Stark saw the fires, and the humped shapes of skin tents already dusted with snow.

"That is where we wish to go," said Hargoth. "That is why we will not sell you to the Wandsmen. You will lead us, to the stars."

He bent his head humbly before Stark. But his eyes, looking upward, were not humble.

15

STARK WALKED halfway down the slope, so that Hargoth was obliged to follow. Then he stopped.

"I will lead you," he said, "after we have taken the Citadel. Not before."

The wind moaned against the ridge, sending a frozen spindrift of white crystals across it that drifted down on Stark and the Irnanese, on Hargoth and his lesser priests. There was an instinctive movement, each group gathering apart from the other. After that, they stood very still.

Hargoth said, "The ships are in the south."

Stark nodded. "Unfortunately, that gate is shut. There is war in the south. Other men beside you wish to follow those star-roads, and the Wandsmen are saying they cannot. They are killing, in the name of the Lords Protector. The only way to open that gate is to take the Citadel, destroy the Lords Protector, and the Wandsmen along with them. Otherwise, you will go south only to die."

The wind moaned and the fine white spindrift fell.

Hargoth turned to Gerrith. "Sun Woman, is this all true?"

"It is true," she answered.

"Besides," said Stark, suddenly very weary of trying to cope with people who stubbornly insisted on getting in his way, "if Skaith were an open world, certain kinds of ships could land anywhere on the planet instead of being confined to the enclave at Skeg. There would be no need for your people to go south. It would be much easier for ships to come to you."

Hargoth did not answer this. Stark had no idea what he might be thinking. He was only certain of one thing, that he would not be taken captive again by anyone if he had to die fighting. He shifted his weight slightly, wishing that his muscles were not quite so stiff with cold.

"You are wise in your knowledge," Hargoth said at last. "What shall I call you?"

"Stark."

"You are wise in your own knowledge, Stark, but I am wise in mine. And I tell you that Thyra lies between us and the Citadel."

"Is there no way around? The land seems broad enough."

"Until it narrows. Thyra bestrides that narrowness. Thyra is strong and populous. And greedy." He paused, and then added harshly, "They have dealings with the Wandsmen. The same word that came to us would have come even sooner to them."

Stark nodded. He stared at the ground, scowling.

"South," said Hargoth. "That is the only way."

His voice held an inflexible note of triumph. Stark kept his peace, answering only with a shrug, into which Hargoth could read any meaning that pleased him.

Apparently he read acquiescence, because he turned and started down the slope. "The fires are warm, the shelters are ready. Let us enjoy them. Tomorrow, at his rising, we will ask a blessing of Old Sun."

Stark perforce followed Hargoth this time. There was nothing of menace in what the man had said, yet Stark felt a twinge of unease. He looked at Gerrith, walking beside him with the long braid swinging. Sun-colored braid beneath the frost. Sun-colored woman. What did Hargoth want of her?

He was about to speak to Gerrith. But she gave him a warning look, and then Hargoth glanced over his shoulder at them, giving them a sharp-edged smile.

Blank-faced, they followed him down.

The folk in the camp were all young men. Women, children, and older men, they were told, were already making preparations for the migration, packing the belongings, dismantling the homes in the broken towers, drying meat and making journey-bread, choosing the beasts that would be saved from the present slaughter to support them later on.

They were singing, said Hargoth, the very ancient hymn preserved from times beyond remembrance, taught once in each lifetime but never sung until now. The Hymn of Deliverance.

The Promised One shall lead us
Down the long roads of the stars,
Toward a new beginning . . .

The men sang it around the fires as Stark and the others came in. Their faces were flushed, their eyes brilliant, fixed upon this stranger from the far places of heaven. Stark felt embarrassed and more than a little annoyed. Ever since he had landed on Skaith people had been forcing shackles on him, shackles of duty that he had not himself chosen and did not want. Damn these people and their prophecies and legends!

"Our forefathers were men of knowledge," said Hargoth. "They dreamed of star-flight. While the world died around them they continued to dream, and to work, but it was too late. They left with us the promise that, though we could not go, one day you would come to us."

Stark was glad when the hymn ended.

Gerrith refused food and asked to be shown to her shelter, alone. Her face had that remote prophetess look on it. Stark saw the skin flaps of the tent fall shut behind her with a feeling of chill between his shoulder-blades.

He ate the food that was given him, not because he was especially hungry but because the hunting animal never knows how long it may be until the next meal. He drank the strong drink that seemed to be made of fermented milk. The Irnanese sat near him in a close group. He sensed that they wanted to talk but were inhibited by Hargoth and his people, who crouched or moved among the fires like slender ghosts with their high stooping shoulders and their gray-masked faces all alike and without expression. Despite the fact that the People of the Towers had rescued them from Amnir's shackles,

Stark did not like them. There was a touch of madness in them, born of the long dark and the too-long-held faith. It made him feel no easier that their madness was centered on him.

The flaps of Gerrith's tent opened. She came and stood in the firelight. She had thrown off her heavy outer garments, and her head was bare. In her hands she held the small ivory skull, still speckled with the slaughter of Irnan.

Hargoth had risen. Gerrith faced him, and her eyes meeting his were like two copper sunrays meeting ice.

She spoke, and her voice rang sweet and clear as it had that day when Mordach tried to shame her and died for it.

"Hargoth," she said. "You intend to give me to Old Sun as a gift, to buy his blessing."

Hargoth did not look aside, though he must have heard Stark and the Irnanese getting to their feet, clapping hands to weapons.

"Yes," he said to Gerrith, "you are a chosen sacrifice, sent to me for that purpose."

Gerrith shook her head. "It is not my fate to die here, and if you kill me you and your people will never walk the star-roads nor see a brighter sun."

Her voice carried such conviction that Hargoth hesitated over whatever words he had been about to say.

"My place is with the Promised One," said Gerrith. "My path lies northward. And I tell you there will be blood and enough to feed Old Sun before this is finished."

She held the skull higher in her two hands, over the fire, and the flames turned a sullen red, staining them all with the color of death.

Now Hargoth looked uncertain. But he was proud and obstinate. "I am king," he said. "And high priest. I know what must be done for my people."

"Do you?" asked Stark quietly. "Can you be sure? You know only the dream. I am reality. How do you know that I am truly the Promised One?"

"You come from the stars," said Hargoth.

"Yes. But so does the stranger who was brought to the Citadel, and he is the one who tells the ships to come, not I."

Hargoth stared at him for a long moment in the red glare of the fire.

"He has that power?"

"He has," said Stark. "How can you be sure that *he* is not the Promised One?"

Gerrith lowered her hands and stepped back from the fire. The flames returned to their normal color. She said calmly, "You stand at the crossroads, Hargoth. The path you choose now will determine the fate of your people."

A heavy and sententious statement, Stark thought, but he felt no desire to smile at it. It was the simple truth, and it involved his own and Ashton's fate as well as that of Hargoth's people.

His hand closed over the hilt of the sword taken from one of Amnir's men. He waited for Hargoth's answer. If the stupid man insisted on sacrificing Gerrith and going south, Old Sun was going to have some victims here and now.

Hargoth's gaze flicked uncertainly between Stark and Gerrith—the chill, flat, shining gaze of madness, of fanatic conviction. The lesser priests who had assisted him at Amnir's camp were gathered nearby, their masked faces immobile, watching. Suddenly Hargoth turned on his heel and joined them. They went apart. Their backs formed a wall that hid whatever they might be doing, but the movement of their shoulders indicated that some sort of ritual was being performed. They chanted, a low sonorous murmuring.

"Lacking a live victim," Gerrith said, "they're consulting some other augury."

"It had better be favorable," said Halk, and drew his swordblade hissing from the sheath.

The silence lengthened. The guttering fire hissed as snow and frost fell into it. The People of the Towers stood in the blowing darkness beyond, and waited.

The priests made one long moaning sigh. They bowed to some invisible Presence. Then they returned to the fire.

"Three times we have cast the sacred finger-bones of the Spring Child," said Hargoth. "Three times, they pointed north." His eyes showed a desperate, thwarted rage. "Very well. We will go up against the Thyrans. And if we win past them, do you know what waits beyond Thyra, to keep us from the Citadel?"

"Yes," said Stark, "I know. The Northhounds."

A shadow crossed Gerrith's face. She shivered.

"What is it?" asked Stark.

"I don't know. It seemed—that when you spoke that name, one heard it."

Across the desolate miles to the north, a great white shape had paused in its measured padding through blowing snow. It turned and swung a huge, fanged muzzle southward, questing across the wind.

16

As Hargoth had said, the broad land narrowed. It began to rise sharply toward a series of ridges, and on either hand were rough hills and deep gullies choked with tumbled ice. The track of Amnir's wagons still followed the ancient road. Apparently the summer thaw was strong enough to cut the road in many places. It had been remade across the beds of wider channels, the narrower ones filled in with stones, a tribute to the hard work and enterprise of Amnir's men. And much good it had done them in the end.

With Hargoth's people, the party now numbered thirty-six: two tens of fighting men and their captain, armed with slings and javelins; the Corn King and eight priests, armed with magic; and the original six from Irnan, counting Stark, who would just as soon have dispensed with his new allies. The force was too large to move easily in secret, and too small to be effective as an attack unit. Still, he thought the Corn King and his priests might be useful in one way, when they came to meet the Northhounds. The breath of the Goddess might at least slow down these legendary demons. In any case, he had had no choice.

The narrow men in gray proved to be nearly tireless. Their marching gait was a sort of springy trot that was difficult at first for Stark and the others to keep up with after the long days of captivity. But they fell into the pace gradually, feeling strength and elasticity returning. Only Halk, who had suffered the worst confinement, stumbled along at the rear, sweating and cursing. He was so vile-tempered that Breca gave up trying to help him and rejoined the others.

"How far to Thyra?" asked Stark.

"Three long marches." Hargoth had not been to Thyra himself, but Kintoth, captain of the fighting men, had. He wore lightning-strokes on the cheeks of his mask and he carried an iron sword.

"We go there somewhiles to trade for tools and weapons," Kintoth said, slapping his sword-hilt. "The Thyrans are great smiths. We always go in force. We trade them dried meat as well as hides and cloth, but in the old days before the trader we were afraid of being added to their foodstocks ourselves. Now that Amnir is dead, we shall have to start worrying again. The Thyrans keep beasts and trade knives to the lichen-gatherers for fodder but there's never enough in the starving times."

"We trade women, too," said Hargoth. "A matter of necessity, though neither we nor the Thyrans like it. We must both have fresh blood to survive. There was a third city once that neighbored us, but the people kept too fiercely to themselves and finally they died."

He trotted on for some time in silence. Then he added, "Sometimes the Wandsmen bring us women from the south. They don't live long here. Usually we give them to Old Sun." And he looked at Gerrith.

"What about the Citadel?" asked Stark, not missing the look.

"We've never seen it. No one has. Not even the Harsenyi. There are the Northhounds, to guard against strangers. And there is the mist."

"Mist?"

"Thick mist that boils like steam above a cauldron and never lifts. It is a strong magic. The Citadel is always hidden."

"But you know the way there?"

"I know what the Harsenyi have said. Some of their people serve the Wandsmen."

"But you don't really know. Do the Thyrans?"

"I have told you. The way is known, and not known."

"What about the women from the south?"

"The ones they give us are never taken to the Citadel, but brought straight on." Hargoth's mouth was a thin line. "The gifts of the Wandsmen! They bring us more than women. Small phials and pretty powders, joy and dreams for all, and perpetual slavery. They tempt our young ones to go south and join the Farers. We are not fond of the Wandsmen."

Hargoth studied the strangers. Old Sun was above the horizon now, and his gaze moved from one face to another, not hurrying, seeing in the rusty daylight what he had not seen by starlight or by the flickering gleam of the fires.

"You have come a long way to destroy them. Why?"

They told him.

Hargoth listened. When they had finished he said, "You Southrons must be soft indeed to let yourselves be so badly ruled."

Gerrith held up a hand to forestall Halk's angry outburst. She looked coldly at Hargoth and said, "You've heard of the Farers. You've never seen them. You've never seen a mob in action. Perhaps you will before you're through. Tell me your opinion then."

Hargoth inclined his head.

"The Lords Protector," Stark said. "What do you know of them?"

"I think they're a lie, told to keep the Wandsmen in power. Or if they ever lived, they've been dead a thousand years. That's why I would call this a fool's errand, except that I know the Wandsmen are real. And if, as you say, they intend to keep us from the stars—."

Apparently he was still not quite convinced. And he continued to glance sidelong at Gerrith from time to time, in a manner that Stark did not care for.

"My lord Darkness, my lady Cold, and their daughter Hunger," Stark said. "You worship the Goddess and she sends her power through you. Yet you also worship Old Sun?"

"We need him to keep the darker gods at bay. Otherwise we would die. Besides, the Sun Woman was to be a parting gift."

Long after Old Sun's setting they went aside from the road and found a secure hollow in the hills. The warriors built tiny fires of what dead mosses and lichens they could find among the wind-scoured stones. They had not expected to be so long away from the Towers and so the rations were short. No one complained. They were all used to hunger.

When it was time to crawl into the skin tents for sleep, Stark said to Gerrith, "You'll shelter with me. I think Hargoth still has notions."

She accepted that without protest. Stark saw Halk watching, wise and sneering, as he followed Gerrith into the tent.

Their two bodies crowded the small space, and Stark realized that this was the first time since that bloody day in the square of Irnan that he had been alone with Gerrith. On the way to Izvand there had been the Irnanese and the troop of mercenaries, and not so much as a hand's breadth of privacy. Halk and Breca pleasured themselves as the fancy took them, without embarrassment, but theirs was an old relationship. Stark and Gerrith had no relationship beyond their two roles as Wise Woman and Dark Man, one hardly conducive to intimacy, and he was not at all sure that she wanted any other. Her status as prophetess set her apart, surrounding her with a certain aura of untouchability. Besides, it had been most hellishly cold.

Afterward, as Amnir's captives, they had had no opportunity even for conversation, let alone anything else.

Now, in the shelter, with a minuscule lamp for light and each other for warmth, he felt something totally new. He was conscious that they touched, at thigh and hip and shoulder. Their breath mingled in faint clouds of vapor. Animal heat rose from their living flesh. Lying close, he felt her stop shivering, and he put his hand on hers.

"Has your gift told you yet why it was you had to come all this weary way?"

"Let's not talk about it now." She turned her head and looked at him. "Let's not talk about anything now."

He drew her to him. She smiled and did not resist. With his fingertips he traced the outline of her cheek and jaw; thin, he noticed, with the beautiful structure of the bones quite clear beneath the wind-browned skin. Her eyes were enormous, her mouth soft and sweet, welcoming.

He kissed her, a first tentative touching of the lips, and her arms came around him fiercely, and after that nothing was tentative. She was strong and hungry, warm life in that place of cold and death, giving and taking without stint. And Stark knew that this had been going to happen right from the beginning, from the moment when Mordach ripped away the robe and left her clothed in nothing but her magnificent and indestructible pride.

Neither of them spoke of love. Love is for a long future. They slept in each other's arms and were content.

In the black morning they were away again, following the green star. They halted briefly for the ritual greeting of Old Sun at his rising, when Hargoth looked regretfully at Gerrith, who was surrounded by Stark and the Irnanese. At noon they halted a second time to rest and chew their journey rations, hard chunks of edible lichens pressed into cakes and a strong-flavored mixture of fat and meat fibers pounded together with bitter herbs.

Stark discussed strategy with Kintoth.

"You see here," said the captain, making out a rough map in the snow with his finger. "This is the road we're on now. It winds about so, and here is Thyra, sitting on a dozen hills. The old city, that is. The new one is dug in and around." His finger made vague marks on the perimeter.

"How old is the new city?" asked Stark.

"Not as old as ours. No. Say only a thousand years, or so. The People of the Hammer came out of nowhere, the bards tell us, and took up these ancient cities . . ."

"More than one?"

"There are several tribes. The Thyrans are the only ones we have to do with, but it is said that there are more in other places, and that they all have the same god, Strayer of the Forges."

"They all have the same madness," said Hargoth, "and that madness is for iron and the working of it. They mine the bones of the cities, and the metal is more than wealth to them, it is life."

"All right." Stark looked at the map. "The road. Thyra, old and new. What else?"

Kintoth sketched stylized mountains on the far side of Thyra. "These are called the Witchfires, for a reason you will understand when you see them. They mark the boundary between the darklands and the high north. Here is the pass that we must take to cross them, if we ever reach it."

Thyra stood like a wall before the mouth of the pass.

"Is there no other way across the mountains?"

Kintoth shrugged. "There may be a hundred. This is the only one we know, and the Citadel lies somewhere beyond it. Now, on the road, here . . ." He drew fortifications across the approach to Thyra. "This post is strongly held. And all around the city are sentry posts." His finger poked random little holes in the snow. "I don't know the exact locations. The Thyrans live in and around the edges of the ruins, and they're more vulnerable than we in the Towers. They take care to guard their wealth and their precious flesh, lest both be devoured."

The land seemed totally deserted. Stark asked, "What enemies have they here?"

"This is the northern edge of the darklands," said Hargoth. "We live all our lives in a state of siege. Anyone, anything, may come. Sometimes the great snowdragons, with the frost white on their wings and their hungry teeth showing. Sometimes a band of Outdwellers who run demented across the world and take whatever they can lay claws on. And there are creatures who wait, hidden just out of sight, smelling the warm food that walks and hoping they can snatch it."

"It doesn't do to show weakness or inattention," said Kintoth. "The Harsenyi, for instance, might be tempted to attack if they thought they could gain by it. The other tribes of the Hammer might become greedy. And of course, the Thyrans have a bigger worry than most."

He stabbed his finger at the sketched-in range of the Witchfires. "They have neighbors here among the mountains. The Children of Skaith-Our-Mother."

Stark stared at him in the brassy twilight of the hollow. The wind blew snow in vagrant clouds.

Halk laughed, a harsh and jarring sound.

"Perhaps you will be lucky a second time, Dark Man!" he said, and laughed again.

17

SHADOWS LAY long across the road, pointing north. Soft-shod, the party moved quietly. Wind scoured, their tracks faded away as soon as they were made.

"What are they like, these Children of Skaith-Our-Mother?"

Hargoth shook his narrow head. "The Thyrans say they're monsters. They have many tales of them, all horrible."

"Are they true?"

"Who can say?"

"You have no knowledge yourself? Haven't any of your people gone into the mountains? Through the pass?"

"In the darklands," said Hargoth, "it is difficult enough to stay where one is. One does not travel for any reason other than survival."

"The Harsenyi seem to manage it."

"They're nomads, it's their way of life. They're strong enough to fight off the brainless attackers, the hungry mouths, and the rest of us thank them. They're the only link we have with the outer world.

They bring things we haven't got and can't make, and most of all they bring news. Being nomads, they don't compete with us for food and shelter. Besides, we're used to them."

"And they cross the Witchfires."

"And more. It is said that they even trade with the Hooded Men on the far side of the Bleak Mountains." He paused, considering. "It is *said* that they trade with the Children of Skaith."

Stark kept his voice free of irritation, though with an effort. "And what do the Harsenyi say of the Children?"

"That they are monsters, and greater magicians than we. That they have power over stones and all things belonging to the ground, which they can cause to shake whenever they wish. They say—"

"They say. The Harsenyi are doubtless the fount of all wisdom, except that traders have been known to lie before now in order to keep their markets secret. Does anybody know?"

"If you mean, can I give you firm knowledge of the Children—no, I cannot."

"You're trying to talk them away, Dark Man," said Halk. "They will not go so easily."

Stark glanced at him, but did not bother to reply. He wondered if he looked as trail-worn and hollow-eyed as did Halk and the others. The sturdy furs bought at Izvand had turned mangy with use, showing bare spots where the thongs had rubbed. The men had stopped shaving, perforce, since Amnir had allowed them nothing in the way of knives or razors. Since their release they had been content to enjoy beards and longer hair as a protection against the cold. The women covered their faces with wrappings against the cold. Breca walked steadily beside Halk. Gerrith, now, walked beside Stark, and her eyes smiled. She alone seemed alive, here and now. The rest were like automatons, waiting for someone to press the buttons.

Stark felt much the same way himself. Land and sky lay upon him like a burden: cold, empty, without promise.

And no one knew what had happened in the south.

The shadows lengthened. The wind blew down from the high north, skirling dry snow.

They came to a place, and Kintoth caught Stark's arm. "There! See there? In the sky, Stark. Look up!"

Stark looked, and saw a glitter and dazzle of pale gold.

"Those are the Witchfires."

The peaks disappeared again as the road bent.

Two of Kintoth's men who had gone ahead as scouts came racing back down the road, loping like greyhounds.

"A party, coming from Thyra."

"How large?" asked Kintoth.

"Large. We saw them only from a distance."

In a few moments they were off the road, settling themselves among the rocks and hollows. Stark left it to Kintoth to make sure there were no betraying marks. He found himself a vantage point where he could overlook the road. Halk lay down beside him. A short distance away Hargoth watched and waited, and presently Kintoth joined him.

The Thyrans were audible a long way off. Drums beat a steady marching pace, accompanied by the intermittent squealing of some shrill-voiced instrument and the clashing of metal on metal. After a while the party came round a bend in the road.

Stark estimated the Thyrans at half a hundred men, including pipers and drummers and cymbal-clashers. All were armed with iron weapons. All wore iron caps, and iron-studded back- and breast-plates over their furs. Iron-bound targes were slung behind the left shoulder. Banners and pennons lashed in the wind above them, barred scarlet and black, with the device of a hammer. They were short broad men who had a look of power about them, and they marched with a driving purposefulness that had in it something chilling, like the march of army ants. They were not, one felt, accustomed to defeat.

Behind the soldiers came a party of unarmed men hauling iron-framed carts loaded with supplies.

"They'll be going to meet the trader," said Halk, low-voiced even though the drumming and clashing would have drowned any other sound. "I wish them joy when they find him."

Stark waited until the last clanking cart had vanished along the road, and then he went to Hargoth.

"Do the Thyrans send out an escort every year for the trader?"

"No. We keep watch for large parties of armed men."

"That is so," said Kintoth. "Once or twice we've watched the trader almost to the gates of Thyra, and they've had no more than the usual lookouts. There's no way of telling just when the wagons may come, and anyway, Amnir had a force sufficient for his safety."

"Nevertheless," said Stark, "Halk thinks that's where they're going." He pondered. "Could they be going to attack, say, the Towers?"

"Not with fifty men. I'd say Halk's right."

"Yet as you say, Amnir had a force sufficient for his safety. This force is large enough to overcome, or at least overawe, Amnir's force. It looks as if they have a very special interest in the trader this year, perhaps connected with something he might have that the Thyrans might want to take away from him—something of unusual value. I wonder if the Thyrans have had some late word from the Citadel about us."

"We were undoubtedly followed to Izvand," said Gerrith. "Fast messengers could have taken word up the Wandsmen's road that Amnir left there in search of us."

"Fast or slow, it makes no difference," said Halk. "We'll never get past Thyra anyway unless we can make ourselves a new road."

"We start on that right now," said Stark. The old road had suddenly become menacing. There might be any number of patrols and lookout posts. Stark tried to calculate how long it would take the armed escort to find whatever was left of Amnir and his wagon-train, and get word of the disaster back to Thyra. Presumably they would send a runner. And then what? Would the Thyrans start scouring the hills?

He reckoned they had better be through the Witchfires as quickly as possible.

They struck away from the old track. It was not difficult to keep direction. Old Sun smeared the southwestern sky with dull red-ochre, and when that had faded the green star shone hugely, almost as bright as a little moon, in the northeast. Stark depended on Kintoth to tell him where Thyra ought to be. The going was by turns fairly easy, and very rough, and often the way was barred completely by a sheer cliff or an impassable gorge. This made for weary backtracking. Progress was discouragingly slow.

There was no love-making that night. They did not stop at all except when weariness forced them to, and then only until enough strength returned to let them go on again. There was no complaint, even from Halk. They all seemed to feel that the hills were dangerous, too dangerous for peaceful rest, and they were anxious to be out of them.

The Lamp of the North climbed higher. The aurora, brilliant in the sky, flared white and rose-pink and ice-green. And there was a new presence in the night.

The peaks of the Witchfires stood tall in the north. They caught these delicate colors on their ice-sheathed flanks and sent them gleaming and glimmering back in flashes of many-faceted light, a wonder born of the cold.

"The Witchfires are sacred to the Goddess," said Hargoth, "though we see them seldom."

Along toward midnight, Stark found a trail.

18

It was a furtive, cunning sort of trail, such as animals make, and it was only because Stark had lived his life in the wild places that he saw it at all. The trail was going the way he wanted to go and so he decided to follow it for the time being. It was very narrow, sliding up and down the slopes, twisting cleverly to avoid the cliffs and canyons. After a while he realized that it was not a single trail but one of a network of footways through the hills.

He asked who might have made them, and Hargoth said, "Out-dwellers, probably, though other beings may use it. Cities attract them, as I told you. There is always the hope of food."

It was impossible to tell if the trail had been recently used. The bare ground was frozen too hard, and where the snow lay there was no sign of prints. If there had been any, the wind or some other agency had wiped them out.

Stark went ahead of the party, trusting to no one but himself.

He caught a taint of smoke in the clean air. Going more cautiously, he saw a ridge ahead. Sounds came from beyond the ridge. Unbelievable sounds.

He went back to warn the others, then crept on his belly up to the top of the ridge.

He looked down into a shallow bowl between the hills. A fire of dead lichen burned small at one side, within a ring of blackened stones. The tiny flickering it made was no more than a pinpoint. The bowl brimmed with the light of the aurora and the green star. The Witchfires sparkled against the north. Snow covering the slopes of the bowl sparkled more faintly, and in that shadowless gleaming a score of figures danced to the wild thin music of a reedy pipe.

They danced in a wide circle, moving widdershins round the slopes. They leapt and whirled, and when they did so they laughed and their tatters flew: the height and the lightness of their leaping, and the grace and the swift rushing joy of it made them seem to take wing upon outstretched arms. Joyousness, Stark thought, was a rare thing anywhere, and he had seen little of it on Skaith. But this was a curious place in which to find it.

There was no set pattern to their dancing, except that they kept the circle. Now and again two or more would join together and go skittering hand in hand, with the laughter spilling out of them in long trills like birdsong, to caper about the piper, who leapt and whirled by himself in the center of the dance. Sometimes he would do a contra-step with them, and sometimes he would do a circle of his own, clockwise against the circle's turning.

After a while it seemed to Stark that there was something more than joy in their frolicking. A certain quality. What was the word Hargoth had used? Demented?

He turned as someone slid softly up beside him. He could see the twin lightning strokes on the mask. Kintoth peered over the ridge and then drew back.

"Outdwellers," he said.

Stark nodded. "They seem to know every inch of these hills. Perhaps they know of a way around Thyra."

"It's worth a try," said Kintoth, "but remember, they're an unchancy lot. Don't turn your back on them, even for a moment." He added, "And remember, the Wandsmen may have spoken to them about you."

"That had occurred to me," Stark said. "Tell the others to come up and stand along here, where they can be seen. Weapons ready."

Kintoth hurried away. Stark waited a moment or two. Then he rose and began to walk down the slope.

He could not say who saw him first. But the piping wavered away, and the dancing stilled. The dark figures stood quietly in the beautiful shining from the sky. They watched him, not speaking, and their tatters ruffled in the wind like feathers.

Stark gave them the formal greeting. "May Old Sun bring you warmth and life."

One of the Outdwellers came forward. It was a woman, he thought. They were a thin people, with wild locks hanging under curious little caps, and their coverings were not revealing. The coverings, he saw now, were made of many small skins sewed together, and the tatters were the legs and tails flapping free. The woman's face was narrow and pale, with a pointed chin and enormous eyes that slanted upward. There were no whites to the eyes, only irises of lambent green with hugely expanded pupils that seemed to reflect the night entire.

"Old Sun is well enough," she said carelessly. Her accent was strange, difficult to follow, and her mouth was strange too, with exceedingly sharp protruding teeth. "We worship the Dark Goddess. May the night bring you life and joy."

Stark hoped that it would. He did not count on it. "Who is your leader here?"

"Leader?" She cocked her head on one side. "We have all sorts. What's your fancy? A leader for singing the clouds and stars, a leader for catching the wind and one for setting it free again, a leader . . ."

"One for the making of trails," said Stark. "I wish to pass by Thyra, unseen."

"Ah," she said, and looked past him over his shoulder, to the rim of the bowl. "You alone? Or with these others I see: Gray Warlocks of the Towers and five persons unknown."

"All of us."

"Unseen?"

"Yes."

"And unheard?"

"Of course."

"But you are not as fleet as we, nor as light of foot. We can go where a snowflake would be heard, and it falling."

"Nonetheless," said Stark, "we will try."

She turned to her people. "The strangers and the Gray Ones would pass by Thyra in secret. Slaifed?" She sang the name.

A man came to her, laughing, kicking the dry snow. "I will lead them." They were a small people, these night-dancers, the tallest of them reaching no higher than Stark's shoulders. Slaifed looked him up and down and across and made a rude sound. "I can do that, but I can't make your great hoofs be silent. That is up to you."

"And their weapons," said the woman. "Don't forget their weapons."

"No one forgets weapons," said Slaifed, and laughed again, a peculiarly lilting sound that somehow sent a shiver across Stark's nerves. Slaifed himself bore no weapons, at least none that Stark could see, except for a knife such as everyone carried for the necessities of daily life.

"Follow me," said the Outdweller, "if you can."

He went gusting away across the snow, seeming to ride the wind. The others of his tribe returned to their dancing, all but the woman, who came with Stark. The thin voice of the pipe was audible for some time, fading slowly with distance.

Hargoth's people and the Irnanese went very quickly, in spite of Slaifed's doubting. They went with their hands on their weapons and their eyes alert.

The scarecrow figure of the Outdweller flitted ahead. The Witchfires gleamed and glittered under the shaking aurora.

The woman looked up sidelong at Stark. "You are from the south."

"Yes."

"From the south, and not from the south." She circled him, her small nose lifted. She walked backward, studying the Irnanese. "*They* are from the south. They smell of Skaith." She turned to Stark again. "Not you. You smell of the dust of heaven and the sacred night."

Stark was not aware that he smelled of anything except a lack of soap and water. But he did not miss the significance of the remark . . . unless the Outdwellers were clairvoyant. He said, "You're given to fancies, little sister." His gaze roved constantly over Slaifed, the trail, the ever-shifting hills. The piping had ceased now, perhaps because it was too far away to be heard. "How are you called?"

"Slee," she said. "Slee-e-e-e . . . like the wind running over a hill."

"Were you always wanderers, Slee?"

"Since the beginning. Our people have never had roofs to prison them. All this is ours." Her wide arms touched everything, hills and sky, the Witchfires, the darklands behind them. "In the time of the Great Wandering we were the free plunderers who fed on the roof-dwellers."

Stark thought that probably she meant that quite literally. She was proud of it. She danced with pride, going a little ahead of him. Slaifed was even farther ahead. This part of the trail was fairly straight, with a steep hillside on the right and a sharp drop-off to the left, into a ravine with a frozen stream at the bottom. The hillside could be climbed at need, but not easily.

A hundred feet or so on, the trail bent around a jutting shoulder of rock. Suddenly Slaifed began to run.

So did Slee.

So did Stark.

Slee's hands were at her breast when Stark caught her and flung her aside with a swinging slash of his hand, never breaking stride. Slaifed looked back, not believing that anyone but an Outdweller could move so swiftly. He reached into the breast of his tunic, still going like the wind.

Stark caught him halfway round the rock. It was like catching a bird. He sank his fingers into the long thin neck that was all cord and muscle, and set his feet, and did a thing that made Slaifed's body snap upward as one snaps a whip.

Stark saw the Outdweller's absolutely incredulous face, saw a double set of iron talons, only half drawn on over thin fingers, drop to the ground. Then he had flung the body against Slee, turning as she came into his back.

Her iron claws were in place and slashing. He felt the metal, still warm from her flesh. Then she fell under Slaifed's dead weight and Stark killed her with one blow. She stared up at him from the white ground, the great dark pupils still reflecting the night, though not so brightly.

The column, headed by the Irnanese, had come to a halt. Weapons were rattling along the line. Stark touched the angle of his jaw where Slee's claws had cut him, two shallow grooves just above the neck. The blood was already beginning to freeze. He drew his sword and went on around the rock.

The trail led straight on, straight to the walls of a Thyran guardpost. There were streaks of light from slitted windows. There were men on the walls and on the squat watchtower. The post filled all the space between the hills and the ravine.

Stark turned back.

Tattered shadows came streaking down the hillside, to leap with outstretched talons onto the marchers. The Outdwellers had decided not to spend the night dancing in the hollow. There was an eruption of noise and violent motion.

Almost at once the harsh bellowing of iron horns sounded from the guardpost.

19

THE OUTDWELLERS, inferior in numbers and armament, were relying on their speed and agility. They skittered back and forth and up the hillside out of reach. Kintoth's slingers and javelin-throwers were hampered by the close quarters. They were forced to use the javelins as stabbing weapons, forming a bristling circle around Hargoth and the priests. Kintoth rallied his rear-guard. The Irnanese closed ranks, more dangerous with their swords and spears. The attackers avoided them.

Some few of the Outdwellers fell or were wounded in that first rush, some few of the gray men of the Towers were slashed or forced over the edge of the ravine. That was all. The Outdwellers were fighting a nuisance action, to disrupt the column and hold them for the Thyrans.

Stark joined the Irnanese.

"What's ahead?" asked Halk.

Stark told him.

"How many men?"

"I don't know. But we're in a trap here, we've got to run one way or the other."

"What's behind us but more traps?" said Halk.

"Move, then," said Stark, and ran back along the line, shouting to Kintoth. The men began to move, slowly at first, then more and more rapidly. By the time Stark got back to the head of the column they were going at a run.

They swept around the shoulder of rock and charged headlong into the Thyran soldiers who were coming from the guardpost.

The impact scattered the Thyrans, a dozen or so squat, thick-armed warriors. Stark and the tall Irnanese hewed with the strength of desperation, blades ringing on iron. Kintoth's light-armed troop had a bit more room to work in here and javelins were finding unprotected legs and throats. If this dozen, ten soldiers and their officers, had been the whole of it, the guardpost would have fallen.

Stark and the Irnanese were almost at the gate when the second ten came through, a solid wedge of leather and metal. This would be the off-shift, the delay just long enough for them to turn out and get their gear on.

Weight of shield and armored bodies bore the swordsmen back. Short blades stabbed, cutting through thick furs. The first lot of Thyrans rallied, the seven or eight who could still fight. They concentrated on the tall Southrons, beating them back into the lines of the gray men.

The brothers fell, almost in the same moment. Halk went to one knee, his hand at his side where blood poured out through a rent in his tunic. Heavy boots kicked him down and trampled over him. Breca screamed like an eagle. Her long blade took the head clean from a Thyran's shoulders and then she went down beneath a wall of shields.

Stark had lost sight of Gerrith. He was among the gray warriors now, the ones who had formed a guard around the Corn King and his priests. These were pressed back against the cliff, standing quietly with folded arms. Stark, running sweat and blood, beating aside the short stabbing swords that forced him ever backward, shouted furiously to Hargoth, "Where is your magic, Corn King?"

Hargoth answered, "Where are your stars?" And his eyes shone like bitter ice through the holes of his mask.

The gray men fell, or were driven into the claws of the Outdwellers, who slashed them from behind, or pushed them over the edge into the ravine. Their slings were useless, their javelins spent or broken against the Thyran armor. Stark caught a glimpse of the twin lightning strokes being separated by a blow that split Kintoth's narrow skull to the jawbone. He felt rock against his back. The wall of shields came in against him. He struck up and under, felt the blade go home, and lost it as the man fell, taking the sword with him. The shield-wall battered him with iron bosses, drove the breath from his lungs. He snarled and clawed and bit, all humanness lost in pain and a growing dark. The Thyrans came on, as merciless as time. And at last, the darkness was all.

When light returned to him, it was the light of Old Sun, running rusty on the stones of a square courtyard enclosed by thick walls. He was inside the guardpost. He was cold and he hurt, and he had bled somewhat onto the stones where he lay. He was not dead, and he thought after a while that he was not dying. A name came into his head.

Gerrith.

A stab of fear contracted his belly. He tried to sit up, and found that his hands were bound. He wondered if a man could learn to live his whole life with his hands bound.

He did not sit up, but he achieved a wider view.

Halk leaned against the wall nearby. His eyes were shut and he breathed through his mouth, shallow careful breaths. His face had a gray pallor; it seemed to have fallen in around the bones. His tunic was open, showing a rough wad of bandage. Beyond him, Hargoth and his priests sat in a group. They appeared soiled and bruised but not wounded, and their masks had been left on them. A guard stood over them, watchful against sorceries. In another place were such of their warriors as had survived, only seven and most of them wounded. All were bound.

He did not see Gerrith.

He called her name, and she spoke from behind him. "I'm here, Stark." He floundered about, pushing his back up against the wall, and she tried to help him. Her hands were tied. She did not seem to be hurt, except for bruises, and her hair hung loose around her face.

"Why," he asked her, "in the name of all the starry hells of space did you insist on coming?"

He was furious with her.

There was much activity in the courtyard, almost a holiday air. Thyran soldiers went about various sorts of business. Their dead and wounded were laid out on litters. A cluster of Outdwellers, like ragged crows, stood by a doorway and grabbed for bundles of provisions being handed out to them. Their payment, no doubt, for betrayal.

One of them saw that Stark was conscious. He came over and looked down with malevolent pleasure. It was the piper. Stark could see the instrument peeping out from his untidy wrappings.

"Why?" asked Stark.

"They told us to watch for you. They told us how you looked. They promised to pay us. But we would have done it for nothing."

The pupils of his eyes had contracted. They reflected nothing now but hate.

Again Stark asked, "Why?"

"The stars are sacred," said the piper. "They are the eyes of the Goddess. When our souls take flight the bright eyes see them, and the arms of the Goddess reach out to gather them in. You wish to defile the stars and rob us of all bliss."

Stark said wearily, "I don't think you understand." Normally he was tolerant of tribal fancies, but he felt no great tenderness for the Outdwellers. "The stars are already defiled. They're only suns, like that one over your head. They have worlds around them, like this one under your feet. People live on those worlds, people who never heard of Outdwellers or their footling goddess. And the starships fly between them. It's all going on out there, this second as you stand here, and nothing you can do will stop it."

The piper carried his peculiar weapons, along with his pipe. He thrust one hand in and out of his garments so swiftly that Stark could barely follow the motion. Sharp claws flashed upward, ready for the death-stroke, and Stark had just time enough to consider the wisdom of his remarks. Then a hairy fist closed on the piper's broomstick arm, and a Thyran officer with an iron torque around his neck said cheerfully, "Do you drop it, or do I break your wrist?"

The piper wriggled his fingers and let the claws go clacking onto the stones.

"This one's worth more alive," said the Thyran, and let go. He wiped his hand on his breeches. "Go along with you, filth."

The piper gathered up his armament and went. The Outdwellers began to file out through the gate, glancing back as they did so with hateful leers at the captives. Stark suddenly sat up straighter and looked again around the courtyard.

"I see your dead," he said to the Thyran. "I do not see ours."

"Don't worry, friend. The Outdwellers will give them useful burial." The Thyran examined him with interest. "You put us to some pains to keep from killing you."

"Why did you?"

"That was the order. Dead if necessary, alive if possible and double the reward. Same for the woman, and for this man. The others—" He shrugged. "Dead was good enough."

Halk's eyes had opened. "Breca was my shield-mate. The men were my comrades. You killed them. That was fair enough, since we came against you. But to give them to those vermin for—" He could not finish the sentence. Rage choked him. Incredibly, he came to his feet and was reaching for the Thyran's throat with his bound hands. His wound betrayed him and he fell again, to stare half blind at Stark with such hatred as might kill a man where he sat.

"Prophecies!" Halk said, and sobbed once, a racking sound that shook his whole body. Then he fainted.

Stark wished that he had left Halk and the others in Amnir's wagons, sleeping the sleep of the Goddess.

Hargoth and the priests were watching him, and he could not bear that gaze, either, even though he had never asked for their faith. He asked the Thyran, "Who are 'they' who gave you the orders, and what are we waiting for?"

The Thyran smiled. "As to 'they,' you'll meet them soon enough. And we're waiting for men to come up from the city, to take over the post while we go down with you and our wounded. You left us short-handed."

There was a second gate, in the wall opposite the one through which the Outdwellers had gone. A couple of soldiers were up above, keeping an eye out over whatever country lay beyond. The Thyran glanced at them, and then he laughed.

"You wanted the Outdwellers to show you a way around Thyra. There isn't any way around. We guard ever trail, every approach. Not a puff of wind can get past us. Otherwise, anyone could creep in and nibble away our wealth."

He kicked Stark experimentally, studied the dried blood that showed on him, cocking his head from side to side. He stepped back, turning to Hargoth.

"I don't believe he's from the stars at all. He's just meat like the rest of us. And none too bright, either, to take up with the Gray Maggots. A fine lot altogether, to make big talk about flying up to heaven!"

His broad face beamed with the scornful smugness of absolutely sublime stupidity. Stark hated him.

"Aren't you even curious?" he asked. "A million worlds out there with more wonders than I could tell you in a million years, and you don't even want to ask a question?"

The Thyran shrugged, heaving his weight of iron bosses up and down. "Why should I care what's out there? What more could I find anywhere than I already have here in Thyra?"

He walked away. "Well," said Stark, "and there's no answer to that." He leaned back against the wall, infinitely tired. "What do you say now, wise woman?"

Hargoth gave her no chance to speak. "The only way was south. South! South where the ships are."

"The Spring Child told you otherwise."

"A false augury. A punishment. Because of your lust for that woman, you cheated Old Sun of his gift. He sent us a curse instead of a blessing."

The eight heads of the priests nodded solemnly. Nine pairs of eyes pierced him with malevolence.

"You are not the Promised One."

"I never claimed to be," said Stark. "Was it because of your anger that you didn't use your magic to help us?"

"The Goddess does not send us power like a lightning bolt. It is a slow magic. We had no time."

"You have time now."

Impatiently Hargoth said, "How can we perform the ritual? How stand as we must, and think as we must? You know little of sorcery."

Stark knew enough of it not to depend on it. He gave up the conversation.

"Have faith," said Gerrith softly.

"Faith?" said Stark. "Will it produce us another miracle that leads nowhere?"

The guards above the gate sang out. Stark heard the marching drumbeat in the distance. Presently the gate was opened and the replacements tramped in. A period of ordered chaos followed as the change-over was made. The outgoing force formed ranks. The litters were picked up. Urgently the captives were made to rise.

Halk was conscious again. He fell twice trying to get up, with a Thyran boot to help him. Stark swung his hands in a short vicious arc and knocked the soldier clanging against the wall.

"He needs a litter," said Stark, "and don't draw that blade. I'm worth double alive and your officers won't thank you for robbing them."

The sword hesitated, halfway out of the sheath. The officer with the iron torque came up.

"Put that away," he said to the soldier, and then he hit Stark backhanded across the face. "You trade overmuch on your value."

"He needs a litter," Stark said.

Halk swore that he did not and tried again to get up. He fell a third time. The officer shouted for litter-bearers.

"Now, then," he said, "move!" He shoved Stark into line.

The drummers picked up the steady beat. The company marched out through the gate.

The path on this side of the guardpost ran for a time under the flank of a ridge that shut off any view of what lay beyond. Then it swung around a curve and the prospect opened up, suddenly and with spectacular effect.

The Witchfires thrust sharply into the sky, throwing back Old Sun's sullen gleaming. At their feet, covering a portion of the foothills and spreading out across a broad valley, was the ruin of a city.

It had probably begun, Stark thought, as a strong fortress in the days when fighting men and caravans moved back and forth through the pass of the Witchfires, which was like a wide notch between the peaks. Later it had become a city, and then a metropolis, and then a dead and silent corpse, sinking in upon itself with the weight of wind and frost and endless time, until all its original form was lost and it was only a great, dark, many-humped mound beneath the mountains.

Then from somewhere the Thyrans had come, Strayer's men, the People of the Hammer; and the city had taken on a strange new life. Now, in the dim coppery glare of day, the guardian of the pass appeared more like a doorkeeper at the gate of hell. All around the base of the city, and into its ugly flanks, and among its heaped debris, were fumaroles from which came plumes of smoke and red glarings that pulsed and shook.

"The forges are never cold," said the Thyran officer. "We are all smiths, even as we are all soldiers. We work and we guard. This is how Strayer taught us."

It sounded a dull life, but Stark forebore to say so. The inside of his mouth was still bleeding.

Some two hours of marching brought them into the new city.

It lacked beauty. Some of the dwellings were underground, some partly so. Others, built of stone from the hills and debris quarried from the old city, were above ground but squat and low, with few windows to take the cold.

A vast straggle of frozen lanes ran between the dwellings. There were places for pens and livestock, and near them a band of hairy folk leading a string of animals made way for the soldiers, staring out of filthy faces at the prisoners. The animals bore great stacks of dried lichens.

There was a lot of smoke, blowing constantly, and a muffled sound of hammering that went on like heartbeats. Huge piles of rusty scrap metal bulked here and there, and over all was the old city, a tangled mountain blotting out part of the Witchfires. Over the centuries the Thyrans had chewed and tunneled the mountain ragged round its edges, and dug dwellings into this raggedness like caves, opening dark mouths into the deeper bowels of the ruin. Stark thought of a community of rats living in the biggest junkyard in the world. If the Thyrans were able to reclaim even a small fraction of the countless tons of metal buried in that junkyard, they could keep themselves busy for another thousand years.

The company swung into what was evidently the street that led up from the main gate. It was much wider than the lanes, and it ran almost straight.

The thudding of the drums became sharper, the pace of the men smartened. People were swarming out to see them go by. They were chiefly of the same heavy build, though occasionally there were individuals of a different shape and coloring to attest to outside blood. The women were no more prepossessing than the men. Stark had no idea what the women of the Towers looked like, but they could only have been an improvement. These people shouted to the soldiers, crowding in to stare and push at the captives. The fur-clad children yelled insults and threw things.

The soldiers shoved the people back with bone-breaking good nature. The crisp beat of the drums never faltered. The company marched up the straight street, straight to the Iron House.

The dark walls of the Iron House were burnished like a shield. The metal sheathing of the roof shone with a dull luster in the light of the ginger star. A guard of twelve men was drawn up before massive iron doors that bore the hammer device. The House was rectangular, some eighty feet long by half that many wide, the long way oriented north and south. The doors were in the southern front. At the northern end, close against the ruins, were lower wings of stone and rubble.

The drums sounded a long roll. The heavy doors swung open. The company marched into a great hall.

Fires burned in pits, giving out heat and smoke. At the far end of the hall was a dais, with a high seat and several places of honor. The high seat was made of iron, strong, square, without grace or ornamentation. A man wearing an iron collar and pectoral sat in it; he was also strong and square and without grace. The pectoral on his barrel chest was in the form of a hammer.

There were others on the dais, in the seats of honor, and Stark saw with no surprise at all that the man on the right of the high seat was Gelmar of Skeg.

20

PEOPLE CAME into the hall behind the soldiers. The chief men beat and shouldered their way through the press to crowd up onto the dais or take their places below it, according to rank. Lesser men filled the body of the hall. Women remained outside, and small boys who darted in were pitched out bodily. The iron doors clanged shut. As though that were a signal, the men began shouting, "Strayer! Strayer and the forges!" They stamped their feet and slapped their weapons. "Strayer!"

After that ritual shout the hall settled gradually to a breathy silence, undertoned with rustlings and coughings. The smoky air became charged with a smell of heat and sweat, wool and fur and leather.

A clear space had been left around the soldiers. The officer drew his sword and lifted the hilt in salute.

"These are the captives, Ironmaster."

The Ironmaster wore a fine purple robe. The cloth must have come up from the south in Amnir's wagons; the local weave was coarse and undyed. He nodded his grizzled head and the officer put away his sword.

The Ironmaster turned to Gelmar. "Are these the ones you wanted?"

Gelmar rose and came down from the dais. He wore a tunic of the somber red Stark remembered from Skeg, and he carried his wand of office. He came without haste, and he looked at Stark with cool deliberation. On the dais were three other Wandsmen, wearing green.

One of them, in a seat next to Gelmar's, had a face deep-scarred and half blinded by a sword cut that had left an ugly groove from forehead to jaw. The wound was healed, but still showed an angry color. This man leaned forward in his chair, with the hunched quiver of an animal about to spring.

Gelmar looked into Stark's eyes, and his own were dark and somehow veiled, lacking the fire of triumph Stark had expected. Yet there was a cold ferocity about them that was frightening.

"I know this man," said Gelmar. "Yes. Concerning the others—" He beckoned to the scarred man on the dais. "Vasth?"

Vasth came quickly to peer into Gerrith's face.

"There were two women," said the Thyran officer. "One of them fought like a man. A shield-bearer, as we had been told. These Southrons defy all morality, allowing women to handle swords. We were forced to kill her."

"No matter," said Vasth. "This woman is Gerrith, the daughter of Gerrith. And this—" He turned to Halk on his litter. "This one is Halk, a ringleader, a killer of Wandsmen. I have cause to remember him." He traced the groove of the scar. "He gave me this."

"A pity my hand was weak in that moment," said Halk. He had not stood the journey well. He looked past the green Wandsman to Gelmar. "What has happened to Irnan?"

"Irnan has fallen," said Gelmar, and his mouth was cruel. "So much for all your trouble."

"And Ashton?" asked Stark.

"Ashton," said Gelmar, and smiled, a small twisting of the lips as one might twist a knife blade in the yielding flesh. "The Lords Protector were discussing what should be done with him when I left the Citadel. That decision will have been made by now. Perhaps he lives, perhaps he is already dead. I can't tell you. But you'll know soon enough." He turned from Stark to face the Corn King and his priests.

Stark made one violent movement and was instantly quelled.

Gelmar took no notice of him. "You were with these rebels, Hargoth, coming to attack us at the Citadel. Why did you do this folly?"

"Because we want the freedom of the stars."

Hargoth still had his pride. His narrow head was as erect as ever, his eyes met Gelmar's defiantly. "The man Stark and the Sun Woman told us that you, the Wandsmen, forbade this and so we must destroy you. We believed an omen; we believed them. But they were false prophets. They would not go south where the ships are. They cheated Old Sun, because of the lust of their bodies. And because we believed them, we have been punished."

Gelmar nodded. He said, "The ships are gone from the south, Hargoth. Do you understand that?"

"I understand."

"The ships are gone. The foreign men and their ways are gone with them. The star-roads are closed. Our way lies as it always has, with Skaith and Old Sun. Do you understand that?"

Hargoth said, "I understand." In his voice was the deadness of understanding.

"Then go and tell your people, Hargoth."

Hargoth bent his head.

Gelmar spoke to the dais, to the man in purple who watched smiling, pleased by the humbling of the gray men of the Towers.

"Open your doors, Ironmaster. Let them go."

"I had rather see them slain," said the Ironmaster. "But—" He shrugged and ordered the doors to be opened.

The priests and warriors formed their meager ranks, beaten men, acquiescing not with patience but with anger.

And Hargoth said, "Wait."

He faced Gerrith. "You prophesied for me, Sun Woman. Now I prophesy for you. Your body will yet feed Old Sun, though not as a parting gift."

Gerrith's expression had changed. All the way from the guardpost she had looked tired to exhaustion, merely enduring. Now she seemed to be listening intently to some inner voice. Yet she heard Hargoth and answered him.

"That may be. But your people must find themselves a new Corn King, for you lead them badly. You cast the finger-bones and you prophesy, but you do not know truth from falsehood."

Her head came erect, and her voice rang out strongly.

"Irnan has not fallen. The ships have not gone from Skaith. The star-roads are open. New things are here, and the Wandsmen are afraid. In the end—"

Vasth struck her, viciously. Blood sprang from her mouth and she fell, past Stark with his bound hands, into the arms of a Thyran soldier, who caught her awkwardly.

"We have had enough of wise women," said Vasth.

The hall had become suddenly still. In that stillness Gelmar spoke softly to Hargoth.

"Will you go?"

Hargoth turned and went, his priests and the remnant of his warriors following after.

Gelmar clapped his hands.

Men came in through a leather-curtained doorway at the side of the hall. They wore saffron-colored tunics and richly ornamented collars of some bright metal. They were of a breed that Stark had not seen before, one of the many things on Skaith he had not seen—beautiful men, beautifully proportioned, with aquiline faces almost too perfect, and they were so much alike that it was difficult to tell one from another, except for the color of the hair. This ranged from black to a reddish blond, but all had copper-colored eyes. The eyes were too wide apart and too long for their faces, and there was something odd about them. As they came closer, Stark saw what it was. They were like the inlaid eyes of statues, startlingly lifelike but without life, showing brilliance but no depth.

As though they understood without orders what they must do, two of them picked up Halk's litter, and another helped Gerrith to her feet. Two more replaced the Thyran soldiers beside Stark. They had daggers at their belts, and smooth muscles showed powerfully beneath their tunics. A sixth man stood by, and it was to him that Gelmar spoke.

"Take them now. Guard them."

Stark saw Gelmar's face clearly, very clearly. The lines, the tautness, the weariness. Some of that proud high confidence that he remembered from their first meeting had been left forever in the sea where Stark had taken him.

Stark said, "Gerrith is right. You are afraid."

Gelmar's men had them moving almost before the words were said, and Gelmar ignored him. No one beyond their small group had even heard him. But Stark knew that what he said was true.

New things had come, things the Wandsmen could neither control nor comprehend, and they felt their ancient power threatening to slip away from them. They must grasp it now and hold it firmly, regardless of the cost, or else it would be gone.

And grasp it they would, with all their strength, in whatever way seemed best to them. The fear, and the uncertainty, would only make them more dangerous.

And might already have cost Ashton his life.

The captives were taken into one of the adjoining wings, to a room rudely furnished with sleeping mats and a few random articles. The Thyrans seemed not to indulge themselves in luxury but the mats at least offered some comfort.

The men in the saffron tunics stayed, all six of them, to guard a woman and two men, and one of those wounded. It was a measure of their importance.

Gerrith was making a dazed and fumbling attempt to wipe some of the blood from her face. Halk said,

"Gerrith, what you said about Irnan—was it true?"

Answering for her, Stark said harshly, "Of course it's true. Why else would they want us alive? If the revolt were really over, dead would be good enough."

In a curiously gentle voice, one of the bright-eyed men said, "Do not talk."

Halk ignored him. He seemed to have recovered a measure of strength, even of eagerness. "Yes, I see. If Irnan still stands, then perhaps other city-states have joined her—"

He broke off with a gasp of pain as the man nearest him kicked the frame of the litter.

If that were so, thought Stark, it would not be enough for the Wandsmen to announce that the wise woman and the Dark Man and the ringleaders of the revolt were all dead and the prophecy come to nothing. They would have to produce real evidence, and parade it before people who knew and could attest to its authenticity. Gerrith alive, the Dark Man alive, one undoubted ringleader alive—all captives of the Wandsmen, proof that the prophecy was a lie and the power of the Lords Protector invincible. Gelmar and his aides could keep the three of them in cages for the rest of their lives, dragging them up and down the roads of Skaith. Or a fitting end could be devised for them, a very public end, with recantings and repentance—an end to remain vivid for generations in the minds of the people.

Then, if hope of the fulfillment of the prophecy had anything to do with keeping the revolt alive, it would collapse very quickly. Irnan would fall, and that would be the end of it. For the present, at least.

The Wandsmen obviously believed that that hope was keeping the revolt alive. Stark believed it too. Not because the Irnanese were childishly superstitious, but because if the Citadel and the Lords Protector were not destroyed, they could not hold out alone against the mobs of Farers and whatever mercenary troops the Wandsmen would send against them. Their allies, present or potential, among the other city-states then would fall away. Jerann himself had said that these others would wait and see what happened.

The Citadel and the Lords Protector. It all came back to them. They were the symbol of permanence—the unchanging, the holy and unseen and forever inviolate power.

The power that would by now have pronounced judgment on Ashton.

Was it, after all, a power that a man could fight? Even if he were free?

Stark looked at his bound wrists. The thongs were wet with his blood. The six men crowded the small room, watching. They had orders not to kill him, he didn't doubt. But there are worse things to do to a man than killing him.

Six men between him and the door. Beyond the door, the Iron House, and beyond that, Thyra. With every gate and every path guarded. Not a puff of wind could get through.

Halk had had second thoughts. "Why would Gelmar lie to Hargoth?"

Again the litter was kicked.

Again Stark answered, speaking rapidly, eye on the nearest guard. "Does he want the People of the Towers marching south . . ."

He dodged the first blow, stiffened fingers aimed at his throat.

". . . singing the Hymn of Deliverance?"

The second blow he could not dodge. He didn't try. He caught the vicious fingers between his teeth.

He learned one thing. These too-perfect creatures were not automatons. They bled.

So did he.

After a time a healer came, a Thyran in a tunic both undyed and unwashed. He wore a chain of office around his neck and was followed by two boys bearing pots of ointment and bundles of rags. The healer tended their hurts, spending long minutes over Halk, grumbling at wasting his time and talents on a non-Thyran who would probably die anyway. When he was finished, servants came and fed them, and then they were told to rest in preparation for a journey. Gelmar seemed to be in great haste.

The room was stiflingly close. The powerful bodies of the men in the saffron tunics were oppressive in the confined space. The smell of them was repulsive to Stark. They smelled like snakes. Nevertheless, he managed to sleep until men came in with new manacles for them, fresh from Strayer's forges. Gelmar's man with the bitten hand held his sword-point at Stark's groin while the irons were fastened on; his face had still shown no expression, not even pain.

Gerrith seemed to have awakened from a dream, and not a pleasant one. She was careful not to look at Stark.

When the Lamp of the North was above the peaks, they were taken out of the room and marched along a corridor to a yard beside the Iron House, where men and beasts were waiting. The beasts were small, with shaggy hair that swept the ground and sharp horns tipped with metal balls to prevent them hooking. The men who led them wore bulky garments of skins with the fur inside, and only their eyes showed between heavy caps and thick tangled beards. The beards were flocked with white as though the snow had got into them; it did not seem to be a sign of age. Stark guessed that these were Harsenyi, in the service of the Wandsmen.

For a moment the prisoners were close together, and Gerrith managed to touch Stark's hand and smile at him. A strange smile.

It was as though she had said goodbye.

21

THE BEASTS shuffled and blew, breath puffing white in the icy air. Stark and Gerrith were made to mount, with a guard on either side, afoot. Halk was transferred to a traveling litter slung between two of the animals. He appeared to be unconscious or asleep most of the time. Even so, he had been manacled like the others, and a guard stood at the head of his litter.

Gelmar, cloaked and hooded for the journey, came and bent over him, feeling Halk's throat where the life beat in it.

"Cover him well," he said to the beautiful man by the litter. "If he reaches the Citadel alive, we can heal him."

The beautiful man, with sword and dagger belted now over a rich outer tunic, covered Halk carefully with furs.

Gelmar and the lesser Wandsmen mounted. The retainers, twelve in all, portioned themselves out along the line, walking near the Harsenyi but obviously disdainful of them.

An escort of Thyran troops tramped up, banging the inevitable drum. The cavalcade started.

They passed through the gate and turned north toward the night-sparkle of the Witchfires. The escort saw them past the outer guardpost, then saluted and went drumming and clanking back to the city.

The path lay ahead, climbing a long gradient to the summit. Somewhere on the other side of the mountains was the Citadel. In a way, Stark thought, getting there was going to be easier than he had thought. At least he would not have to worry about the North-hounds.

No wagons had come this way in centuries, and the track was narrow. The hard little hoofs of the beasts clattered steadily on the frozen ground. The sky was a glory of shifting color.

It was bright enough to see quite clearly the shapes that thronged the pass.

For geological ages the forces of wind and water, thaw and freeze, had worked at the rock walls, scouring, carving, polishing, wearing away. Sheathed in ice, the sculptures seemed alive in the shaking light of the aurora. Great faces watched with deep-gouged eyes. Towering pinnacles soared and tottered, gargoyle wings spread out to shadow the little humans passing beneath. In the wider places, where softer strata had been carried off, whole crowds of cowled and hooded forms seemed to whisper together. The wind from the high north blew down the pass, chuckling and singing, talking to the shining creatures it had helped to create.

Stark's human reason told him that these monsters were no more than lumps of eroded stone. His mind knew that. His primitive gut said otherwise. And his animal senses told him that other beings not of stone were close by.

The Children of Skaith-Our-Mother?

He could not see anything, but a regiment might have hidden itself in the eccentricities of the rock. Still, the Wandsmen and their retainers, even the beasts, moved on confidently. If there was something here, they were accustomed to it and not afraid.

The manacles weighed heavily on Stark's wrists. The sky flared. White, pure as the veils of angels. Pale green, delicate as shoal-water. Red, like a fire of roses. From time to time the shimmering curtains drew apart to show the velvet darkness beyond, with the green star glowing.

Gerrith rode ahead of him, sitting her little beast quietly, her head bowed as though she rode toward an ordeal. He wished he knew what she had dreamed.

At length, just below the summit, at the right-hand side of the pass, he saw a tall pinnacle standing, canted forward until it seemed that it must fall of its own weight. It had the form of an elongated man in an attitude of prayer, and about its base irregular groups and lines of hooded figures stood as though they listened.

In the shifting light and shadow of the aurora, three of the figures moved, detached themselves from the stone, came into the center of the pass and stood barring the way.

And now the little beasts snorted and danced. The cavalcade came to a halt beneath the leaning man.

Gelmar rode forward. "Kell à Marg," he said. "Skaith-Daughter." His voice had a flat quality, as though he were holding it in rigid check. "Fenn. Ferdic."

The figures were cloaked against the wind but their heads were bare except for diadems of wrought gold. The diadem of the foremost figure was set with a great smoky jewel. There was something peculiar about the three faces, very pale in the aurora-light.

Kell à Marg said, "Gelmar." The voice was like chiming bells. It was a woman's voice, imperious in spite of its music, with the innate arrogance of unquestioned power. A match for Gelmar, Stark thought. He had made out the peculiarity of the faces. They were covered in fine white fur, and the features, while not unpleasing, were distorted subtly from the human—the noses blunted, the jaws prominent. The woman had eyes as huge and dark and glowing as the jewel she wore. Night-creature's eyes. She said to Gelmar,

"Did you think to pass through our mountains without pause?"

"Skaith-Daughter," said Gelmar, and now there was just the faintest edge of irritation in his voice, "we have an urgent mission and time is short. I thank you for this honor, but—"

"No honor," said Kell à Marg. She looked past him at the captives. "These are the wicked ones you were seeking?"

"Kell à Marg—"

"You've been setting the whole of the north by its ears; it's small wonder we know. Even in our deep caverns, we're not deaf."

The edge of irritation had sharpened. "Kell à Marg, I told you—"

"You told me there was a threat to Skaith, something new and strange that only you of the Citadel could deal with. You told me only because I asked you—because the Harsenyi had brought us tales we could not understand."

"There was no need to concern yourself."

"You take too much on your shoulders, Gelmar. You intend to settle the entire future of Skaith-Our-Mother without consulting us, her Children."

"There is no time, Kell à Marg! I must take these people south as soon as possible."

"You will make time," said Kell à Marg.

There was a silence. The wind from the high north whined and chuckled. The hooded figures listened dutifully to the endless prayer of the leaning man. The cloaks of the Children fluttered.

Gelmar said, "I beg you not to interfere." Irritation had become desperation. He knew this woman, Stark thought. Knew her and feared her, disliked her intensely. "I understand these people, I've dealt with them, I know what must be done. Please, let us pass."

The ground shook, ever so slightly. Above their heads the leaning man seemed to sway.

"Kell à Marg!"

"Yes, Wandsman?"

A second small quivering. Pebbles rattled down. The leaning man bowed. The Harsenyi began hastily to move themselves and their beasts out from under those tons of rock.

"Very well!" said Gelmar furiously. "I will make time."

Kell à Marg said briskly, "The Harsenyi may enter and wait in the usual place."

She turned and walked with a lithe, undulant stride toward the cliff. There was a sort of lane between the stone figures. She went along it, with Fenn and Ferdic, and the cavalcade followed meekly. Gelmar's stiff back was eloquent of stifled rage.

Gerrith had straightened up. Her head was high. High and proud. Stark felt a qualm of alarm not connected with the Children or the threatening quality of the cliff which, he knew, was about to swallow them. They had already alarmed him, but this was different. He wondered again what she knew, and damned all prophetic visions for the thousandth time.

Halk's voice came from the litter, weak but still jeering. "I told you you could not escape the Children by talking them away."

A great slab of stone opened in the cliff face, moving easily on its pivots. The cavalcade passed through.

The door swung shut. Kell à Marg flung back her cloak. "I do so hate the wind!" she said, and looked at Gelmar, smiling.

They were in a large cavern, evidently the place where the Harsenyi customarily came to trade with the Children. Lamps burned dimly in the quiet air, giving off a scent of sweet oil. The walls were rough, the floor uneven. At its inner side there was a second door.

"The lesser Wandsmen are not needed," said Kell à Marg. "I think we'll get little good from the wounded man, so he may stay here as well. Those two—" She pointed to Stark and Gerrith. "The wise woman and the one called, I believe, the Dark Man. I want them. And of course, Gelmar, I require your counsel."

The green Wandsmen accepted their dismissal with bad grace; Vasth looked poisonous but held his tongue. Gelmar's jaw was tightly set. He could barely control his anger.

"I shall need guards," he said, cutting the words very short. "This man Stark is dangerous."

"Even in irons?"

"Even in irons."

"Four of your creatures, then. Though I fail to see how he could hope to escape from the House of the Mother."

There was a shuffle of dismounting. Kell à Marg stood easily, waiting with her courtiers. Stark knew without being told that she did not often stand this way, in this outer cavern, with the nomads. This was a special occasion, one of sufficient urgency to make her break precedent. She was looking at him with frank curiosity.

He looked at her. The cloak tossed back over slender shoulders revealed a lean body as arrogant as her voice, clad in its own sleek white fur and ornamented with a light harness of the same wrought gold as the diadem. A beautiful animal, a voluptuous woman. A great royal ermine with wicked eyes. Stark felt no stirring of excitement.

She lifted a shoulder daintily. "This one may or may not be as dangerous as you say, but it's bold enough." She turned and led the way to the inner door. It swung silently open.

Kell à Marg strode through it. Gelmar, his two captives, and his guards followed after, with the wiry white-furred courtiers bringing up the rear.

Attendants who had opened the door swung it shut again behind them, and they were closed into a strange and beautiful world.

Stark shivered, a shallow animal rippling of the skin.

The House of the Mother smelled of sweet oil, of dust and depth and caverns.

It smelled of death.

22

THEY WERE in a corridor, wide and high, lighted by the flickering lamps. A group of people were waiting there. They bent their heads with the pale fur and the close-set ears and the golden diadems that varied in size and splendor according to rank. A murmur of voices repeated reverently, "Skaith-Daughter. You have returned."

Stark thought they had been waiting a long time and were tired of standing. At one side he noticed four of the Children gathered together, apart from the others. They bore themselves with a separate pride. They were clad in skull-caps and tabards of some black material, close-belted with golden chains, and they did not bow. Their collective gaze went immediately to the strangers.

Courtiers and officials, when they straightened up, also fixed Stark and Gerrith with cold and hostile eyes. Wandsmen they were apparently used to, for they spared Gelmar only an unwelcoming glance. The strangers seemed to disturb them deeply.

"I will speak with the Diviners," said Kell à Marg, and gestured the courtiers out of the way.

The black-clad ones fell in around Kell à Marg. They five walked ahead, speaking in low voices. The courtiers and officials had to be content with the last place in line.

They walked for what seemed a long while. The walls and roof of the corridor were covered with carvings, some in high relief, others almost in the round. They were done with great artistry. They appeared to have something to do with the history or the religion of the Children. Some of the history, Stark judged, might have been stormy. There were places where the carvings had been damaged and repaired, and he counted six doors in the first stretch that could be closed against invaders.

Chambers opened off the corridor. They had magnificently carved doorways, and what he could see of their interiors gave an astonishing impression of richness. Pierced lamps of silver picked out gleams of color, of inlay and mosaic, touched the *outré* shapes of things that Stark could only guess at. One thing was certain; these Children of Skaith-Our-Mother had little in common with their cousins of the Sea. Far from being animals, they had what was obviously a complex and highly developed society, working away here beneath the glittering peaks of the Witchfires.

Or ought he to say "had once had?"

Some of the chambers were unlighted. Others had only one or two lamps in their large darkness. There was that subtle odor of dust and death, a feeling that the comings and goings glimpsed in the branching corridors and the work, whatever it might be, that was going on, were all less than they should be in the House of the Mother.

The corridor ended in an enormous cavern, a natural one where the fantastic rock formations had been left untouched. There were lamps enough here, and a royal path of marble blocks set into the floor. Beyond was a series of jewel-box ante-rooms, and then the vaulted chamber that must belong to Kell à Marg, Skaith-Daughter.

It was perfectly plain. Walls and floor were faced with some luminous white stone, without carving or ornamentation. It was completely bare. Nothing was allowed to distract the eye from the focal point of the room, the high seat.

Kell à Marg climbed the broad steps to the dais and sat herself.

The high seat was carved from rich brown rock the color of loam, and the shape of it was a robed woman, seated to hold Skaith-Daughter on her knees, her arms curved round protectively, her head bent forward in an attitude of affection. Kell à Marg sat with her hands on the hands of Skaith-Mother, and her slim, arrogant body gleamed against the dark stone.

The Diviners stood in a little group at her right, the others were scattered around the spacious emptiness, close to the high seat; Fenn and Ferdic were at her left. Gelmar, Stark, Gerrith, and the guards were together at the foot of the steps.

"Now," said Kell à Marg, "tell me again of this danger that has come to Skaith."

Gelmar had taken firm hold of himself. His voice was almost pleasant.

"Certainly, Skaith-Daughter. But I would prefer to do it more privately."

"These about me are the Keepers of the House, Gelmar. The Clan Mothers, the men and women who are responsible for the well-being of my people. I wish them to hear."

Gelmar nodded. He looked at Stark and Gerrith. "Only let these two be taken out."

"Ah," said Kell à Marg. "The captives. No, Gelmar. They stay."

Gelmar began an angry protest, smothered it, inclined his head, and began to tell the story of the ships.

Kell à Marg listened attentively. So did Fenn and Ferdic, the Clan Mothers and the counselors. Under the attentiveness was fear, and something else. Anger, hate—the instinctive rejection of an intolerable truth.

"Let me be clear about what you say," said Kell à Marg. "These ships. They come from outside, from far away?"

"From the stars."

"The stars. We had almost forgotten them. And the men who fly in these ships, they also come from outside? They are not born of Skaith-Mother?"

The glowing eyes of the Clan Mothers and the counselors looked at Stark, looked at blasphemy.

"That is so," said Gelmar. "They are alien to us, completely. We let them stay because they brought us things we lack, such as metals. But they brought us worse—off-world ways, foreign ideas. And they corrupted some of our people."

"They corrupted us with hope," said Gerrith. "Skaith-Daughter, let me tell you how we live under the rule of the Lords Protector and their Wandsmen."

Gelmar would have liked to stop her, but Kell à Marg silenced him. She listened while Gerrith spoke. When she had finished, Kell à Marg said,

"You and your people wished to get into these ships and fly to another world, away from Skaith? You wished to live on alien soil, which never gave you breath?"

"Yes, Skaith-Daughter. It may be difficult for you to understand. We looked upon it as salvation."

It was the wrong thing to say. She knew it. Stark knew it. Yet it had to be said.

"We found a different salvation," said Kell à Marg. "We returned to the womb of the Mother, and while your people starved and clawed and died under Old Sun, we lived warm and fed and comfortable, secure in the Mother's love. Do not expect me to weep for you, nor to care about what the Wandsmen do in their own place. I have a larger concern than that."

She turned to Gelmar. "This revolt still goes on."

Reluctantly, he said, "It does."

"Well," said Stark, "and we knew that."

Kell à Marg continued. "You intend to take these people south. Why?"

"There was a prophecy—"

"Yes," said Kell à Marg. "The Harsenyi brought us some gossip about that. It concerned this man, did it not?" She looked at Stark.

Gelmar appeared anxious to hurry by this point. "It sparked the revolt. If I prove to them that the prophecy was false—"

Kell à Marg interrupted him, speaking to Gerrith. "Was this your prophecy, wise woman?"

"My mother's."

"And what did it say about this man?"

"That he would come from the stars," said Gerrith, "to destroy the Lords Protector."

Kell à Marg laughed, silvery spiteful laughter that touched Gelmar's cheekbones with a dull flush.

"I can see your concern, Gelmar! Too bad if he destroyed them before you had your turn."

"Skaith-Daughter!"

"But surely they know?" She turned to the strangers, wicked eyes alight. "Surely you know by now? The Lords Protector are only Wandsmen grown older."

Stark's heart gave a great leap. "They're human?"

"As Gelmar. That's the great reason they must remain invisible, here in the hidden north, behind their mists and their myths and their demon Northhounds. Invisibility is a condition of godhead. If folk could see them, they would know the truth, and the Lords Protector would cease to be divine. Or immortal. They would be only Wandsmen, clever enough and ambitious enough to put on white robes and spend their declining years at the Citadel wrapped in all the rewards that faithful service to their God of Goodness can bring. And these rewards are many."

Stark laughed. "Human," he said, and looked at Gelmar.

Gelmar's expression was venomous. "You need not mock, Skaith-Daughter. We serve the needy, which is more than the Children do, who serve only themselves. In the time of the Great Wandering you were asked repeatedly to give sanctuary here in the House of the Mother to folk who were dying for the lack of it, and you turned them all away."

"And so we have survived," said Kell à Marg. "Tell me, how many sufferers were taken past the Northhounds into the Citadel, to save their precious lives?"

"The Citadel is sacred . . ."

"So is the House of the Mother. The Children were here before the Citadel was built . . ."

"That is only your tradition."

". . . and we intend to be here still when it is gone. Let us return to the subject in hand. Surely a simple way exists to end your revolution. Send the ships away."

Gelmar said between his teeth, "Give me credit for some wisdom, Skaith-Daughter. Sending the ships away would solve nothing, because—"

"Because," said Stark, overriding him, "he could not make them stay away. Isn't that so, Gelmar? Isn't that why, as the wise woman said, the ships are still there, in the south?"

Again Kell à Marg held up her hand to silence Gelmar. Her hand was slender, with curving nails. There were no rings on it. The palm was pink and naked. The hand beckoned Stark to come closer, up the steps. The guards came with him.

"You are truly from another world?"

"Yes, Skaith-Daughter."

She reached out and touched his cheek. Her whole body seemed to recoil from that touch. She shivered and said, "Tell me why Gelmar could not keep the ships away."

"He has not the power. The ships come into Skeg because that is where the first ones landed, that is where the port is and the foreign enclave and the market where trading is done. It's easier and more convenient. And the Wandsmen have the appearance of control there. At least they can see what's going on."

She seemed to understand. She nodded, and said sharply to Gelmar, "Let him speak."

"If Skeg is closed to the ships, there is nothing to prevent them going anywhere else the captains think they might pick up a profit. Most ships, the smaller ones, can land where they will. The Wandsmen couldn't keep track of them; they couldn't have their mob of Farers everywhere."

"They might land even here?"

"Not in the mountains, Skaith-Daughter. But close enough."

"And they would do this for profit. For money."

"You know about those things."

"We are students of the past," she said. "Historians. We know. It is only one of the things we left behind us, that need for money."

"It's still a powerful need among men, no matter where they come from. And I think what Gelmar fears the most is that some of these ships might begin taking away people who want to leave Skaith and are willing to pay for it."

Stark was watching Gelmar's face. It was closed now, closed tight, and he thought that his guess was close to the truth.

"These ships couldn't evacuate whole populations, as the Galactic Union could, but it would be a start. Gelmar's got his fist in the dam and he's trying to hold it there, hoping that the first little drop never gets through. That's why he's so desperate to put down the revolt at Irnan before it becomes a movement. If the whole south falls into civil war, it will be the off-worlders who gain, not the Wandsmen."

Or the Lords Protector, who were only Wandsmen grown older. An unbroken chain since the first founders, renewing themselves with each generation. In that sense, they were eternal and unchanging, just as Baya had said. As eternal and unchanging as the human race.

And as vulnerable.

The room was like the inside of a great pearl, glowing softly white. Kell à Marg sat at the center of it, on the brown knees of Skaith-Mother, between the encircling arms. Her eyes were on Stark, huge and sweating and uncouth in his chains and his heavy furs, the man not born of Skaith-Mother.

He said brutally, "The thing is done, Kell à Marg. Your world has been discovered; it cannot be undiscovered. New things are here and will not go away. The Wandsmen will lose the battle in the end. Why should you help them to fight it?"

Kell à Marg turned to her diviners. "Let us ask help from the Mother."

23

The Hall of the Diviners lay at the end of a long corridor in a section of the Mother's House given over to their exclusive use. The chambers Stark could see as they passed were austere and dim, occupied by students and acolytes and lesser Diviners. The chambers had been designed for much larger numbers. Branching corridors led only to silence.

The Hall itself was round, with a vaulted roof from which a single great lamp hung, gleaming silver, intricately pierced. Beneath the lamp was a circular object, waist-high and about three feet across, covered with a finely-worked cloth. The walls, instead of being carved or faced, were covered by tapestries, apparently of a great age and holiness. A benign and gigantic woman's face looked out of them, many times repeated, made wraithlike by the fading of time but disturbing none the less, with eyes that seemed to follow every move of the people in the Hall. The great lamp was not lighted. Smaller ones on pedestals burned feebly around the circumference of the room.

No one spoke.

Acolytes entered. Reverently they lighted the silver lamp and removed the worked cloth from the object beneath it, chanting all the while.

"The Eye of the Mother," murmured the Diviners, "sees only truth."

The Eye of the Mother was a crystal, enormous, set in a massive golden frame. It was clear and lucid as a raindrop, and the light from the lamp went sparkling down into it. The Diviners ranged themselves beside it, heads bowed.

There was no high seat here. Even Kell à Marg stood. Fenn and Ferdic stood behind her. Gelmar, Stark and Gerrith, and the four guards formed a separate group, close inside the door.

Kell à Marg spoke, and the hatred in her voice was distributed about equally among the outsiders.

"You are all strangers in this House. I trust one no more than another, and all of you speak of things I do not understand and cannot judge, since they are not within my experience."

"Why would I lie, Skaith-Daughter?" Gelmar asked.

"When did the Wandsman ever live who would not lie if it suited him?" Her gaze went to Gerrith, then settled on Stark. "Gelmar I know. The woman does not pretend to be other than Skaith-born, nor does she pretend that she has seen these ships. The man does so pretend. Search his mind for me, Diviners."

The imperious hand gestured to Fenn and Ferdic, who approached Stark. The two guards who flanked him did not move. Ferdic glanced at Gelmar, who snapped something to the guards. They moved aside, but they followed as Stark was led to stand beside the crystal.

"Look," said the Diviners, "into the Eye of the Mother."

Light from the pierced lamp came and went within those lucid depths, now shallow, now deep, ever shifting, drawing the gaze down and down. "The crystal is like water, let the mind float upon it, let the mind float free . . ."

Stark smiled and shook his head. "I can't be caught that easily."

The Diviners stared at him, startled, angry.

"Do you want my memories, the things that cannot lie?" he asked them. "You may have them, freely."

Every world had its methods. He had seen too many of them and mastered too few, but he knew a little. Telepathy and mind-touch he had encountered often and was not afraid of them. The important thing was never to lose control.

He shared his memories with them, the ones that were impersonal enough for sharing.

They stood with their heads bent, but they were only pretending to look into the crystal now. That was for later on. Now they were absorbed, listening to what his mind had to tell them. The truth, for Kell à Marg. Remembering.

Remembering, briefly, the worlds of his youth and Sol, his parent star, a warmth of brilliant gold.

Remembering space, as it had first burst upon him through the simulators in the passenger quarters of a starship outbound for Altair. The stunning magnificence of myriad suns ablaze in the black sea of infinity where they swam forever on their appointed ways. The clusters, like cosmic hives of burning bees. Bright nebulae sprawled across the parsecs, piled clouds of glorious fire. Dark nebulae, where the drowned suns glimmered pale as candles. The island galaxies, unthinkably distant. The deep, wide universe with no rock roof to close it in.

Remembering finally that incredible world-city, Pax, and her incredible moon, symbols of the power of the Union.

The Diviners cried out, between agony and terror. "He has seen! He has seen, Skaith-Daughter! The night-black gulfs and the burning suns, the skies of foreign worlds." They looked at Stark as though he were a demon.

Kell à Marg nodded, very slightly. "So much we are sure of, then. Now I wish to know why this man came here."

"To search for a friend, Skaith-Daughter. Someone he loved. The Wandsmen took him, the Wandsmen may have killed him. He has a great hatred for the Wandsmen and the Lords Protector."

"I see. And the prophecy. Where is the truth of that?"

"He does not know."

"The prophecy," said Stark, "and all the trappings of a fated man were put upon me through no will of my own."

"Yet they were put upon you. Why you alone, of all the strangers?"

"I don't know. But I mean you no harm, Skaith-Daughter. Neither does Gerrith. The Wandsmen are a danger to you and the whole planet, because they don't understand at all what they're dealing with."

Gelmar said, "He lies. There is no danger to you, if you will only let us go!"

Kell à Marg stood for a long time, silent, brooding, the great royal ermine pondering over its prey. At last she said,

"You mistake me, Gelmar. I am not afraid. I am not interested in your Southrons and their revolt. I care nothing for your assurances. This man is part of a new force in the world. He may, or he may not, be important to the future of the Children, and that is all I care about. When I know, then I shall decide who goes and who does not."

She turned to the Diviners. "What does the Eye of the Mother see?"

Now they looked in earnest, deep into the heart of the crystal.

The hall became silent, so still that Stark could hear every breath that was drawn. A great uneasiness took him. This mad she-thing had complete power here, and that was not a pleasant thought.

The many faces of Skaith-Mother watched dimly from around the walls. They did not comfort him.

The waiting became intolerable. No one moved. The Diviners might have been carved from wood. The weight of the mountain pressed down on Stark. He was hot, and the manacles were heavy, broad iron cuffs with a length of chain between. He turned his head, but he could not see Gerrith, who was still behind him somewhere, near the door.

One of the Diviners drew in a sudden breath and let it out again. Something was happening to the Eye of the Mother.

Stark thought at first that it was the lamp. But that glowed as brightly as ever, and yet the light was draining out of the great crystal, the luster dimming, dulling, darkening, going from pellucid clarity to an ugly curdled red. And Stark remembered another time, another cave, and Gerrith's Water of Vision.

"Blood," said the Diviners to Kell à Marg. "Much blood will be spilled if this man lives. Death will come to the House of the Mother."

"Then," said Kell à Marg quietly, "he must die."

Stark began gathering the chain into his hands, carefully, so that it might not clink.

Gelmar stepped forward. "And he shall die. I shall see to it myself, Skaith-Daughter."

"I shall see to it," said Kell à Marg. "Fenn! Ferdic!"

Both had jeweled daggers at their belts. They drew them and went light-footed to Gelmar. And Kell à Marg said, "Tell your creatures to kill the man, Wandsman."

Desperately, furiously, Gelmar cried, "No, wait—"

For a moment, the beautiful men of the Citadel did not know what to do. They all watched Gelmar and waited.

Stark did not wait.

He spun around, swinging his clenched hands with the iron weight of the manacles and the chain into the body of the guard who was a little behind him to his right. He felt the flesh break. The man's breath went out in a harsh scream. He dropped and Stark hurdled him, charging for the door. There were sudden shouts behind him.

The two guards who were with Gerrith ran forward to intercept him. Gerrith, forgotten for the moment, moving swiftly, snatched one of the small lamps from its pedestal and flung it at the wall.

Flaming oil splashed, spread, caught. The hangings, centuries dry, exploded into smoke and flame.

One of the guards turned back and struck Gerrith aside, much too late. Stark saw her fall and then he lost her. Smoke choked him, blinded him. Voices were rising in terror and urgent cries. The many faces of the Mother twisted, blackened, vanished. Two of the Diviners threw themselves upon the crystal, shielding it with their bodies. The others ran to beat futilely at the flames. One of the beautiful men was on fire; another, rushing to Gelmar's voice, blundered into Stark and went on without pausing. Stark called Gerrith's name but there was no answer, and then he stumbled over her. He caught her tunic and dragged her through the doorway, into the hall. A great gout of smoke came with them.

He thought for a moment she was dead. But she coughed and then said distinctly, "If you don't go now, this will be the end of it."

The tumult in the Hall grew louder as those inside fought their way toward the door. Students and acolytes came out of their chambers along the corridor. Stark bent over Gerrith.

She struck at him. "Get gone, damn you! I gave you this chance. Will you throw it away?"

Stark hesitated. Alone he might make it. Burdened with Gerrith, he could not. He touched her briefly. "If I live—" he said, and left her there, and ran.

He went down the corridor, huge and murderous, iron shackles swinging. White-furred bodies scattered before him or were swept aside. They were young, these student Diviners, and their teachers were old, and all were unused to combat. Stark went through them like a gale through chaff.

Behind him he heard fresh shouts and cries. Gelmar and Kell à Marg, at least, had won free of the burning Hall. Looking back, he saw two of the guards running after him. Them he could not fight, their swords against his irons.

He plunged into a branching corridor, running hard. A flight of rock-cut steps led him downward, into another corridor, dustier, more dimly lighted. He followed that into a maze of rooms, tunnels, and stairways, the rooms crowded with objects, the passages deserted, lighted by fewer and fewer lamps.

He stopped at last and listened. All he could hear now was the hammering of his own heart. For the moment, at least, he had lost them. He took one of the lamps from a wall niche and went on, deeper and deeper into the House of the Mother.

24

THE CHILDREN must have spent innumerable generations gnawing away here in the bowels of the Witchfires. They must have been vastly more numerous than they were now, and Stark remembered Hargoth's comments on the necessity of fresh breeding stock. The Children would have cut themselves off from that, certainly by choice and probably by the alteration of their genes as well. Artificial mutants, they might be unable to cross-breed with humans. The Children of the Sea-Our-Mother might have undergone the same deprivation, but he had no way of judging that.

It was unpleasantly quiet. The silence of centuries hung here as thick as dust. Yet the air was breathable. The Children had seen to it that ventilation was adequate. Their engineering instincts had been sound as well, probably bred into them. They had a feeling for stone and how to use it. Their warren of caverns and passages seemed capable of enduring as long as the Witchfires.

Except for the lamp he carried, it was now totally dark. Stark moved on, having no idea where he was going, fighting down a growing panic. The House of the Mother would make a handsome tomb. Probably they would never even find his body.

In spite of that, curiosity as well as necessity compelled him to stop and examine some of the things that crammed these forgotten chambers.

He realized that he was in a museum.

What had Kell à Marg said? *We are students of the past. Historians.* They must have looted the dead and dying cities of the north. Perhaps even before they were abandoned by the people fleeing south in the Great Wandering, the Children had begun their collecting. Art objects, statuary, paintings, jewelry, musical instruments, fabrics, pots and pans, machines, toys, tools, books, constructions of wood and metal and plastic—anything of a size to be handled through the corridors, whole or piecemeal, and stored away in the caverns. The history and technology, art and ideas, of a totally destroyed civilization survived here in these buried vaults, the pleasure and the mania of a dying race.

Stark thought that whether he himself lived or died, the Children of Skaith-Our-Mother were going to have much trouble as time went by, trying to guard their incredible hoard.

He was looking for two things, a weapon and some tools to get the shackles off. There were plenty of weapons, most of them useless, lacking the technology that had made them work. Constant temperature and humidity had preserved most things remarkably well, but there was inevitable deterioration. He finally found a knife that did not come apart at the tang, and he thrust that into his belt.

The tools were easier. Mallet and chisel could endure a bit of punishment. But there was no way that he could use them by himself. He stuck the chisel in his belt beside the knife and carried the mallet. It made a serviceable weapon in itself.

There was no one to use it on.

Neither was there any water, nor any food. Thirst began to be a problem, with hunger not far behind. He was used to both, and he knew his potential. It would take him some time to die. But he ceased to reproach himself about Gerrith.

He had hoped to find another lamp, but they had all been neglected too long and the oil had evaporated. The level of the one he carried went slowly, steadily down. He did not stop longer than he had to. He wanted to keep going as long as he had light.

Then, as he passed the mouth of a narrow tunnel, a strong draught of air blew it out.

The air was fresh and cold. Stark felt his way into the tunnel. After a little time he saw that there was light ahead. Daylight.

It came through an arched opening at the end of the tunnel. A wild surge of hope sent Stark running toward it.

Once lookouts might have been stationed here, keeping watch over the turbulent north. Or the Children might have taken the air after their work in the museum rooms, to see again the sun and the stars they had left behind. Now there was nothing but a high solitude. The tiny balcony was no more than a niche in the northern face of the Witchfires. Far too high, and that northern face too sheer, for any thought of getting down it.

Stark saw an immense white landscape, infinitely forbidding. From the feet of the Witchfires a naked plain tilted upward, gashed with the scars of old erosions. The wind blew fiercely across it, raising snow-devils that danced and whirled. Some of them had a peculiar look; these were not snow-devils at all, but pillars of steam rising out of the ground, to be shredded and torn away.

A thermal area. Stark became excited, remembering Hargoth's words about the magic mists that hid the Citadel. He looked up across the plain, to a distant range of mountains much higher and more cruel than the Witchfires. And he saw, to the northeast, low against the mountains' flank, a great boiling of white cloud.

He stood on his high lonely perch, and looked, and swore.

He saw, when he turned his head, a string of tiny figures moving across the vast whiteness of the plain, from the direction of the Witchfires.

Gelmar, going to the Citadel.

A driven man, Stark left the small niche. Turning his back on the light, he went again into the darkness of the corridors.

Now he prayed for steps to lead him down. He had been trying from the first to work his way back to ground level, and he was appalled to find himself still so high. The devil of it was that, feeling his way along in the pitch blackness, he might be passing any number of steps to one side or the other without knowing it.

Hunger and thirst became more insistent. He was forced to stop now and again to sleep, as an animal sleeps, briefly but totally relaxed. Then he would get up and go on again, every nerve and every sense stretched fine to catch the slightest hint of anything that might guide him back to life.

He had slid and stumbled along what seemed like miles of passages, blundered horribly through crowded rooms that tried to swallow him in a tangle of relics, half fallen down infinite numbers of steps, when the faintest of faint sounds touched his ears.

He thought at first that it was only weariness, or the whisper of his own blood in his veins. Then it went away and he didn't hear it again. He had just come down a flight of steps. That was at his back. He could feel the carvings of a wall on both sides, so the corridor went ahead, and that must be where the sound had come from. He began padding along it, stopping frequently to hold his breath and listen.

The sound came again. It was unmistakable. It was music. Someone in this catacomb of dust and age and darkness was making music. Very peculiar music, atonal, twanging, quavering. It was the most beautiful music Stark had ever heard.

Twice more the music stopped, as though whoever was playing the instrument had halted in annoyance over a wrong note. Then it would begin again. Stark saw a gleam of light and approached without sound.

There was a carved doorway. Beyond was a small chamber well lighted by several lamps. One of the Children, an old man with slack skin and prominent bones, bent over an oddly shaped instrument with numerous strings. Beside him was an antique table strewn with ancient books and many parchments. There was also an untouched plate of food and a stone jug. The old man's fingers caressed the strings as if they were stroking a child.

Stark went in.

The old man looked up. Stark watched the slow advance of shock across his face.

"The Outside has come into the House of the Mother," he said. "It is the end of the world." And he set the instrument carefully aside.

"Not quite," said Stark. "All I want of the House of the Mother is to leave it. Is there a northern gate?"

He waited while the old man stared at him, great luminous eyes in a moth-eaten face, the fur of his crown rubbed up untidily, his whole being wrenched cruelly away from where it had been. Finally, Stark made a threatening movement.

"Is there a northern gate?"

"Yes. But I can't take you there."

"Why not?"

"Because I remember now. I was told—we were all told—an enemy, an outsider, was in the Mother's House and we were to watch. We were to give the alarm, if we should see him."

"Old man," said Stark, "you will not give the alarm, and you will take me to the northern gate." He placed his powerful hands on the frail instrument.

The old man stood up. In a soft and very desperate voice he said, "I am trying to recreate the music of Tlavia, Queen City of the High

North before the Wandering. It is my life's work. That is the only Tlavian instrument known. The others are lost somewhere in the caverns. If it should be destroyed—"

"Consider yourself the guarantee of its safety," Stark said. "If you do exactly as I tell you—" He took his hands away.

The old man was thinking. His thoughts were almost visible. "Very well," he said. "For the sake of the instrument."

Stark gave him the mallet and chisel. "Here." He laid his wrists on the antique table, which had a fine marble top and seemed sturdy. He regretted the sacrilege, but there was no other choice. "Get these things off me."

The old man was clumsy, and the table was considerably damaged, but in the end the manacles came off. Stark rubbed his wrists. Hunger and thirst had become painful. He drank from the stone bottle. It was some sort of dusty-tasting wine; he wished it had been water, but it was better than nothing. The food he thrust into his pockets, to be eaten along the way. The old man waited patiently. His acquiescence had been too quick, too unemotional. Stark wondered what mischief lurked in his transparent mind.

"Let us go," he said, and picked up the instrument.

The old man took a lamp and led the way into the corridor.

"Are there many like you?" Stark asked. "Solitary scholars?"

"Many. Skaith-Mother encourages scholars. She gives us peace and plenty so that we may spend our whole lives at our work. There are not so many of us as there used to be. Once there were a thousand at the study of music alone, thousands more at history, the ancient books, art and laws. And of course, the cataloguing." He sighed. "But it is a good life."

In a short time they were back in the inhabited areas. The old man did not have far to go to find his solitude. Stark took a firm hold on his worn harness with one hand, holding the instrument precariously in the other.

"If anyone sees us, old man," he said, "the music of Tlavia dies."

And the old man led him cunningly enough, skirting the edges of the busy levels, the caverns of the lapidaries and goldsmiths, sculptors and stonemasons, the nurseries and schools for the young, the strange deep-buried farms where fungoid crops flourished in perpetual musty dampness. These lower levels, Stark noticed, were definitely warmer, and the old man explained that the thermal area extended beneath part of the Mother's House, giving them many gifts, such as hot water for the baths.

He also told Stark other things.

The nomad trail used by the Harsenyi ran between the pass of the Witchfires and the passes of the Bleak Mountains, the big range that Stark had seen. It was at the western side of the Plain of Worldheart; Stark remembered the little black dots of Gelmar's party moving along it. The trail was safe for the Harsenyi as long as they did not wander from it, and they had a permanent village in the foothills, which was as close as any of them ever got to the Citadel. The plain was called Worldheart because the Citadel was built on it, or above it. The old man had never seen the Citadel. He had never seen a Northhound. He thought that they did not range too far from the Citadel unless they were attracted by an intruder. They were said to be telepaths.

"They hunt in a pack," the old man said. "The king-dog's name is Flay. At least, it used to be. Perhaps the lead dog is always Flay. Or perhaps the Northhounds live forever."

Like the Lords Protector, Stark thought.

He felt a difference in the body of the old man, where his hand touched it. It had become tense, the breathing tight and rapid.

They were in a broad passageway, not very well lighted, obviously not much frequented. Ahead he could see the opening of another passage to the right.

The old man said innocently, "The northern gate is there, along that corridor. It's seldom used now. The Wandsmen used to come from the Citadel more often. Now they come to the western gate, when they come at all." He held out his hands for the instrument.

Stark smiled. "Wait here, old man. No noise, not a word." Still carrying the frail instrument, Stark went noiselessly to the branching corridor and looked along it.

There was a great stone slab at the end of it, where it widened out into a guard chamber. And a guard was there. Half a dozen of the Children, male, young, armed, patently bored. Four of them were occupied with some game on a stone table. The other two watched.

The old man had begun to run. He did not even stop to see what became of his precious instrument. Stark set it down unharmed.

He took the knife from his belt and went down the corridor, moving fast, shoulders forward, all his attention fixed on that slab of rock that stood between him and freedom.

The Children probably had not had to fight in their own defense since the last of the Wandering. They were out of practice, babes comfortable and soft in the womb of the Mother. He was almost on top of them before they knew he was there. They sprang up to face him, eyes large with sudden fear, pawing for their weapons. They had not really believed that he would come. They had not really believed that if he did come he would try to kill them. Surely their six against his one—

They had not *really* understood what killing is.

Stark slashed one of the players across the throat. He fell across the table, tangling his mates with his thrashings, making dreadful noises. They stared at the blood, and Stark struck down another with his fist and caught up the light wiry body and threw it against the others. He went past them like a bull to the slab of stone and pushed against it. It moved. Two of them came at his back and he turned and fended them off, the knife blade and his heavy furs turning most of their sword cuts; their blades were light like their bodies, made more for beauty than for killing. He kept pressing his shoulder against the slab and it kept turning and in a moment they were hitting stone and he was through the opening. He slammed the stone shut on their screaming faces, and began to run.

They would spread the word through Kell à Marg's great House that he had escaped, but he did not think that anyone would come after him, at least not very far.

Not here on the Plain of Worldheart, where the Northhounds prowled.

25

OLD SUN was below the peaks, and the northern face of the Witchfires was gray and ugly, a sheer frowning wall at his back. The mountain shadow made a long darkness across the plain. The wind was a knife, a scream, a madness bewailing eternal winter. The flogged snow-devils danced in desperation to appease it.

The region of boiling cloud that hid the Citadel was visible, small and bright against the flank of the Bleak Mountains, catching the last of the westering light.

The Citadel.

He did not know exactly how long he had been wandering in the House of the Mother, and the old man had not been able to tell him in terms that he could understand. They had their own view of time in those dark catacombs. But it was long enough for many things to have happened.

There was no point in asking himself questions for which there could be no answers until he reached the Citadel. If he reached it.

Stark fixed the bright patch of cloud as a mark in his mind's eye, northeast across the plain. He set out toward it.

The shadow of the Witchfires stretched longer and darker ahead of him. He would not outrun it. It would soon be night, and the Children were staying safe, as he had thought they would, in their Mother's House. Why risk their lives when the Northhounds would certainly deal with him? The Bleak Mountains burned with a bloody glow that dimmed quickly to ashen dullness. The first stars showed.

Stark lost his view of the Citadel-clouds and took his bearing from a star. The whole landscape faded into that insubstantial bluish-gray that comes over the snowlands at twilight, where everything slides away at the edges of sight. The sky turned darker, turned black. The Lamp of the North rose up in it, a huge green lantern, and the plain became white again, a diminished white but much more clearly seen now that the glimmery grayness had gone. The first twitching of the aurora appeared overhead.

Stark moved forward as steadily as he could, watching for the plumes of steam marking the thermal areas he had seen from the balcony. The wind tore at him, beating him with hammer blows. It sent the snow-devils against him, and at these times he dropped face down on the ground until the blinding buffeting whirl of snow-dust passed over him. At other times the wind picked up lower clouds of snow and mixed them cunningly with the thermal plumes so that all was a formless whiteness. Several times he stopped short, sensing a bareness and a tremor beneath his feet, to find a gaping blow-hole lying just ahead, ready to swallow him.

The ravines, those ancient gashes of erosion he had seen, were less dangerous. The bedrock of the plain was hard and had not scoured out too deeply. Wind and snow had worn the edges down. Nevertheless, Stark went carefully when he had to cross one. A fall here in the darkness of Worldheart could mean cheating the Northhounds of their pleasure.

He was happy, in a strange sort of way. The end of his journey was in sight, and he was free, unencumbered. His body and his skills were his to use to the limit, without regard for others. The battle against cold and wind and cruel terrain was a clean one, uncluttered by ideas, ideals, beliefs, or human spite. For the moment he was less Eric John Stark than he was N'Chaka, wild thing in a wild place, perfectly at home.

Perfectly at home, perfectly functional, wary and watchful. His gaze roved constantly, never straining against the night, never looking straight at an object but always past it, never trying to hold it steady, only sensing its shape and whether or not it moved.

Twice the wind brought him a hint of something other than the cold smells of snow and frozen ground.

The banners of the aurora snapped and quivered. The heads of the snow-devils seemed to touch them. Colors shifted, green, white, rose-fire. Plumes of steam shot high out of the rock, now to his right, now to his left, glimmering, shredding, vanishing. Sometimes he thought that dim white shapes stalked him between snow and steam. For a long while he could not be sure.

There came a time when there was no longer any doubt.

He had come, treading delicately, out of a cloud of mingled steam and snow, and he looked up along the tilt of the plain, and a great white thing stood there watching him.

Stark stopped. The thing continued to watch him. And a cold beast-thought touched his mind, saying,

I am Flay.

He was big. The ridge of his spine would have reached Stark's shoulder. His withers were high and powerful. The thick neck drooped with the weight of the massive head. Stark saw the eyes, large and unnaturally brilliant, the broad heavy muzzle, and the fangs, two white cruel rows of them, sharp as knives.

Flay stretched out a foreleg like a tree-trunk and unsheathed tiger claws. He tore five furrows in the frozen ground and smiled, lolling a red tongue.

I am Flay.

The eyes were bright. Bright. Hell-hound eyes.

Swift panic overcame Stark, loosened his muscles, weakened his joints, dropped him helpless on the ground with cold nausea in his belly and a silent scream in his brain.

I am Flay.

And this is how they kill, Stark thought, with the fleeting remnants of sanity. Fear. A bolt of fear as deadly as any missile. This is how they were bred to kill. The size, the fangs and claws, are only camouflage. They do it with their minds.

He could not draw his knife.

Flay sauntered toward him. And now the other shapes were visible on the tilting plain, the pack, six, ten, a dozen, he couldn't count them, bounding and leaping, running.

Fear.

Fear was a sickness.

Fear was a dark wave rolling over him, taking sight and hearing, crushing mind and will.

He would never reach the Citadel, never see Gerrith. Flay would give him to the pack and they would play with him until he died.

I am Flay, said the cold beast-mind, and the red jaws laughed. Huge paws padded silently in the blowing snow.

Far down beneath the dark mass of fear that destroyed all human courage, another mind spoke. Cold beast-mind, not thinking or reasoning, mind alive and desperate to live, mind feeling self as bone and muscle, cold and pain, a hunger to be fed, a fear to be endured. Fear is life, fear is survival. The end of fear is death.

The cold beast-mind said, *I am N'Chaka.*

The blood beats, hot with living, hot with hate. Hate is a fire in the blood, a taste in the mouth of bitter salt.

I am N'Chaka.

I do not die.

I kill.

Flay paused, one tentative forefoot lifted. He swung his head from side to side, puzzled.

The human thing ought now to be inert and helpless. Instead it spoke to him; it groped and tottered and rose from the ground, rose to its hands and knees and faced him.

I am N'Chaka.

The pack halted their playful rush. They formed a semicircle behind Flay, growling.

Fear, said Flay's mind. *Fear.*

They sent fear, deadly killing fear.

Cold beast-mind let the fear slide over it. Cold beast-eyes saw Flay, coarse-furred Flay looming in the night-gleaming.

I have seen the great rock lizard open his jaws to take me, and he has not taken me. Why should I fear you?

The pack growled, looking sidelong. *Flay, Flay! This is not a human!*

The N'Chaka thing got to its hind legs, crouching. It circled, making beast sounds. It sprang at Flay.

Flay struck it sprawling with one sweep of his paw.

The thing rolled over twice. Blood came out of rents in its fur. It bounded up and drew the knife from its belt. It came again at Flay.

The pack could not understand. Human victims did not fight. They did not challenge the king-dog, only a member of the pack did that. This thing was not a member of the pack, but neither was it human. They did not know what it was.

They sat down to watch, while N'Chaka fought the king-dog for his life.

They would not send more fear. This was up to Flay.

Flay had realized, not believing it, that fear was useless. He tried once more, but the N'Chaka thing came at him without pause, slashing at him, dodging, circling, darting in and out, wary now of the claws. It was fighting; there was nothing left in its mind but fight, fight and kill.

It enjoyed the fighting. It meant to kill.

Now it was Flay who feared.

In all his long life he had never failed to take his prey cleanly. No single victim had ever fought back.

Now this N'Chaka thing defied him. And the pack was watching, and he had no weapons but his claws and teeth.

And those he was not used to using, except in play. None of the young dogs had yet dared to challenge him.

Fear! he said to the pack. *Send fear!*

They only watched, moving restlessly, the wind tearing at their fur.

In a fury, Flay struck at the N'Chaka thing with his terrible claws.

The thing was ready this time. It leapt back and slashed with the knife. It slashed so that Flay howled and went on three legs.

The pack smelled his blood and whined.

A measure of humanity was creeping back into Stark's mind, now that he had mastered the fear. And along with it came a savage sense of triumph.

The Northhounds were not invincible.

Perhaps the Citadel would not be invincible, either.

Because he knew now that he was going to reach it.

He knew that he was going to kill Flay.

Flay knew it too.

The wounded paw had slowed the Northhound. But he was still formidable. He bared the double row of fangs and made rushes. His jaws snapped on empty air with a frightening sound. They would crush a man's thigh-bone like a dry stick. Stark circled him, making him turn against that bad foot, and twice he darted in and slashed at the face. His eyes held Flay's eyes, the hell-hound eyes that were bred for terror, and he thought. *How close the knife comes, Flay! How it flashes! Soon—*

The heavy head dropped lower. The terrible eyes wanted to look away. The paw bled and the pack whined, red tongues hanging.

Stark feinted, ceased to hold Flay's eyes, and the big head turned aside. Stark flung himself onto Flay's high bony back.

He was only there for a second or two before he was thrown off, but that was long enough for the knife to go in. Flay whirled, snapping at the hilt standing out behind his shoulder, and then he staggered and went down and blood came out of his mouth.

Stark pulled out the knife and let the pack have the body. He stood apart, waiting. Their shallow minds had already told him what they would do.

He waited until they were finished.

They gathered then, keeping their eyes carefully averted lest they should seem to challenge him. The largest of the young dogs came belly down and licked Stark's hand.

You will follow me?

You killed Flay. We follow.

But I am human.

Not human. You are N'Chaka.

You guard the Citadel.

Against humans.

And how many lost and hungry wayfarers have those jaws snapped up, Stark wondered. The Lords Protector defended their privacy too well. *You defend against humans, but not against N'Chaka?*

We could not kill N'Chaka.

Will you kill Wandsmen?

No.

They had neither love nor loyalty, but their breeding held them true. Fair enough.

The other men, who serve the Wandsmen?

They are nothing to us.

Good.

He considered their well fleshed bodies. There were certainly not enough human victims to keep them fat, and there was little game on the Plain of Worldheart where they ranged. Someone must feed them.

Where do you kennel?

At the Citadel.

Come, then.

With the pack at his heels, Stark set off toward the mountains.

26

THE BOILING CLOUDS turned copper with the rising of Old Sun. The Northhounds trotted unconcerned through a wilderness of humped rock and gaping blow-holes. Stark went with them while the ground boomed and shook and the steam spurted.

He had not planned it this way. He had not thought that a direct attack on the Citadel would be possible. But this unexpected, and highly uncertain, weapon had been put into his hand, and he had decided to use it.

Now.

As swiftly and brutally as possible.

The thermal area seemed to go on forever. Then suddenly they had passed through it, and the mountains were there, and the Citadel.

Dark and strong and solid, clinging to the mountain flank, the compact shape of its walls and towers looking like an outcrop of the native rock. The fortress and fountainhead, from which a handful of men ruled a planet.

He could understand why it had been built here, hidden behind its perpetual curtain. In the days of the Wandering, when everything was chaos, this place would have been isolated from the main streams of migration, and therefore relatively safe. Tall crags protected the Citadel at back and side, the thermal pits guarded its front. With all that, and the Northhounds, the Lords Protector need not have worried overmuch about bands of plunderers coming south over the passes. From the size of the Citadel, they would have garrisoned fewer than a hundred men, and they would not have needed more.

How many men would be there now, after all these centuries of peace? He did not know. He looked at the Northhounds and hoped that they would be adequate. Otherwise, any number would be too many against one man with a knife.

There were sentries on the walls, bright-eyed men with blank faces. They saw Stark at the edge of the cloud with the pack behind him, and even over the roaring of the vent-holes Stark could hear their sudden shouting.

Hurry! he told the Northhounds.

No hurry, said the young dog, whose name was Gerd.

The Northhounds trotted on toward the base of the Citadel, courses of stone laid in upon the rock.

They will kill you, Stark told them, and ran, dodging this way and that.

Arrows began to fly from the walls. In the roiling copper shadow they flew. None hit Stark, though he felt the wind of them. Some stuck in the ground. Two hit Northhounds.

I said they would kill you.

He was under the base of the Citadel now, where the arrows could not reach him.

Why, N'Chaka?

It was a cry of puzzled anguish. The Northhounds began to run.

They believe you have come to attack them.

We have always been faithful.

A third hound rolled over screaming, an arrow through his flanks.

They doubt you now.

And small wonder. For the first time since the first whelp of them was born, they had let in an intruder. They had *brought* in an intruder.

The Northhounds bayed.

There was a hole in the rock. They ran into it. The cave was large and dry, sheltered from the wind. It smelled of kennel and there were troughs where the hounds were fed. At the back was a door of thick iron bars with heavy bolts on the inner side.

Stark went to the door. He could sense the bewilderment and rage in their beast minds.

They tried to kill you. Why did you not send fear to them?

Gerd growled and whimpered. He was one of the first two hit. The arrow had gashed his rump painfully. *We never sent fear to those. We will now.*

Stark reached through to the bolts and began to draw them.

Are there humans in the Citadel?

Gerd answered irritably, *With Wandsmen.*

If they were with the Wandsmen, or the Lords Protector, it was no concern of Gerd's.

But there are humans? You can touch their minds?

Human. One mind. Touch.

One mind. One human.

Gerrith?

Halk?

Ashton?

Stark opened the door. *Come and kill for N'Chaka.*

They came.

There was a hall with storerooms on either side, and then a rough stair that went up into darkness. Stark climbed as fast as he dared, much faster than was wise, his knife in his hand. The people of the Citadel were surprised, shocked, off-guard, and he wanted to use that advantage. At the top was a massive iron door to be shut if anyone managed to pass living through the Northhound's kennel, and a windlass arrangement to drop a section of the stair. Beyond was a chamber cluttered with the debris of long occupancy, things working their way down the scale to eventual burial in the thermal pits. A barred slit let in daylight, which was only a little better than no light at all.

A broader stair led up from this room, into a long low hall lighted at intervals by lamps. There were no windows. Row upon row of wooden racks crammed the space, leaning and sagging under the weight of endless rolls of parchment.

The records, Stark guessed, of generations of Wandsmen who had come to the Citadel to report and confer concerning their work in the world.

They looked as though they would burn well. So did the enormous timbers that sustained the roof.

There was a stair on the opposite side of the hall. He was halfway to it when a body of men came plunging down. They might have been on their way to close that iron door.

They stopped dead when they saw the Northhounds. The hounds never came inside the Citadel. They could not conceive of such a thing happening. Yet it had happened.

Their faces and their bright eyes remained expressionless even after the Northhounds had sent fear.

Kill, said Stark, and the pack killed. They were very angry, very swift. When they had finished, he picked up a sword, leaving belt and scabbard untouched. The sword would wipe clean.

He started up the stair.

Gerd spoke in his mind. *N'Chaka. Wandsmen—*

He saw *white* in his mind and knew that Gerd meant the Lords Protector. The hounds did not distinguish between Wandsmen.

Wandsmen say kill you.

He had expected this. The hounds were loyal to the Wandsmen. How strong was his own hold over them? If the Wandsmen were stronger, he would finish here as the blank-faced men had finished.

He turned to Gerd, looking straight into the hell-hound eyes.

You cannot kill N'Chaka.

Gerd stared at him steadily. The bristled lips pulled back to show the rows of fangs. There was still blood on them. The pack whined and whimpered, clawing the stones.

Who do you follow? Stark asked.

We follow the strongest. But Flay obeyed Wandsmen—

I am not Flay. I am N'Chaka. Shall I kill you as I killed Flay?

He would have done it. The sword point was aimed straight for Gerd's throat and he was as hungry for blood as they were.

Gerd knew it. The fiery gaze slid aside. The head hung down. The pack became quiet.

Send fear, Stark said. *Drive away all but the Wandsmen and the human. Drive away the servants who kill you. Then we will talk to the Wandsmen.*

Not kill?

Not the Wandsmen, not the human. Talk.

But Stark's hand gripped the sword.

The Northhounds obeyed him. He felt the air vibrate with their sending.

He led them up the stair.

Some men were at the top. Terror was on them, an agony in the gut. The Northhounds tore them leisurely. Gerd picked up the leader and carried him in his jaws like a kitten.

No one else stood against them. All the others had had strength enough to run.

Stark came at length into another hall, higher than the one that held the records but not so long, with windows open onto the eternal mist. It was sparsely furnished, ascetic, a place for meditation. Kell à Marg, spiteful daughter of Skaith, had been wrong. There was no hint here of secret sin and luxury, either in the hall or in the faces of the seven white-robed men who stood there in attitudes of arrested motion, overwhelmed by the swiftness with which this thing had happened.

There was an eighth man, not wearing a white robe.

Simon Ashton.

Gerd dropped what he was carrying. Stark put his left hand on the hound's great head and said, "Let the Earthman come to me."

Ashton came and stood at Stark's right hand. He was thinner than Stark remembered and he showed the strain of long captivity. Otherwise he seemed unhurt.

Stark said to the Lords Protector, "Where is Gerrith?"

The foremost of them answered. Like the others, he was an old man. Not aged or infirm, but old in work and dedication as well as years. His thin hard jaw and fierce eyes reflected an uncompromising and inflexible toughness.

"We questioned her, and the wounded man, and then sent them south with Gelmar. It was not believed that you could survive the Children in the House of the Mother."

He looked at the Northhounds. "This too would not have been believed."

"Nevertheless," said Stark, "I am here."

And now that he was here, he wondered what he was going to do with them. They were old men. Unyielding old men, devoted to their principles, ruling with the iron rod of righteousness, cruel only to be kind. He hated them. If they had killed Ashton he could have killed them, but Ashton was alive and safe and he could not see himself slaughtering them in cold blood.

There was another factor. The Northhounds. They felt his thoughts and growled, and Gerd leaned his massive shoulder against Stark's side, to hold him.

The man in white smiled briefly. "That instinct, at least, is too strong for you. They will not let you kill us."

"Go, then," said Stark. "Take your servants and go. Let the people of Skaith see the Lords Protector for what they are, not gods or immortals but only seven old men cast adrift in the world. I will pull down this Citadel."

"You may destroy it. You cannot destroy what it stands for. It will remain a symbol. You cannot destroy us, for the work we do is greater than our physical bodies. The prophecy is false, man from the stars. You will not prevail. We shall continue to serve our people."

He paused. "My name is Ferdias. Remember it."

Stark nodded. "I'll remember. And prophecy or not, Ferdias, you have served too long."

"And what do you serve? The littleness of one man. For one man, you set our world in turmoil." He looked at Ashton.

"He too is only a symbol," said Stark softly. "The symbol of reality. That is what you're fighting, not one man, or two. Go and fight it, Ferdias. Wait for the stars to crash in on you. Because they will."

They turned and left him. He stared after their proud and stubborn backs, and the Northhounds held him, whimpering.

"You are a fool, Eric," Ashton said, and shook his head. "As Ferdias said, it does seem a lot for one man."

"Well," said Stark, "before we're done, you may wish I'd left you with the Lords Protector. What made them decide against killing you?"

"I convinced them I'd be more valuable to them alive. They're very worried men, Eric. They know they're threatened by something big, but they don't know how big. They don't really understand. The whole concept of space-flight and the Galactic Union is too new and strange. Really shattering. They don't know how to deal with it, and they thought I might be of some help to them since I'm part of it. I pointed out that they could always kill me later on."

He looked at the Northhounds and shivered. "I won't ask you how you did that. I'm afraid I know."

"Of all men, you ought to," said Stark, and smiled. Then he asked, "How long ago did Gelmar leave, with Gerrith?"

"It was yesterday."

"They won't have got far ahead of us, then. Not with Halk slowing them down. Simon, I know that the Ministry cannot condone the vandalism I am about to commit, but you won't try to stop me, will you?"

Again Ashton looked at the pack. "Not likely. Your friends might be annoyed."

Stark set about destroying the Citadel as well as he could, and it was well enough. The furnishings, the hall of records, and the great timber beams burned hotly. Most of the outer walls would be left, but the interior would not be habitable, and in any case the sacred isolation of the Citadel was gone for all time, as was the superstitious awe that went with it.

He thought the destruction of the Lords Protector might be just as complete. He was glad, when he considered it, that he had not been able to kill them. They would have remained forever a potent and holy legend. The truth, when the people saw it, would kill them more certainly than the sword.

The Northhounds did not attempt to interfere with his burning of the Citadel. Their guardianship seemed to have been associated only with the pleasurable aspects of keeping intruders away from it.

Stark stood with Ashton on the road outside the Citadel, watching the flames lick at the window-places, and he said,

"So far, so good. There is still Gerrith, and a long walk south, and then we'll see what we can do about Irnan and the freedom of the stars. Not to speak of getting ourselves safely away from Skaith."

"It's a large order," said Ashton.

"We have allies." Stark turned to the Northhounds, to Gerd. *What will you do now that there is nothing left for you to guard?*

We will follow the strongest, said Gerd, licking Stark's hand.

And so you will, thought Stark, until I fall sick or wounded, and then you will do to me as you did to Flay. Or try to.

He bore them no ill-will for that. It was their nature. He laid his hand on Gerd's head.

Come, then.

With Ashton at his side, Stark set his face to the passes of the Bleak Mountains and the Wandsmen's Road beyond. Somewhere on that road was Gerrith, and at its end, the starships waited.

The Hounds of Skaith

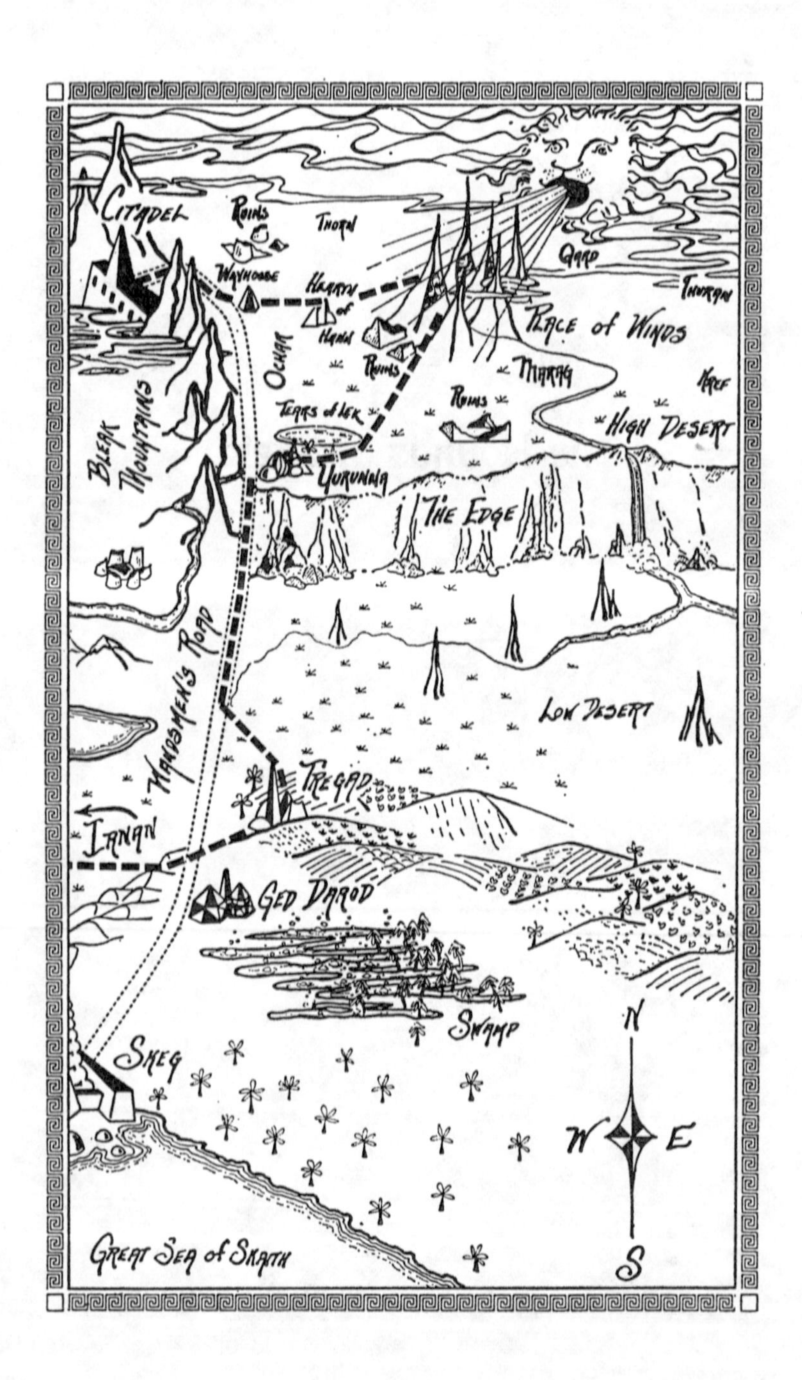

Citadel
Ruins
Thorn
Wayhouse
Hearth of Hann
Qard
Thuran
Place of Winds
Ochar
Ruins
Marag
Kref
Ruins
Terrs of Lek
High Desert
Yurunna
Bleak Mountains
The Edge
Low Desert
Wandsmen's Road
Tregad
Ianan
Ged Darod
Swamp
Skeg
N
W
E
S
Great Sea of Skaith

1

In her great hall, deep in the mountain heart of the glimmering Witchfires, Kell à Marg Skaith-Daughter sat upon the dais. Her throne was carved from rich brown rock the color of loam—the shape of it was a robed woman, seated to hold Skaith-Daughter on her knees, her arms curved protectively, her head bent forward in an attitude of affection. Kell à Marg sat with her hands on the hands of Skaith-Mother, and her slim white-furred body gleamed against the dark stone.

Below, at the foot of the dais, Yetko the Harsenyi sweated in his heavy garments, keeping his eyes averted from the Presence. He was overwhelmed by the crushing weight of mountain above him and by the labyrinthine strangeness of the House of the Mother, of which this luminous white chamber was the core and center. He was overwhelmed by being there at all. Yetko and his people had traded with these Children of Skaith-Our-Mother for generations, but the trading was done in a place outside the sacred House and never by such exalted ones as were gathered here—the Clan Mothers and the counselors, the Diviners, Skaith-Daughter herself—all glittering in their fine harness and jeweled badges of rank. No other Harsenyi had ever stood where he was standing. Yetko knew that his being here was neither right nor normal, and he was afraid. But this was a time for fear and for fearful happenings, a time of breaking and sundering. He had already beheld the unthinkable. His having been brought here was surely a part of the madness that walked upon the world.

Kell à Marg spoke. Her voice was musical, with a sound of bells, but it was a voice of power nonetheless.

"You are the headman of the village?"

They both knew that she meant the permanent camp on the other side of the Plain of Worldheart. There was no other. The Harsenyi were nomads, carrying their houses with them as they moved. Yetko said:

"I am."

He was uneasy with these creatures, terrified lest he show it. Their forebears had been human, even as he was, but by some lost magic of the ancients their bodies had been altered so that they might live and be happy in these beautiful sunless catacombs, the protecting womb of the goddess they worshipped. Yetko was a child of Old Sun and the wide cruel sky; he could not understand their worship. The fine white fur that covered them disturbed him. So did their smell, a faint dry pungency. Their faces were distorted subtly from what Yetko considered the human norm—noses too blunt, jaws too prominent, eyes too large and glowing in the lamplight.

"From our high northern balconies," said Kell à Marg, "we have seen flames and smoke on the other side of the plain, behind the mists. Tell us what has happened."

"One came," said Yetko. "He overthrew the Lords Protector. They fled from him through the passes of the Bleak Mountains, along the road to Yurunna; and he burned their Citadel that has been since before the Wandering, so that only the empty walls still stand."

A sigh went around the hall, a sound of astonishment and shock.

Kell à Marg said, "Did you see this person?"

"I saw him. He was very dark and tall, and his eyes were like the ice that forms over clear water."

Again the sigh, this time with a note of vicious hatred.

"It was Stark!"

Yetko glanced sidelong at Skaith-Daughter. "You know him?"

"He was here, a prisoner of the Wandsman Gelmar. He has brought death to the House of the Mother, killing two of our young men when he broke free by the northern gate."

"He will bring more death," said one of the Diviners. "The Eye of the Mother has seen this." He stepped forward and shouted at Yetko. "Why is it that the Northhounds did not kill him? Why,

why? Always they guarded the Citadel from intruders. Why did they let him live?"

The Clan Mothers and the counselors echoed him, and Kell à Marg said:

"Tell us why."

"I do not know," said Yetko. "The Lords Protector told us that somehow he had slain the great king-dog Flay and taken control of the pack. They said he was more beast than man. Certainly the hounds went with him to the Citadel, and certainly they killed a number of the servants there." A deep shudder shook him as he remembered. "Certainly when he came to our camp to take riding animals from us, the Northhounds followed at his heels like puppies."

"He is not Skaith-born," said Kell à Marg. "He comes from another world. His ways are not ours."

Yetko shuddered again, partly because of her words, but mostly because of the tone in which she spoke them.

"He followed the Lords Protector?"

"Yes, with the hounds. He and another man. The other man came long before, up the Wandsmen's Road from the south. He was a captive in the Citadel." Yetko shook his head. "That one also was said to have come from beyond the sky. Mother Skaith is beset by demons."

"She is strong," said Kell à Marg, and laid her head against the breast of the brown stone woman. "There are many dangers, I believe, beyond the Bleak Mountains."

"Yes. The Hooded Men permit us to come only as far as the first wayhouse, but that is a week's journey and dangerous enough because of the Runners, which are terrible things, and because of the sandstorms. The Hooded Men themselves are man-eaters; and the Ochar, who keep the road, are a powerful tribe."

"So that with good fortune the man Stark may die in the desert."

Yetko said, "It is likely."

"What of the Wandsman Gelmar? He left the House of the Mother with two prisoners."

"He crossed the Bleak Mountains before the attack on the Citadel. He had a Southron woman with him, and a wounded man in a litter. There were also three lesser Wandsmen and the servants."

"Perhaps I was wrong," said Kell à Marg, speaking to herself aloud, "not to let Gelmar keep the man Stark, as he wanted. But

Stark was in chains. Who would have believed that he could escape our daggers, and then survive even the Northhounds?"

For the first time Yetko understood that the Presence was afraid, and that frightened him more than her strangeness or her power. He said humbly, "Please, if there is nothing more you require from me . . ."

Her dark unhuman eyes brooded upon him. "Now that the Citadel has fallen, your people are preparing to abandon the village?"

"We kept the village only to serve the Wandsmen and the Lords Protector. If they come again, so will we. In the meantime, we will only come for the trading."

"When do you go?"

"With Old Sun's next rising."

Kell à Marg nodded slightly and lifted a slender hand in a gesture of dismissal. "Take him to the outer cavern, but see that he stays there until I send word."

The two white-furred man-things who had brought Yetko from the camp to the great hall took him out again, through long hollow-sounding corridors with carved walls and ornamented ceilings and myriad doorways into dimly lighted rooms filled with half-glimpsed unknowable things. There was a smell of dust and of the sweet oil that fed the lamps. Yetko's thick feet went faster and faster, in a hurry to be gone.

Kell à Marg sat upon the knees of Skaith-Mother. She did not move or speak; her courtiers stood waiting, silent and afraid.

At last she said, "Fenn. Ferdic."

Two lordly men stepped forward. They wore shining diadems. Their eyes, too, shone with anguish, because they knew what she was about to say to them.

Skaith-Daughter leaned forward. "The threat is greater than the man Stark. We must know the true nature and extent of the danger. Go with the Harsenyi as far south as you may, and as quickly. Go on to Skeg. Learn about these starships. Do all in your power to have them sent away to whatever suns they came from."

She paused. They bent their furred and handsome heads.

"Seek out Gelmar," she said. "He will know if Stark has somehow managed to survive the desert. And if he has, do anything, pay any price, to have him killed."

Fenn and Ferdic bowed. "We hear, Skaith-Daughter. Even this we will do, in the service of the Mother."

Men condemned to death, they withdrew to make their preparations for the journey.

First of these was a ceremony in the Hall of Joyful Rest, where the Children were laid to sleep in the embrace of the Mother. It had been so long since anyone had been forced to leave the sacred House that the officiating Diviner had difficulty in finding the proper scrolls for the ritual. The stone knife and small jeweled caskets had been untouched for centuries. Still, the thing was done at last. The severed fingers were buried in hallowed ground, so that no matter where death might overtake them on the outside, Fenn and Ferdic could know that they were not lost entirely from the tender love of Skaith-Mother.

2

GERD THRUST his massive head against Stark's knee and said, *Hungry.*

The Northhounds had been ranging ahead of the men. Born telepaths, they were able to communicate well enough for most needs; but sometimes their talk, like their minds, was overly simple.

Stark asked, *Gerd is hungry?*

Gerd growled and the coarse white fur bristled along his spine. He looked uneasily at the emptiness surrounding them.

Out there. Hungry.

What?

Not know, N'Chaka. Things.

Out there. Things. Hungry. Well, and why not? Hunger was the great constant over most of this world of Skaith, senile child of the ginger star that spilled its rusty glare out of a dim cold sky onto the dim cold desert.

"Probably a pack of Runners," Ashton said. Having been up this road as a prisoner some months before, he knew the hazards. "I wish we were better armed."

They had helped themselves to what they needed from the Citadel before Stark put it to the torch. Their weapons were of excellent quality, but Skaith's poverty-stricken technology, sliding backward through long centuries of upheaval and dwindling resources, could now offer nothing more sophisticated than the sword, the knife and the bow. Stark, being a mercenary by trade, was proficient with all these; the wars he fought in were small and highly personal affairs, involving tribes or small nations on as-yet-uncivilized worlds beyond the fringes of the Galactic Union. Simon Ashton, who had done all his fighting years ago and in uniform, would have felt happier with something more modern.

"We have the hounds," Stark said, and pointed to a rise ahead. "Perhaps we can see something from there."

They had been driving hard ever since they left the smoking ruins of the Citadel. The passes through the Bleak Mountains led them first north and then east, and the mountain chain itself made a great bend to the southeast, so that the lower range now stood like a wall at their right hands. The Wandsmen's Road came up from Skeg straight across these eastern deserts, a much shorter route than the one Stark had followed on his own journey north from Skeg to find the hidden Citadel where Ashton was being held. He had had perforce to go first to Irnan, which was somewhat westerly, and then more westerly still, with his five comrades, to Izvand in the Barrens. After that he had made a long traverse in the creaking wagons of the trader Amnir of Komrey, who had taken them to sell for a high price to the Lords Protector, through the darklands on an ancient road. Stark's way up from Skeg had described roughly the curve of a broken bow. Now he was going south again along the straight line of the bowstring.

He whacked his shaggy little mount to a faster pace. At first, where the frozen ground was hard and stony, they had made good time. Now they were among the dunes, and the Harsenyi beasts with their sharp little hoofs were laboring.

They topped the rise and halted. By the time the westerlies came across the barrier mountains, they had dropped most of their moisture. In place of the snows on the other side there was dun-colored sand with only a splotching and powdering of white. The air was no less cold. And in all that bitter landscape, nothing moved. The cairns that marked the Wandsmen Road marched away out of sight. The Lords Protector were still well ahead.

"For old men," said Stark, "they're traveling well."

"They're tough old men. Let the beasts rest a bit, Eric. It won't help anyone if we kill them."

The exodus of the Lords Protector and their servants had taken more animals than the Harsenyi could well spare. Only fear of the Northhounds had induced them to part with three more, two for riding and one to carry supplies. They were strong little things, with thick hair that hung down as though they were wearing blankets. Bright button eyes peered through tangled fringes. Sharp horns were tipped with painted balls to prevent hooking. Their air of patient martyrdom was well spiced with malice. Still, they bore their burdens willingly enough; and Stark reckoned they would do, for the time being.

"We'll borrow some from Ferdias. But we must catch up with Gelmar before he reaches the first wayhouse. If we don't, we'll never see him, not in this desert."

"Gelmar won't be sparing his animals, either. Ferdias will have sent one of the Yur ahead to tell him what happened. He'll know you're coming after him."

Stark said impatiently, "He's traveling with a badly wounded man." Halk, the tall swordsman, albeit no friend of Stark's, had come north with him for the sake of Irnan, and he was one of the two survivors of the original five. The other was the wise woman Gerrith. They had been caught with their comrades in Gelmar's trap at Thyra, and Halk was sorely hurt in that battle.

"He must be carried in a litter. Gelmar can't travel too fast."

"I don't think you can count on that. I believe Gelmar would sacrifice Halk to keep you from taking Gerrith back. She's a vital part of their whole strategy against Irnan." Ashton paused, frowning. "Even so, I think the Wandsmen would be willing to sacrifice Gerrith if they could take you. Ferdias had the right of it, you know. It was madness to try and turn an entire planet upside down for the sake of one man."

"I've lost two fathers," Stark said, and smiled. "You're the only one I've got left." He kicked his mount forward. "We'll rest farther on."

Ashton followed, looking in some wonderment at this great dark changeling he had brought into the world of men. He was able to remember with vivid clarity the first time he had seen Eric John Stark, whose name then was N'Chaka, Man-Without-a-Tribe. That had been on Mercury, in the blazing, thundering valleys of the Twilight Belt where towering peaks rose up beyond the shallow atmosphere and the mountain-locked valleys held death in an amazing variety of forms. Ashton was young then, an agent of Earth Police Control, which had authority over the mining settlements. EPC was also responsible for the preservation of the aboriginal tribes, a scanty population of creatures kept so much occupied with the business of survival that they had not had time to make that last sure step across the borderline between animal and human.

Word had come that wildcat miners were committing depredations. Ashton arrived too late to save the band of hairy aboes, but the miners had taken a captive.

A naked boy, fierce and proud in the cage where he was penned. His skin was burned dark by the terrible sun, scarred by the accidents of daily living in that cruel place. His shaggy hair was black, his eyes very light in color—the clear, innocent, suffering eyes of an animal. The miners had tormented him with sticks until he bled. His belly was pinched with hunger, his tongue swollen with thirst. Yet he watched his captors with those cold clear eyes, unafraid, waiting for a chance to kill.

Ashton took him out of the cage. Thinking back on the time and effort required to civilize that young tiger, to force him to accept the hateful fact of his humanity, Ashton sometimes wondered that he had possessed enough patience to accomplish the task.

Records of Mercury Metals and Mining had given the boy's identity and his name, Eric John Stark. Supposedly, he had died along with his parents in the fall of a mountain wall that wiped out the mining colony where he was born. In fact, the aboes had found him and reared him as their own, and Ashton knew that no matter how human his fosterling Eric might look on the outside, the primitive N'Chaka was still there, close under the skin.

That was how Stark had been able to face the Northhounds and kill their king-dog Flay. That was why they followed him now, accepting him as their leader, beast to beast. Seeing the nine great white brutes running beside Stark, Ashton shivered slightly, sensing the eternal stranger in this, the only son he had ever had.

Yet there was love between them. Stark had come of his own free will, to fight his way across half this lunatic world of Skaith and free Ashton from the Lords Protector at the Citadel.

Now a long road lay before them, full of powerful enemies and unknown dangers. In his heart Ashton felt sure they would never make it back to Skeg, where the starport offered the sole means of escape. And he felt a moment of anger that Stark had put himself in this position. For my sake, Ashton thought. And how do you think I will feel when I see you die, for my sake?

But he kept this thought to himself.

When their mounts had begun to flag noticeably, Stark allowed a halt. Ashton watered the riding animals and fed them with cakes of compressed lichens. Stark fed the hounds sparingly with strips of dried meat brought from the Citadel. Gerd was still muttering about *Things*, though the landscape remained empty. The men chewed their own tough rations, moving about as they did so to stretch muscles cramped by long hours in the saddle.

Stark said, "How far have we come?"

Ashton looked at the faceless monotony of the dunes. "I'd guess we're more than halfway to the first shelter."

"You're sure there isn't any other way to go, to get ahead of Gelmar?"

"The road was laid out in the beginning along the shortest route between Yurunna and the Citadel. It hardly bends an inch in a hundred miles until it hits those mountain passes. No shortcuts. Besides, if you lose the guideposts you're done for. Only the Hooded Men and the Runners know their way around the desert." Ashton drank water from a leather bottle and handed it to Stark. "I know how you feel about the woman, and I know how important it is to keep Gelmar from taking her back to Irnan. But we've all got a long way to go yet."

Stark's eyes were cold and distant. "If Gelmar reaches the wayhouse before us, he will get fresh mounts. The tall desert beasts, which are much faster than these. Am I right?"

"Yes."

"He will also see to it that there are no fresh mounts for us, and the tribesmen will be warned to look for us."

Ashton nodded.

"Perhaps, with the hounds, we might overcome those difficulties. Perhaps. But the next wayhouse is seven days beyond?"

"Not hurrying."

"And Yurunna is seven days beyond that."

"Again, not hurrying."

"Yurunna is a strong city, you said."

"Not large, but it stands on a rocky island in the middle of a fat oasis—or what passes for a fat oasis hereabouts—and there's only one way up. The wild tribesmen look upon it with lust, but it's so well guarded they don't even raid much around the oasis. The Yur are bred there, the Well-Created. Some more of the Wandsmen's nastiness; I don't believe in breeding humans like prize pigs even to be the perfect servants of the Lords Protector. The Northhounds are bred there, too, and sent north along the road to the Citadel as they're needed. How would meeting their old kennelmates and the Houndmaster affect your friends?"

"I don't know. In any case, the hounds alone would not be useful against a city."

He put away the bottle and called the pack. The men climbed again onto the saddle-pads.

"There's another good reason for hurrying," Stark said. He looked at the wasteland, at the dim sky where Old Sun slid heavily toward night. "Unless we want to spend the rest of our lives on Skaith, we had better get back to Skeg before the Wandsmen decide to send the ships away and close the starport down for good."

3

Starships were a new thing on Skaith. Only in the last dozen years had they arrived, a shattering astonishment out of the sky.

Before that, for its billions of years of existence, the system of the ginger star had lived solitary in the far reaches of the galaxy, untouched by the interstellar civilization that spread across half the Milky Way from its center at Pax, chief world of Vega. The Galactic Union had even embraced the distant little world of Sol. But the Orion Spur, of which Skaith and her primary were citizens, had remained largely unexplored.

In her young days, Skaith was rich, industrialized, urbanized and fruitful. But she never achieved space-flight; and when the ginger star grew weak with age and the long dying began, there was no escape for her people. They suffered and died, or if they were strong enough, they suffered and survived.

Gradually, out of the terrible upheavals of the Wandering, a new social system arose.

The consul of the Galactic Union, who spent a few brief hopeful years at Skeg, wrote in his report:

> The Lords Protector, reputed to be "undying and unchanging," were apparently established long ago by the then ruling powers as a sort of superbenevolence. The Great Migrations were beginning, the civilizations of the north were breaking up as the people moved away from the increasing cold, and there was certain to be a time of chaos with various groups competing for new lands. Then and later, when some stability was reestablished, the Lords Protector were to prevent a too great trampling of the weak by the strong. Their law was simple: Succor the weak, feed the hungry, shelter the homeless—striving always toward the greatest good of the greatest number.
>
> It appears that through the centuries this law has been carried far beyond its original intent. The Farers and the many smaller nonproductive fragments of this thoroughly fragmented culture are now the greater number, with the result that the Wandsmen, in the name of the Lords Protector, hold a third or more of the population in virtual slavery, to supply the rest.

A slavery from which there was no escape, until the starships came.

Skaith was starved for metals, and the ships could bring those, trading iron and lead and copper for drugs with fantastic properties that were grown in Skaith's narrow tropic zone and for antiquities looted from the ruins of old cities. So the Wandsmen let them stay, and Skeg became a marketplace for the off-worlders.

But the ships brought with them more than iron pigs. They brought hope. And that hope was a corrupting influence.

It led some folk to think of freedom.

The people of Irnan, a city-state in the north temperate zone, had thought of freedom so strongly that they asked the Galactic Union, through its consul, to help them emigrate to a better world. And that precipitated the crisis. The Wandsmen reacted furiously to dam this first small trickle, which they foresaw would turn into a flood as other city-states saw the possibilities of escape. They took Ashton, who had come out from Pax as representative of the Ministry of Planetary Affairs to confer with the Irnanese, and sent him north to the Citadel for the Lords Protector to question and deal with. With his ready-made mob of Farers, Gelmar, Chief Wandsman of Skeg, shut down the GU consulate and made Skeg a closed enclave which no foreigner might leave. Other Wandsmen, under Mordach, punished the Irnanese, making them prisoners in their own city. And when Stark came to find Ashton, the Wandsmen were waiting for him.

Gerrith, wise woman of Irnan, had prophesied that a Dark Man would come from the stars. A wolf's-head, a landless man, a man without a tribe. He would destroy the Citadel and the Lords Protector for the sake of Ashton.

For that prophecy the wise woman died, and Stark came very near to dying. He fitted the description. A mercenary, he owned no master. A wanderer of the space-roads, he had no land of his own. Orphaned on an alien world, he had no people. Gelmar and his Farers had done their best to kill him at Skeg before he could begin his search. Word of the prophecy had been carried far and wide among the scattered peoples of Skaith. It had dogged Stark all the way north, so that he was alternately considered a savior to be worshipped and encumbered, a blasphemy to be destroyed out of hand and an article of value to be sold to the highest bidder. The prophecy had not in any way helped him.

Nevertheless, he had managed to do what the prophecy had said he would do. He had taken the Citadel and gutted it with fire. Because of the Northhounds and their inbred loyalty, he had not been able to kill the Lords Protector. But they would be destroyed in another sense when it became known to the people that they were not at all supernatural beings, undying and unchanging, but only seven Wandsmen who had achieved the positions of supreme authority for ordering the affairs of the Fertile Belt—seven old men cast out now upon the world by no greater power than that of an off-planet adventurer.

So far, so good. But the wise woman had not said what would follow the fulfillment of her prophecy.

Of the six who had left Irnan to find the Citadel, only three survived: Stark himself; Gerrith the daughter of Gerrith, who had become the wise woman in her mother's place; and Halk, that strong man and slayer of Wandsmen, comrade of the martyred Yarrod. The rest had died when the men of Thyra took Stark and the others captive for Gelmar. Thanks to Gerrith and the interference of Kell à Marg Skaith-Daughter, who had insisted that Gelmar bring the strangers into the House of the Mother so that she might learn the truth of the rumored starships, Stark had escaped from the Wandsman. He had almost died in the dark catacombs under the Witchfires, in endless rooms and corridors long abandoned and forgotten by the Children of Skaith themselves. But he had at last made his way out by the north gate, to face the Northhounds and take the Citadel.

Gelmar still held Halk and Gerrith and was hurrying them south to be displayed before the walls of Irnan as evidence of the failure and folly of the revolt which had flared so suddenly into bloody violence. Irnan still stood against the anger of the Wandsmen, defying siege, hoping for allies and waiting for word from the north. When it became known that the Citadel had truly fallen, that the Lords Protector were human and vulnerable even as other men, then other city-states would be encouraged to join with Irnan in striking out for the freedom of the stars.

Stark knew that he could count on the Lords Protector and the Wandsmen to do everything in their power to stop him. And their power was enormous. Here in the thinly populated north they maintained it by bribery and diplomacy rather than by strength. But in the Fertile Belt, the green girdle that circled the old planet's middle zones and contained the bulk of her surviving peoples, their power was based on long tradition and on the mob rule of the Farers, those wayward charges of the Lords Protector who lived only for joy beneath their dying sun. Where necessary, the Wandsmen also employed well-armed and disciplined mercenary troops such as the Izvandians. The farther south Stark went, the more formidable his enemies would become.

Stark's mount was beginning to give out. He was just too big for it. Ashton's was in better case, having less to carry. In spite of his years Ashton retained the rawhide leanness Stark remembered from the beginning, the same tough alertness of eye and mind and body. Even after numerous promotions had landed him in a soft job with the Ministry of Planetary Affairs, Ashton had refused to become deskbound. He continued stubbornly to do his researches into planetary problems in the field, which was why he had come to Skaith and run himself head-on into the Wandsmen.

At least, Stark thought, he had gotten Ashton out of the Citadel alive and safe. If he did not get him back to Skeg and off-planet the same way, it would not be for lack of trying.

The wind blew stronger. The sand moved under it with a dreary restlessness. The hounds trotted patiently: Gerd, who would have been king-dog after Flay; Grith, the great grim bitch who was his mate; and the seven other survivors of the attack on the Citadel—hellhounds with deadly eyes and their own secret way of killing. Old Sun seemed to pause on the rim of the mountain wall as if to rest and gather strength for the final plunge. In spite of himself, Stark felt a passing fear that this descent might be the last one and that the ginger star might never rise again, a common phobia among Skaithians which he seemed to be acquiring. Shadows collected in the hollows of the desert. The air turned colder.

Gerd said abruptly, *Things coming.*

4

THE HOUND had stopped in his trotting. He stood braced on forelegs like tree trunks, high shoulders hunched against the wind, coarse fur ruffling. His head, which seemed too heavy for even that powerful neck to support without weariness, swung slowly back and forth. The dark muzzle snarled.

The pack gathered behind him. They were excited, making noises in their throats. Their eyes glowed, too bright, too knowing—the harbingers of death.

There, said Gerd.

Stark saw them, strung along a rib of sand in the grainy light. A second before nothing had stood there. Now, in the flicker of an eyelid, there were eleven . . . no, fourteen bent, elongated shapes, barely recognizable as human. Skin like old leather, thick and tough, covered their staring bones, impervious to wind and cold. Long hair and scanty scraps of hide flapped wildly. A family group, Stark thought—males, females, young. One of the females clutched something between pendulous breasts. Other adults carried stones or thigh-bones.

"Runners," Ashton said, and pulled out his sword. "They're like piranha fish. Once they get their teeth in—"

The old male screamed, one high wild cry. The ragged figures stooped forward, lifted on their long legs and rushed out across the shadowed sand.

They moved with incredible speed. Their bodies were drawn and thinned for running, thrusting heads carried level with the ground and never losing sight of the prey. The upper torso was all ribcage, deep and narrow, with negligible shoulders, the arms carried like flightless wings outstretched for balance. The incredible legs lifted, stretched, spurned, lifted, with a grotesque perfection of motion that caught the throat with its loveliness even as it terrified with its ferocity.

Gerd said, *N'Chaka. Kill?*

Kill!

The hounds sent fear.

That was how they killed. Not with fang or claw. With fear. Cold cruel deadly mind-bolts of it that struck like arrows to the brain, drained the gut, chilled the blood-warm heart until it ceased beating.

The Runners were like birds before the hunters when the guns go off.

They dropped, flailing, writhing, howling. And the Northhounds went playfully among them.

Ashton still held the unnecessary sword. He stared at the pack with open horror.

"No wonder the Citadel remained inviolate for so long." His gaze shifted to Stark. "You survived *that?*"

"Barely." Once again he was back on the nighted plain, with the snow beneath him and the bitter stars above, and Flay's great jaws laughing while he sent the killing fear. "I almost went under. Then I remembered being afraid before, when Old One was teaching me to live in that place where you found me. I remembered the rock lizards hunting me, things as big as dragons, with bigger teeth than Flay. It made me angry that I should die because of a hound. I fought back. They're not invincible, Simon, unless you think they are."

The hounds were snapping the grotesque bodies back and forth like rags, playing toss and tug-of-war. Stark caught a glimpse of the female with the hanging breasts. What she had clutched between them was an infant, its tiny browless face snarling savagely even in death.

"There are some worse than that in the darklands on the other side of the mountains," Stark said, "but not much worse." Scraps and remnants of old populations left behind by the Great Migrations had solved the problems of survival in numerous ways, none of them pleasant.

"The Hooded Men hate and fear the Runners," Ashton said. "They used to range much farther north, but now they're in bitter competition for what few resources are left in this wilderness. They can run down anything that moves, and anything that moves is food: humans, domestic animals, anything. The weaker tribes are suffering the most, the so-called Lesser Hearths of the Seven Hearths of Kheb. They've taken to raiding south, all the way to the cliff villages below Yurunna, along the Edge. The Ochar, who call themselves the First-Come, fare much better because of the supplies they get from the Wandsmen. The Lesser Hearths do not love them. There is war between them and between each other. And the Ochar will not love you, Eric. They're hereditary Keepers of the Upper Road, and their existence depends on the Wandsmen. With the Citadel gone and no more traffic between it and Yurunna . . ." He made an expressive gesture.

"So far," said Stark, "I've found very few on Skaith to love me."

Only one, in fact.

Her name was Gerrith.

When the hounds were done with their gamboling and their crunching, Stark called them to heel.

They came reluctantly. *Good play, full belly,* Gerd said. *Now sleep.*

Later sleep, Stark answered, and looked into the bright baleful eyes until they slid aside. *Now hurry.*

They hurried.

The last dull glow faded. Stars burned in the desert sky, dimmed intermittently by the flaring aurora. Skaith has no moon, and the Three Ladies, the magnificent clusters that ornament the more southerly nights, gave no light here. Nevertheless, it was possible to follow the markers.

The wind dropped. The cold deepened. Warm breath steamed white, froze on the faces of the men and the muzzles of the beasts.

Gerd said, *Wandsmen. There.*

The hounds could not distinguish between the different grades of Wandsmen, except that Gerd pictured *white* in his mind, which was the color of the robes worn by the Lords Protector.

Presently Stark made out a trampled track in the sand, and he knew that they were very close.

The riding animals had begun to stagger with weariness. Stark called a halt. They fed and rested and slept a while. Then they went on their way again, following the broad trail over the dunes.

The first coppery smudge of dawn showed in the east. It widened slowly, dimming the stars, staining the land like creeping rust. The rim of the ginger star crawled up over the horizon. And from somewhere ahead, Stark heard voices chanting.

"Old Sun, we thank thee for this day. For light and warmth we thank thee, for they conquer night and death. Abandon not thy children, but give us many days in which to worship thee. We worship thee with gifts, with precious blood . . ."

From the top of a dune Stark looked down and saw the camp: a score of servants, a huddle of beasts and baggage and, some distance apart by the remains of a fire, the seven old men—the Lords Protector, their rich robes of fur over white garments, offering the morning prayer. Ferdias was pouring wine onto the last of the embers.

He looked up at the Northhounds and at the two Earthmen on the back of the dune. Stark saw his face clearly, a strong face, proud and implacable. The dawn wind stirred his robes and his mane of white hair, and his eyes were as cold as winter ice. His companions, six dark pillars of rectitude, looked up also.

The chant did not waver. ". . . with precious blood, with wine and fire, with all the holy things of life . . ."

Wine hissed into the hot ashes, steaming.

And Gerd whined.

What is it? Stark asked.

Not know, N'Chaka. Wandsmen angry. Gerd lifted his head, and his eyes caught the light of Old Sun so that they burned like coals.

Wandsmen want to kill.

5

Very quietly Stark said to Ashton, "Don't make any threatening moves. Stay close to me."

Ashton nodded, looking uneasily at the nine gaunt giants who stood almost as tall as the riding animals. He settled himself in the saddle and took a firmer grip on the rein.

Stark forgot him for the moment.

The Northhounds were incapable of understanding the complexities of their betrayal. According to pack law, they had followed a new leader, one who had established beyond doubt his right to lead. They had followed him to the Citadel; and the servants, the Yur, to whom they owed no loyalty, had attacked them with arrows. They did not understand why. They only understood the wounds, and their rage had been deadly. But they had offered no threat of harm to the Wandsmen, the Lords Protector. They had forbidden N'Chaka to touch them. As they saw it, they had been loyal to their trust. They were to prevent all humans from reaching the Citadel, but they did not regard N'Chaka as human. They saw nothing wrong in allowing him to go there.

Yet, when Ferdias ordered Gerd to kill N'Chaka in the Citadel, Gerd had wavered dangerously. Only the knowledge of what N'Chaka had done to Flay decided the outcome.

Now there would be another test.

Stark thought of Flay, of the death of Flay, torn and bleeding on the plain. He made the thoughts strong. And he said:

Watch the servants. They may send more arrows to us.

Gerd's lips pulled back. He growled. The gash across his own hip was still raw and painful.

We watch.

Stark kicked his beast into a walk, down the slope of sand toward the Lords Protector. Ashton followed. The hounds padded beside Stark, carrying their heads low, snarling.

The Yur remained motionless, staring at the pack with their shining copper-colored eyes that were like the inlaid eyes of statues, reflecting light but no depth. Their faces were beautiful to see, but so alike that they were all the same face, a face totally lacking in expression. Yet Stark could smell the fear, the rank sweat of it upon them. They had not forgotten what the Northhounds had done to their brothers.

Old Sun had completed his rising. Ferdias poured out the last of the wine. The chanting stopped. The seven old men waited by the ashes of the fire.

The Earthmen and the hounds reached the bottom of the slope and halted before the Lords Protector. Stark slid off the saddle-pad, coming to the ground with the easy grace of a leopard.

"We will have six of your beasts, Ferdias," he said. "The best and strongest. Have your servants bring them now, but bid them take care." He put his hand on Gerd's high shoulders.

Ferdias inclined his head slightly and gave the order.

Nervous activity began among the Yur. Ashton dismounted carefully. They waited.

The Lords Protector looked at the Earthmen as at two incarnate blasphemies.

Especially they looked at Stark.

Seven iron men, they were believers in a creed and a way of life, the only ones they knew. Skaith was their world, Skaith's peoples their people. They had served all their lives to the best of their considerable abilities, honoring the ancient law—succor the weak, feed the hungry, shelter the homeless, strive always for the greatest good of the greatest number.

They were good men. Not even Stark could question their goodness.

He could question the lengths to which that goodness had been carried. Lengths that had made the blood-bath at Irnan inevitable and had brought about the deaths of equally good men and women who wanted the freedom to choose their own path among the stars.

Despite his hatred, Stark felt a certain sympathy for the Lords Protector. A little more than a decade was hardly time enough in which to absorb the enormous implications of what had happened. Skaith's little sky had been a tight-closed shell for all the ages of its existence. Uncounted generations had lived and died within that shell, seeing nothing beyond. Now, with a single dagger-stroke, that sky was torn open and Skaith stared out upon the galaxy—stunning in its immensity, thronged with unimagined worlds and peoples, ablaze with the glare of alien suns, busy with life where Skaith was concerned only with her long dying.

Small wonder that new thoughts were stirring. And small wonder that these well-nigh all-powerful men were desperately afraid of what the future might hold. If Irnan succeeded in her revolt, and other stable populations, those who supplied the food and commodities to support the vast army of Farers, should join with her in emigrating to freer worlds, all the dependents of the Lords Protector would be left destitute and the whole order would be destroyed.

"It is not right or decent," said Ferdias slowly, "that any creature in human form should control the Northhounds on their own level, as a beast."

"He will not control them long," said a small lean man with intense black eyes. "They cannot live where Old Sun is stronger."

"That is true," said Ferdias. "They are bred for the cold north."

Stark shrugged. He was not worried about that day. He was worried about this one. Gerd moved uneasily, and Stark let his hand slide down to the hound's broad head.

"Why do we not kill this person here at once?" said the black-eyed man. "The hounds will not touch us."

"Can you be sure?" said Ferdias. "We have never killed a Northhound, and they regard him as one of their own."

"Besides," said Stark, "I'd set them on the Yur. Then you'd be alone, at the mercy of the Runners, the bellies without minds. Even the Lords Protector are not safe from them."

Another one of the six spoke up, a tall gaunt man whose wild hair was blowing across his face. His eyes glared out through it as from a thicket. He shouted at Stark.

"You cannot hope to live. You cannot hope to see Irnan again or the ships at Skeg."

Ferdias said, "I think it is useless to argue with Stark that he has no hope of doing whatever it is he intends to do. This was argued when he determined to fulfill the prophecy of Irnan."

"A prophecy of traitors!" cried the wild-haired man. "Very well, he has fulfilled it. He has taken back the man Ashton and burned our sacred roof over our heads. But that is the end of the prophecy, and the end of the Dark Man. He is no more fated."

"Unless there should be another prophecy," said Ferdias, and smiled without the slightest warmth or mirth. "But that is hardly likely. Gerrith goes to her own fate. And by her words, since Mordach destroyed the Robe and Crown, there is no longer a wise woman for Irnan."

"Wise woman or not," said Ashton, "and prophecies be damned, the change will come. Skaith herself will force it on you. The change can be peaceful, controlled by you, or it can be hideously violent. If you have the wisdom and the foresight to bring Skaith into the Union—"

Ferdias said, "We have listened to you for many months, Ashton. Our opinions have not been altered, not even by the fall of the Citadel." His gaze dwelt again on Stark, and the hounds muttered and whined and were restless. "You hope to destroy us by revealing to the world that we are not immortals but only men, only Wandsmen grown older. Perhaps this may come about. It has not happened yet. The Harsenyi nomads will carry the tale of the Citadel's fall in their wanderings, but it will be a long time in the telling. No doubt you sent messengers of your own, or tried to, to take word swiftly to Irnan. Messengers can be intercepted. Irnan is under siege. We hold all the Fertile Belt. We hold Skeg, your only hope of escape, and the starport is under guard at all times—you can hardly hope to reach it without being captured. And Skaith herself is your enemy. She is a cruel mother, but she is ours, and we know her. You do not."

He turned abruptly. "The beasts are ready. Take them and go."

Stark and Ashton mounted.

Ferdias spoke aloud to Gerd, so that Stark too might hear him. "Go now with N'Chaka. You will come back to us when it is time."

The Earthmen rode out of the camp with the hounds behind them.

They rode for some distance. The camp was lost behind them in the dunes.

Stark's muscles relaxed as the adrenaline stopped flowing. Sweat broke out on him, clammy beneath his furs. Ashton's face was a study in hard-drawn lines. Neither man spoke. Then at last Ashton sighed and shook his head and said softly, "Christ! I thought surely they'd try to turn the brutes against us."

"They were afraid to," Stark said. "But there will be another time."

The hounds trotted peacefully.

"It seems such a primitive idea," Ashton said, "setting them to guard the Citadel."

"That's what they wanted. The Lords Protector had men-at-arms in plenty to defend them during the Wandering, but men will face other men and weapons they can see. The great white hounds appearing suddenly out of the snow—wraiths with demon eyes and a supernatural power to kill—was something most men preferred to avoid, and of course the ones who didn't, died. In time the legend became even more effective than the fact."

"The Lords Protector must have killed many people who only wanted help."

"The Lords Protector have always been realists. The important thing was that the Citadel should remain sacrosanct, a mystery and a power hidden from men. A few lives had to be sacrificed for the good of the many." Stark's face hardened. "You weren't at Irnan,

Simon, tied to a post, waiting to be flayed alive by the will of Mordach, the Chief Wandsman. You didn't hear the mob howl, you didn't smell the blood when Yarrod was slaughtered and torn."

Gerrith did. Gerrith was there, stripped naked but not shamed before the mob, defying Mordach, calling out to the people of Irnan in the clear strong voice of prophecy. *Irnan is finished here on Skaith, you must build a new city, on a new world, out among the stars.* She had waited there for death, beside him. As had Halk, and those three who had died at Thyra trying to reach the Citadel.

Ashton had his own bitter memories of captivity and threatened death. He was only alive himself because the Lords Protector had not quite dared to be deprived of his knowledge of this new and unknown foe they had to deal with—the vast Outside.

"I know how they think," he said. "But they're not being realists about the future. The viable surface of this planet gets smaller every year. The marginal peoples are already beginning to move as the cold drives them and the food supplies dwindle. The Lords Protector are perfectly aware of this. If they don't act in time, they'll have another slaughter on their hands, such as they had at the time of the Wandering."

"It was the slaughter that gave them their power," Stark said. "They can accept another one as long as they retain their power which they will never give up."

"We're asking them to do more than give up power. We're asking them to cease being. Where does a Lord Protector go when he has nothing left to protect? They have meaning only in the existing context of Skaith. If we take away that context, they disappear."

"That," said Stark, "is the best fate I could ask for them."

He picked up the reins. The road markers marched away in the morning. Gelmar was somewhere ahead.

With Gerrith.

The men made much better time now, changing mounts frequently. The pack load was shared between two led animals. The beasts were by no means fresh, but they were stronger than the ones that had been left behind. Stark pushed them without mercy.

Gelmar was pushing, too. Three times they came upon dead animals. Stark half-expected to find Halk's body left by the wayside. The man had taken a great wound at Thyra, and this pace would no doubt finish him.

"Perhaps Halk is dead," Ashton suggested, "and they're carrying the corpse. They can display him just as well, pickled in wine and honey."

The wind blew fitfully, veering with a kind of spiteful malice so that it could kick sand in their faces no matter how they turned them. Toward noon a haze came out of the north and spread across the sky. Old Sun sickened, and the face of the desert was troubled.

Ashton said, "The Runners often come with the sandstorms. In force."

They drove their mounts to the limit and beyond, passing each marker as an individual triumph. The beasts groaned as they went. The hounds ran with their jaws wide and their tongues lolling.

The haze thickened. The light of the ginger star yellowed and darkened. The wind struck at the men with vicious little cat's-paws. Sky, sun and desert lost definition, became merged into one strange brassy twilight.

In that distanceless and horizonless half-gloom Stark and Ashton came to the top of a ridge and saw Gelmar's party ahead, a line of dark figures clotted together, puffs of blowing sand rising beneath them as they moved.

6

STARK SAID to Gerd, *Run. Send fear to the servants if they fight. Hold them all until I come.*

Gerd called his pack together. They fled away, nine pale shadows. They bayed, and the terrible voices rang down the wind. The people of Gelmar's party heard and faltered in their going.

Stark handed his lead-reins to Ashton and flogged his beast into a lumbering gallop.

A spume of sand had begun to blow from the tops of the dunes. The wind was settling into the northeast quadrant. Stark lost the voices of the hounds. For a time he lost sight of the party, because of a dusty thickness in the lower air that came down like a curtain on the flat below the ridge. When he saw them again, blurred shapes of men and animals rubbed with a dark thumb on an ocher canvas, they were standing perfectly still. Only the hounds moved, circling.

Stark rode up to the group. The face he was looking for was not the first one he saw. That was Gelmar's. The Chief Wandsman of Skeg sat his mount a little apart from the others, as though perhaps he had turned to intercept the hounds. The strain of the journey showed on him and on the three other Wandsmen who accompanied him. Stark knew them all by sight but only one by name—that was Vasth, who had wrapped his ruined face in a scarf against the cold. Halk had struck him down at Irnan, on that day when the city rose and killed its Wandsmen. Vasth was apparently the only survivor. His remaining eye peered at Stark, a vicious glitter between the wrappings.

Gelmar had changed considerably since Stark first met him, tall and lordly in his red robe, secure in his unquestioned authority, ordering the mob at Skeg. The Wandsman had taken his initial shock that night, when Stark laid violent hands on his sacred person and made it clear to him that he could die as easily as any other man. He had received further shocks, all connected with Stark. Now he looked at the Earthman, not as would a superior being with power unlimited, but as a tired man, one who was exasperated, thwarted and quite humanly angry—seeing another defeat, but not beaten. Gelmar was not ever going to be beaten as long as he could breathe.

Gerd ranged himself at Stark's side. *Wandsmen angry we follow N'Chaka.*

Angry with N'Chaka. Not you.

Gerd whined. *Never angry at Flay.*

Flay is dead. Ferdias say follow me, for now.

Gerd subsided, unsatisfied.

Gelmar smiled briefly, having understood Gerd's side of the exchange. "You'll have difficulty holding them. They're not equipped to serve two masters."

"Would you care to put it to the test now?"

Gelmar shook his head. "No more than Ferdias did."

The Yur, ten or eleven of them scattered along the line, were standing quiet. Some were on foot, and they seemed less tired than the mounted Wandsmen. But they were bred for strength. They stared at the hounds with their blank bright eyes, and Stark thought they were puzzled rather than afraid. They knew what had happened at the Citadel, but they hadn't seen it. They were armed with bows and light lances, swords and daggers at their belts.

"The servants," Stark said, "will lay down their arms, very carefully. If any hostile move is made, the hounds will kill."

"Would you leave us at the mercy of the Runners?" cried one of the lesser Wandsmen.

"That concerns me not at all," said Stark. "You have a dagger at your own waist. Discard it." He motioned to Gelmar. "Give the order."

"The hounds will not harm us," said Vasth. His voice came muffled through the scarf.

Gelmar said with cold impatience, "There is a sandstorm blowing. We need the Yur." To Stark he said, "The Runners come with the storms, living where other creatures would die. They come in strength, devouring everything in their path."

"So I have heard," said Stark. "Give the order."

Gelmar gave the order. The Yur dropped their weapons into the blowing sand. Gelmar loosened his own belt.

Stark kept his eyes on Vasth.

Gerd said, *Wandsman throw knife, kill N'Chaka.*

I know. Touch him, Gerd.

Not hurt Wandsman.

No hurt. Touch.

Gerd's baleful gaze turned to the Wandsman. Vasth was stricken with a sudden trembling. He made a strangled sound and let the dagger fall.

"Stand quiet now," said Stark, and called, "Gerrith!"

There was a covered litter slung between two animals. She came from beside it, shaking back the fur hood that covered her head. The wind picked up thick strands of hair the color of warm bronze. She smiled and spoke his name, and her eyes were like sunlight.

"Come here by me," he said.

She reined her beast to the side away from Gerd. Her face had been thinned by the long journeying, all the way from Irnan, across the Barrens and through the haunted darklands to the Citadel. The fine bones were clear under honed flesh and taut skin colored by the winds of Skaith to a darker bronze than her hair. Proud and splendid Gerrith. Stark was shaken by a stabbing warmth.

"I knew you were coming, Stark," she said. "I knew the Citadel had fallen, long before Ferdias' messenger reached us. But we must go on now, quickly."

"I have no mind to stay." The wind had strengthened, driving the sand. The weapons were already half-buried. The world had become much smaller. The twilight had deepened so that even the faces of the Wandsmen and the Yur were indistinct. "Is Halk living?"

"Barely. He must have rest."

Ashton appeared dimly out of the murk with the led beasts. "Let them go, Simon," Stark said. "Gerrith, can you two handle the litter?"

They went at once and took the places of the two servants who had been leading the animals. Then they rejoined Stark.

"Gelmar. Tell your people to move."

The cavalcade moved, reluctantly, thinking of weapons left behind. Riders hunched in saddles, covered faces from stinging sand. Little drifts piled on Halk's litter.

They passed a marker, and Stark was squinting ahead trying to see the next one when Gerd said:

Humans. There.

Stark rode closer to Gelmar. "What humans? Hooded Men? The wayhouse?"

Gelmar nodded.

They went on.

When Stark reckoned they were far enough away from the buried weapons to make impractical any attempt to recover them, he reached out and caught Gelmar's bridle.

"We leave you here. Follow too closely and your servants die."

Kill Yur? Gerd asked hopefully.

Not unless I tell you.

"After you have secured the wayhouse," Gelmar said, "what then?"

"He will leave us to die in the sand," said Vasth. "May Old Sun shrivel the men from the stars!"

The cavalcade had halted, bungling together behind Gelmar.

"I would prefer to show you the same mercy you have shown us," said Stark. "But if you make it to the wayhouse, I'll not deny you shelter."

Gelmar smiled. "You could not. The hounds would force you to let us in."

"I know," said Stark. "Otherwise I might be less generous."

He rode away from the party, with Ashton and Gerrith and the litter.

Lead us to humans, he said to Gerd, knowing that Gelmar would be following the same mental beacon. They could forget about the markers.

They plunged on, across whaleback dunes that blurred and shifted shape beneath them. The litter swayed and jolted. Stark was sorry for Halk, but there was no help for it. The desert cried out in torment, a great hissing gritty wail rose and circled and fell away again to a deep moaning.

Then, abruptly, the wind dropped. The lower air cleared in the sudden stillness. Old Sun shone raggedly above. From the top of a ridge they saw the wayhouse half a mile or so ahead, a thick low structure of stone with a series of drift-walls about it to keep the desert out.

Ashton pointed away and said, "God Almighty."

A *tsunami,* a tidal wave of sand, rushed toward them out of the northeast. It filled the whole horizon. Its crest of dusty foam curled halfway up the sky. Below, it was a brightish ocher shading down through dirty reds and browns to a boiling darkness at the bottom that was almost black.

Stark saw a scudding of many shapes that ran fleetly before the edges of that blackness.

For the second time Gerd said, *Things come.*

Gelmar's party appeared on the back trail, clear in the placid air. They paused and looked northeastward, then came on again at a run.

Stark lashed the beasts forward. The wave had a voice, a roaring almost too deep for the human ear to register. The heart felt it, and the marrow of the bones, and the spasming gut. Even the animals forgot their weariness.

All at once Gerd spoke urgently in Stark's mind.

Wandsman says come, N'Chaka. Come now or things kill.

He turned with the pack and raced away down the back trail, answering Gelmar's call.

7

STARK SAID, *Gerd, come back!*

The hounds ran on.

Danger, N'Chaka. Guard Wandsmen. You come.

"What is it?" shouted Ashton, his voice a thin thread against the far-off roaring. "Where are they going?"

"To guard the Wandsmen." The overriding imperative, the instinct bred in the bone. And Gelmar's cry for help must have been urgent enough, what with his escort unarmed and the Runners coming. Stark swore. If he let the pack go without him, N'Chaka might never regain his authority. He could not make the hounds return to him. Neither could he afford to let Gelmar get control of them.

"I have to go with them." He waved the others on. "Get to the wayhouse, Simon." Gerrith's face, pale under the bronze, and framed in dark fur, stared at him. The litter careened wildly, the muffled form within it so still that Stark wondered if any life was left. "Go!" he yelled. "Go!" He reined his beast around and sent it staggering after the hounds, his thoughts as black as the base of the sand wave.

He met Gelmar's party in a space between two dunes. All the Yur were on foot now, running more strongly than the beasts. Two ran at the head of each Wandsman's mount, helping it along. The Northhounds hovered on the flanks.

Gelmar looked at Stark with a certain cruel amusement. "I wondered if you'd come."

Stark did not answer. He fell in at the head of the party, sword in hand. The crest of the wave, outspeeding the base, began to spread overhead. Dirty veils of grit trailed down from it. The air was thickening again. When they topped a dune, Stark could see the wall of sand sweeping nearer.

The Runners scudded before it as if riding a sandstorm gave them even more pleasure than sex or feeding. It was a game, such as Stark had seen strong-winged birds play with storm winds, and there was a sinister beauty in the flickering movement of bending shapes, a sort of dark dance, swift and doomsome. He could not count the creatures, but he guessed at half a hundred. Perhaps more.

They were not moving at random. They had a goal.

"The wayhouse?"

"There is food there. Men and animals."

"How do they attack?"

"With the stormfront. While their victims are stunned and suffocating, they feed. They survive the dust, and they seem to enjoy the violence. They strike like Strayer's Hammer."

Strayer was a god of the forges worshipped by certain iron-working folk on the other side of the mountains. Stark had had some experience of that hammer.

"We must have shelter," he said, "before the sand wave hits, or we'll be so scattered that even the hounds won't be able to help us."

From the next ridge Stark made out the smudged images of Ashton, Gerrith and the litter. They had reached the walls and begun to pass through a gate. Stark lost sight of them as he came sliding down to the flat. Flying grit blinded him. The ground shook. The huge solemn roaring filled the world.

Half a mile.

Seven and a half minutes walking. Half of that running flat out for your life.

Stay close, Gerd! Lead to humans!

Gerd's head pressed his knee. He felt the hound tremble.

No worse than snowblind storm on Worldheart. Lead, Gerd!

Grith came shouldering up beside her mate. *We lead.*

The air was a darkening turmoil. They fled across the face of the storm, toward the walls they could no longer see.

Things come, N'Chaka.

Kill?

Too far. Soon.

Hurry, then!

Wind plucked at them, trying to lift them into the sky. Stark counted seconds. At one hundred and seventy a wall loomed in the murk, so close that they almost came against it. The gate. The gate!

Here, N'Chaka.

An opening. They passed through it. Now that they were within the walls the fury of the wind seemed to abate somewhat, or else there was a space of dead air just before the wave. They could see the squat stone house ahead, beyond an inner wall and forever out of reach. They could see, much closer to them, some long low pens for the sheltering of animals, roofed over and open to the south, empty.

They could see the wave burst over the northeast walls in great boiling spouts of sand, dun-colored against black.

The Runners came with the boiling sand spouts, skimming the ground with outstretched arms. They were filled with a demoniac energy, as though they drew strength from the dynamics of wind and erupting desert.

Stark dropped from the back of his foundering beast and caught tight hold of Gerd's coarse neck-fur with his left hand. The Yur were behind him, fairly carrying the Wandsmen, the hounds hanging close, shoulders jostling. The pens offered no security but they were shelter of a sort, better than the open. They flung themselves under the nearest roof, against the nearest wall.

The wave hit.

Black, roar, dust, cracking, shaking, world falling. The wind hated them for cheating it. The air beneath the roof was thick with sand, and the sand had faces in it, gargoyle faces, film-eyed and browless, with great snapping teeth.

Kill!

The hounds killed.

Part of the roof ripped away. Runners were there, kicking, tearing. Their strength was appalling. The hounds killed, but some of the Runners plummeted down through the holes, onto the prey beneath. The Yur had placed the Wandsmen in a corner and formed a human wall across their front. They had only their hands to fight with. Runner jaws clamped on the living flesh and did not let go.

Stark killed with a furious loathing, slashing at anything that moved in the blind dust. There was a foul stink. The screaming of the Runners in rage and hunger and deadly fear came thin and terrible through the storm.

The hounds killed until they were tired.

Too many, N'Chaka. Strong.

Kill, kill, or Wandsmen die!

He did not care if the Wandsmen died. He only wanted to live himself.

The hounds killed.

The last of the Runner pack went whimpering away after the passing storm, to seek easier prey. There were heaps of ugly bodies left behind. But the hounds were too weary for play. They sat and hung their heads and let their tongues loll.

N'Chaka, we thirst.

Spent and shaken, Stark stood staring at the pack.

"They have their limits," said Gelmar. His face was ashen. "Of course they have." One of the Yur was beside him. "Give him your sword." And again, impatiently, "Your sword, Stark! Unless you wish to do the thing yourself."

The Wandsmen were unharmed. Two of the Yur were dead. Three others had been torn beyond hope. Runner corpses were still attached to them, blood dripping from obscene jaws.

Stark handed over his sword.

Quickly and efficiently the Yur gave each the mercy-stroke. The eyes of the victims watched without emotion and became only a shade less bright in the beautiful blank faces as death overtook them. The uninjured servants stood by impassively. When he was finished, the Yur wiped the blade and returned the sword to Stark.

And it had all happened in the space of a few minutes. The concentrated savagery of the attack had been shocking. Stark realized that Gelmar was looking at the Runner bodies with a sort of horrified fascination.

"Never seen them before?"

"Only from a distance. And never . . ." Gelmar seemed to hesitate over some inner thought. "Never so many."

"Each year they come in greater numbers, Lord."

It was a new voice, authoritative and strong. Stark saw that four men had appeared in the open side of the pen. They were little more than shadows in the blowing dust. Hooded cloaks of leather, dyed the color of bittersweet, whipped about tall lean bodies. Faces were hidden behind wrappings of cloth of the same color, all but the eyes, which were blue and piercing. The man who had spoken stood in the chief's place ahead of the others. Pendant upon his forehead, under the hood, was a dull orange stone set in gold, much scratched and worn.

"We saw you just before the storm struck, Lord, but we were not able to come."

He was staring, as they all were, at the bodies of the Runners. "The Northhounds did this?"

Gelmar said, "Yes."

The Hooded Man made a sign in the air and muttered something, glancing sidelong at the great hounds. Then he straightened and spoke to Gelmar. But his cold gaze had turned to Stark.

"In the house are two men and a woman who came just before you. The gray-headed man we saw before, when the Wandsmen brought him north some months ago. They admitted they had been your prisoners. They told us that this stranger leads the Northhounds, so that they no longer obey you, and that we must take orders from him. We know, of course, that this is a lie."

He tossed back his cloak to show a sword, short and wickedly curved, and a knife whose iron grip looped over the knuckles for striking and was set with cruel studs.

"How do you wish us to take this man, Lord—alive or dead?"

8

GERD MOVED his head and growled, catching the man's thought.

N'Chaka?

Send fear. Him! Not kill.

Gerd's hellhound gaze fixed on this tall chief of the Ochar, First-Come of the Seven Hearths of Kheb, and crumpled him sobbing into the dust like a terror-stricken child. His companions were too astonished to move.

"No!" cried Gelmar. "Stop it, Gerd!"

The hound whined irritably. *N'Chaka?*

Stark dropped his sword and caught Gerd's head, both sides, by the skin of his jowls.

Wandsmen not threatened. N'Chaka is. Who do you follow?

Have it out now, Stark thought. Now. Or we're back where we started, all of us—Gerrith, myself, Simon, Halk—all prisoners of the Wandsmen.

He drew houndskin tight between his fingers, stared into hot hound eyes.

Send fear.

The Ochar chief gasped and groveled in the sand.

"No," said Gelmar, who came and put his hand on Gerd's shoulder. "I forbid you, Gerd. You belong to us, to the Wandsmen. Obey me."

The Ochar chief ceased to struggle. He continued to sob. The three other men had moved away from him, as if he had been suddenly bewitched and they feared to be caught by the same spell. They appeared bewildered, unable to believe what they saw.

Gerd made an almost human cry. *N'Chaka! Not know.* He was tired, and the fight had left him edgy and upset. The smell of blood was strong. He pulled against Stark's hands. He threw himself from side to side, and his claws tore the dust.

Stark held him. *Choose, Gerd. Whom do you follow?*

A dangerous light had begun to kindle in Gerd's eyes. Abruptly the hound stood still, quivering in every muscle.

Stark braced himself.

The pack, by custom, would not interfere. The matter was between himself and Gerd. But they would see to it that no one else interfered, in a physical sense. There would be no danger of a knife in the back.

"Kill, Gerd," said Gelmar, his hand on the hound's shoulder. "This man will lead you all to death."

And Stark said, *You cannot kill me, Gerd. Remember Flay.*

The bolt of fear struck him. It shriveled his brain and turned his bones to water. It set his heart pounding until it threatened to burst against his ribs. But he held his grip. And a fierce cry came from out of his deep past, *I am N'Chaka. I do not die.*

The fear kept on.

Stark's pale eyes changed. His mouth changed. A sound came from his throat. He was no longer seeing Gerd as Gerd. He was seeing older, faraway things, the Fear-Bringers—the eternal enemy with all his many faces of dread, hunger, storm, quake, deadly night, deadlier day, the stalking hunter snuffling after heart-blood.

All life is fear. You have never felt it, hound. Death never feels it. Hound, I will teach you fear.

His grip shifted suddenly to Gerd's throat, gathered loose skin on either side, gathered and twisted, twisted and gathered, until the hound began to strangle, and still his fingers worked, and he said:

Do you see, Gerd, how it feels to die?

N'Chaka . . . !

The fear stopped.

Gerd dropped down, jaws wide, muzzle drawn in a snarling rictus. He put his chin on the ground.

Follow . . . strongest.

Stark let go. He straightened up. His eyes were still strange, all the humanness gone out of them. Gelmar stepped back, as though retreating from something unclean.

But he said, "You will not always be the strongest, Stark. Human or beast, your flesh is vulnerable. One day it will bleed, and the hounds will tear you."

The Ochar chief had risen to his knees. He wept tears of rage and shame.

"Do not let me live," he said. "You have put disgrace upon me before my tribesmen."

Stark said, "There is no disgrace. Is one man stronger than all these?" He pointed to the Runner bodies.

The Ochar chief got slowly to his feet. "No. But just now you withstood."

"I am not of your world. No man born of Skaith can stand against the Northhounds. And lest your tribesmen think shame of you, I will show them the truth of that."

Gerd squatted on his haunches, stretching his neck and hacking. Stark called the pack and they came around him, eyes averted lest they should seem to challenge him.

He gave an order, and the three Ochar were smitten with a palsy. They opened their mouths beneath the orange wrappings and cried out. They ran stumbling away.

"Now," said Stark to the chief, "we will go to the house. Gelmar, take your people. Walk ahead of us." To the Ochar he said, "How are you called?"

"Ekmal."

"Stay by me, Ekmal. And remember that the hounds hear your thoughts."

He ordered the hounds to watch but not to kill unless he told them to.

The Wandsmen went ahead, hating him. The Yur, beautiful and blank, walked with the Wandsmen. Ekmal walked beside Stark, his hands well away from his girdle and the sharp blades. The hounds came at Stark's heels. The wind still blew and the air was brown, but a man could move in it if he had to.

Men in cloaks of orange leather were bringing animals out of the house, where they had been taken for safety. The animals were tall, with long legs and wide paws splayed and furred for the sand. They stepped daintily. They were all colors, black and yellow and brown, barred and spotted. Their arched necks bore slender heads set with intelligent amber eyes.

The men leading them had met the three Ochar who were fleeing from the hounds. They stood shouting at each other with much gesticulating. Then they all turned and stared, and some of them reached for weapons.

Stark said, "Speak to them, Ekmal."

"Put down your arms!" Ekmal cried. "These demon dogs have killed a hundred Runners. Obey this man or he will set them on us."

The men muttered among themselves, but they took their hands from their hilts. Ekmal turned to Stark.

"What do you wish of us?"

"Water for the hounds. Have all your beasts brought out and fitted to carry us—myself and your three captives. Have food . . ."

"All the beasts? We cannot!"

"All the beasts. With food and water."

"But without beasts we're prisoned here!" Ekmal had the desert man's horror of being left afoot.

"Exactly," said Stark. "And so will the Wandsmen be, and the Lords Protector when they come, if they survived the storm."

Ekmal stopped. His eyes widened. "The Lords Protector? Coming here?"

Gelmar said, "This off-worlder has pulled down the Citadel, Ekmal. He has burned it, and the Lords Protector are cast out."

A stillness came over the Hooded Men. They stood stiff and stricken in the wind.

Ekmal wailed and lifted his hands to the sky. "The Dark Man has fulfilled the prophecy. He has destroyed the Citadel, and there will be no more keeping of the road above Yurunna. He has destroyed us, the hereditary Keepers, the First-Come of Kheb. Our wives and our sacred mothers, our tall sons and blue-eyed daughters, all will die. Our villages will disappear beneath the sands. Even the Fallarin will not remember us."

All the Hooded Men cried out. And from within the house came a new lamenting in the voices of women.

There was a shrill scream, and something fell with a clatter onto stone, beyond the open doorway.

He had a bow, N'Chaka. To send arrows.

"Wait!" said Gelmar in his strong far-carrying voice. "Do nothing now. The hounds will strike you down. But your day will come. The Lords Protector do not abandon their children. The Citadel will be rebuilt, and there are no more prophecies. Skaith is old and strong. No one man, not even a stranger from the stars, can prevail against her. Let him go now. He will find his death in her arms."

"May she bury him deep," said Ekmal. "May Old Sun shrivel his bowels. May Runners eat him."

Stark said, "Give the orders."

Ekmal gave them, shooting sharp words like darts through the cloth that hid his face. The men obeyed, but their eyes held death, or rather the hope of it, for Stark. There were eleven of them besides the chief. They led out all the animals, to the number of eighteen.

Ekmal said, "The well is inside."

Watch, Gerd.

The stonework of the house was solid and very old. Endless chafing of wind and sand had eroded it in whorls and pits. The edges of the doorway were worn round. On either side of the door, the wall wandered off to enclose a straggle of connected buildings that rose here and there to a second low story. Window places had been blocked up. At one corner was a little tower with many openings, and Stark could hear from within it a dim murmuring, as of birds. The wooden doors that worked on a pivot stone were enormously heavy and sheathed in iron brought by Harsenyi traders from Thyra beyond the mountains. The metal, far more valuable than pure gold, was scratched and scarred by Runner claws.

Inside, the air was still and warm, with pungent odors of animals and smoke and cooked foods. The stable area was off to the right, beyond a partition. The four Harsenyi beasts were there, standing with their heads down and their flanks heaving. The well had two stone troughs, one for the stable and one for humans.

The main room was large and neatly kept, with a dung fire smoking on a raised hearth. Weapons were ranged ready to hand. There were hangings and trophies on the walls, along with ornaments, some of them so exotic that they must have been brought up from the south over the Wandsmen's Road. Bags of grain, jars of wine and oil and other stores were kept in walled enclosures. At the back, the large room opened into a series of passageways leading to other quarters. The Wandsmen, Stark was sure, would have apartments fitted with every comfort. All in all, it was a pleasant place to rest from the rigors of travel.

A group of women, some holding small children to them, was gathered just inside the door. They wore long bright-colored garments of wool, and they did not cover their faces, which were thin-featured and handsome and fiercely hostile. They were clustered about one woman who knelt on the floor comforting a boy of about eleven. He wore a woolen tunic with an orange girdle, and he had not yet hidden his face behind the man's veil. He was trembling, biting back his sobs, and when he saw Stark he reached out for the bow he had dropped on the stones.

"No!" said Ekmal, and snatched up the bow. He touched the boy's bright head. "This is my son Jofr. I beg you—"

"Water the hounds," said Stark.

The women drew aside to let him pass. They bore themselves proudly. Their tawny necks and arms sounded when they moved with the soft clacking together of metal and darkling stones. Jofr rose to his feet and stood staring until his mother pulled him back.

Halk's litter had been set down close to the fire. Gerrith knelt beside it holding a cup. Ashton stood by her. Both had been watching, taut as bowstrings, to see who came in. They must have known something of what had gone on outside, but they could not be sure until they saw Stark and knew that he had survived the Runners and was somehow still in control.

Halk was watching, too.

"Over there," Stark said to Gelmar. "Sit down and be quiet." The hounds were lapping out of the trough. Hate and the death wish were as strong in the air around him as the smoke.

Watch, Gerd!

We watch, N'Chaka.

Stark walked to the fire, and the blue eyes of the women cursed him. Weariness gnawed at him, a corrosion in his bones. "Is there wine?"

Gerrith poured from a clay jug and handed him the cup. Ashton's gaze moved uneasily from the Wandsmen to the Hooded Men who came and went with gear and provisions.

"We must go on now," Stark said. "I can't stay awake forever, and I dare not risk the hounds." He bent over the litter. "Halk?"

Halk looked up at him. A tall man, taller than Stark, he lay under the furs like a withered tree. The bones of his face stuck out through folds of skin where the flesh had dropped away. His huge hands were stiff bunches of twigs bound with purple cords. But his eyes were as hard and bright and contentious as ever, and his bloodless lips still managed the old fleering smile.

"Dark Man."

Stark shook his head. "The Citadel is gone, so is the Dark Man. The prophecy is finished, and I am no more fated. This choice is yours, Halk. Will you go with us, or must we leave you here?"

"I'll go," said Halk. His voice came groaning and whispering out of his hollow chest like wind from a cave. "And I'll not die, neither. I've sworn before Old Sun's face that I'll live to make of you an offering to the shade of Breca."

Breca had been Halk's shieldmate, struck down in the battle with the Thyrans. Those iron men had given her splendid body to the cannibal Outdwellers, mutton for the spit. Halk might have borne her death, but not that. And he blamed the Dark Man of the prophecy for having led them all to disaster.

"When do you plan to make this offering?" Stark asked.

"On the day when you are no longer useful to Irnan. Until then I'll fight beside you, for the city's sake."

Stark nodded. "I'll remember." To Gerrith and Ashton he said, "Gather your belongings." He called to two of the Hooded Men and told them to carry Halk's litter outside.

The hounds came dripping and slobbering from the trough.

Gelmar said, "Stark. They will not follow you below Yurunna. Then you will be two men and a woman with a half-dead burden to bow your backs and only your six hands between you to fight with when the Yur come to take you." He turned suddenly to Gerrith. "Has the wise woman something to say?"

She stood frozen in the act of pulling up her hood. She had the look of a prophetess once more, her eyes at once seeing and not seeing, fixed on Gelmar, her lips open to form words.

Stark said her name sharply. She started. Then for a moment she seemed bemused, like one waking suddenly from sleep in a strange place. Stark put his hand on her shoulder, guiding her toward the door. He did not answer Gelmar. There was nothing to say, except that what would happen would happen; and that they all knew anyway.

They passed the women and children. Jofr stood straight, a small thing of prey already shaped for his world.

Gerrith stopped. "Take the boy," she said.

The women screamed like eagles. Ekmal came, one hand for the boy and one for his dagger. Gerd growled.

Stark said, "I will not."

"No harm will come to him," Gerrith said, and her voice rang like a far-off bell. "Take him, Stark, or Mother Skaith will bury us all."

Stark hesitated. Then reluctantly he reached out for the boy. Gerd growled louder.

"You heard the wise woman," Stark said. "No harm will come to him. Do not make me use the hounds."

The boy's mother spoke, one word, the deadliest one she knew. Ekmal's hand hovered over his knife. The hounds growled.

Stark said, "Come."

Jofr looked at his father. "Must I?"

"It seems so."

"Very well," said Jofr, and smiled. "I am an Ochar."

He stepped forward alone to Stark's side.

They went out into the yard. The animals were ready, linked by leading lines, three of them saddled with the high desert saddles, covered in worked leather with designs of many colors tempered by sun and wind. The litter was suspended between two of the animals, and Halk was once more an inert bundle, his face hidden beneath the hood.

They mounted. Stark took Jofr before him in the saddle. They rode away from the house, past the heaps of Runner bodies by the pens, past the gnawed and scattered bones of the Harsenyi beasts.

Ekmal and the Hooded Men stood watching them until they vanished beyond the walls. Then Ekmal went into the house and spoke to Gelmar.

"Lord, is it true that he and that other are not born of Skaith-Mother?"

"That is true."

Ekmal signed the air. "Then they are demons. They have taken my son, Lord. What must I do?"

Without hesitation Gelmar said, "Bring the Swiftwing."

Ekmal went along one of the tunnels of the house. The tower of murmuring birds lay to his right, but he did not go to it. They were base creatures, fit only for food. He turned to the left and climbed narrow steps to a high apartment with window slits that let in the light of Old Sun and the wind of the desert. There were hangings of faded crimson on the walls, and trophies of weapons and skulls. Some of the skulls were brittle and yellow with age, crumbling dustily at the rims of the jaws and eyeholes.

In the center of the room, on an iron perch, sat a creature that seemed itself to be all of iron and bronze, a martial armor of shining feathers. Even with the great wings closed it had a look of speed and power, one sharp clean stroke from the crown of its snaky head to the last of its tapered tail. One of these dwelt in the house of every chief among the Ochar. Fed from the chief's table, with its slender collar of gold, it was the badge and sign and pride of chieftainship, ranking equally with honor and before life, wife, mother or child.

"Swiftwing," said Ekmal. "Sky-piercer. Wind-rider. Lightning-brother."

The creature opened eyes like two red stars and looked at Ekmal. It opened its beak and cried out stridently the only word it knew:

"*War!*"

"Of course, war," said Ekmal, holding out his arm.

9

THE BEASTS were fresh and strong, striding easily over the sand. The hounds trotted quietly. The wind continued to drop, diminishing the brownness of the air.

Stark rode like a thundercloud, one arm about the small ferocity of Jofr, who sat straight and unbending, his body yielding only to the motion of the beast.

Gerrith said, "You are angry about the boy."

"Yes," said Stark. "I am angry about the boy. And I'm angry about something else—the visions."

"Let the boy go," Ashton said. "He can find his way back easily enough."

Gerrith sighed. "Do that if you will. But none of us will ever see Yurunna."

Ashton turned and studied her face. He had known many peoples on many worlds. He had seen many things that he could neither believe nor disbelieve, and he had acknowledged his ignorance.

"What did you see," he asked, "before Eric woke you?"

"I saw Eric . . . Stark . . . in a strange place, a place of rocks. There were Hooded Men there, but their cloaks were of different colors, not the orange of the First-Come. They seemed to be hailing Stark, and someone . . . something . . . was performing a ritual with a knife. I saw blood . . ."

The boy had stiffened in the circle of Stark's arm.

"Whose blood?" Stark asked.

"Yours. But it seemed to be shed in promise, in propitiation." She looked at Jofr. "The boy was there. I saw upon his forehead that he was to be your guide. Without him you would not find the way."

"You're sure of this?" Ashton said.

"I'm sure of what I saw. That is all I can be sure of. Has Stark told you? My mother was Gerrith, the wise woman of Irnan. She prophesied in the fullness of power. I do not. My gift is small and fitful. It comes as it will. I see, and I do not see." She turned to Stark. "You are angry about visions! I'm sick of them. I'd prefer to go blundering ahead without sight, as you do, trusting nothing but my own hands and brain. Yet these windows open and I look through them, and I must tell what I see. Otherwise . . ." She shook her head violently. "All that time in the stone house, with those things clawing and screaming to get in at us, I kept seeing you being torn apart and I couldn't tell whether it was the true sight or only my own fear."

Ashton said, "I had the same vision. It was fear."

"The hounds passed a miracle," Stark said. He was watching the boy's bright head, which was poised now with a new alertness.

Gerrith shuddered. "They'll come again."

"Not in such numbers, and the hounds will watch."

"If there's another sandstorm," said Ashton, "let's pray there's somewhere to hide. The next wayhouse is a week's journey."

"You'll not reach it," Jofr said. "My father will send the Swiftwing."

"Swiftwing?"

"The bird of war. All the clans of the Ochar will gather. Your demon dogs will kill many, no doubt, but there will be many more." He twisted around and smiled at Stark, his small white teeth showing sharp as a knife-edge.

"Um," said Stark. "And what of this place of rocks, and the Hooded Men who are not of the First-Come?"

"Ask the wise woman," said Jofr contemptuously. "It is her vision."

"Your father mentioned the Fallarin. Who are they?"

"I am only a child," said Jofr. "These things are not known to me."

Stark let it go. "Simon?"

"They're a winged folk," said Gerrith suddenly.

Ashton glanced at her. "Yes. Undoubtedly a controlled mutation like the Children of the Sea and the Children of Skaith. They seem to be held in some sort of superstitious awe by the Hooded Men. They are important to tribal life but in what way I was never told. The Ochar are closemouthed with strangers, and the Wandsmen respect their tabus. Anyhow, I had other things to think about. But I do know one thing, Eric."

"What?"

"When that boy said *I am an Ochar*, he was doing more than stating a fact or making an affirmation of courage. He was also saying that an Ochar knows the ways of the desert, sharing its powers; that an Ochar destroys his enemies, never turning aside from sacred feud as long as he has breath. That's a blue-eyed viper you hold there, and never forget it."

"I've known desert men before," said Stark. "Now let me think."

The wind dropped. The face of the desert became peaceful. The veils of dust fell away from Old Sun, and the rusty daylight showed the markers of the Wandsmen's Road marching on ahead, never so far apart that if one was buried the next one, or the one beyond that, could not be seen.

Stark said, "Simon, what lies beyond Yurunna? You spoke of something called the Edge."

"The plateau we stand on drops away, four thousand feet or so. It's much warmer below, and there are places where springs make cultivation possible. There are cliff villages—"

"Where the Hooded Men raid?"

"Not the villages themselves, they're out of reach, but they try to catch people in the fields, or steal their harvest. Beyond that is more desert until you come to the Fertile Belt."

"The good green land of the Farers."

"I was brought straight up the road from Skeg, so I didn't see too much of the country. The only city I saw was Ged Darod, the city of the Wandsmen. It was quite a place."

"A place of pilgrimage," Gerrith said. "Sanctuary, whorehouse, foundling home, spawning ground of more Wandsmen. That's where they're trained and taught, and every scrap of windblown rubbish in the world that drops there is made welcome."

"The whole of the lower city is crammed with Farers and pilgrims from all over Skaith. There are pleasure gardens—"

"I've heard of it," Stark said. "But first comes Yurunna."

Happy as a bird, Jofr's clear voice said, "You will not reach Yurunna."

He flung his arm skyward, a gesture of triumph. Where he pointed, high up, a winged shape of bronze and iron glinted and was quickly gone.

"It will go first to the nearest clan chiefs, and then to the farther ones. From its collar they will know that it belongs to my father. They will raise up their men at once, to come to him. You cannot pass through them on the way to Yurunna."

"Then we must go another way," said Stark. "And if there's no safety for us among the Ochar, we'll have to seek it among their enemies. Perhaps Gerrith's vision has purpose after all."

Ashton said, "You'll go to the Lesser Hearths?"

"It seems the only choice."

Jofr laughed. "The Ochar will still come after you. And the folk of the Lesser Hearths will eat you."

"Perhaps. What about you?"

"I am of the blood. I am man, not meat."

"What will they do to you?"

"I am a chief's son. My father will buy me back."

"Then will you guide us to the Lesser Hearths? Or at least to the nearest one."

"Gladly," said Jofr. "And I myself will share in the feasting."

Stark said to Gerrith, "This guide you have chosen for me does not inspire trust."

"I did not choose him," Gerrith snapped. "And I did not say he would guide you out of love."

"Which way?" asked Stark of Jofr.

Jofr considered. "The Hearth of Hann is nearest." He indicated a northeasterly direction, frowning. "I must wait for the stars."

"Does that sound right to you, Simon?"

Ashton shrugged. "Judging from where the Ochar lands are. They have the best, of course."

"The Lesser Hearths are weak," said Jofr. "The Runners eat them. When they are gone, we shall have all the land and water."

"But that time is not yet," said Stark. "Let's go."

They left the markers of the road behind them.

They moved on across boundless desolation while Old Sun slid down to the mountaintops and vanished in a cold brassy glare that streaked the land and then gave way to blackness and starshine and the dancing aurora.

Jofr studied the sky. "There. Where the big white one hangs under a chain of three. That is the way we must go."

They altered course toward the star.

"Have you been this way before?" asked Ashton.

"No," said Jofr. "But every Ochar knows the way to the hearths of his enemies. The Hearth of Hann is five days' journey. The Hann wear purple cloaks." He said it as though "purple cloaks" was a scatological term.

Stark said, "Do you know the name of that star?"

"Of course. It is Ennaker."

"The folk who live on its third world call it Fregor. Those who live on the fourth world call it Chunt. The folk of the fifth world also have a name, but I cannot shape their speech with my mouth. All the names mean sun."

Jofr set his jaw. "I do not believe you. There is only one sun, ours. The stars are lamps he has set to guide us."

"All those lamps are suns. Many of them have planets, and many of the planets support life. Did you think that Skaith was all alone, and you the only people in the universe?"

"Yes," said Jofr passionately. "That is the way it must be. There have been stories about flaming eggs that fall from the sky and hatch demons in the form of men, but they are not true. My mother said they were only idle tales and not to be listened to."

Stark bent his head above Jofr, dark and grim in the night. "But I am a demon, boy, out of a flaming egg."

Jofr's eyes widened, reflecting the starlight. He caught his breath sharply, and his body seemed to shrink within the circle of Stark's arm.

"I do not believe," he whispered. He turned his face away and rode huddled and silent until they made camp.

Halk was still alive. Gerrith fed him wine and broth, and he ate and laughed at Stark. "Take a dagger to me, Dark Man. Else I shall live, as I told you."

They tied Jofr as comfortably as possible. Stark set the hounds to watch and said good night to Ashton, who looked up at him with a sudden unexpected grin.

"I'll tell you true, Eric. I don't think we'll make it, and I don't think I'll ever see Pax again; but it's good to get back to the old ways. I never was much for office work."

Stark said, "We'll fill you up with the other kind." He put his hand on Ashton's shoulder, remembering other nights by other fires on other worlds a long time ago. Ashton had learned about the pacific administration of wild worlds by doing, and Stark had gained his early knowledge of tactics and the art of dealing with all manner of peoples from his growing-up years with Ashton along the frontiers of civilization.

"Set your superior mind to work, Simon, and tell me: how do three men and a woman and a pack of hounds take over a planet?"

"I'll sleep on it," Ashton said, and did.

Stark went and stood by the fire. Halk was asleep. Jofr lay curled in his furs with his eyes shut. Gerrith sat watching the smoke rise from the glowing embers. She stood up and looked at Stark, and they went away a little from the fire, taking their furs with them. Gerd and Grith roused and followed. When they lay down together, the two hounds lay beside them.

There were many things to be said between them, but this was not a time for words. This was the coming together after separation, after captivity and the fear of death. They did not waste life in talking. Afterward they slept in each other's arms and were happy, and did not question the future. The deep-shared warmth of being was enough, for as long as they could have it.

On the second day after leaving the Wandsmen's Road, the character of the desert began to change. Underlying ridges rose up and became hills. The restless dunes gave place to eroded plains gashed with old dry riverbeds. Stark and his people rode through a haunted land.

There had been cities here. Not so many as in the darklands, which had been rich and fertile in their day, nor so large, but cities nonetheless, and their bones still lay along the riverbanks. Runners nested in them. Jofr seemed to have an instinct for cities. He seemed almost to smell them on the wind. But he said it was only that every Ochar boy was made to memorize the ancestral maps as well as the star-guides, so that no Ochar could ever be lost in the desert no matter what befell him. Stark tried to make him draw a map in the sand. He refused. Maps were tabu except for the Ochar.

The boy had been given a beast of his own to ride, and not the swiftest. He appeared to be content to lead. Stark trusted him not at all but he was not afraid. Gerd would tell him when the boy's mind contemplated treachery.

In the meantime Stark brooded, riding long hours without speaking, and then talking far into the night with Ashton and sometimes with Gerrith and Halk. It was after all their world.

Twice they waited until dark to skirt the ruins of a city, because the Runners did not hunt by night. At other times they saw roving bands of the creatures, but the hounds killed them or drove them off. And on a morning, suddenly, when they had been no more than two hours on the way and Old Sun was barely above the horizon, Gerd said:

N'Chaka. Boy think death.

At the same moment Jofr made an excuse to dismount and go apart. "Go straight on," he said. "I'll follow in a moment."

Stark looked ahead. There was nothing but a flat place of sand between two low ridges, and nothing unusual about the sand except that it was perfectly smooth and the color perhaps a shade lighter than the surrounding desert.

Stark said, "Wait."

The party halted. Jofr paused in the act of hiking up his tunic. Gerd came and stood beside him, dropping his huge jaw onto the boy's shoulder. Jofr did not move.

Stark dismounted and climbed one of the ridges. He picked up a large flat stone and threw it out onto the smooth sand.

The stone sank gently and was gone.

Gerd said, *Kill, N'Chaka?*

No.

Stark came back and looked at Gerrith, and Gerrith smiled. "I told you Mother Skaith would bury us all if you didn't take the boy."

Stark grunted. Much subdued, Jofr mounted again. They went around the sinking sand, and after that Stark kept an eye out for smooth places.

He knew that they were entering the territory of the Hann when they came upon the remains of a village. There had been wells and cultivation not so long ago. Now the small beehive houses were broken and gutted by the wind, and there were bones everywhere. Bones crushed and snapped and fragmented until there was no telling what sort of flesh they had once supported. The sand was full of gray-white chips.

"Runners," Jofr said, and shrugged.

"Surely the Runners attack Ochar villages," said Ashton. "How will your people hold all this land when you take it?"

"We're strong," said Jofr. "And the Wandsmen help us."

They passed two more villages, dead and disemboweled.

Beyond the third one, in midafternoon of the fifth day, with Halk propped up in his litter wide-awake, they saw ahead of them, on the top of a hill, a knot of riders in dusty purple.

Jofr whipped his beast forward, his voice screaming high and thin. "Slay these men! Slay them! They are demons, come to steal our world!"

10

STARK SAID to the others, "Wait." He went forward slowly. Gerd paced at his right knee. Grith trotted out of the pack and came on his left. The seven other hounds came behind him. He rode with his right hand high and his left holding the rein well away from his body. Up on the hill one of the men snatched the yelling boy from his beast.

Stark went half of the distance between them and stopped. He counted eight purple cloaks. They did not move for a long while, except that the man who held Jofr cuffed him once, hard. The hounds sat in the sand and lolled their tongues, and no one reached for a weapon.

They know us, N'Chaka. They fear us.

Watch.

One of the men on the hill picked up his rein and moved down the slope.

Stark waited until the man halted before him. He was much like Ekmal, sinewy and blue-eyed, sitting his tall beast with the limber grace of the desert man whose life is made up of distances. His face was covered. The pendant stone on his brow that marked him a chief was a lighter purple than his leather cloak.

Stark said, "May Old Sun give you light and warmth."

"You are in the country of the Hann," said the chief. "What do you want here?"

"I wish to talk."

The chief looked from Stark to the Northhounds and back again. "These are the deathhounds of the Wandsmen?"

"Yes."

"They obey you?"

"Yes."

"But you are not a Wandsman."

"No."

"What are you?"

Stark shrugged. "A man from another world. Or if you wish, a demon, as the little Ochar said. In any case, no enemy to the Hann. Will you make truce according to your custom and listen to what I have to say?"

"Suppose I do that," said the chief, "and my people do not like what they hear."

"Then I shall bid them good-bye and go in peace."

"You swear this?"

"By what? The word of a demon? I have said what I will do."

The chief looked again at the hounds.

"Have I a choice in the matter?"

Stark said, "No."

"Then I will make truce and the Hann shall hear you. But the hounds must not kill."

"They will not unless weapons are drawn against us."

"None shall be drawn." The chief held out his right hand. "I am Ildann, Hearth-Keeper of the Hann."

"I am Stark." He clasped the chief's wiry wrist, felt his clasped in return and knew that Ildann was testing his flesh to see what it was made of.

"From another world?" said Ildann scornfully. "Many tales have come up from the south and down across the mountains, but they're no more than tales told round a winter fire. You're flesh and blood and hard bone like myself—no demon, and not a man either by our standards, but only meat from some Southron sty."

Stark's fingers tightened on the man's wrist. He said softly, "Yet I lead the Northhounds."

Ildann looked into Stark's eyes. He looked away. "I will not forget that."

Stark released his grip. "We will go to your village."

The two groups joined uneasily together, side by side but not mingling. And Jofr said incredulously, "Are you not going to kill them?"

"Not immediately," said Ildann, watching the hounds. Gerd gave him one baleful glance and a warning growl.

The village was in a wide valley, with a glimpse of mountains farther on beyond its rim of hills; not great mountains like the barrier range, but a curiously gnawed-looking line of peaks. In old times there had been a river here. Now it was dry except at the spring flooding, but there was still water in deep tanks dug in the riverbed. Beasts walked patiently around great creaking wheels, and women were busy with the preparation of the soil for the spring sowing. Herds of beasts cropped at some dark scanty herbage that looked more like lichen than grass; perhaps it was something in between, and Stark wondered what sort of crops grew in this place.

The women and the beasts alike were guarded by bowmen in little watchtowers set about the fields. And Stark saw the outlines of old cultivation abandoned to the sand and wrecks of old waterwheels beside dry holes.

"Your land draws in," he said.

"It does for all of us," said Ildann, and glanced bitterly at Jofr. "Even for the Ochar. Old Sun grows weaker, no matter how we feed him. Every year the frosts are with us longer, and more water stays locked in the mountain ice, so that there is less for our fields. The summer pastures shrink—"

"And every year the Runners come in greater numbers to eat up your villages."

"What have you, a stranger, to do with our troubles?" Ildann's gaze was fiercely proud, and the word he used for "stranger" bore connotations of deadly insult. Stark chose to ignore them.

"Is it not the same for all the Lesser Hearths of Kheb?"

Ildann did not answer, and Jofr said impudently, "The Green Cloaks are almost wiped out, the Brown and the Yellow are—"

The man whose saddle he was sharing slapped him hard across the side of his head. Jofr's face screwed up with pain. He said, "I am an Ochar, and my father is a chief."

"Neither statement is a recommendation," said the man, and cuffed him again. "Among the Hann little whelps are silent unless they are told to speak."

Jofr bit his lips. His eyes were full of hate, some for the Hann, most of it for Stark.

The village was protected by a wall that had watchtowers set at irregular intervals. The beehive houses, little more than domed roofs over cellars dug deep in the ground for warmth and protection against the wind, were painted in gay designs, all worn and faded. Narrow lanes dodged and twisted among the domes, and in the center of the village was an open space, roughly circular, with a clump of gnarled, dusty, leather-leaved trees growing in the middle of it.

In the grove was the mud-brick house that held the Hearth and the sacred fire of the tribe of Hann.

Ildann led the way there.

People came out of the houses, away from the wells and wineshops, the market stalls and the washing stones. Even those who had been in the fields came in, until the space around the Hearth-grove was filled with the purple cloaks of the men and the bright-colored skirts of the women. They all watched while Ildann and Stark and the others dismounted and Halk's litter was set carefully on the ground. They watched the grim white hounds, crouching with their eyes half-closed and their jaws half-open. The veiled faces of the men were shadowed beneath their hoods. The faces of the women were closed tight, expressing nothing. They merely watched.

Ildann spoke. A tall woman with proud eyes came out of the Hearth-house, bearing a golden salver on which lay a charred twig. Ildann took up the twig.

"Hearth-right I give you." He marked Stark's forehead with the blackened end of the twig. "If harm befalls you in this place, the same must befall me." He replaced the twig, and the woman went back to tending the Hearth. Ildann spoke to the crowd.

"This man called Stark has come to speak to you. I do not know what he has to say. We will hear him at the second hour after Old Sun's setting."

The crowd made a muttering and rustling. Then it parted as Ildann led his guests away to a house that was set apart from the others. It was larger than most and had two sides to it, one for the chief, the other for guests. The Hooded Men were seminomadic, herdsmen and hunters spending much of the summer on the move after game or pasturage. The bitter winters shut them perforce between walls. The rooms of the guesthouse were small and sparsely furnished, gritty with the everlasting dust but otherwise clean and comfortable enough.

"I'll keep the boy with me," said Ildann. "Don't worry, I'll not waste a fat ransom just to satisfy my spite. Your beasts will be cared for. Everything needful will be brought to you, and I'll send a healer if you wish, to see to your friend there. He looks like a fighting man."

"He is," said Stark, "and I thank you."

The small room had begun to smell strongly of hound, and the minds of the pack were uneasy. They did not like being closed in. Ildann seemed to sense this.

"There is a walled enclosure through that passage, where they can be in the open. No one will disturb them." He watched them as they filed out. "Doubtless you will tell us how it is that these guardians of the Citadel have left their post to follow at your heels."

Stark nodded. "I wish the boy to be there when I speak."

"Whatever you say."

He went out. Halk said, "I wish to be there, too, Dark Man. Now help me out of this damned litter."

They got him onto a bed. Women came and built fires and brought water. One came with herbs and unguents, and Stark watched over her shoulder as she worked. The wound in Halk's side was healing cleanly.

"He needs only rest and food," the woman said, "and time."

Halk looked up at Stark and smiled.

At the second hour after Old Sun's setting, Stark stood under the trees again. Gerd and Grith flanked him to right and left. The remaining seven crouched at his back. Ashton and Gerrith were close by, with Halk in the litter. Ildann stood with the principal men and women of the village, one hand resting firmly on Jofr's shoulder. The Hearth-grove and the open space were lighted by many torches set on poles. The cold dry desert wind shook the flames, sent light snapping and flaring over the folk gathered there, waiting silently, all of them now cloaked and hooded against the chill so that even the faces of the women were hidden.

Ildann said, "We will hear the words of our guest."

His eyes, in the torchlight, were intensely alert. Stark knew that he had spent the last few hours pumping Jofr dry of all the information he possessed. The boy's cockiness had gone; he now appeared angry and doubtful, as if the water had got far too deep for him.

The faceless, voiceless multitude stood patiently. Wind rubbed their leather cloaks together, rattled the tough leaves of the trees. Stark rested his hand on Gerd's head and spoke.

"Your chief has asked me how it is that the Northhounds, the guardians of the Citadel and the Lords Protector, have left their posts to follow me. The answer is plain. There is no longer a Citadel for them to guard. I myself put it to the torch."

A wordless cry went round the crowd. Stark let it die away. He turned to Ildann.

"You know this to be true, Hearth-Keeper."

"I know," Ildann said. "The Ochar boy heard, and saw. This man is the Dark Man of the prophecy of Irnan, which has been fulfilled. He and his hounds brought four Wandsmen captive into the way-house, and they told Ekmal and his folk that the Lords Protector are fugitives and homeless. There will be no more keeping of the Upper Road by the Ochar, and their lament is very loud."

The cry that came now from the crowd was one of savage pleasure.

Jofr shouted at them furiously. "The Wandsmen have promised us! The Citadel will be rebuilt. My father has sent the Swiftwing, and all the clans of the Ochar will come against you"—he stabbed his finger at Stark—"because of him!"

"That is likely," Stark said. "And I tell you that the Wandsmen would pay a high price for me and for my comrades." He placed his left hand on the head of Grith. "But you would first have to over-come the hounds. Ildann, ask the boy how many Runners were killed by the pack? He saw the bodies."

"I have asked him," Ildann said. "At least half a hundred."

"So you see," Stark said, "that reward would not be easily won. But I can offer you another and greater reward. I offer you freedom from the greed of the Ochar, who want your lands. I offer you free-dom from the oppression of the Wandsmen, who support the Ochar. I offer you freedom from the Runners, who eat up your villages. I offer you freedom from hunger and thirst. I offer you Yurunna."

There was a startled silence. Then every tongue began to wag at once.

"Yurunna!" said Ildann fiercely. "You think we have not looked at that place, and often? You think we have not tried? In my father's time, in my grandfather's time . . . The walls are strong. There are many Yur to defend the walls, and they have great machines that scatter fire to burn men where they stand. They have the kennels where the demon hounds are bred, and even the whelps are deadly. How should we take Yurunna?"

"For the Hann alone, or for any of the Lesser Hearths alone, it would not be possible. For all the Lesser Hearths banded together . . ."

Voices rose, shouting about old enmities and blood feuds, raids and killings. The crowd became turbulent. Stark held up his hands.

"If your blood feuds are more important to you than the survival of your tribe, then cling to them! Let the last ember perish from your Hearth, for the sake of them. But why be so foolish? All together, you could be powerful enough to fight the Ochar, to fight anyone except Mother Skaith herself, and you have no choice but to run from her, and that is south. The cold drives the Runners down on you, and you in turn are driven to raid even as far as the Edge. Why should you suffer all this when Yurunna is there for the taking? Would it not be better for Yurunna to feed you, rather than the servants of the Wandsmen?"

There was an uneasy, mumbling quiet while they thought about that.

Ildann voiced the vital question. "Who would lead? No chief of the Lesser Hearths would endure to be made less than any other."

Stark said, "I would lead. I wear no cloak of any color and am at feud with none. I want neither land nor loot, and when my task is done, I leave you." He paused. "It has been foretold that a winged being will blood me among the Hearth-Keepers of Kheb."

Again he waited until the reaction subsided.

"The decision is for you to make. If you decide against me, then I will go and speak to the others. And now I have finished." He turned courteously to Ildann. "What will you have us do?"

"Return to your quarters and wait. We must talk among ourselves."

Back in the guesthouse, they did little talking among themselves. This was the strategy that had been discussed and agreed upon. As fugitives with no resources of their own, they could hope for very little in the way of success, or even survival. With a base of power, even a small one, the odds improved significantly. Yurunna was the bait.

Stark had offered it. Now they could only wait and see what the tribesmen would do with it.

"It will go your way," said Gerrith. "Don't worry."

"If it does," said Halk, "well and good. If it doesn't, what has Stark got to worry about? He is no longer the Dark Man, no more fated. He can leave us and run alone back to Skeg. Animal that he is, he might make it. Or again, he might not. No matter. Bring me food and wine. I'm hungry." He lifted his hands and flexed them stiffly. "If we do march south, these must be ready to hold a sword again."

All that night Stark kept waking to hear the sounds of the village, droning and stirring like a disturbed wasp's nest. After Old Sun had been sung up and given wine and fire to begin his day, the summons came from Ildann. Stark went to the house of the chief, and Ashton and Gerrith went with him, as did the two hounds, who would not be left behind.

Ildann had sat all night with his village leaders, both men and women. His eyes were red-rimmed and blinking, but Stark saw in them a glitter of ambition and excitement.

There was something else, too, and its name was fear.

"What do you know of the Fallarin?"

"Nothing," said Stark, "except that the name means 'Chained.'"

"They are the true rulers of this desert. Even the Ochar must bend their stiff necks and pay tribute, as we do."

He brooded. Stark stood patiently.

"They're a blighted race, the Fallarin. In old times the wise men knew how to change people in some sort. They became different—"

"It's called controlled mutation," Stark said. "I've met others. The Children of the Sea-Our-Mother, who live in the water, and the Children of Skaith, who burrow under the Witchfires. Neither meeting was pleasant."

Ildann lifted his shoulders in a peculiar motion of distaste. "The Fallarin wished to be Children of the Sky, but the change was not . . . not as they wanted it. For centuries they have sat in their dark bowl in the mountains, talking to the winds. They are great sorcerers, with power over all the moving air when they wish to use it. We pay them when we sow, when we harvest and when we go to war. All of us. Otherwise they send the sandstorms—"

He looked up sharply. "Is it true, the foretelling of the winged man with the knife?"

"It is true," said Gerrith.

"Well, then," said Ildann, "if the Fallarin will blood you chief, giving you windfavor, the Lesser Hearths will follow wherever you lead."

"Then," said Stark, "I must find the Fallarin."

Ildann nodded. "Tomorrow I go on the spring pilgrimage to the Place of Winds. The Keepers of all the Hearths gather there, under truce. It is forbidden to anyone not of the blood to come there, but I will break custom and take you, if you wish. However, I tell you this."

He leaned forward. "The Fallarin have powers to overcome even your hellhounds, and if they decide against you, you'll end in the flames of the Springfire which is lighted there for Old Sun."

"That may be," said Stark. "Nonetheless, I will go."

"You alone," said Ildann. "The other men have no reason to go, and women are not permitted there. The occasion of the Springfire involves death, and according to our custom women have to do only with the things of life."

Stark did not like the separation, but there seemed no help for it, and Gerrith said:

"All will be well."

Wishing that he could believe that, Stark rode out of the village with Ildann and Jofr and sixty warriors, the Northhounds, a meager string of pack-beasts and two condemned men in cages, to follow the pilgrim standard to the Place of Winds.

11

THE PILGRIM standard led the way east. A man whose hereditary honor it was rode ahead of the company with the tall staff that bore a pair of outstretched wings. They were wrought in gold with fine workmanship, but they had grown frail with long use, and the wings had been several times broken and clumsily mended. The standard rendered the party safe from attack by members of other tribes. The purple cloaks of the riders drew a streak of somber color across the drab land. They made excellent time. The winds touched them gently. It was always so, Ildann said, when they rode to the gatherings.

Jofr was quiet, glancing frequently at Stark with a certain pointed hopefulness.

Old Sun watched Stark, too, a dull eye full of senile malice. *I'm none of yours,* Stark thought, *and you know it, and you're thinking of the Springfire, like the boy.* He laughed at his own fancy. But the primitive N'Chaka did not laugh. The primitive N'Chaka shivered and was cold, smelling danger on the dim air.

The primitive N'Chaka did not place much faith in visions.

He let the Northhounds run pretty much as they would, keeping Gerd or Grith always by him. Before many miles a pack of Runners appeared. The party was too strong for them to dare an attack. They hung on beyond bowshot, hoping for a straggler or an injured beast. Stark let the eager hounds go at them, and the Hann were impressed. That was the first time the hounds killed along the way. It was not the last. The Runners cared nothing for the pilgrim standard.

Early on the third day a grim wall of mountain rose out of the plain, dark and jagged and alone. It had a look of thunder about it even though the sky was clear, and there as a cleft in the middle of it, like a narrow gate.

At the foot of the cleft, enclosing a kind of bay, a thick stone wall had been erected. Within the wall were the tents and banners of a considerable encampment.

The cavalcade halted, straightened lines, shook dust from cloaks. Purple banners took the wind. A trumpeter set a curved horn to his lips and blew a harsh neighing call of three notes. Stark called the pack to heel. The company moved on toward the wall.

In the wide space between it and the cliff five camps were set up, each one separate with its own staff and its banners, red, brown, green, white and burnt orange for the Ochar. Jofr leaped and cried out; his mount was held tightly so that he could not run.

In the center of the space was a structure of stone slabs perhaps six feet high and twice as broad, with three upright stones set in it, and the whole blackened and stained and cracked from the heat of Old Sun's spring feasting. At least ten cages were dropped haphazardly around the base of the structure, each one holding a man.

Cloaks of the five colors turned out to see the Hann come in. It was a minute or two before they saw Stark and the hounds, and a minute or two more before they believed what they had seen. Then a great cry of anger burst out, and the motley-colored crowd surged forward. The hounds bristled, close around Stark.

Kill, N'Chaka?

Not yet . . .

Ildann held up his arms and shouted. "Wait! It is for the Fallarin to say what shall be done. It has been foretold that they will blood this man a chief . . . Listen to me, you sons of offal! This is the Dark Man of the Southron prophecy, do you hear? The Dark Man! He has brought down the Citadel!"

The crowd stopped its surging and began to listen.

Ildann's voice rang against the cliffs, crying the good news.

"The Citadel has fallen. There'll be no more keeping of the Upper Road—it's dead as a lopped branch above Yurunna, and the Ochar are lopped with it!"

Red, brown, green and white roared with fierce, astonished joy. The roar was followed by a babble of voices. And then, out of a knot of orange cloaks, a tall man spoke.

"You lie."

Ildann thrust Jofr forward. "Tell him, boy. Tell the almighty Romek, Keeper of the Hearth of Ochar."

"It is true, Lord," said Jofr, and bowed his head. "I am Ekmal's son, from the north house—" He stammered out what he knew, and the whole crowd listened. "But the Wandsmen promised, Lord!" he finished. "The Citadel will be rebuilt. And my father has sent the Swiftwing among the clans . . ."

He was drowned out by another roar from the folk of the Lesser Hearths. Stark could see that each of their numbers was less than that of the Ochar. He estimated some hundred and twenty of the orange cloaks, with Ildann's sixty the next largest. All together, the Lesser Hearths did not greatly surpass the Ochar. The Yellow Cloaks were not in yet, but he doubted that they would add more than another twenty or so. These were chief's escorts, the men of honor, but they were probably a fair reflection of the relative numbers of fighting men available to the tribes.

The Ochar closed their ranks, groups of them flowing together out of the press until they formed a solid block of color. They spoke among themselves; and the eyes of Romek, hard cold blue above his facecloth, sought Stark's.

The Lesser Hearths were stirred by currents of motion as men discussed and questioned and thought about the meaning of Ildann's words.

Behind them all was the cleft. Shadows clotted thick there. Stark could not see into it. The wind made strange sounds passing through. Stark could imagine that it talked a secret language of its own, telling all that happened below. And if the wind talked, surely someone listened.

Romek stepped forward. He questioned Jofr, making him tell again the story of how Stark and the hounds came to the wayhouse. Then he said:

"It seems certain that this outlander has done a great wrong. Since it touches us, it is for us to deal with him."

"And take him back to the Wandsmen, no doubt," said Ildann, "to make your masters happy."

"He is nothing to you," said Romek. "Stand aside."

"You're forgetting the Northhounds," said Ildann. "Surely you know them? But try if you like."

Romek hesitated. Nine pairs of baleful eyes regarded him. Ildann shouted again to the red cloaks and the white, the brown and the green.

"The Dark Man has brought down the Citadel. Now he will bring down Yurunna."

"Yurunna!" they cried. "How? How?"

"If we will join our forces together, he will lead us. If the Fallarin blood him. Only if the Fallarin blood him! He is not of our race, and his feud is only with the Wandsmen. Because of that feud he offers us Yurunna. Yurunna! Food, water, safety from the Runners. Life! Yurunna!"

It sounded like a battle cry.

When he could make himself heard, Romek said, "That would mean war with the Ochar. We would sweep the desert clean."

"Perhaps not!" shouted the chief of the Brown Cloaks. "And if we should take Yurunna, the First-Come would be the Last!"

Hate was in the laughter that followed. Old and bitter hate. Romek heard it. He took it as a thing of pride. He looked at the Northhounds, and he looked at Stark, and he nodded his cowled head.

"All this will happen only if the Fallarin blood him. Very well. Let him go to the Fallarin and ask them for windfavor. And when they've heard him out, we shall see where he goes—to Yurunna, or to the Springfire."

"He will go to the Fallarin when he is bidden," said Ildann.

"No," said Stark. "I will go now."

"But you cannot," said Ildann, all bravery gone from his voice. "No one enters there without permission."

"I will," said Stark.

He rode forward with the hounds beside him. The sound in their throats was like muted thunder, and the Hooded Men stood back to let them pass. Stark did not look back to see whether Ildann came with him. He moved without haste past the place of the Springfire and the cages where the victims waited, stripped of cloaks and wrappings so that he could see their despairing faces white as snow except for a ludicrous band of brown across the eyes.

He moved toward the cleft, the narrow gateway in the cliff.

Ildann did not follow him into that windy darkness.

The way was only wide enough for a single rider, and very steep. The soft furred paws of the beast and the pads of the hounds made only the smallest scuffling on bare rock. It was cold there, with the tomb-chill of sunless places, and the wind talked. Stark thought that he could understand the words.

Sometimes the wind laughed, and the laughter was not friendly.

Things, said Gerd.

I know. There were galleries high up under the ragged streak of sky. He was aware of movement there, crouchings and scuttlings. He knew, although he could not see them, that there were piles of boulders ready to be sent crashing on his head.

Watch.

N'Chaka! Cannot watch. Minds not speak. Cannot hear!

And the wind talked.

The cleft ended at a wall of rock that had a single opening through which one man might pass.

Stark left the beast. Beyond the opening was a stair that spiraled sharply upward into darkness.

Stark climbed, the hounds behind him, alarmed, muttering, their breathing loud in the closed space. At length he saw the top of the stair and a tall thin doorway with light on the other side.

A creature sat in the doorway looking down at him from under slitted eyelids.

12

IT WAS hairless and horny; and it had four arms that appeared to be very limber and strong, without joints, each arm ending in three tentacular fingers. It opened a beaky mouth and said:

"I am Klatlekt. I keep the door. Who comes to the Place of Winds?"

"I am Stark," he said. "A stranger. I seek audience with the Fallarin."

"You have not been bidden."

"I am here."

The blinking green-gold gaze shifted to the hounds. "You have with you four-footed things whose minds are black and burning."

N'Chaka! It does not fear. Mind not touch.

"They will do no harm," Stark said, "unless harm is done."

"They can do no harm," said Klatlekt. "They are harmless."

N'Chaka. Strange . . .

The hounds whimpered. Stark mounted one more step.

"Never mind the hounds. Your masters wish to see me. Otherwise we would not have reached this door."

"For good or ill," said the doorkeeper. "Come, then."

It rose and led the way. Stark followed, through the tall thin door. The hounds padded after, reluctant.

Cannot touch, N'Chaka. Cannot touch.

They stood in a great bowl surrounded by cliffs of somber rock that shaded from gray to slaty black. The cliffs were high, so that Old Sun never saw the bottom of the bowl, which was carpeted with a moss that felt gravelly rather than soft underfoot.

All around the bowl the rock of the cliffs had been cut and carved into free-standing forms that pulled the gaze upward to the sky, so that Stark felt giddy, as if he might fall that way. It seemed that all the winds of the desert and the currents of the high air had been caught as they passed by and frozen here into stony rising thermals and purling waves and circling whirlwinds that seemed in that twilight to spring and flow. But they did not. They were firmly anchored, and the true air was utterly still. There was no sign of living things except for Stark and the hounds and the one called Klatlekt.

Yet there were living things, and Stark knew it, and so did the hounds.

Things. Watch.

The rock behind the carved wind patterns was honeycombed with secret openings. The hounds growled and shivered, pressing close. They were fearful now for the first time in their lives, their power of death useless against nonhuman minds.

Klatlekt pointed three slender fingers to a raised round platform of stone blocks in the center of the bowl. At the king-point of the circle stood a great carved seat shaped like a wind-devil.

"Go there."

Stark mounted broad steps, the hounds slinking at heel.

Minds up there can touch. Kill?

No!

Klatlekt had disappeared. Stark stood. He listened to the silence that was not quite silent, and the hairs rose at the back of his neck.

A little wind came. It fingered his hair. It went snuffling lightly down the height of him and across the breadth of him, and then it flickered cold across his face, and he thought that some of it went in at his eyes and blew swiftly through the windings of his brain. It pulled free of him with a tiny chuckle and went to pluck at the hounds and set them whimpering with their fur all awry.

N'Chaka!

Still. Still.

It was not easy to be still.

The small wind went away.

Stark waited, listening to sounds he could not quite hear.

All at once there was sound and enough; the rushing susurration of half a thousand pairs of wings a-beat on the air. The Fallarin flitted from their doorways, to stand among their rising thermals and graceful whirlwinds.

Stark continued to wait.

One came alone, from between two curling ribbons of stone that overarched the largest opening. He wore a brief kilt of scarlet leather. A golden girdle clasped his waist, and a king's torque circled his neck. Otherwise he was clad in close dark fur against the cold. His body was small and spare and light. The wings that sprang from his shoulders were dark-leathered and strong, and when he descended to the platform his movement was assured, if not beautiful. But Stark knew why they were called the Chained. The genetic alteration their ancestors had undergone, hoping to give their descendants new life on a dying world, had cheated them cruelly. That inadequate wingspan would never know the freedom of the high air.

"Yes," said the Fallarin, "we are clipped birds, a mockery above and below." He stood before the high seat, looking straight up into Stark's eyes; his own were yellow as a falcon's, but too full of a dark wisdom for even that royal bird. His face was narrow and harsh, too strong for beauty, with a sharp nose and jutting chin. But when he smiled he was handsome, as a sword is handsome.

"I am Alderyk, and king in this place."

Round the circumference of the bowl, from lower galleries, a considerable number of the four-armed things had appeared. They stood quietly, watching. They were not being menacing. They were merely there.

"The Tarf," said Alderyk. "Our excellent servants, created by the same hands that made us, though not of human stock, and with greater care, for they function admirably." His gaze dropped. "You also have your retainers."

The hounds felt the force in him and growled uneasily. Alderyk laughed, a sound not entirely pleasant.

"I know you, hounds. You were made, like us, though you had no choice in that making. You are Skaith-born, like us, and I understand you better than I do your master."

The yellow eyes, somber-bright, returned to Stark.

"You are the future standing there, a strange thing, full of distances I cannot plumb. A black whirling wind to break and scatter, leaving nothing untouched behind you, not even the Fallarin."

His wings spread wide, rustling, then clapped shut. A buffet of air came from nowhere and struck Stark's face like an open palm. "I do not altogether like you."

"Liking is neither here nor there," said Stark mildly. "You seem to know me."

"We know you, Stark. We live solitary here in our eyrie, but the winds bring us news from all the world."

And perhaps they do, thought Stark. And there are also the Harsenyi and the Ochar to peddle whatever tales go up and down the roads of Skaith. The whole north had known about Ashton being brought to the Citadel, a man from another world, and the prophecy of Irnan had followed hard on his heels. The Wandsmen themselves had spread knowledge of Stark throughout the darklands in their eagerness to capture him. It would have been strange if the Fallarin did not know all about the events that were beginning to shake the foundations of their world.

"We knew of the prophecy," said Alderyk. "It was interesting to speculate on the possibility of its fulfillment."

"If the winds bring you news from as far away as Skeg and the city-states, surely there's a breeze that whispers from your own doorstep."

"We heard all that was said there. And perhaps . . ." He cocked his dark head birdwise and smiled. "Perhaps we heard you speak by the Hearth of Hann. Perhaps, even, we heard the sun-haired woman talk of blooding in a place of rocks."

That startled Stark, though not greatly. The Fallarin had the power to move winds—sorcery or psychokinetics, the name mattered little—and it was not unlikely that they could see and hear farther than most, even if it was simply a matter of reading his mind.

"Then you know why Ildann brought me here. You know what I want from you. Tell me what you want from me."

Alderyk ceased smiling. "That," he said, "we have not yet decided." He turned and signaled to one of the Tarf. It scuttled quickly into a doorway, and up on their high perches the Fallarin clapped their thousand wings, and an angry gale whirled snarling around the cliffs. The hounds whined dismally.

The Tarf came back, bearing something on one of its arms. It climbed to the platform and came to Alderyk, who said:

"Let him see the thing clearly."

The thing was a huge proud bird, feathered all in bronze and iron. It fretted because its feet were bound and its head hooded with a bit of cloth. Ever and again it opened its beak and cried out harshly, and Stark understood the word it spoke.

"It is a Swiftwing," he said, remembering the bronze-and-iron flash in the sky, "and it calls for war. It belongs to a chief named Ekmal."

"I think it is his son you have out there."

"I was told that he would be my guide to this place. No harm has come to him."

"Nonetheless, Ekmal calls the clans to war."

Stark shook his head. "The Wandsmen call for war because of the

Citadel. They are determined to have me prisoner, or dead, along with my friends. The boy is safe enough, and Ekmal knows it."

"A fine witches' brew you've set boiling in our northland," Alderyk said. The Fallarin hissed, and again the wind surged angrily. "The Swiftwing came to seek out Romek, the Ochar Hearth-Keeper. We brought it here instead. The creatures are winged powerfully, but they cannot fly against our currents. We wished to know more before we let Romek have its summons."

He motioned the Tarf away. It withdrew to the east point of the platform, gentling the great bird. Alderyk's eyes held Stark's, yellow and cruel.

"You ask for windfavor as war chief of all the Lesser Hearths, to take Yurunna from the Wandsmen. Why should we grant it, when it means war with all the Ochar? Why should we not give you to Romek for the Wandsmen, or to the Springfire to feed Old Sun?"

Stark said, "Old Sun will grow no stronger no matter how you feed him. He is dying, and the north closes in. This is true for you as it is for the Lesser Hearths, and for the Ochar, too, though they don't accept it—they think the Wandsmen can keep them fed forever."

"And can they not?"

"The Wandsmen will decide that, not the Ochar. There is revolt in the south. Things have changed with the coming of the ships to Skeg. Too many folk hate the Wandsmen and wish to find better worlds to live in. There may be a breaking of power."

"Will be," said Alderyk, "if you have your way. Why should we let you use the Lesser Hearths to gain your own ends?"

"You live on the tribute from these people. Surely you know better than I how scant it grows."

There was a rustling of wings and a sigh from the high perches. Alderyk's eyes were two points of yellow fire, burning into Stark's mind.

"Are you saying that we too must leave our place where we have lived for centuries and find ourselves a better world?"

Wind buffeted Stark from all sides, deafened him, caught the breath from his mouth. The hounds cowered. When the wind died away he said, "The northfolk must move sooner or later for their lives. The Lesser Hearths are dying out. The Wandsmen are interested only in retaining their power, and where they must sacrifice to do so, they will. Make your own choice, but you would be wise to leave a road south open for yourselves when you choose to take it. In the meantime there is enough at Yurunna for all, if you control it."

Silence. The stillness of dead air.

"And you would lead?"

"Yes."

There was a sudden commotion among the Tarf, and one of them came rushing across the open and onto the platform, to crouch at Alderyk's feet.

"Lord," it said, clicking and rattling in its shocked haste, "there has been a killing below. The pilgrim truce is broken, and the Ochar hold the entrance to the cleft."

13

For one long moment Alderyk neither moved nor looked away from Stark.

"A black wind, to break and scatter . . ."

Up along the high perches the ranks of the Fallarin moved and shifted, with a hissing of wings and voices. Stark braced himself for an assault. None came. Yet the air was so charged that he looked for lightning bolts to play between the twilit cliffs.

As though he had come to some decision, Alderyk turned abruptly to the Tarf.

"Bid Romek come to me with no more than six of his men of honor. And say that if the peace is not kept, I will send such wrath upon them as they have never seen."

The Tarf went away.

Stark wondered what had happened below, and how many were dead, and whether Ildann was among them.

"Stand back," said Alderyk. "There. And keep your hellhounds quiet."

He sat himself on the high seat that was like a wind devil, and there was thunder on his brow.

Stark went where he was told, to the west point of the circle, opposite the place where the Tarf still gentled the Swiftwing. The hounds were unhappy, sensing great forces about them that they could neither understand nor fight. It was all Stark could do to hold them. His own muscles were tight with strain, and the sweat ran on him. He was acutely aware of the high cliffs and the one narrow door. If things went against him, it was not going to be easy to fight his way out.

He hated the Tarf with their round unhuman heads and their unhuman brains that cared not a fig for Northhounds.

The Ochar, at least, were no more than human.

They entered the bowl, bright orange cloaks dulled in that sunless gloom. They walked across the mossy open ground and mounted the steps to the platform.

Romek saw the Swiftwing and checked. Then he spoke angrily to Alderyk.

"Why have you held this summons from me?"

"Because I wished to," Alderyk said, "and why have you broken truce?"

"Ildann stirred up mischief among the Lesser Hearths. There were high words, and then blows, and some hot head drew a knife. My man only defended himself."

It crossed Stark's mind that if the Fallarin knew all that happened on their doorstep, Alderyk must have known this, too. Had he been unable to prevent it? Or had he let it happen?

"How many are dead?"

"One only." Romek's shoulders lifted slightly. "A Brown Cloak."

"One or a hundred, it's death and forbidden." Alderyk's head went sidewise, in the way Stark was beginning to know. "What are your men defending now?"

A wind, very soft and tigerish, prowled the cliffs.

"The peace," said Romek, and looked at Stark.

"Ah," said Alderyk. "You think there might be trouble if Stark is brought to the Springfire."

In a cold flat unflinching voice Romek said, "There will be worse trouble if he is not. You see the Swiftwing. All the clans of the Ochar are rousing for war, and this man is the cause. If he dies now in the Springfire, with the Keepers of the Lesser Hearths there to see it, then the threat will end."

"But suppose," said Alderyk, "just suppose that we have decided to give him windfavor?"

"You would not be so foolish," Romek said.

"Wise Romek. Tell me why."

"Because it is on the tribute of the Ochar, more than all the others, that you stay alive—and that tribute comes from the Wandsmen more than it does from us." The orange cloth hid Romek's face, but even so it was plain that a smile was on his mouth and that the smile was insolent. "No matter how the winds blow, the Ochar will be fed."

"I see," said Alderyk. "And we will not?"

Romek's hand made a sweeping gesture. "I didn't say that."

"True, you didn't say it."

"There can be no such talk between allies. Give us the man, Alderyk, and we'll see that the peace is kept."

Stark held tight to Gerd's bristling neck on the one side and Grith's on the other.

Wait. Wait . . .

Alderyk stood up. In spite of his smallness he seemed to overtop the towering Ochar. He spoke to his people, calmly and without passion.

"You have heard all that has passed here. We are given a choice, between peace and war, between starvation and the bounty of the Ochar. How do you choose, then? Which shall I give to Romek—Stark or the Swiftwing?"

Dark wings clattered. Winds whirled around the cliffs, reached out to catch at Romek's cloak and hood and tear away his veil so that he stood naked-faced, white and shamed before them all.

"Give him the Swiftwing!"

Alderyk motioned to the Tarf, which moved forward and held out its arm.

Romek took the Swiftwing. With steady fingers he undid the thong that held the bird's feet and loosed the wrapping from its head. It opened eyes like two red stars and looked at him and cried out, "War!"

"Yes," said Romek softly. "War."

He flung the bird upward. It took the air, beating powerfully, circling higher and higher until it gained the sunlight and was gone.

Alderyk said, "From this day the Place of Winds is barred to the Ochar. Now go."

Romek turned and stalked out with his men.

"Come here," Alderyk said to Stark, and sat again upon the high seat, his face hard and grim. "We too have watched the north close in. We have had our eyes on Yurunna and the growing insolence of the Ochar. We lacked two things, strength and a leader. You offer us both. So we gamble, because if we do not we shall become the cut dogs of the Wandsmen even as the Ochar have." His yellow gaze struck deep into Stark, and a shiver of air ran whirling up the stony curves of the seat. "We gamble, Stark. Let us hope we don't lose."

They waited until the yellow Qard came in, just before sundown. That night, while torches flared and light spilled from all the high doorways of the Fallarin, Stark was blooded war chief of the Lesser Hearths of Kheb, mingling his blood with the blood of the Hearth-Keepers, beginning with Ildann, and sprinkling a little more on the stones for Old Sun. Alderyk held the knife. When all else was done, he made a slash in the dark fur of his own wrist and marked Stark's forehead with a purling line.

"I give you windfavor. May you use it well."

Off to one side, where he had been brought for safekeeping, Jofr crouched and hugged his knees and wept with rage and hate.

A little more than three weeks later, duly ransomed, he sat beside his father on the crest of a long dune and saw what made him forget his tears.

Splashed across the dun landscape below, in patches of faded color, was an army, mounted, glittering with spears. The patches of color were purple and red and brown. One-half of the six Lesser Hearths.

Spread out along the dune, a great mass of burnt orange, was the army of the Ochar. Even the inexperienced eyes of a boy on his first warfaring could see that the extent of the orange line was double that of the purple and red and brown together.

Jofr laughed and drummed his heels on the flanks of his mount.

Farther away on that height Gelmar of Skeg looked down and spoke to Romek.

"Good. The First-Come have done well." He was robed and hooded like an Ochar, having no wish to draw attention to himself.

"We could always move more quickly than that rabble," said Romek, and added contemptuously, "So far, the Fallarin have done nothing to hinder us. Perhaps they have been remembering where their interests lie." He sought out the distant purple banner that marked Ildann's place in the line of battle that was being formed out of the interrupted march. "The man Stark will be there, most likely."

But Stark was nowhere in that army.

14

Stark was herding Runners.

After he was blooded, he had let the Hooded Men do what they would at the ceremony of the Springfire, taking no part in it himself. The Ochar had left in a tremendous hurry. Romek would be setting about organizing his army as swiftly as possible. Stark had talked strategy with the Fallarin. During those talks he had come to the conclusion that the Fallarin had acquired, down through the centuries, a streak of madness.

He had sent the Hearth-Keepers away from the Place of Winds to gather their men as quickly as they might, knowing even then that the Ochar, who had begun mustering days before and were less widely scattered, would be ready in force sooner than they could be no matter how they ran. Purple Hann, brown Marag and red Kref could gather most quickly. The other three Hearths were more distant.

By common consent a rendezvous was chosen, a place called the Tears of Lek, a salt lake not far above Yurunna.

But it was certain, unless the Ochar had lost all their skill and Gelmar of Skeg all his cunning, that the army of the Lesser Hearths would not be permitted to join its several parts together at its leisure.

Ildann said, "We three—Hann, Marag and Kref—being the nearest, will surely bear the brunt. We're strong fighters and not afraid to die, but no amount of courage will stand off the Ochar for long."

Alderyk smiled his sharp cruel smile, and the wings of the Fallarin beat up a laughing howl of wind.

"We'll see to it that you have help."

And Stark had stroked Gerd's ugly head and nodded, hoping that he was not lying. Because if he was, the fierce-eyed chiefs would be leading their people to certain death, in his name.

So now, like a careful shepherd, Stark moved across the dunes on the broad track of the Ochar host; and the Northhounds ran free, bounding at the edges of the stinking, tattered and thoroughly cowed flock, flicking them with the lash of terror.

They had gathered up between three and four hundred of the things, cleaning out three nesting cities with fire and wind and hound-fear. Beside Stark and the pack, one hundred and fifty Fallarin—with Alderyk at their head and twice as many Tarf to serve them—managed the Runners with small bursts of sandstorm, guiding them and holding down their speed.

The Fallarin rode, like Stark. When they did take the air, their flight was short and skimming. The Tarf went on their own limbs, and they could outrun anything except the Runners. Stark had used them as scouts, depending on their information for the timing of this unlikely operation. He had considered the whole idea insane, but the Fallarin had been serenely confident, knowing their own skills and the habits of Runners.

"Runner packs always go *with* the sandstorms, and just ahead," Alderyk said. "They never go against them. We can drive them wherever we wish them to go, using the wind for a whip."

And so far they had done just that. Whenever the Runners tried to turn or scatter, they were met by a rush of stinging sand, and they turned again to go before it.

Now Alderyk rode up beside Stark and said, "Look at them. They smell meat."

The runners had begun to move faster. They were forgetting the hounds. Some of the old males made hooting cries.

"Suppose it's our own people they hit," Stark said. The Tarf had kept him in close touch with the movements of both armies, and he knew that Ildann's force was facing the Ochar.

"They won't," said Alderyk. "Be ready about your hounds, and keep out of our way."

Two Tarf came racing back, kicking spurts of sand. "Beyond that next rise, Lord, we could see a great patch of orange moving."

Alderyk said, "I will go myself."

One of the Tarf caught his bridle. He launched himself with a leathery flapping and rose heavily into the air; not high, but high enough to see farther than anyone on the ground.

He went a little distance forward and then came back in a great hurry.

"Now!" he said to Stark. "Ildann's army lies there, to your left, across two ridges." He cried out a shrill cry to the Fallarin.

Stark called in his hounds.

War-horns sounded out of sight beyond the dunes, hoarse and bawling.

The Fallarin were ranged in a wide crescent whose points enclosed the Runners. Stark rode through their line, out of the way of it. He saw them spread their wings. He heard them begin to sing, a strange wild crooning storm-song, and underneath the singing the wings beat a broken cadence.

The hounds howled.

Within the crescent the wind rose shrieking and the sand rose with it in a blinding wall. The blurred mass of the Runners moved, picking up speed, all the narrow bodies thrust forward, the incredible legs churning.

The sand hid them. Wind and cloud rushed away. Stark put his beast into a loping run, the hounds beside him.

He cleared the first dune, plunged in the hollow beyond it, going at a tangent behind that flying wall of sand. He began to hear noises, horns blowing, a confusion of shouts and cries almost lost in the wind-roar. When he reached the crest of the second dune, he could see what was happening.

Ildann had drawn his line on a wide flat. The Ochar had launched their attack from the height, throwing out wings on either side to take advantage of their greater numbers and envelop the smaller army.

The sandstorm of the Fallarin, with its several hundred Runners, hit the Ochar left wing before it was halfway down the slope of the dune.

The shock was audible. The mass of burnt orange disintegrated in a boiling of sand and leaping bodies. Hideous sounds came out of that turmoil, where the Runners tore, and fed, and died.

War-horns bellowed. Men shouted. The sounds were thin and lost. The charge faltered as the line staggered, struggled to reform itself.

Momentum carried right and center down the slope. Arrows flew from both sides. Ildann's line wheeled, raggedly but with savage enthusiasm, purple and brown taking the brunt of the shock while the red Kref spurred up to drive a wedge between the Ochar center and the totally demoralized left.

They struck hard. But Stark's heart sank when he saw the solid wall of orange that still confronted them.

He kicked the beast into a run, going down the slope toward the battle.

The sand was settling. Knots of men and beasts and Runners heaved and floundered, inextricably mixed, among the dead and dying. Suddenly at the Ochar rear a whirlwind rose and struck, spouting up more sand. Torn scraps of orange flew out of it like winter leaves. The Fallarin had moved on to fresh endeavors. The Ochar line swayed and shifted, and the men of the Lesser Hearths howled like wolves.

With his spear leveled and the hounds death-baying around him, Stark went into the fight.

He went bareheaded and barefaced, and that alone marked him. The Red Cloaks cheered and shouted his name. The hounds killed a way for him through the orange, toward where Romek's standard showed above the melee, opposite Ildann's center.

Many of the men on both sides fought on foot now. The ground was littered with dead beasts and the dusty cloaks of the fallen. Over the roar of battle came the sound of the whirling winds, dancing their devil's dance, stripping men of their garments, beating and blinding them, tossing them like chaff, driving their mounts mad with fear.

The Ochar flinched and reeled. Battered from all sides, they began to break and scatter, and the whirlwinds drove them. The men of the Lesser Hearths pressed furiously against the yielding line.

Romek's standard still stood. He had his clansmen by him, a hundred or more still unwounded. He saw Stark, at the head of the Purple Cloaks and coming strongly. Romek raised his standard and shouted. His men charged Ildann's center.

Romek came straight for Stark.

Let be, said Stark to the hounds. *Guard yourselves*.

He spurred forward to meet the Keeper of the Hearth of Ochar.

The first spear clash snapped shafts against small round shields and toppled both men unhurt from the saddle. Drawing blade, they fought on foot, with the tides of purple and orange flowing round them on all sides and a banshee screaming of wind beyond. Romek was a tall cold fury quite careless of life if he could only take Stark with him.

Kill? said Gerd, clawing the ground. *Kill, N'Chaka?*

No. This one must be mine.

There were plenty of others. The hounds killed themselves weary.

Gradually Stark became aware of a small quietness in which he and Romek circled and slashed and parried. There was only the stamp of their feet and the ringing blades and a huge sound of breathing. They were surrounded by Purple Cloaks.

Romek, steel and rawhide, cut and slashed until his arm began to tire. Stark moved like a wraith. The level light of Old Sun caught in his pale eyes, and there was a patience there as terrible as time.

Romek's soft boots shuffled in the trodden sand. Shuffled, missed step. Stumbled.

Stark leaped forward.

Romek struck, low and viciously, out of that feint.

Stark leaned aside, as an animal shifts weight in mid-spring. The blade sang past him. His arm whipped down. The curved edge of his blade took Romek between shoulder and jaw.

Gerd came and sniffed at the severed head. Then he licked Stark's hand.

Ildann, his cloak torn and bloody, shook his sword in the air.

"Where are the Ochar? Where is the pride of the First-Come?"

A great wild shout went up. The men would have taken Stark on their shoulders; something held them back, and it was not entirely the presence of the hounds.

Stark thrust his blade into the sand to clean it. The battle was over, except for the noisy business of stamping down the last bits of it and slaughtering those Runners that were still alive and too stupid to escape. The whirlwinds danced over the dunes, flogging the surviving Ochar on their way.

Stark said to Ildann, "Where are my companions?"

"Yonder behind the ridge, there." He pointed across the flat. "We left them with the baggage train and a strong guard. They'll be coming soon."

"Did you see . . . Was there a stranger with Romek at any time?"

"A Wandsman? No, I saw none."

"Pass the word along. If a stranger is found among the dead, I want to know it."

Ildann passed the word. But Gelmar was not among the dead. He was fighting hard to stay among the living, clinging to his racing beast and thinking of Yurunna and the Lords Protector.

Jofr was not among the dead, either. Some of the Hann found him half-dazed where the wind had flung him, and they brought him to headquarters instead of slitting his throat because they remembered the ransom.

Stark was there with Gerrith and Ashton and Halk, and the three Hearth-Keepers, and Alderyk of the Fallarin. He looked at the boy, all beaten and drooping between the tall men.

"Let him sit," he said. There was a tiny fire and the air was chill. "Bring him food and water."

Jofr kept his head bent down and would not touch what was brought to him. Ashton sat by and watched him.

Stark asked Gerrith, "Do we have any further need of this one?"

"No."

Stark turned to Alderyk. "Perhaps some of your Tarf could take him where he can find his own people."

"That would be easy enough. But why do you want to save him?"

"He's only a child."

"Very well, if you must. They can start now."

The three chiefs began to talk about ransom.

Stark said to the boy, "Is your father living?"

"I don't know. I lost him when the wind struck."

"You see?" said Stark to the chiefs. "And even if Ekmal did survive, he will have little to spare for ransoms. Think of the loot of Yurunna. Get up, boy."

Jofr sighed and made as though to rise. Instead, he flung himself across the fire, straight at Stark's throat, and there was in his hand a small knife with which he was used to cut meat.

Stark caught his hand and Ashton his feet. The knife dropped.

"That's why he refused your bread and salt," said Ashton. "I told you it was a blue-eyed viper."

Stark smiled. "It's a brave one, at any rate." He shook the boy and set him on his feet. "Get home to your mother."

Jofr went away with his guards, and he was weeping again, this time with sheer frustration. The blade had come so close.

Hann, Kref and Marag slaughtered the too sorely wounded with due honor and ceremony and buried their dead. Runners came out of nowhere to dispose of the Ochar.

The army gathered itself and moved on, traveling swiftly toward the bitter lake.

The Tears of Lek shone sullenly under Old Sun like an unpolished shield dropped in the midst of desolation. Its heavy waters never froze even in the dead of winter. White salt pans gleamed, scarred by generations of quarrying. On the unfriendly surround of stiff sedges and sand, the camps of green Thorn and white Thuran were set up. The yellow Qard as usual, were late.

Camp was made, and the men began celebrating their victory. Thorn and Thuran were as savagely joyful as the actual victors. They sang harsh yelping songs and did leaping dances to the rattle of small drums and the shrilling of pipes. This went on all night, and there was almost a second war when it seemed to Hann, Marag and Kref that their newly made and so far non-fighting brothers were taking too large a part in the rejoicing.

In the red morning Stark and Ashton, with Alderyk and the chiefs, rode out to a line of untidy hills and climbed to a place where they could overlook Yurunna.

From this distance it was not the city that took the eye so much as the oasis that surrounded it.

There was water, in plenty. Sunlight glinted on irrigation ditches, a spidery pattern amid the fields. Things were a lot further along here than at Ildann's village. Color smeared the land in patches; sickly yellow, greenish black, dusty ocher, leprous white. There were orchards of spiny twisted trees. To Stark, it was supremely unlovely. To the tribesmen, it was paradise.

In the midst of this ugly garden, some careless titan had dropped a huge grim rock, and on top of the rock someone had built a darkness. There was little detail to be seen this far away, but that was the impression Stark had, a walled and brooding darkness above the gloomy fields.

"You see how it stands, Eric," Ashton said. "Not pretty, but rich and fat all the same. And alone. Every hungry tribesman who ever passed this way has looked at it and plotted how to take it."

"And sometimes tried," said Ildann. "Oh, yes, tried."

"The Wandsmen keep the city well prepared. A caravan came in while I was there, bringing military stores, oil and the stuff they call *kheffi*, some kind of resinous fiber that makes the spreading fire when it's soaked and lighted. There were timbers and cordage to repair the ballistas, and there were weapons. They train the Yur well and keep them trained, about a thousand of them. Yurunna is vital to their presence here in the north, and they know that even the best-bought loyalty, such as they have from the Ochar, ought not to be tempted with weakness."

"Very formidable," said Alderyk.

"Yes."

"Impregnable?"

"Certainly difficult."

"For ordinary humans, yes," said Alderyk.

He clapped his wings and cried a vaulting cry. Dust whipped across the desert, and a long while later Stark saw trees in the oasis bend to a sudden gust.

The yellow Qard came in that afternoon. The next day the army marched and set down before Yurunna.

15

HIGH ON ITS ROCK, the city scragged the sky like the top of a shattered tree stump. A wall encircled it, high and tight. Buildings stretched up to peer over with narrow eyes. Steep roofs gave back a hard gleaming in the rusty light of Old Sun, except where there were empty gaps.

A single road, wide enough for a cart, zigzagged up the western face of the rock to the single gate. The gate, Ashton said, was fashioned of black iron and very strong. It was set deep between two flanking towers. On the tops of these towers great cauldrons were set, with engines for casting the spreading fire.

At other places around the wall other engines were set. Yur in polished leather manned the wall, and now and again a Wandsman passed along it with a couple of hounds in leash. The wall was sheer and smooth, thirty feet or so atop seventy or eighty of sheer cliff.

Lacking modern weapons, lacking even primitive siege engines, the invaders faced a city that seemed impregnable.

But that night the attack on Yurunna began, though not one man of the Lesser Hearths dight himself for war.

The men drummed and danced and piped and sang or did otherwise as it pleased them. But there was another singing, and that came from the camp of the Fallarin, where the Tarf stood guard in a silent circle, armed with four-handed swords.

The singing was sprightly and wicked and mischievous and cruel, and under it like a whispering base was the sound of wings a-beat.

Up in the city a small wind began to prowl.

It skipped on roof tiles and ran along narrow streets. It poked and whined into holes and corners. It climbed old walls and felt the texture and the weakness of them. It puffed at cressets, torches, lamps. It snuffed wood.

It grew.

It became a hundred winds.

Yurunna was old, a palimpsest, city built upon half-obliterated city as this people and that came down from the north and took it and held it and then left it again for the next wave of wanderers. Some of the buildings were stout, solid stone. Some were built in part of timber brought up from the south, using one or two walls of an older shell so that the wooden structures resembled the nests of mud-dauber wasps plastered to the stone. In the center of the city and in the area around the gate the buildings were used and lived in. In the small outer quarters of the small city the buildings were unused, except along the wall where the sinews of war were stored ready to hand. These buildings were sound, and kept so. Of the others, some had fallen. Some were ready to fall.

All night long the werewinds laughed and gamed in the narrow ways of Yurunna, and the Yur looked up with their copper-colored eyes like the eyes of dolls and saw deadly roof tiles spin like autumn leaves, shied down at them by the fingers of the wind. Chimneys crumbled. Old walls swayed and shook until they toppled. The dark was full of clatterings and crashings. The Yur women wept in their great house, trembling when the shutters banged open and the curtains blew, scurrying to protect their screaming young.

The Wandsmen, two score of them who oversaw the breeding of Yur and Northhound, the training of the young, the ordering of city and field, were at first scornful of the power of the Fallarin. No wind could threaten their strong walls. They became uneasy as the night wore on and their own city seemed to have been turned against them; had in fact become a weapon in the enemy's hands.

The Northhounds on the wall and in the dark streets shivered, though they had felt far colder winds. They howled dismally, and when walls fell on them they died, and there was no enemy they could strike at. The face of the Houndmaster, already set in the grim lines of a heartstricken man, became more grim.

And that was not the worst.

The werewinds played with fire.

Cressets fell. Torches blew down. Lamps were knocked over. Flames sprang up, and the werewinds blew upon them, fanned them, sucked them up into whirling gold-red storms. The black sky brightened above Yurunna.

The Wandsmen fought the fires with fewer Yur than they would have liked. They dared not strip the wall of defenders for fear of winged men, who might scale the unscalable and let down ropes for the wingless.

Toward dawn, when the fires were to some degree controlled, the werewinds struck in several places, oversetting the cauldrons of oil and the supplies of the spreading fire on the wall, then tossing down the huge basket-torches that burned beside the emplacements. The resultant fires destroyed some of the ballistas, ate their way into some of the nearby storerooms, where there was more oil and more of the *kheffi* for the spreading fire. Wandsmen and Yur had no rest by day.

Stark assumed that the Fallarin rested. He made no attempt to find out. He rode among the tribes, making sure that certain preparations were being carried out.

By evening, the defenders of the city had repaired the damage on the wall, dragging up new ballistas, setting more cauldrons and containers.

When it was full dark, the gay sadistic song began again, with the beating of wings. Again the werewinds prowled and frisked, and destroyed, and killed wherever they could.

Fires were harder to set because this night there were no torches or cressets or lamps in the city. They managed even so. They puffed old embers to life and tumbled more cauldrons and torches, throwing ballistas and crews from the wall and from the towers by the gate. At dawn there was a pall of smoke over Yurunna, and no rest within it.

For three long nights the werewinds made Yurunna their playground. On the morning of the fourth day Alderyk, gaunt and strange-eyed, came like a moulting eagle to Stark's tent and said:

"Now you must get off your hunkers, Dark Man. You and your Lesser Hearths and your demon hounds. We have broken the path for you. Tread it."

He went back to his camp, angry cat's-paws striking up sand at every flapping step. Halk looked after him.

"That little man makes an evil enemy."

He had spent his idle days creaking and groaning at martial exercises. He had not yet got back his full strength, but half of Halk's strength was greater than most men's. Now he made steel flicker around his head.

"When we enter the city, I'll bear shield beside you."

"Not you," Stark said, "and not Simon, either. If I should fall, there'll be things for you to do."

Stark sent word to the chiefs. He spent time with Ashton. He spent time with Gerrith. He ate and slept, and the day passed.

For Yurunna that night began like the others—as it seemed to the Wandsmen, a year of others, with the whirling winds dancing death around them and over them, and sandy sleeplessness in their smoke-stung eyes, and their limbs aching. Then they began to perceive that there was movement in the darkness.

They tried to follow it. The winds kicked and trampled, blinding them with dust, wreaking havoc along the wall. Twice and thrice the Wandsmen had replaced the defenses of the gate-towers, clearing away scorched wreckage from the square below to give the Yur fighting room. Now again cauldrons and spreading fire were thrown down to smoke and blaze in the square. Gusts of wind pounded at the iron gate, so that it moved with a deep groaning.

Things, said the hounds of Yurunna, where the Houndmaster and two handlers and two apprentice boys held them at the back of the square, away from the fires. *Things come.*

Kill, said the Houndmaster.

The hounds sent fear.

Thirty Tarf, fifteen on a side, bearing a ram made from a green tree trunk cut beside Yurunna's springs, came up the zigzag road to the gate. Twenty more came with them, holding the turtle roof above their heads. They did not flinch from the sending of the hounds.

The hounds said, *Things do not fear us.*

And they became afraid, with a new fear added to the ones they already had, of strange winds and noises and the smell of death.

The Houndmaster said, *Those will come who do.*

He was a tall Wandsman. The tunic under his dented mail was the somber red that marked him next in rank below the Lords Protector. From the time he had been a gray apprentice up from Ged Darod he had lived and worked with Northhounds. He loved them. He loved their ugliness and their savagery. He loved their minds, to which he had become so closely attuned. He loved sharing their simple joy of slaughter. His heart was broken for each hound he had lost to the werewinds.

For the nine traitor hounds he had lost to an off-world monster called Stark, who was neither man nor beast, more than his heart was broken.

The Lords Protector had come, the august and holy men he had served all his life, tending the hounds and training them and sending them north to guard the Citadel from all intruders. His hounds—his hounds!—had not guarded, had betrayed, had followed after this sky-born blasphemy who flouted their power; and the Citadel was a burnt-out ruin, the Lords Protector driven shamefully to seek refuge at Yurunna.

They had been kind. They had absolved him of fault. Still, the hounds were his.

The dishonor was his.

After the Lords Protector, Gelmar came, in such haste that he killed his beast within sight of the gate. The Ochar were broken. Yurunna stood alone against the host of the north, and the leader of that host was Stark, with his nine faithless hounds.

Gelmar and the Lords Protector had fled on, down the road to Ged Darod. Now, as they had feared, Yurunna was tottering to its fall. And the Houndmaster had seen from the battlements a big dark man on a dappled beast riding a circuit of the walls, with nine white hounds running by him.

He spoke to his own hounds, the twenty-four that were all he had left, and less than half of them full-grown. He spoke to them gently, because the young ones trembled.

Wait, he said. *There will yet be killing.*

The ram began to swing. The deep drum-sound beat out heavily over Yurunna.

Muster-horns blew, calling the Yur to defend the gate.

The defenses along the wall, already thin, were thinned still more. Many of the storerooms were gutted, and the emplacements destroyed. Because of the blocking of streets where fire and wind had brought down buildings, bodies of men could no longer be moved quickly back and forth. They could only move freely on the wall. Now many of those who manned it were drawn to the gate.

When the wind dropped, it was seen that masses of men had gathered in the plain below and were already on the zigzag road.

Stark was under the wall with his hounds and fifty Tarf, led by Klatlekt. Half the Fallarin, with the rest of the Tarf and one-third of the tribal army, waited in the fields.

Kill, said Stark. *Clear the wall.*

The hounds ranged on either side, sending fear to the Yur above.

When the chosen section of the wall was cleared, the Fallarin hop-flapped up the sheer cliff, up the unscalable wall, and made fast ropes of twisted hide around the crenels of the firestep.

Tarf swarmed up the ropes, swords and shields hung at their backs. Some spread out to hold the wall. Others hauled up rope ladders or helped the tribesmen climb.

Stark forced the growling hounds to submit while he fitted slings under their bellies. The Tarf hauled them up, careless of their rage and fear. Stark climbed beside them. On either side now came red Kref and green Thorn.

The Fallarin returned to their mounts and rode away.

On the broad top of the wall Stark gathered his party: Klatlekt and twenty Tarf and the hounds. He set out toward the gate.

The hounds forgot the indignity of the slings. There was a dark excitement in their minds, a wildness mixed with fear.

Many minds, N'Chaka. Too many. All hate. All red. Red. Red.

In the square, where the ram was a wincing thunder in their ears, the hounds of Yurunna said:

Things come. There along wall. And men. And hounds.

Hounds?

Yes.

The Houndmaster stroked rough heads. *Good,* he said. *That is good.*

He passed word to the Wandsman captains that invaders were on the wall. He snapped orders to his two handlers and the apprentice boys, all Wandsmen, though of lesser and least rank, and thus safe like himself from the Northhounds. All were leaden with weariness, and the boys were all but useless with fright. However, the time would not be long. They would do.

He did not call up any of the Yur. The renegade hounds would only kill them before they could shoot arrow or lift spear, and the captains would need every one.

He spoke to his favorite hound, an old wise bitch.

Hounds, Mika.

Mika made an eager growling and led the way.

Up on the wall Gerd said suddenly, *N'Chaka. They come to kill.*

16

STARK HAD COME far enough around the curve of the wall to be able to see the top of the north gate-tower above the roofs. The tribesmen were coming strongly behind him, pouring up onto the wall, helped by the strong arms of the Tarf. They could still be thrown back if the hounds of Yurunna spread death and terror among them.

Stark went down stone steps, down off the wall, into the street below. Klatlekt and the twenty Tarf came with him.

The hounds slunk, whining.

Houndmaster, Gerd said. *Angry.*

Dim faint memories stirred, of old days, of running in couples with littermates, of an overmastering mind that gave orders and engendered a respect that was as near to love as a Northhound could feel.

He will kill us, Grith said.

How?

With hounds. With his great sword.

Kill N'Chaka, Gerd said.

Not N'Chaka, Stark answered. And, contemptuously, *Stay, then, if you fear the Houndmaster. N'Chaka will fight for you.*

N'Chaka understood that he had little choice about fighting in any case. That was why the Tarf were there. But he felt a responsibility toward these fangy horrors who had become his allies. He had deliberately seduced them into betraying their masters, knowing that they could not comprehend what they were doing. They had followed him, they had served him, they were his. He had a duty to fight for them.

To the Tarf he said, "Do not touch mine."

He set off along a street that led inward from the wall. He had no worry about finding the hounds of Yurunna. They would find him. He wanted it to be as far as possible from the tribesmen.

Gerd howled. Then he bayed, and Grith bayed, and the others took it up. They followed Stark, and that deep and dreadful challenge rang ahead of them along the silent stony ways with no other sound in them but the drumbeat of the ram.

The hounds of Yurunna heard. The young ones whined, partly from fear and partly from excitement, feeling a new ferocity rise within them. The old ones lifted their own voices, and their eyes glowed with a deadly light. The old relationship was long forgotten. These were strangers invading their territory, crying a pack cry, following a strange leader who was neither hound nor Wandsman.

The Houndmaster said kill. They would kill gladly.

The streets were not too much encumbered. The stout stone buildings here had resisted the winds and fires. Both parties moved rapidly, hound-minds guiding eagerly toward a meeting.

The Houndmaster knew the streets, and Stark did not.

The Houndmaster spoke. Handlers and struggling apprentices forced the hounds to a reluctant halt. Ahead of them was a small open space, a little square where four streets met.

The Houndmaster waited.

In that one of the four streets that led from the wall, Gerd said, *There!* and rushed ahead into the square.

Nine hounds running, heads down, backs a-bristle. N'Chaka would have held them. But N'Chaka was fighting his own fight.

When the Northhounds fought each other, as the males did for leadership of the pack, they used every weapon they had. Fear would not kill a Northhound, but it served as a whip to wound and drive, the stronger against the weaker. The hounds of Yurunna did not at first send fear against the invading hounds. By order of the Houndmaster they sent it all against the alien leader.

N'Chaka struggled to stand erect, to breathe.

To live.

"Slip them," said the Houndmaster, and the hounds of Yurunna went free.

Twenty-four against nine, in the small square. Twenty-four encircling and overlapping nine, carrying them back by sheer weight into the mouth of the street whence they had come. Twenty-four and nine inextricably mixed. To the Tarf, indistinguishable.

The Houndmaster followed them with his great sword raised high, and to him each hound was as well known as the hairs and scars and pits upon his own face.

Three hounds of Yurunna, with the Houndmaster's old bitch Mika leading, burst out of the boiling mass into the street where the Tarf stood crammed between the walls, their effective force reduced by the constriction to no more than five or six.

At their forefront Klatlekt stood by Stark, blinking his green-gold eyes.

He warded the enemy hounds' first rush with his sword, while Stark sobbed for breath and stared blindly with the icy sweat beading his face.

"We must have fighting room," said Klatlekt. Hound-fear could not harm him. The fangs and the ripping claws could. He plucked at Stark with one powerful hand. "Come. Or we go without you."

The hounds attacked again, two feinting to draw Klatlekt's blade, the bitch driving straight for Stark's throat.

In the square the sword of the Houndmaster flashed down. And up. And down again.

N'Chaka saw death coming, smelled death, heard it. Sheer brute reflex, the dangerous last blind outlashing, brought his own sword forward.

Houndmaster! Kill, Gerd! Kill, or we all die.

The Houndmaster, untouchable Wandsman belly deep in hounds, swung his sword.

Gerd, torn and bleeding, with N'Chaka's cry ringing in his mind, saw the flash of that blade above him and broke the unbreakable commandment.

The Yurunna bitch-hound shrieked, an almost human sound, as the life-long mind-bond snapped. She turned her head, searching, crying out, and Stark ran her through the neck, clumsy and vicious with the black terror on him.

He went forward, shouting to his hounds, and they flung themselves in a frenzy of guilt and triumph on the hounds of Yurunna, sensing that the Houndmaster's death had robbed them of their strength.

The guilding presence was gone, the strong firm voice that had spoken in their minds since they first saw light.

Stark became that voice.

Go back to your kennel. Back, or we kill.

The hounds of Yurunna begged help from the handlers. The handlers no longer spoke. Gerd had learned how easy it was to kill Wandsmen.

Back to your kennel! Go!

The apprentices had fled long ago. The hounds of Yurunna were quite alone. The strangers and their strange leader fought fiercely. The things fought with them, the unhuman things that wielded long sharp swords and were not touched by fear.

Go, said the strong commanding voice in their minds.

The young hounds, already fearful and with no master to give them courage, did as Stark told them. There were eight still able to run.

The old hounds died there, full of rage and grief, and Stark knew that if the Houndmaster had been present on the Plain of Worldheart, he would never have made himself leader of Flay's pack.

The small square fell quiet again. Gerd and Grith came panting to Stark's side. Only three others came with them, and not one unmarked. Stark and Klatlekt and several more of the Tarf had taken wounds, but none was disabled.

Klatlekt blinked heavy eyelids and said, "If this is finished, we will return to the wall."

"It is finished," Stark said, knowing that more than this fight was finished. The face of the Houndmaster stared white and accusing from amid the rough sprawled carcasses. As a terror and a menace, as a weapon of the Wandsmen, the Northhounds were finished forever.

Stark took Gerd's head between his hands. *You have killed Wandsmen.*

Gerd's teeth showed, even though he trembled. *Houndmaster killed us.*

So. Other Wandsmen will kill.

With a strange echo of despair, Gerd said, *We kill them.*

Grith?

We kill.

Come, then, Stark said, and went off after the quick-footed Tarf, who had not waited for him. He was conscious of his hurts and of his weariness, but he was exhilarated by this triumph over the Wandsmen. He ran swiftly, his heart beating hot, eager for more.

The booming of the ram had stopped. In its place was the confused uproar of men fighting. The tribesmen were making their attack.

Most of them had come down off the wall to strike the Yur in the streets and the square. A strong party of tribesmen and Tarf had gone on to the tower and were fighting their way into it. Down below it housed the mechanism that controlled the gate, which was standing firm in spite of the battering.

Stark and his hounds lent aid where it would help the most. He took a particular pleasure in picking out the Wandsman captains and saying, *Kill.* It was time they felt the weight of the weapon they had used for so long against other men.

The north tower was taken. The clanking mechanism hauled open the iron gate, and the tide of purple and white, brown and yellow, poured through it into the square. The zigzag road was a solid river of men rushing upward, yelping, howling, brandishing sword and spear, and below the road more men came from among the warty crops and spiny orchards to jostle for a place.

Nothing could stand against that tide. The bodies of tribesmen spitted on Yur spears hung there with no room to fall. The defenders were forced back, back against stone walls, out of the square, into the streets, where the bands of Hann and Marag, Kref and Thuran, Thorn and yellow Qard hunted them and killed.

When the killing was done, the looting began. Most of the fat storehouses where food and drink were kept had escaped the damage of the werewinds, being in the heart of the occupied section of Yurunna; many of them were in underground chambers cut in the rock. The tribesmen pillaged the storerooms, and the houses, and the public places. The Keepers of the six Hearths did what they could to maintain order.

Even so, things happened.

The men found the great walled house of the Yur women and battered down its doors. Instead of the orgy of pleasure they had anticipated, they found creatures like obscene white slugs that stared at them with empty eyes and screamed without ceasing, clutching their unnatural young like so many identical blank-faced dolls. Overcome with disgust, the tribesmen made a silence in the place and never once thought of these degraded things as food.

That was the end of the Yur, the Well-Created servants of the Wandsmen. Some of the men still lived, but there would be no more breeding.

Stark had no part in this. He had gone to the kennels.

The gray-clad apprentices were there, boys up from Ged Darod only that year. One of them, a sullen heavy-faced youth, was crouched in a corner hugging himself and waiting to die, with hate and fear and nothing else at all in his eyes.

The other was with the hounds. He was slight and dark, his boy's face still unformed, his boy's hands too large and knuckly. He was afraid. There was no reason why he should not be. He was hollow-eyed and red-eyed and pale with exhaustion. But he was with the hounds where he belonged. And he met Stark's gaze with what dignity he could muster, even though he knew that those five grim blood-dabbled beasts at Stark's heels might kill him where he stood.

"How are you called?" Stark asked.

"Tuchvar," said the boy. And again, more clearly, "Tuchvar."

"Where from?"

"Tregad."

Tregad was a city-state, east of Irnan and north of Ged Darod.

Stark nodded and turned to the young hounds. They whined and glanced at him furtively with their hellhound eyes that had not yet come to their full evil brightness.

You know me.

They did.

I am N'Chaka. I lead you now.

The hounds appealed to Tuchvar. *Houndmaster?* They knew that that mind had ceased to speak to them. They could not yet grasp the fact that it would never speak again.

Tuchvar said aloud, "This man is master now."

N'Chaka? Master?

Master, Stark said. *These old ones will teach you the law.*

Gerd moved forward, stiff-legged and growling. The young hounds said, *We will obey.*

Stark spoke now to Gerd and Grith. *Will you go with me below Yurunna?*

It was their turn to be uneasy. *Not know. Hound-kind never sent but to Citadel.*

Stark said, *You cannot stay here. Things with swords will kill you, things that do not feel fear. You must go with me.*

Go with N'Chaka or die?

Yes.

Then we go.

Good.

He didn't know whether it was good or not. They were cold-weather beasts, and he had no idea how well they would adjust to warmer climates. Some animals managed very well. In any case what he told them was true. Neither the Fallarin nor the Lesser Hearths of Kheb would consent to having a pack of Northhounds loose and leaderless to prey on them and their cattle. The Tarf would see to that.

Gelmar and the Lords Protector had not counted on the Tarf.

He explained all this to Tuchvar. "Will you come with the hounds, at least as far as Tregad? Or do you serve the Wandsmen too loyally?"

"Not," said Tuchvar carefully, "so loyally that I want to die for them right here." He had been listening to the sounds outside and not liking them. He did not see what good it would do for him to die. It could not help the Wandsmen. It would certainly not help him.

The other apprentice spoke up from his corner, voice pitched high with fear and spite.

"He serves no one loyally but the hounds. Even at Ged Darod he was thinking all the time about starships and other worlds and listening to the heresies of Pedrallon."

Stark went over and yanked him to his feet.

"Stop shivering, boy. Nobody's going to kill you. What's your name?"

"Varik. From Ged Darod." Pride stirred in the lumpish face. "I was born there, at the Refuge."

"Farer's get," said Tuchvar. "They haven't any fathers."

"The Lords Protector are my fathers," said Varik, "and better than yours, sitting fat behind walls and trying to hide away food from the hungry."

"My father's dead," said Tuchvar bitterly, "but at least I know who he was, and he worked."

"All right," said Stark. "Now. Who is Pedrallon?"

"A red Wandsman," said Varik, "with the rank of Coordinator. The Twelve took away his rank and put him to doing penance for a year. It was supposed to be a secret, of course; they said Pedrallon had been relieved of his duties because of his health, but nothing stays a secret in our dormitories, not for very long."

Busy little apprentice Wandsmen, Stark thought, nibbling up crumbs of forbidden gossip like mice in a cupboard.

"What was his heresy?"

Tuchvar answered.

"He said the migrations were beginning again. He said that some of Skaith's people would have to go, to make room for others. He said it was wrong to stop the Irnanese."

17

THERE WAS a complex of buildings where the two score Wandsmen had lived, with such women as they might have from time to time. The quarters lacked nothing of comfort. Stark and his party and the Keepers of the six Hearths had lodged themselves here. The Fallarin, ever exclusive, had found themselves another place.

At the center of the complex was a wide hall furnished with handsome things brought up from the south. The Hearth-Keepers had managed to keep their men from looting here. Rich carpets were on the floor. Hangings brightened the dark stone of the walls. Many lamps lighted it, in a profligate squandering of oil. Braziers gave off warmth. Tarf and tribesmen mingled, carrying food and wine to the tables, where the conquerors of Yurunna were celebrating their victory.

The hall was crowded. Everyone who could possibly force his way in had done so. They stuffed themselves on the plenty of the Wandsmen's storerooms, washing it down with Southron wine and bitter beer. When the feasting was done, some of the men danced with flashing swords while drums thumped and pipes shrilled. Others rose and sang boasting songs. They began to drink to their leaders, each Hearth vying with the others in claims to bravery and prowess in battle.

They drank to the Fallarin.

They drank to the Dark Man.

Ildann put down his goblet and said, "Now Yurunna is taken, we remember your promise, Stark."

He spoke so that the words were a challenge, intended to be heard by all. He waited until the hall became quiet, with every head bent toward him, listening, and then he asked:

"What will you do now?"

Stark smiled. "Have no fear, Ildann. You have Yurunna. I leave to you and your fellows the task of sharing out the loot and the land, the placing of villages and the method of ruling them. You're at full liberty to kill each other if you choose. I've done my part."

"You go south, then?"

"To Tregad. To raise an army for Irnan. If we succeed, there will be war with the Wandsmen." He looked out over the hall, at all the masked faces. "War. Loot. High pay. And at the end, the starships. The freedom of the stars. That may mean nothing to you. If so, stay and make bricks for the villages. If any wish to come with me, you will be welcome."

Ildann had three sons. The youngest rose to his feet. His name was Sabak. He was slender as a reed and light as a roebuck in his movements, and he had fought well. He said:

"I will go with you, Dark Man."

Ildann crashed his fist on the table. "No!"

Sabak said, "I have a mind to see these ships, Father."

"Why? What do you want with other worlds? Have I not fought to bring you the best of this one? Yurunna, boy! We have taken Yurunna!"

"And that is well, Father. I too fought. Now I wish to see the ships."

"You're a child," said Ildann, suddenly quiet. "Men must feed and breed wherever they are. One world or another, feeding and breeding are the most of a man's life, along with the fighting that goes with them. No matter where you go, you'll find nothing better than what you have."

"That may be, Father. But I will see for myself."

Ildann turned on Stark, and Gerd, crouched by Stark's feet, sprang up snarling.

"I see now why the Wandsmen wish to kill you," Ildann said. "You bring a poison with you. You have poisoned my son with dreams."

A puff of wind made the lamps flicker. Alderyk had risen. The light gleamed gold at his throat and waist and in his falcon eyes.

"The boy has wisdom enough to understand that there is something beyond the walls of his sty, Ildann. Feeding and breeding are not enough for everyone. I too will go with the Dark Man. I am a king, and I have a duty to be as wise as Ildann's youngest son."

There was a clamor of voices. Ildann shouted furiously.

Again the lamps flickered and the cloaks of the men rustled as the small wind admonished them.

"The ships are there," Alderyk said. "The men are there, men from other worlds. We cannot pretend that things are still as they were before the landing, or ever will be again. We must know, we must learn." He paused. "There is another matter."

He spoke now to Stark, his eyes agleam with cruel mirth.

"I said you were like a black whirling wind, to break and shatter. It's our world you blow across, Dark Man, and when you fly away among the stars, we'll be left to deal with whatever wreckage you may have devised. So it seems my duty to be with you."

A buffet of air slapped Stark about the head, tossing his hair, making him blink and turn aside.

"I control winds, you know," said Alderyk.

Stark nodded tranquilly. "Very well." He stood up. "Let the word be passed. I leave Yurunna tomorrow, when Old Sun is at his highest. Let every man who wishes to come south with me be in the square beside the gate at that time, mounted, armed and with three weeks' provisions."

He left the hall, with Ildann's angry voice raised again behind him. Ashton came, too, and Halk and Gerrith.

Halk said, "I think I'll go into the streets and drum up trade." In the quiet of the corridor, the sounds of celebration came clearly from outside. Through the windows Stark could see fires burning and men moving about them, dancing, chanting, drinking. Grith and the three rose stiffly from where they had lain on watch.

"Take Gerd with you to watch your back," Stark said. "The Hearth-Keepers may object to this stealing of their men."

"Keep your grimhound," Halk said, and touched his sword. "This is enough."

"Will you argue?" Stark asked, and Gerd swung his heavy head to stare at Halk.

Halk shrugged. He walked away. Gerd followed. Halk did not look back or notice him.

"What will you get?" Ashton asked.

"A few boys like Sabak, with stars in their eyes. Malcontents, troublemakers, the restless types who would rather fight than make bricks. Not too many, probably." He smiled briefly. "Alderyk I'll be glad to have, in spite of his thorns."

He said good night and went to his quarters. He sat for a time, brooding. He knew that Gerrith would be waiting for him. He did not go to her. Instead, he took a lamp and made his way quietly, with the hounds, along the chilly corridors and down several flights of steps until he reached the cellars, cut deep into the rock. The Wandsmen had had no need of prison cells and so there were none. Some of the smaller storage chambers had been pressed into service as dungeons, to hold the handful of Wandsmen who had survived the fall of Yurunna.

Half a dozen of the yellow-cloaked Qard were lounging on piles of grain sacks, by way of being guards. Two of them played a game with varicolored pebbles, tossing them into a space marked out with intricate patterns drawn in the dust of the floor. The others made bets.

One of them looked up. "Hey," he said. "The Houndmaster!"

They all left off what they were doing and stood. Stark stared at them with displeasure.

"How long have you called me by that name?"

"Since we first heard it from the Hann, who first saw you with the Northhounds," said one of the men. "Didn't you know?"

"No. What else am I called?"

"Herder of Runners. Dark Man. Some even call you Starborn, but most of us don't believe that."

"Ah," said Stark. "You don't."

The man shrugged. "It may be. But it's easier to think that you came from the south."

"What do you know of the south?"

"There are great cities there, as high as mountains, and forests between them where there are all sorts of monsters and the trees eat men. Old Sun burns there with great heat, which is itself unnatural. I think anything might come from the south."

"Well," said Stark, "in a manner of speaking, I did come from there. What will you do now that you have Yurunna?"

"Build a village." The city was too large, too dark and cheerless for the tribesmen. They would build in the familiar pattern, at the edge of cultivation, close to their fields and herds. "We'll bring our women to tend the crops; men can't do that, you know. The land bears only for women. It is the same in the south?"

"I can name you a dozen places where it's so, and another dozen where it isn't." And not only in the south, friend, Stark thought. All over the galaxy.

The man shook his head. "You and your companions are the only strangers I've ever seen. There are different thoughts behind your eyes. I hadn't ever wondered about people living and thinking in other ways. Our way seems the only one, the only *right* one . . ."

One of the other men leaned forward. "Say truly, Dark Man. Are you from the south, or from another world?"

"From another world," said Stark. "Look up into the sky some night and see the stars; think of the ships going back and forth between them. Maybe some day you'll get tired of fighting the cold and the Runners and decide to go out there yourselves."

The men muttered and glanced at each other.

"We are Qard," said the first man. "We have a place in the tribe, we have a set of laws to live by. If we went to some other place . . ."

"'The land shapes us,'" Stark said. "'If we were in another place, we would be another people.'" He remembered Kazimni, the wolf-eyed Izvandian, captain of mercenaries at Irnan, who had said that. "And of course it's true. Yet there are those who have lived for centuries with the hope that someday the star-roads would be open."

He remembered the ruins of the towers away in the darklands, and the madness of Hargoth the Corn King, who had seen the ships in his Winter Dreaming, shining beside the sea. He and his people had been ready to migrate all the long way south to Skeg, singing the Hymn of Deliverance, to find those ships. They had hailed Stark as the savior come to lead them, until that black day at Thyra and Gelmar's cruel lie. The Corn King and his priests had left there stricken men, believing that the ships were already gone and that their endless waiting must continue.

"Anyway," said the tribesman, "the ships are far away, if they exist at all. The choice will not be made in my lifetime."

And perhaps not in mine either, Stark thought, and said, "I will speak to the red Wandsman."

There was only one of that rank among the survivors. His name was Clain, and he had been one of the administrators of the city. He was intelligent and well controlled; a rather cold and rigid man, too proud to show the rage and despair he must be feeling. Which was not true of the lesser Wandsmen. They were all to be kept alive with a view to ransom or as possible trade goods in future negotiations.

Clain was alone, at his own request, and not uncomfortable in his confinement. He stood when Stark entered, stiff with unwelcome, looking bitterly at the hounds. Stark left the three outside, taking only Grith with him into the cell. He shut the heavy door.

"Can you not leave me in peace?" the Wandsman asked, and Stark felt sorry for him in a way. Battered, exhausted and soiled, Clain was the model of painful defeat.

"I've already told you that Irnan still fights. I've told you all I know about what forces have been sent against her. I've told you there was talk among the Lords Protector, in their short visit here, concerning the starport at Skeg . . ."

"They spoke of closing the starport if Irnan should be relieved and the revolt widened."

"I told you that."

"They are guarding the starport closely, hoping that my friend and I may come there."

"I told you that, too."

Stark shrugged. "We knew it anyway. Now tell me about Pedrallon."

Clain sighed. "I have told you that I don't know Pedrallon."

"He's a red Wandsman. Surely there aren't so many of you at Ged Darod that you haven't at least heard of him."

"My place was not at Ged Darod, it was here . . ."

"One of your colleagues has told us that you went down to Ged Darod eight months ago, at about the time Pedrallon was disciplined by the Twelve."

"That's true. But I am not in the confidence of the Twelve."

"Really. Yet the gray apprentices knew all about it."

Clain's mouth made an icy pretense of a smile. "I suggest that you return to the kennels, then, for further information."

Stark frowned. "You have no idea of the basis of Pedrallon's heresy?"

"I am not concerned with such matters. I went to Ged Darod to see about increasing the supplies we send—did send—to the Ochar. Their crops have suffered . . ."

"You don't know why he was disciplined so severely?"

"I only heard that he was ill."

"And you don't know what his penance was?"

"I told you—"

"Yes," said Stark, "you did indeed. Grith . . ."

All this time Clain had been avoiding the sight of the Northhound, as though he knew what must happen because of her. Now his skin became even grayer than before.

"I beg you—"

"I believe you do," said Stark. "I'm sorry." *Grith, touch. Not kill. Touch.*

The massive head lifted. Stark could have sworn she smiled, pulling her dark lips back from gleaming fangs. Her bright eyes grew brighter still, smoky fires under heavy brows.

Clain went on his knees and wept. "They were our servants," he said between chattering jaws. "Ours. This is evil. Wrong."

Touch him, Grith.

In no more than five minutes Stark had everything he wanted.

He left Clain curled up, shivering on his pallet. He nodded to the Qard and went up the stairs again. He knocked at Ashton's door and went into the room.

Noises filtered through the shuttered windows from the streets of Yurunna. The tribesmen were still joyful. Ashton looked at Stark's face and sighed.

"What have you found out?"

"Pedrallon was sentenced to a year of menial duties at the Refuge as well as being stripped of his rank. They seem to have considered executing him, but didn't—Wandsmen are hardly ever sentenced to death. The small number of Wandsmen who openly supported his position were also punished, in lesser ways. There may have been others who were not open."

"Well?" said Ashton.

"Pedrallon was accused of being in secret communication with the star-captains at Skeg. He denied it. He was also accused of having a group of adherents on the outside. He denied that, too. If there was a conspiracy, it was a small one, and it may be out of business entirely. But from what Clain said, there is a possibility that Pedrallon had secured a transceiver from one of the captains and that some of his group had it hidden in or near Ged Darod. If so, it's still there. The Wandsmen never found it."

"A transceiver," Ashton said, and sighed again.

"If the Wandsmen send the ships away, as they promise to do, we'll be cutting our own throats if we succeed in raising men at Tregad. If we don't, if you and I just run for Skeg, our chances of getting through their cordon are about nil."

"Do you know there's a transceiver?"

"I said it's a possibility."

"Ged Darod. The heart and center. And you're thinking of going there."

"I don't think there's any way out of it," Stark said, "if we hope to leave Skaith alive. Or dead."

18

THE WANDSMEN'S ROAD was old. Above Ged Darod it ran through the barren places where survival was difficult, so that even during the Wandering and the unsettled times that followed, the road had not been too much exposed to attack by marauding bands. The system of wayhouses made travel on the road swift and comfortable for those authorized to use it. For the unauthorized, it was death.

Over the centuries there had been much coming and going along the road: Wandsmen and their armed escorts and mercenaries on the Lower Road, Yur and Ochar above; caravans bringing goods and supplies up to Yurunna, with their escorts and companies of lower-grade Wandsmen; caravans bringing women for the Wandsmen at Yurunna and for the distant peoples of Thyra and the Towers, beyond the mountains in the haunted darklands. Special parties, outwardly indistinguishable from the ordinary, conveyed each new Lord Protector north to the Citadel, which he would never leave until in his turn he was laid to rest among the thermal pits of Worldheart. But never had there been such a company on the road as went upon it now from Yurunna.

Stark rode at the head, on a dappled beast. Thirteen great white hounds followed him, with the gray apprentice Tuchvar to whip them in. With Stark at the head of the column were Ashton and Gerrith, and Halk with a great sword slung at his back, the hilt standing up over his shoulder; somewhere in the storerooms of Yurunna he had found a blade to his liking for size and weight. Alderyk rode where he would, Klatlekt and half a dozen Tarf trotting attendance beside him.

Next were fifty Fallarin, with their rich harness shining and dust in the folds of their wings, and five score Tarf with their four-handed swords and curiously stubby bows from which they could fire a deadly stream of arrows.

After them came the tribesmen, purple Hann with Sabak at their head, red Kref and green Thorn, white Thuran and yellow Qard, brown Marag, all in dusty leather. One hundred and eighty-seven of them, divided into groups according to their tribe, the day's place in line of each group chosen by lot in the morning. Stark hoped that they would become a single body of fighting men, but that time was not yet. He humored their pride.

South from Yurunna, at the great scarp of the Edge, the mountain wall on their right hand came to an end. Four thousand feet below, the desert spread away to the horizon without a break, except for abrupt upthrusting fangs of rock, worn thin with endless gnawing at the wind. The sand was streaked and stained in many colors, black and rust red, poison green, sulphur yellow. It was chillingly devoid of life, but the markers of the road marched out across it, a line of tiny dots.

At the foot of the Edge, just below them, where springs ran from beneath the cliffs, there were patches of cultivation and areas where a brownish sward covered the sand. A multitude of speckles on these areas were the herd-beasts of Yurunna, which had been driven to pasture here out of the way of the army. Men would come presently to drive them back.

The company wound its way down a steep and tortuous road cut in the sheer rock.

It was warmer at the foot of the scarp. The smell of water was strong in the dry air. High above the fields, where the face of the cliff was eroded into open caves, inaccessible dwellings squatted in remoteness and mystery; clusters of uneven walls with inscrutable windows at which no faces showed. Whether or not the star-roads were open made little difference here.

The company refilled waterskins at the springs and went on.

They moved swiftly, yet the desert seemed to have no boundaries. The wayhouses had been abandoned, beasts driven off, supplies carried away or destroyed. By this they knew that spies had been left to watch Yurunna, and that word of its fall had gone ahead of them. The wells had been blocked with boulders or choked with sand. Water supplies ran short. Men sickened of the hard stony waste with its deathly colors like the skin of a poisonous reptile. The beasts became footsore. There began to be grumbling and discontent. The hounds panted in the warmer air and the tribesmen threw open their leather cloaks. The Fallarin sulked and wished for water to wash their fur glossy again.

As Stark had guessed, most of the tribesmen were the restless ones, the trouble makers, and the Hearth-Keepers had not been too sorry to see them gone. At night Stark went among them, talking to them, telling tales of marches and battles on worlds far away, imbuing them with as much of his own strength of purpose as was possible, binding them to himself by sheer force of personality.

Nevertheless, he watched them.

Gerd roused him one night. A dozen or so hooded forms were stealing away from the camp, on foot, leading their animals. Stark let them get a certain distance away and then sent the pack. The deserters came crawling back to camp herded by thirteen grim white hounds. The attempt was not repeated.

Yet Stark could not blame them. Sometimes at night he stood, with Gerd and Grith by him, and listened to the stillness and felt the empty leagues around him and wondered what he was leading his small legion into. If they survived this ugly desolation, their way to Tregad was by no means clear. Gelmar had a long head start. Gelmar would have the news from Yurunna. Gelmar would look at a map, consider the logistics and assume that Tregad, being the nearest possible source of help for Irnan, would be Stark's most likely destination. Surely he would think of some way to intercept him.

They were three days without water at the last. Then they came to the first stream, with a line of stunted trees twisting along its course, and knew that they would live.

Stark had brought maps from Yurunna. As soon as was possible he left the Wandsmen's Road and struck out southeast for Tregad.

The land was not hospitable. In the Barrens to the west there had at least been an abundance of water and edible mosses for the beasts. Here there was little in the way of forage except along the stingy watercourses. Still, the beasts were hardy and they managed, and the men grew more cheerful even though their own bellies were pinched. The deathly colors had been replaced by an honest gray-brown. The Fallarin splashed and fluttered like birds at the cold pools and sleeked their fur until it glistened. The hounds had remained well so far. Here they hunted and found game, small shy creatures that might outrun the hounds' feet but not their fear.

The Three Ladies now ruled the sky again, glorious clusters brighter than moons, so that the nights were filled with a milky radiance. To Stark and the Irnanese they were like old friends. To the Fallarin and the tribesmen they were an astonishment.

With startling abruptness the nature of the country changed. They came out of the barren places and into the northern edge of the Fertile Belt not far above the latitude of Irnan. Here were grass and water and arable land.

Here, for the first time, they found villages, walled, dourly squatting above their fields, with watchtowers here and there to guard against predators—chiefly, the Wild Bands.

Several times the hounds gave warning. Stark and his men could catch glimpses of them, furtive slinking forms all hair and tatters, loping along at a distance, eyeing them.

Sabak said, "They're no better than Runners."

"Not much," Stark agreed, "but some. They're not as brainless, they haven't got such big teeth and they're not anything like as fast." He added, "Don't straggle."

Using the hounds and the Tarf as scouts, Stark was able to hit the villages before they could shut their gates. At each one he spoke to the people. The Dark Man of the prophecy told them of the fall of the Citadel and of the taking of Yurunna. They were a small dark people here, quite different from the tall Irnanese, and their manner was not friendly. Yet when they heard of the news their faces brightened. They too chafed under the yoke of the Wandsmen, who came at every harvest time to take a portion of their meager crops so that they were always on the edge of hunger. Many of the people had gone, to become Farers. Slowly the villages were dying. The hardness of the life and the small rewards had left ruins here and there and fields abandoned to the greedy weeds.

In each village a few of the folk picked up what arms they had or could improvise, and they joined with Stark's company. And along the paths and the herdsmen's tracks and the hunters' ways, messengers took the words of the Dark Man among scattered settlements.

Other messengers were abroad, too.

One night a signal fire flared atop a distant hill, its light paled by the lovely glow of the Three Ladies. A second fire kindled to life farther away, and then a third, a tiny pinpoint. The fourth Stark could not see, but he knew it was there, and a fifth—as many as were needed.

"They've seen us," Halk said. "They know where we are and where we're going. Wherever they choose to be waiting for us, there they will wait."

Stark found the main road to Tregad, and the company went down it like a thunderbolt.

It had been spring when Stark and his companions left these latitudes, with orchards just in blossom and the fresh green blanketing the fields. Now grain was yellowing toward harvest and fruit was heavy on the boughs.

Deep summer. Yet there was no one but themselves on the road to Tregad, where there ought to have been traders and drovers, wandering mountebanks and the bands of Farers. The gates of the villages they passed hung open, but the people had gone to hide themselves in the hills and the fields were untended.

Stark, with the hounds and some of the Tarf, scouted ahead, alert for ambush.

The hounds were not as tireless as they had once been. The young ones especially had become thin and listless. They suffered from fluxes, and Tuchvar worried and nursed them with infusions of herbs and green bark from a particular shrub. The old hounds fared better, though they suffered in the midday heat, mild as it was in this temperate climate. Still, they went obediently as they were told, and Stark rode with them far in advance of the troop.

There was no ambush. Woods and narrow defiles held no enemy.

"But of course," said Ashton, "Gelmar knows you've got the hounds, so an ambush wouldn't work—they'd warn you."

"He must meet us somewhere," Halk said. "He or his people."

"No doubt they will," said Stark.

And they did.

Tregad, when they came to it in the middle of an afternoon, was a city much like Irnan, stone-built and solid behind massive walls. Irnan was gray; the stone of Tregad was honey-colored so that it appeared far less grim, glowing warmly in the sunlight with the broad fields and orchards at its feet and its head halfway up the shoulder of a mountain, and a wide dark lake beyond.

Four thousand Farers thronged the fields and orchards. They trampled the standing crops into the ground, tore the fruiting branches from the trees. They howled and screamed and surged in irregular waves upon the gates of the city, which were shut against them.

There were some scraps of color on the city wall just below the battlements. Stark made out the bodies of six men hanging there, one in a red tunic, five in green.

"It looks," he said, "as if Tregad has hung up her Wandsmen."

Halk's great blade came rasping from its sheath. His face, still gaunt and craggy, shone with exultation.

"Tregad has revolted, then! Well, Dark Man, there are allies beyond that Farer trash! What will you do? Attack? Or run away?"

19

HALK LEANED FORWARD, his jaw thrust out, challenging. Stark had an idea that if he said run, the long blade would be for him.

Farer trash or not, the odds were staggering. He did not know what had happened in Tregad, though he could make a guess. Presumably, having slain their Wandsmen for whatever reason, the people of the city were committed to revolt. Presumably, when they saw a small force attacking the Farers, they would make a sally to support it. If they did not, or if they came too late, the results would be unpleasant.

Stark sighed and said, "Alderyk?"

The Fallarin had been staring at the mob, his aristocratic nose wrinkling with disgust.

"I think we must have a wind," he said, "to blow away the stink."

He rode back to his people. They began to move out, forming the familiar crescent—a much smaller one this time, and with no Runners ahead of it to drive against the enemy. Stark sent Tuchvar with Grith and half of the pack to stay by Gerrith and Ashton, both of whom were armed and ready. He himself rode back along the line, snapping orders.

The Farers began to be aware of the newcomers.

They were drawn from every race of the Fertile Belt, in all colors, sizes and shapes. They were of all ages, except young children and the very old. They were dressed, or not dressed, in every conceivable fashion, each according to his taste; rags, body-paint, flowing things, flapping things, no things. Some were shaven bald as eggs, others had hair to their knees. Some were adorned with flowers or plucked branches hung with fruit. Some affected tufts of leaves, or feathers or garlands of the potent love-weed. These were the blessed children of the Lords Protector, the weak to be succored, the homeless to be sheltered, the hungry to be fed. Happy children, blowing free with the winds of the world, living only for the day because the years of Old Sun were numbered and there was no time to waste on anything but love and joy.

Their other name was mob.

The ones in the outer fields saw Stark's troop first. They stopped their trampling and stared. The stopping and staring spread gradually inward toward the wall, until the whole motley crowd of them had fallen quiet.

They stared across a level space of turf at the company that had appeared so suddenly from among the low hills above Tregad. They saw the Dark Man on the dappled beast, the huge white hounds, Halk and the sun-haired woman and the off-world man, the winged Fallarin glinting with gold in the sunlight, the Tarf with their striped bellies and four-handed swords, the tribesmen in their leather cloaks, the villagers with crude weapons and faces full of hate.

They stared, startled and agape, until they realized how small a troop it was and who was leading it.

A single voice, a woman's voice, cried out, "The Dark Man and the whore of Irnan!"

Mob shout, mob yell.

"The Dark Man and the whore!"

A woman, slim and naked, with body-paint laid on in whorls of pink and silver, pushed her way from the crowd and leaped onto a farm wagon abandoned in the fields. She was graceful and young and her hair was like a dark cloud around her head.

Stark knew her. "Baya."

So did Halk. "I told you then to kill her, Dark Man. Did I not?"

Baya shouted to the mob. "I was at Irnan! I saw the arrows fly. I saw the Wandsmen butchered. I saw the Farers slain . . . *because of them!*"

She flung out her arm toward Stark and Gerrith, her body bent like a bow.

"The star-spawn and the red-haired bitch whose mother made the prophecy!"

The mob gave tongue, a strange wild high-pitched scream.

Gerrith said, "That is the girl you brought from Skeg?"

"It is." Baya had made the first contact there with Stark, leading him to Gelmar and a deadly trap beside the milky sea. She had led the search for him after he escaped, when Yarrod and his group from Irnan hid him among the ruins beyond the river. Stark remembered how he had broken up a particularly nasty business involving two of Baya's Farer companions, high on love-weed, and had then been faced with the choice of killing the girl to keep her mouth shut or bringing her along on the journey to Irnan. He had chosen to do the latter. Mordach, Chief Wandsman of Irnan, freed her when he took Stark and Yarrod's people prisoner. Stark had not seen her again. He had wondered if she survived the slaughter in the city. Now he knew.

"These are the ones we came to take!" she was crying. "Let the traitors of Tregad rot behind their walls, we don't need them. Kill the Dark Man! Kill the whore! Kill! Kill! Kill!"

She leapt from the wagon and began to run across the turf, naked and lithe and light, hair flying behind her. Her name meant Graceful, and she was. Gerd snarled and lifted his hackles, his head against Stark's knee.

N'Chaka. Kill?

The blood-cry of the mob shook the heart. The Farers began to move, not as one man, but in groups, patches, swirls, until the whole of the mass was in motion. They were armed only with such things as stones and sticks and knives, an assortment of weapons as haphazard as themselves. But they were a good four thousand strong. They were not afraid.

The Fallarin had formed their crescent. They began to chant.

The tribesmen had swung into a V formation, with Stark and Halk at the apex and the villagers between the wings.

"Archers," said Stark. "And keep together. Head straight for the gate. Above all, don't stop."

Arrows were nocked to strings. The mob streamed toward them, a flapping bobbing grotesque multitude with that single slender form fleeting ahead.

The first sharp gust of wind knocked Baya from her feet. Her pink-and-silver body rolled on the green turf. The Fallarin moved forward, hunched in their saddles, dark wings beating, voices harsh and commanding. Magic or mind-force, the winds obeyed it. They whirled and beat, lashing hair and garments, pelting the Farers with leaves and twigs and heads of broken grain, chaff to sting and blind the eyes.

The mob mass faltered and began to stumble. The winds drove group against group, spreading confusion which fed upon itself.

Stark raised his arm, and a tribesman in Hann purple put a horn to his lips and blew a strident call.

Stark said to the hounds, *Now kill!*

He kicked his beast into a run, heard the troop move behind him. Gerd ran at his knee. The winds dropped as suddenly as they had begun. Bowstrings twanged. He saw Farers dropping, spinning away. The floundering mob was split before him and he crashed on into the opening.

Fallarin and Tarf closed up swiftly behind the wings of the V. The beasts began to stumble over bodies. Halk was shouting a battle-cry that Stark had heard once before, in the square at Irnan: "Yarrod! Yarrod! Yarrod!" Stark looked at the gates of Tregad, and they were still far away and they were still shut. The mass of Farers seemed to be clotting and compacting ahead, between him and the gate.

There were too many of them. Swords rose and fell with increasing desperation. The hounds could not kill enough, could not kill fast enough. From out the milling screaming horde stones came flying. Stones are cloddish weapons, without grace or beauty, but they function. Stark shouted, urging the men on, fighting off a horrible vision of the mob rolling in like water in the wake of the troop and submerging it by sheer weight of numbers.

Ponderously, with what seemed like dreamlike slowness, the gates of Tregad swung open.

Armed men poured out. A torrent of them. Hundreds of them. No sortie, but a full-scale attack. They fell upon the Farers with the ferocity of a long hatred, spilling blood into the fields as payment for the murdered grain.

Archers and slingers appeared upon the walls. A mounted troop rode out. Farers began to run. The solid mass broke. Bits of it shredded away, and the armed men moved through the chaos, smiting, until the shredding became a rout and the Farers were fleeing for the hills, leaving their dead in heaps amid the wreckage they had made.

A comparative quiet came over the field. Tregadians went among the wounded or leaned on their arms and stared at the strangers. Stark rallied his folk. Some had been hurt by flying stones, and one of the Tarf was dead. Three of the villagers were missing. He sent Sabak and some others to search for them.

Alderyk looked after the Farers, who were still being harried by the mounted troop and the more energetic foot. "The cold north has something to recommend it, after all," he said.

"You have the Runners."

"They don't pretend to be human," Alderyk said, "and we're not obliged to keep them fed."

The mounted troop turned and came back, having seen the Farers well on their way. An old man rode at the head of it, a fierce old man, all eyebrows and cheekbones and jut nose and thrusting chin. Locks of gray hair hung from under a round hard leather cap. His body-leather was worn and stained with use, and his sword was plain, with a broad blade and a sturdy grip, made for a day's work.

His black eyes probed at Stark, darted to Gerrith and Ashton, to the Fallarin and the Tarf, back to the hounds and Tuchvar. Those eyes were startlingly young and bright with angry excitement.

"You bring an interesting assortment of talents, Dark Man."

"Is that why you waited so long?" Stark asked. "To see what we could do?"

"I was impressed. Besides, it was my attack you were interfering with. I might ask you why you didn't wait until we were ready." He sheathed his sword. "I am Delvor, Warlord of Tregad." He bowed with a stiff courtliness to Alderyk and his Fallarin. "My lords, you are welcome in my city." In turn he greeted the others. "You find us at a moment of sudden event. Those ornaments on the wall are still warm."

He faced Stark abruptly and said, "Dark Man. I have heard one story and another story, all from Wandsmen and Farers. Now I want to hear the true one. Has the Citadel fallen?"

"It has. Ask Ashton, who was prisoned there. Ask the North-hounds, who were its guardians. Ask the Hooded Men, who heard of it through Gelmar himself, the Chief Wandsman of Skeg."

Delvor nodded slowly. "I was sure, even though the Wandsmen said no and the Farers said lie. But it is strange, then . . ."

"What is?"

"The Lords Protector. The mighty ones who dwelt at the Citadel. Where are they? Or were they only a myth?"

"They're no myth," Stark said. "They're old men, red Wandsmen moved up to the top of the ladder where there's only room for seven.

They wear white robes and do the ultimate thinking, remote and cool and unhurried by the urgencies of the moment. They make the policies that run your world, but they're making them at Ged Darod now, instead of at the Citadel."

"At Ged Darod," Delvor said. "The Lords Protector, undying and unchanging . . . Seven old men, turned out of their beds and their immortality, running for shelter at Ged Darod. Is this what you're telling me?"

"Yes."

"And yet there is no word of it? No beating of the breast, no crying of woe among the faithful? Those several thousand vermin didn't know it."

"They'll have to know in time," Stark said. "The Wandsmen can't keep it secret forever."

"No," said Halk. "But they haven't got to tell the truth, either." He looked almost himself again, holding the bloody sword, his face streaked with the sweat of battle. He laughed at Stark. "These Lords Protector are going to be harder to destroy than you thought, Dark Man."

"Come," said Delvor. "I forget my manners."

They rode toward the gate, and the soldiers of Tregad raised a ragged cheer.

Stark squinted up at the Wandsmen dangling on the wall. "The red one wouldn't be Gelmar, I suppose?"

"No, that was our Chief Wandsman. One Welnic. Not a bad sort until he bethought him of his duty."

"What happened here?"

Delvor bent his black gaze upon the Farer dead sprawled amid crushed grain. "They came swarming out of the hills this morning. We're used to Farers, the gods know, but they run in small packs normally, drifting in and out. These were in their thousands, and for a purpose. We didn't like the look of them. We shut the gates. One of those—" He pointed to a green Wandsman swinging gently in the breeze, "a one-eyed man, slightly mad, I think, was leading them. He raged at us, and Welnic insisted that he be let in to talk. So we let him through the postern, with the mob howling outside. They'd been sent from Ged Darod. It was thought that you were coming here to try and raise troops for Irnan, and they meant to trap you here in my city. I might not have minded that so much, since no decision had been made . . ."

"You were still waiting," Halk said, "for word from the north."

"Prophecies are all very well," said Delvor coldly, "but one does not go to war on the strength of a simple statement that thus or such will happen."

"We did."

"It was your prophecy. We preferred to wait." He gestured impatiently and got back to the subject. "The Farers had been brought to take over our city, to make sure that you got no help from us. The people of Tregad were to be used as hostages. They felt that you would hesitate to use your several weapons against us, and so you could be more easily disarmed and taken. We refused to have our people so endangered. That madman, that one-eyed swine, told us that if some of them had to die, it was in a good cause, and he bade us open the gate to his mob, which was already screaming threats and damaging our fields. We became even more angry when Welnic told us we would have to obey. When we did not, the Wandsmen tried to open the gates themselves. You see where they ended."

His restless gaze stabbed at them. "They pushed us too far, you see. We might never have gone over. We might have sat debating and havering until Old Sun fell out of the sky. But they pushed us too far."

"So they did at Irnan," said Stark.

As they came under the wall, he was able to distinguish the individual features of the Wandsmen. Distorted and discolored as it was, there was no mistaking one of those faces, with the livid scar marring all of one side from brow to chin.

"Vasth," he said.

Halk, recognizing his handiwork, said harshly, "He will trouble decent men no more. You've done well here, Delvor."

"I hope so. There are many who will not agree."

"One thing puzzles me. Were there no mercenaries quartered on you, as there were at Irnan?"

"Only a token force. The rest had been sent as reinforcements to the siege. The Wandsmen were desperately anxious that Irnan should fall. I keep my men well trained to arms. We were able to deal with the mercenaries."

They passed in through the long tunnel of the gateway, into the square beyond, a cobbled space surrounded by walls of honey-colored stone. People straggled about, looking dazed by the swift turn of things, talking in low voices. They fell silent as the cavalcade came in and turned to stare. At the Dark Man and the whore of Irnan, Stark thought, wondering if Baya had escaped a second time.

Trail-worn and tired, they dismounted from their lean and foot-sore beasts; the tall desert beasts so out of place here. The tribesmen shook the dust from their cloaks and stood proudly, their veiled faces giving an impression of remote impassivity beneath their hoods, fierce eyes fixed resolutely on nothing, refusing to be awed by crowds or buildings.

The Fallarin, dainty as winged cats, stepped lightly down. The hundred Tarf, in quiet ranks, blinked in mild unconcern at the townsfolk.

"I wonder," said Ashton, "that Gelmar didn't come himself to Tregad."

"Probably," Stark said, "he has something more important to attend to." His face hardened. "We all know that as soon as word of this day's work gets back to Ged Darod, Gelmar will be on his way to Skeg to shut down the starport."

20

It was warm in the woods, shadowed and warm and quiet. Branches were thick overhead, screening out Old Sun. The hollow was rimmed with flowering bushes and lined with golden moss. The tiny stream that ran through the hollow whispered and chuckled to itself, almost too softly to be heard. The smells were sweet and drowsy. Now and then a bird called somewhere, or some small creature rustled, or the brown shag-coated riding animals whuffled contentedly at their tethers. It was altogether a pleasant place to sit on an afternoon, after all the cold deserts and bitter winds and hard riding. Tuchvar had difficulty keeping his eyes open.

He had to. He was on watch.

Because he knew the way to Ged Darod and could handle the hounds, the Dark Man had chosen him as guide and companion. Him alone.

The hounds slept, thirteen great white sprawls on the moss. It saddened Tuchvar to see them so gaunt, and he tried to convince himself that they looked better than they had. They twitched and groaned and muttered in their sleep. He was aware of them as they dreamed; fleeting scraps of memory, of hunts and fights and mating and feeding and killing. The old hounds remembered mist and snow and the free-running of the pack.

The Dark Man slept, too, with Gerd's head resting on his thigh and Grith snoring by his other side. Tuchvar peeped at him sidelong, feeling like an intruder and afraid that at any moment those strange clear eyes would open and catch him at it. Even in sleep the man was powerful. Tuchvar felt that if he were to creep toward that muscled body, relaxed and sprawled like those of the hounds, no matter how quietly he went it would spring up all in a second before he could reach it, and those long-fingered hands would have him by the throat.

But they would not kill him until the brain behind the disconcerting eyes had considered and made that decision.

Control. That was the strength one felt in the Dark Man. Strength that went beyond the physical. Strength that the big tall man with the big long sword did not have, and perhaps that was why he disliked the Dark Man so much, because he knew that he lacked this strength himself, and envied it.

Stark's face fascinated Tuchvar. Had, since he first saw it there at Yurunna. He thought it was beautiful in its own way. Subtly alien. Brooding, black-browned, with a structure that might have been hammered out of old iron. A warrior's face, scarred by old battles. A killer's face, but without cruelty, and when he smiled it was like sunlight breaking through clouds. Now, in the unguarded innocence of sleep, Tuchvar saw something there that he had never noticed before. It was sadness. In his dreams, it seemed, the Dark Man remembered lost things and mourned them, not unlike the hounds.

He wondered where, across the wide and starry universe, on what remote and unimagined worlds, Stark might have lost those things, and what they might have been.

He wondered if he himself would ever get beyond the narrow skies of Skaith.

Not if the Wandsmen had their way.

It made him hurt inside to think that with one single word they could make those skies a prison for him, forever.

The Dark Man stirred, and Tuchvar became busy with the fastenings of his blue smock. He had put off the gray tunic of an apprentice Wandsman at Tregad. He had not chosen to wear it in the first place, and he had grown to hate it.

Being an orphan, he had come into the care of the Wandsmen; and Welnic, finding him more intelligent than most, had sent him to Ged Darod to be educated. That was a prideful thing, to be chosen, and even though he was made to study hard and learn the virtues of service and self-abnegation, the off-times in the lower city were a carnival, a fair that never ended.

Then they sent him north to Yurunna, and that was a different story. Cold and bleak, half-lifeless above the unpleasant oasis, the city had oppressed him with a sense of the unnatural. There was no laughter in those cheerless streets, no activity except the Yur, with their blank faces and empty eyes, going about their regimented business. One never saw their women or their young ones. No children played. No one ever sang, or shouted, or quarreled, or made music. There was nothing to do. The senior Wandsmen kept to themselves. The Houndmaster had been a harsh disciplinarian; Tuchvar had wept no tears for him, though he recognized the man's devotion to the hounds. He himself had become attached to the brutes for lack of anything better. Varik had not been much, as an only companion. He had elected with snuffling loyalty to remain with the Wandsman being held at Yurunna, rather than aid the forces of subversion. Tuchvar wondered how he was, and hoped that he was miserable.

It was Pedrallon and the Wandsmen's treatment of him that had made Tuchvar begin to question the system to which he was apprenticed.

His eyes were on the stars. He lived for the day when he could go to Skeg and actually see the ships and the men from other worlds. He was passionately on the side of the Irnanese, and he had worshipped Pedrallon, from his humble distance, for saying that the Irnanese were right and the Wandsmen wrong. And then Pedrallon had been silenced, punished, put to shame. He himself had been given a tongue-lashing by his mentor and soon after had found himself packed off to Yurunna.

He had begun to think, for the first time in his life. Really think, trying to separate the deed from the word and the word from the truth, getting hopelessly confused because here there was nothing one could put one's hand on, only uncertainties and perhapses. But he decided at the last that in any case he wanted the stars more than he wanted to be a Wandsman, and if the Wandsmen were going to forbid him the stars, he would fight them in any way he could.

Beyond the trees, shimmering in the midst of the plain, lay Ged Darod, golden roofs and thronging multitudes, with the great towers of the upper city reared like a benison over all. Memories swept across Tuchvar's mind in a crushing wave, memories of power, deep-seated and very old, as strong as the foundations of the world. His belly contracted with a pang of dismal certainty.

Surely not even the Dark Man could overcome that power.

He wanted to pound his fists against all frustration. Why were grown men so blind, so stupid, so stubborn, when the answers to everything were so clear and simple? He had stayed for hours in the state hall at Tregad, with its fine pillars and sturdy arches carved in patterns of vines and fruit, listening to the speeches and the arguments. Some were still concerned with the rightness or wrongness of what had been done, as though that mattered now. Some demanded that the city take the Dark Man and his companions prisoner and hand them over to the Wandsmen in the hope of buying forgiveness. These people had had to be forcibly silenced when the Dark Man and his people spoke, telling of the Citadel and Yurunna and urging help for Irnan as a means of freeing Tregad from the yoke of the Wandsmen.

And of course that was the thing to do. Tuchvar could not understand why there was any question about it, why they did not at once raise every man they could spare and march to Irnan. Yet still they talked and argued.

Some said they ought to shut themselves up behind their walls and wait to see what happened. Others wrangled about the starships —whether or not they were worth fighting for, whether or not some or all of the people should emigrate, whether or not both those questions were fruitless because in any case the Wandsmen would send the ships away. Men and women yelled and screamed at each other. Finally Delvor had risen, in his iron and worn leather, and fixed them his fierce glare.

"The stars are nothing to me one way or the other," he said. "Skaith was my mother, and I'm over old for fostering. But I tell you this: Whatever you want, life on another world or a better life right here, you will have to fight for it, and not with words or halfhearts, and you cannot fight alone. The first blow has been struck. Let us strike the second. Let us march to relieve Irnan. And let word be sent among all the city-states that the Citadel has fallen, that the Lords Protector are human and vulnerable men, that we fight for our own freedom, and if they want to get the bloody Farers off their backs, they had better damned well join us!"

Someone had yelled, "Tell 'em to try hanging up a few Wandsmen! It's tonic for the soul."

There had been a lot of cheering, and the majority of people in the hall, those who had had little to say, began to shout, "On to Irnan!" Then somebody shouted, "Yarrod! Yarrod!" like a battle cry, and so the decision was finally made in a bedlam of noise, and Tuchvar understood dimly that this had been the only possible decision all along and that the people had known it.

A little later he had asked the off-worlder with the kind eyes, the man called Ashton for whom Stark had a special look, why it had taken them so long.

"The city-states are democracies," Ashton said. "The curse of all democracies is that they talk too much. On the other hand, the Wandsmen haven't got to talk at all. They simply decree."

So now men were marching toward Irnan, and that had pleased the tall warrior Halk.

The wise woman, with her thick bronze braid of hair and her splendid body, had not seemed happy at all when she said good-bye to Stark. Tuchvar thought he had seen tears glint at the corners of her eyes when she turned away.

He could not know it, but the Dark Man was reliving, in his dreams, an earlier moment spent with Gerrith, the two of them quite alone.

"I have seen a knife, Stark."

"You saw one before, remember? And it was good."

"This is not good."

"Where is the knife? Who wields it?"

"I cannot see . . ."

And her lips came against his, and he tasted salt upon them, the salt of tears . . .

Stark woke, and was in the hollow with Tuchvar and the hounds, and Ged Darod out on the plain. He wondered if the knife waited for him somewhere in those streets. Then he shrugged the thought aside. Knives were no new thing to him. Nor was being wary.

While the boy took food from the saddlebags, Stark went through the trees to where the wood ended above a cliff and he could look out over the plain, green and lush, with Ged Darod in the middle of it like a dream. Golden roofs, roofs tiled and lacquered in scarlet and green and cobalt blue, flashed and glittered in the sunlight. The upper city was built on a slight rise, natural or artificial, and the massive buildings there, with their soaring towers, were of a pure whiteness unrelieved by any color. Roads crossed the plain from all directions, converging upon the city, and the roads were thronged with pilgrims, indistinct masses of tiny figures moving in a haze of dust.

He went back to the hollow and said to Tuchvar, "Tell me again where I will find Pedrallon."

"If he's still kept there . . ."

"I understand that. Tell me."

Tuchvar told him, while he ate and drank, and washed in the running stream, and the sunlight slanted lower. Then the boy watched while Stark opened a bundle and took out the things he had brought from Tregad. Tuchvar had a special interest because Stark had consulted with him on what habit might pass without notice among the mass of pilgrims.

A cloak to conceal somewhat his height and his manner of walking. A hood to cover his head, and a mask or veil, after the manner of the Hooded Men, to hide his face. Stark had considered borrowing a cloak from one of his troopers. He decided against it; any member of any one of the Seven Hearths of Kheb would be a matter of interest to the Wandsmen on sight, and the Farers who had seen the troop at Tregad would pose too much of a threat. So he had chosen a cloak of coarse gray homespun, with a deep hood of a different cut and a cloth of faded blue to wrap about his face. Tuchvar had seen pilgrims in every sort of garb; and some hid this, and some that, and some nothing; he thought Stark's choice of garments would not draw notice.

But when Stark turned to him and asked, "Will I pass," Tuchvar sighed and shook his head.

"You are too much you," he said. "Let your shoulders hang, and don't look at anyone straight . . . you have not a pilgrim's eyes."

Stark smiled. He spoke to the hounds, ordering them to stay with the boy and wait for his return. The young hounds were not concerned. The five whined, Gerd and Grith protesting. In the end they obeyed, though not happily.

Guard Tuchvar, Stark said, *until I come.* He went away between the trees, in the deepening dusk.

21

By the time Stark reached the nearest road, far out across the green plain, it was full night. The Three Ladies rode the sky, serene and splendid, shedding a sweeter light than that of Old Sun, a light almost as bright. He was able to see that the number of pilgrims had not diminished. Half of Skaith, it seemed, was on the way to Ged Darod.

He moved through a thin scatter of stragglers dropped out beside the road and slipped into the stream.

His nose twitched, under the veil, to a variety of smells. Warm dust. Bodies washed and scented, bodies unwashed and stinking. Beast-flesh, sweaty, pungent. An underlying heavy sweetness of potent substances smoked or chewed.

The stream was irregular, moving at different speeds within itself. It clotted up around a huge teetering construction like a wheeled temple, drawn and pushed by scores of naked men and women painted the holy brown of Skaith-Mother. It thinned again to a mere trickle of slow-footed walkers. Everyone moved at his own speed. Close to Stark, completely preoccupied, a man in a dirty shift was dancing his way to Ged Darod, three steps forward, leap, whirl, stamp, then three more steps and whirl again. Beyond him, a woman with hair hanging to her heels, all twined with flowers, moved like a somnambulist, arms held stiffly in front of her; she sang as she went in a high clear voice as sweet as a lark's.

A lank holy man, tattooed from crown to foot with sun symbols, cried out ecstatically to Stark, "Rejoice, for we shall be cleansed of evil!"

Stark muttered, "I rejoice," and passed him by, wondering.

There were others in the stream wearing hooded cloaks, others with their faces hidden. No one gave Stark any special notice. Remembering Tuchvar's caution, he tried not to stride too fast, with too much purpose—a purpose which, he knew all too well, might be completely futile.

It was only a guess, based on the incoherent sobbings of a terrified man, that Pedrallon and his people had ever had a transceiver, let alone that they still had it and were in a position to use it. Pedrallon himself might now be dead or incarcerated too deeply for anyone to find. He might have repented his sins and put himself back in the good graces of the Twelve, in which case even to ask about him would be dangerous. Simply entering Ged Darod was a gigantic risk.

Yet it had to be taken. Otherwise he and Simon Ashton could resign themselves to living out such lives as might be left to them on Mother Skaith, and the Irnanese could forget about emigrating. Short of a miracle. True, shutting down the starport and banishing the ships might lead to scattered landings by avaricious star-captains looking for gain. Some of them, or one of them, might land near Irnan or Tregad and might even accept passengers. But it was too much of a gamble to be taken if there was even a slight chance of communicating with Skeg in time.

Tuchvar had told him that the number of folk on the road was not unusual for this season of the year, and perhaps that was so. Yet Stark felt a strange mood among them. Anticipation. The excitement of great events occurring or about to occur; the excitement of being a part of them. He had no idea if some specific word had been spread among them or if he was witnessing one of those mystic hysterias that sweep over the less stable elements of a population from time to time like an air borne plague. Whichever it was, there were curious echoes in the cries he heard.

From a kind of bower at the top of the great creaking temple thing, a priestess, done up with artificial attributes that would have shocked Skaith-Daughter, kept shouting at the night that all blasphemies would be expunged and all blasphemers punished. A carriage of gilded wood went by, carrying a party of folk from the tropic south, slender men and women in bright silks, their rapt small faces cameos cut in amber. They too cried out about punishments and the feeding of Old Sun. Stark went on, and the distant roofs of Ged Darod glistened ahead, in the light of the Three Ladies.

It was strange that there were no folk going the other way, no pilgrims leaving the city.

He passed a group of men all in yellow robes. Podmasters, seeking more sanctity before they took on another mindless and happy group to lead to communal oblivion and the ultimate fulfillment, death.

He passed more dancers, three women this time, holding hands. Their hair covered their faces. Their white limbs gleamed through flowing garments. There was music for them to dance to, a plucking and twangling of strings, a swelling and fading of pipes, where here and there a pilgrim beguiled his way. But the women did not hear that music. They were listening to a secret melody of their own, measured and solemn.

A large band of Farers grabbed at Stark's cloak and cried, "Words, pilgrim! We will hear words tonight. Are you ready for the truth?" Their eyes were glassy, their breathing heavy with sweet drugs. "The truth that casts out lies and castrates evil?"

"I am ready," Stark answered in a voice of thunder. "Are you? Embrace each other! Love!"

They laughed and did as he told them. One of the women flung her arms about him and kissed him, her lips hot through the veil.

"Stay a while, at the side of the road. I'll show you love." She nuzzled at the veil, catching at it with her teeth. "Why do you hide yourself?"

"I've taken a vow," said Stark, and thrust her gently away.

There was a clear space on the road, where only one man walked alone, eyes fixed on the white towers of Ged Darod.

"They succor the weak, they feed the hungry, they shelter the homeless. They are our fathers, the Lords Protector. They give us all we need."

The man repeated this like a litany. Stark looked into his face and knew that he was on his way to die.

Behind him along the road he began to hear a disturbance. He turned. A party of mounted men moved toward him at a businesslike pace, threading their way through the people, sometimes getting off the road entirely to bypass an obstacle. They were not pilgrims.

Stark melted into the nearest group, which drew aside to make room. The hard-ridden beasts came shouldering by, with six riders. Four of them were Wandsmen. The other two were wrapped and hooded in black cloaks.

Glancing up from under his own hood, Stark caught a glimpse of a face, furred, snow-white, with the great shining eyes of a creature who dwells away from the sun.

For a fleeting second he thought those eyes met his, in the gentle light of the Three Ladies.

A stab of alarm shot through him. But the riders went on; there was no outcry, and if the person in the black cloak had indeed noticed him, there had been no recognition. Stark pulled his veil higher and his hood lower and continued on, not happy with what he had seen.

These were Children of Skaith-Our-Mother. Kell à Marg's folk from the catacombs under the Witchfires. He even thought that he knew the one and could make a guess at the other. Fenn and Ferdic, who had come at him with daggers in the Hall of the Diviners.

He didn't know what they were doing at Ged Darod, so far to the south, out in the open world under the sky they had forsaken so long ago. He did know that he had enough enemies already in the city. He did not need any more.

The walls of Ged Darod rose out of the plain, and there was light above them like a glowing dome. The gates stood open, always open. There were a dozen gates, and each gate served a road. The streams of pilgrims poured through them into the City of the Wandsmen.

It was a city of sound as well as light, and the sound was bells. They hung from the edges of the tiered roofs. They climbed the spires and girdled the golden domes. Thousands of them, swinging free to greet with their clapper tongues each passing breeze, so that the air was full of a sweet soft chiming.

Down in the streets was a fragrance of incense and a jostling of crowds that seemed to lack all rancor, in spite of the numbers of pilgrims that continued to be absorbed into them. People squatted or lay against the walls of the buildings. Balconies overhead held more. Runnels of water went everywhere in stone channels, by way of sanitation, and there was a reason for the incense. It was impossible to provide accommodation for everyone, and the Farers preferred the streets in any case.

Stark was only interested in one hostel, and that was the Refuge, where the Farer girls went to have their babes and leave them for the Wandsmen to rear.

He took his bearings, by Tuchvar's instructions, on a scarlet roof with ten tiers and plunged into the teeming streets.

22

As HE WALKED, he became increasingly aware of the mood of the city.

It waited. It waited with held breath. It waited, like a nerve stretched and rasped beyond endurance, for relief. Each fresh incursion of pilgrims seemed to heighten and exacerbate the tension. The city was a catchbasin, filled to overflowing, with everything coming in and nothing going out.

Yet the people were aimless. They wandered through the streets, thronged into the temples, spilled into squares and gardens. They danced and sang and made love. They prayed and chanted. There were many hostels and places where food and drink were dispensed at all hours. The Wandsmen provided everything their children desired, and Wandsmen of the lesser ranks moved about the city seeing that all was in order.

In the quiet enclaves of Ged Darod, between the temple complex and the upper city, were hospitals for the sick and aged, creches for the orphaned and unwanted, homes for the disabled. No one was turned away, though most of the adult inmates were Farers gone in years who had long ago abandoned home and family and so had nowhere else to go when their Faring days were over.

The temples were magnificent. The ones with the golden roofs were sacred to Old Sun. The others, no less beautiful, belonged to Skaith-Mother, Sea-Mother, Sky-Father and several aspects of the Dark Goddess of the high north and antarctic south. Pilgrims eddied slowly through these vast and solemn spaces, staring at richnesses and beauties such as they had never seen. Awed into silence, they made their offerings and did their worship and went away feeling that they had helped their world to live a little bit longer. The true ecstatics remained until they were gently carried away by the temple custodians.

These were the great temples, the powerful deities. There was a multitude of smaller ones. Even Tuchvar could not say who and what all these deities were or how they were worshipped. There were tales told in the apprentice dormitories at night that might or might not be true. Stark doubted nothing. On Skaith, anything at all was possible.

He came to the Great House of Old Sun, the largest of all the temples, a stunning splendor with its golden roofs and white pillars, all reflected in the huge tank that fronted it. A wall surrounded the tank, a stony lacework of tiny niches, and in each niche a candle burned, so that the water gleamed with a million tiny points of fire. People were bathing in the holy water, in the holy candlefire that symbolized the light of Old Sun, who drives away death and darkness.

Stark went along the right-hand side of the tank, past the temple, and into a street where souvenir sellers offered sun symbols in every size and substance. At the end of this street, Tuchvar had told him, he would see the walls surrounding the Refuge.

Purest white in the light of the Three Ladies, the buildings of the upper city stood above the jumbled roofs like a cliff. Rows and rows of small windows, identical in size, betokened the myriad chambers that lay behind that pale facade. There was much more hidden behind it: a vast complex of living quarters, schools, seminaries and administrative offices, forbidden to the public. Crowning it all was the palace of the Twelve, second only to the Citadel in its importance to the Wandsmen.

The street was clogged, like all the others, with far too many people. Stark moved snail-like, not daring to push and shove, keeping his head down whenever one of the Wandsmen appeared. He strained for a sight of the Refuge, hoping that some way would be apparent for him to approach the building without attracting attention.

He never saw it.

A deep-toned bell pealed out from somewhere high up in the white towers. The sweet chiming of the smaller bells was drowned instantly in that mighty tolling, the prattle of cherubs overborne by the voice of God.

It was the summons for which the city had been waiting, and all over Ged Darod people roused from their aimlessness and began to move.

Trapped in that irresistible tide, Stark moved with them.

He was carried by side streets away from the Refuge, into a vast square below the Wandsmen's city, where an arched gateway pierced the white and many-windowed cliff. The gateway was a tunnel, stepped, rising out of sight. At the nearer end above the square there was a platform thrusting out, a kind of stage.

The bell boomed out its call over the shining roofs, steady, mesmeric, echoed in throbbing eardrums and the beating of the blood. The faithful poured into the square until it could hold no more, and the surrounding streets were blocked by solid masses of humanity. Stuck fast, Stark could do no more than try to work his way by slow degrees toward a place at the edge of the square where there were no buildings. The press was so great that he could not see what was hemming in the crowd there. Whatever it might be, that was the direction in which he wanted to go, for it offered the only hope of openness and possible escape from this heaving, breathing, muttering, stinking trap of bodies.

The bell fell silent.

For a moment the sound continued in Stark's ears—then stillness again, and gradually the sweet small tinkling that seemed very far away now, a mere backdrop for the silence.

A company of Wandsmen in blue tunics came down the steps of the gate, bearing torches. They set the torches in standards around the platform. They drew back and waited.

A company of Wandsmen dressed in green paced down the steps and took up places.

A wait, interminable, bringing a whimper as of pain from the crowd.

The red Wandsmen came, a moving patch of dark crimson in the torchlight. They came in procession, four by four, down the steps and onto the platform, some before and some behind; and in their midst were the Lords Protector, spotless white.

A gasp of indrawn breath from the crowd as the seven men in their white robes moved forward, and then the puzzled whispers began, tossing like surf across the square.

"Who are they? What Wandsmen wear white?"

And of course, Stark thought, they didn't know. They couldn't know. Never in the world before this minute had they seen a Lord Protector.

He began to have a cold premonition of what was coming.

A red Wandsman stepped to the front of the platform and lifted his wand of office like a baton.

"My children!"

His harsh and sonorous voice carried clearly for an amazing distance, and when it reached its limits, other voices took up the message and passed it back through the far ranks of the crowd.

"My children, this is a night of great tidings. A night of joy, a night of hope. The messengers of the Lords Protector have come out of the high north to speak to you. Be silent, then, and listen!"

He stepped, giving place to one of the white robes.

Ferdias. Even at that distance there was no mistaking the ramrod stance and the noble head.

The crowd snuffled and panted in its intense effort to be absolutely still.

"My children," said Ferdias, and his voice was a benison, an outpouring of love. "This has been a time of trial. You have heard many things that were difficult to understand—prophecies of doom, news of revolt and disobedience and the slaying of Wandsmen . . ."

The crowd growled like a monstrous beast.

"Now you will hear more tales. Men will tell you that the prophecy of Irnan was a true prophecy, that the Citadel has fallen to the despoiling hands of a stranger and that the Lords Protector themselves are brought down."

Ferdias waited out the response, holding up his hands.

"It is not true, my children! The Citadel has not fallen, cannot fall. The Citadel is not stone and timber to be burned by a careless torch. It is faith and love, a thing of the spirit, beyond the touch of any man. The Lords Protector who dwell there, undying, unchanging, forever watchful over your needs, are beyond the power of any man to harm. We, their humble servants, who are privileged to hear their wishes, are sent now to bid you forget these lies, to let you know that you are, as always, safe in their protecting care."

Under cover of the tumult, Stark managed to worm his way closer to the edge of the crowd, yelling joyfully with the rest, a sick anger gnawing at his belly. So much for his vaunted destruction of the Lords Protector. There had been an excellent reason for keeping the Citadel so remote; he remembered Skaith-Daughter's cynical remark that invisibility was a condition of godhead. Try now to tell this screaming rabble who the seven old men in white really were!

Ferdias was speaking again, his calm strong voice ringing out; father-voice, firm and kind and true.

"All the evil and disruption that beset us stem from one single event—the coming of the starships. The Lords Protector have been patient because of the benefits these ships could bring to you, their children. And because they love all men, they hoped that the aliens, the strange men from worlds beyond our knowledge, might understand and share that love."

The voice suddenly became a whipcrack.

"It was not so. The strange men brought poison. They encouraged our people to rebel. They threatened our faith. They struck at the very foundations of our society. Now the Lords Protector have made their decision. The ships must go from Skaith, they must be forever gone!"

A subtle change in Ferdias' voice, and Stark had the queer feeling that the Lord Protector was speaking directly to him.

"This night the starport will be closed. There will be no more talk of emigration." The voice paused; barbed and toothed, it spoke again. "There will be no more escape."

Raving and yelling like the idiots around him, Stark moved a little farther and saw a stone balustrade at the edge of the crowd. Beyond it were the tops of trees. Farther beyond, somewhere out of sight, were the walls of the Refuge.

And at Skeg, where the starships stood like towers beside the sea, Gelmar would be marshaling his forces.

The red Wandsman had come again to the fore, waving his arms and his wand, signing the crowd to be quiet.

"Be still and listen! There is more. We have reason to believe that the Dark Man himself, the evil man of the prophecy, may be here in Ged Darod, may be among us now. If so, he wears a hooded cloak and all but his eyes are hidden. You will know him by—"

Stark did not wait to hear what they would know him by, if they took the time to look. He charged like a bull for the balustrade and went over it.

The bastard son of Skaith-Our-Mother had noticed him after all.

23

TREE BRANCHES BROKE his fall. Turf soft and springy as a mattress received him twenty feet below. Stark hit rolling and was on his feet and running before the first man after him came down, too swiftly for his own good, and lay screaming over a broken leg.

Thrashings in the trees told of others climbing down more cautiously. Bedlam had broken out in the square above. Only a small number of people would have seen Stark's leap over the balustrade, and even they could not be certain of his identity. Every man in Ged Darod who had chosen to wear a hooded cloak would at that moment be fighting for his life or running for it as Stark was.

Stark kept his own cloak on until he was out of sight of the people above. No point in letting them see him without it. A small private arbor of vines drooping great pendant flowers gave shelter. He stripped off the cloak and mask and thrust them in among rugs and cushions that rather surprisingly covered the floor. Then he ran again, cursing the name of Fenn, or Ferdic, whichever it might be.

That fleeting instant on the road in which their eyes had met must have remained in the creature's consciousness, pricking at him until he noticed it and began to wonder. Then he began to picture to himself the Earthman's appearance, in the Hall of the Diviners, where they had tried to kill him, and before, in Kell à Marg's throne-room, and he began to think, "Yes, those eyes, the very look and color, and I could swear they knew me."

Damn the Three beautiful Ladies. Damn the night-seeing eyes of a burrowing animal.

Not sure. He could not have been sure. But what did he, or the Wandsmen, have to lose by trying? Only the lives of a few pilgrims who would die at the hands of the mob. A small sacrifice for the chance of catching the Dark Man.

Beyond the arbors were more arbors, amid fountains throwing sprays of scented water. There were broad swards set with curious statuary and peculiar apparatus. There were pavilions with curtains of scarlet silk. There were mazes set with little secret bowers. There were silvery pools that promised delight, and gossamer cages swung high from gaily painted poles to dip and bob in the air. Stark knew where he was now. These were the Pleasure Gardens of Ged Darod, and if it had not been for the summons of the bell, the gardens would have been busy with folk playing at various games, in groups and couples.

There was little pleasure here for Stark. He dodged and darted, using every bit of cover. He outdistanced his pursuers. But even though they had lost sight of him, they hung on, fanning out to search every shadow where he might be hiding, yelping at each other like curs on the track of a wolf.

Outside the gardens, Ged Darod would be in a ferment, with crowds rushing this way and that after victims, their blood-lust at fever pitch. Stark felt the living weight of the city all about him, a devouring entity from which he had little chance of escape.

He fled on in the direction of the Refuge, thinking grimly that he might as well. No place else offered any hope at all. If Pedrallon was by a miracle still there, Stark might be able through him to salvage something out of the ruin, in spite of Ferdias.

There was a sunken place within the garden, paved in patterns of lustrous tile depicting various symbols of Skaith-Mother in her aspect as a fertility goddess. Slim pillars of varying heights were set about, and atop each one was a perch where a creature rested and lazily fanned iridescent wings; huge jewel-colored things resembling butterflies, except that each body was luminous. They glowed like silver lamps upon their perches, and their wings fanned perfume.

"They are dazed with nectar," someone said. "Sodden with honey. Their dreams are sweet."

He saw the woman.

She stood beside a pillar, one arm outstretched to touch it. Her garment was mist-gray and it clung to her like mist, softly, with her full, rounded, graceful body glimmering through it. Her hair was black, coiled high and held by an oddly shaped coronet of hammered silver set with a green stone.

Her eyes were the color of a winter sea where the sun strikes it. He had never seen such eyes. They had depths and darknesses and tides of sudden light in which a man might lose himself and drown.

"I am Sanghalain of Iubar, in the White South," she said. She smiled. "I have waited for you."

"Not another seeress!" said Stark, and he smiled, too, though he could hear the yelping pack in the distance.

She shook her head, and then Stark saw another figure among the pillars.

"My comrade Morn," she said, "has the gift of mind-touch. It is the habit of his people, who live where other speech is difficult."

Morn came forward and stood behind the woman, towering above her, huge-eyed and strange. Not human, Stark thought; not mutated by choice like the Children of the Sea. Some sort of amphibian mammal naturally evolved. He was hairless, with smooth-gleaming skin, dark on the back, light on the belly, camouflage against deep-swimming predators. The smooth skin oozed sweat, and the deep chest heaved uncomfortably. He wore a garment of leather, polished black and worked with gold lines, very rich in appearance, and he carried a trident, its long haft inlaid with gold wire and pearls.

"When we first learned that you might be in the city, we realized you must have come to find Pedrallon. Nothing else could have brought you here. So we stayed by the Refuge while Morn tried to find you. There are so many minds. Not until you broke away from the crowd was he able to recognize you and say where you were. Then we came to meet you." She reached out and took his hand. "We must hurry."

He went with Sanghalain of Iubar and round-eyed Morn, moving silently and at a pace that spoke of urgency. The yelping of the pack diminished as they left the Pleasure Gardens and went by narrow ways that brought them abruptly to a courtyard. Stark saw a coach and a baggage wagon, each with a human driver, and an escort of Morn's folk armed and waiting beside their mounts. The night had grown darker, with the setting of the first of the Three Ladies.

"We were on the point of leaving Ged Darod when the word was brought," said Sanghalain. "Quickly, Stark. Into the coach."

He halted. "No. I came to see Pedrallon."

"He's gone. When he learned that your forces had taken Yurunna, he found means to disappear."

"Where is he, then?"

"I don't know. I have been promised that I will be taken to him." An imperious note came into her voice; she was used to command and impatient of obstruction. "We've already risked a good deal to save you, Stark. Get in, unless you wish to die in this madhouse."

A mournful far-off something spoke in his mind like the distant crying of a seabird.

She speaks the truth. We wait no longer.

Morn shifted the heavy trident in his hands.

Stark hesitated only briefly. He got in.

The coach was a heavy thing constructed for long journeys rather than for grace of line. It was made of a black wood, carved and polished, and it had a hood of fine leather against sun and rain. Inside were soft rugs and cushions on a padded floor, so that a lady might ride in comfort, and at the rear was a compartment where things to be used at night or in cold weather could be stored out of the way.

The compartment had been emptied. At Sanghalain's direction Stark crammed himself into it, and she deftly covered him with spare rugs, arranged the cushions and leaned herself against them.

He could feel her weight. Almost before it was settled, the coach began to move. Hard hoofs drummed and clattered on the stones. There was the creak and jingle of harness and the clacking of the wheels. Other than that there was no sound. If Morn and his folk had speech at all, they did not use it.

The company left the courtyard and went a little way at a fair pace. Then the streets of Ged Darod closed around them.

Sounds echoed strangely in Stark's wooden box. Voices boomed and roared, sometimes indistinct, sometimes with startling clarity.

"Irnan! On to Irnan! Save the siege!"

And something was said about the Dark Man.

Fists pounded on the body of the coach. It rocked and jolted where the crowd pushed against it in spite of the mounted escort. Movement was slowed to a crawl. Still, they did move. They moved for a long time. Stark thought they must be nearing one of the gates. Then Sanghalain spoke sharply, just loud enough for him to hear.

"Be very quiet. Wandsmen."

The coach halted. Stark heard the same harsh sonorous voice that had spoken from the platform.

"You're in great haste to leave us, Lady Sanghalain."

Her answer was as cold as the waves that break along the foot of an iceberg.

"I came here to ask help. I did not receive it. I no longer have any reason to remain."

"Would it not have been wiser to wait for morning?"

"If you want the truth, Jal Bartha, I find your city disgusting and your rabble loathsome. I prefer to be away from both as soon as possible."

"You take a harsh attitude, my lady. It was explained to you why your request could not be granted. You must have faith in the Lords Protector. All will be made right in time."

"In time," said Sanghalain, "we shall all be dead and beyond caring. Be kind enough to stand aside, Jal Bartha."

The coach began faltering on its way again. After an interminable period the motion became freer. Noise and jostling subsided. The pace picked up.

Stark dared for the first time to move, easing cramped muscles.

Sanghalain said, "Not yet. Too many on the road." A little later she added, "It will soon be dark."

When the last of the Three Ladies had set, some time would elapse before Old Sun rose. Stark had no idea what direction they had taken from Ged Darod, nor who the Lady Sanghalain was, or where Iubar might be in the White South; and he could not be sure that she was telling the truth about Pedrallon, though it sounded reasonable. The one thing he was sure of was that she had saved his life, and he decided to be content with that. For the rest of it, he was forced to contain his soul and his aching bones in such patience as he could muster—thinking of the ships at Skeg, thinking of the flame and thunder of their going, thinking of himself and Ashton left behind.

The coach turned sharply off the road and went for a long distance over open ground. After a lot of jolting and bouncing it came to a halt and Sanghalain pulled away the cushions.

"It's safe now."

He climbed out as from a coffin, gratefully. It was dark. He made out branches against the sky and the trunks of trees against a lesser gloom beyond. They were in some kind of a grove. The escort had lighted down and were tending their beasts.

"Care was taken that no one should see us leave the road," said Sanghalain. "We are to wait here until the Wandsman comes."

24

Stark stared at the pale blur of her face in the gloom, wishing he could see her eyes, marking the place where her throat would be.

He said very softly, "What Wandsman?"

She laughed. "What menace! There is no danger, Dark Man. If I had wanted to betray you, I could have done it more easily at Ged Darod."

"*What Wandsman?*"

"His name is Llandric. It was he who told me about Pedrallon. Who told me that one of the strangers in the black cloaks thought he might have seen you on the road. Llandric is Pedrallon's man."

"Can you be so sure?"

"Very sure. No one lies to Morn."

"And Morn was present?"

"Morn is always present at such a time. I could not rule Iubar without Morn."

Again the far sad voice in Stark's mind, dim echoing of sea caves under storm.

She tells the truth. No treachery.

Stark let himself relax. "Does Pedrallon still have access to the transceiver?"

"So I was told. I understand it is a thing that speaks over distances almost as quickly as the Ssussminh do." She gave the word a long rolling sound. *Soosmeeng*, like surf on shingle, and Stark understood that she referred to Morn's people.

"Where is it?"

"Wherever Pedrallon is. We must wait."

Wait and be patient, he thought, while Gelmar is sweeping Skeg clean with his broom of Farers.

The driver of the coach brought wine in a leather bottle and two silver cups. They drank, in the mild night, and Stark listened, hearing nothing but the rustle of leaves overhead, the cropping and stamping and blowing of the beasts.

"What brought you to Ged Darod?" he asked her. "What did you want from the Wandsmen that you didn't get?" Her attitude toward the red Wandsman Jal Bartha had indeed been harsh.

"The same thing the people of Irnan asked for and didn't get," she answered. "Our life has become all but intolerable."

"Because of the Wandsmen?"

"No. We're too far away for Farers and oppression, not rich enough to warrant mercenaries. So poor, in fact, and so unimportant that I thought they wouldn't stop our going. I came all this long way north, in the hope—"

She broke off. He sensed her anger, the same futile rage he himself had felt as he battered at the stone wall of the Wandsmen's power. He also sensed that there were no tears ready to come. Sanghalain was too strong for that.

"Where is Iubar?"

"Far to the south, where a peninsula juts into the Great Sea of Skaith. We used to be a prosperous country of fisherfolk and farmers and traders. Our galleys went everywhere, and if we had then to pay our tithes to the Wandsmen, we had enough. Things are different now. The great bergs come from the south, as do the blind mists, to kill our ships. Snow lies deep and long on our fields. The Children of the Sea despoil our fisheries, and the Kings of the White Isles raid our shores. I and my order have some power to protect, but we cannot heal Mother Skaith, who is dying. If we move north, we must fight for every foot of land against the folk who hold it, and they are stronger than we. Whichever way we look, we see death." She paused and added, "A madness has begun to creep among our people, which is even worse."

She was silent for a time. Stark, listening, heard nothing beyond the grove.

She was talking again, her voice low, with a hint of weariness. "Traders and sea gypsies brought us tales of the starships and the men from beyond the sky. We considered, and it seemed that here was a possibility of escape for our people. I took ship and came north to Skeg, to see for myself. The starships were there, and the foreign men, but I was not allowed to approach them. The Wandsmen would not permit it. When I asked them where I could obtain permission, they told me the authority was at Ged Darod. At Ged Darod I was told—but you know what they said, and so my long journey was for nothing, unless Pedrallon can help." She laughed with intense bitterness. "The strangers in the black cloaks had come to ask that the starships be sent away for the safety of Mother Skaith. But the Lords Protector had already taken that step, so they too had made their trip for nothing."

Morn's voice echoed in Stark's mind. *He comes. Alone.*

It was several minutes before Stark's ears picked up the soft thudding of hoofs. A man rode in among the trees, a dim shape, dark on a dark mount.

"Lady Sanghalain?" His voice was young, strained with excitement and an awareness of danger. It broke off, quivering, as he became aware of Stark's bulk beside the woman. "Who is that?"

"Eric John Stark," he said. "I am called the Dark Man."

Silence. Then a letting out of held breath. "You did escape. Ged Darod has been seething with rumors. Some said you were killed . . . I saw several bodies. Others said you were concealed somewhere, or had got away, or had never been there at all. Jal Bartha and the Children of Skaith were all over the city looking at the dead—"

Stark cut him short. "We wish to see Pedrallon."

"Yes. My lady, we'll have to leave the coach and wagon here, and your escort, too."

"Not Morn."

"All right, but no more. Can you ride?"

"As well as you." She caught up a cloak, and Morn lifted her from the coach to the back of one of the beasts. "Give Stark one, too."

"How far have we to go?"

"An hour's hard ride to the east," said Llandric, sounding less than happy that his expected party of two had doubled. Probably he would have preferred to have Pedrallon's permission. If that gave him problems, Stark couldn't help it.

They came out of the grove into the open starlight of the plain; starlight dim enough to prevent them being seen at any great distance.

Even so, Llandric was nervous.

"The Farers are out," he said. "Wandsmen are leading them to the siege. Did Tregad send a force to Irnan?"

"It's on its way now."

"So is an army of Farers, with a short road through the mountains."

Several times they saw torches in the distance, tiny flecks of fire moving across the landscape. Stark hoped that Tuchvar and the hounds were safely hidden in the hollow. The lad would have to use his own judgment if things became threatening.

The country turned rougher and wilder, smooth plain giving way to tumbled hummocks and clumps of tough grass that made bad footing for the animals. Llandric urged them on, peering anxiously at the sky. By Stark's reckoning, a good hour and a bit more had elapsed by the time the rough ground ended at the edge of a vast and pallid swamp, where small dark men quick and wild as otters were waiting for them.

Each one took a beast by the bridle and led it, first along planks that were quickly taken up behind, leaving no trace of hoofprints, and then along some trail that was hidden in knee-deep water. There was a rank wet smell of stagnant shallows and the weedy things that love them. Low-growing trees roofed the riders with pale leaves, shutting out the starshine. Ghost-white trunks loomed faintly, crouching in the water with their knees up. It was pitch black, yet the small men waded on without pause, winding and twisting until Stark had lost all sense of direction.

They came out at last on a muddy island. Dismounting, they walked a short distance along a path with crowding shrubbery on either side, heavy with night-blooming blossoms. Stark saw a glint of light ahead, made out a long low structure all but invisible among taller trees.

Llandric, leading the way, tapped in a ritual sequence on some brittle material that was not wood.

There was a sudden burst of static inside, beyond thin walls, and a voice said clearly:

"They're spreading, getting higher. Half of Skeg must be burning."

A door opened, spilling light. A man looked out at them and said testily, "Come in, come in." He turned away unceremoniously, more interested in what was going on in the room than he was in them. As courteously as he could, to make up for it, Llandric handed the Lady Sanghalain over the threshold. Morn followed her, stooping his bare bullet head almost to his chest. Stark followed him.

The house was built of reeds, bundled and tied or woven to form the ribs and walls. The technique with which it was done was so sophisticated, the patterns so intricate, that Stark knew it must be the age-old art of the dark marsh-dwelling people. Other islands must dot the swamp, where their secret villages were hidden. If outsiders came unbidden, the inhabitants would simply retire, knowing that when the intruders became sufficiently bored with floundering and drowning, they would go away. Or if they preferred, they might smile and agree to lead a search party. The marsh-dwellers could lead it for weeks without bringing it to this particular island, with no one the wiser. No wonder the Wandsmen had not found the transceiver or Pedrallon.

The transceiver stood at the end of the long room, a simple, rugged workhorse with a practically inexhaustible power pack and foolproof controls. The metallic voice was speaking from it again, in accented Skaithian.

"The shop's been shut, Pedrallon. I may as well go home." A pause. "Hear that?"

In the background a roar of thunder split an unseen sky.

"There goes another one. I'm sixth in line."

There was a note of finality, as though he were about to sign off.

"Wait!" The man in the silk robe who sat cross-legged on the reed mat in front of the transceiver all but struck the thing in his urgency. "Wait, Penkawr-Che! Someone has come speak to you." He glanced over his shoulder, and his eyes widened as he saw Stark. "Yes. Someone has come. Will you wait?"

"Five minutes. No more. I've told you, Pedrallon—"

"Yes, yes, you have." Pedrallon had come to his feet. He was a slender man, graceful and quick, with the amber skin of the tropics. Somehow Stark was surprised that the richest, fattest, most comfortable segment of the planet's population would have produced the rebel Pedrallon, whose own people were under no imminent threat of any kind. He became aware at once of the tremendous vitality of the man, an intensity of feeling and purpose that made his dark eyes blaze with fires that were banked only by an iron will.

Pedrallon's gaze noted Sanghalain, rested briefly on Morn, fastened on Stark.

"I expected the Lady of Iubar. I did not expect you."

Llandric said, "He was there. I had to—I thought you would want—" He forced himself to make a complete sentence. "This is the Dark Man."

"I know," said Pedrallon.

Hate showed in his face, naked and startling.

25

In a moment the look was gone, and Pedrallon was speaking with swift urgency.

"I've been in touch with Penkawr-Che for some time. I've not been able to persuade him to join in any scheme for taking people away from Skaith. Perhaps one of you will have better luck."

Stark thrust Sanghalain forward. "Speak to him." She looked uncertainly at the black box, and he pointed to the microphone. "There."

"Penkawr-Che?"

"Make it fast."

"I am Sanghalain of Iubar in the White South. I have authority to promise you half of all my country's treasure, which is in my keeping, if you will take my people—"

The hard metallic voice cut her short. "Take them where? Where would I drop them, on what world that never heard of them and doesn't want them? They would be massacred; and if the Galactic Union caught me, I'd lose my license, my ship and twenty years of my life, along with that half of your country's treasure. The GU frowns on the smuggling of people. Besides . . ." The man took a long breath. When he spoke again, it was with the clenched-teeth distinctness of exasperation. "As I have tried repeatedly to explain, one ship could accommodate only a fraction of your population. Removing any number would require several ships and several landings, and on the second one I have no doubt that the Wandsmen would be waiting for us with a reception party. Two of your five minutes are up."

Sanghalain, flushed with anger, leaned closer to the black box. "But surely you could come to some arrangement, if you wanted—"

"Your pardon, my lady," Stark said, and moved her firmly aside. "Penkawr-Che."

"Who is that?"

"Tell him, Pedrallon."

Pedrallon told him, each phrase as flat and cracking as a pistol shot.

"The off-worlder Stark, the Dark Man of the prophecy, come back from the north. He pulled down the Citadel. He pulled down Yurunna. He drove the Lords Protector into hiding at Ged Darod. He has been at Tregad with an army, Tregad has revolted and sent a force to Irnan to break the siege."

Penkawr-Che laughed. "So much, friend Pedrallon? Yet I hear no joy in your voice. Why is that, I wonder? Old loyalties still twining in the heartstrings?"

"I point out to you," said Pedrallon coldly, "that the situation has changed."

"It has indeed. Skeg is going up in flames, every off-worlder in the enclave has had to run for his life, and we're told that if we ever come back to Skaith, we'll be killed on sight. So?"

"So," said Stark, "I brought Simon Ashton back from the Citadel."

"Ashton?" He could picture the man in the com-room of the ship sitting bolt upright. "Ashton's alive?"

"He is. Take him to Pax, and the Galactic Union will hail you as a hero. Take as many leaders of Irnan and Tregad as you can manage, and be hailed as a humanitarian. As delegates, they can go to Pax with Ashton, and the bureaucrats will deal with all those problems you find so insoluble. They may even reward you. I can guarantee that the Irnanese will pay you well."

"And I," said Pedrallon. "I've already given you one fortune. I'm willing to give another."

"Now," said Penkawr-Che, "I'm interested. Where is Ashton?"

"On the way to Irnan."

"There'll be a battle there. I'll not risk my ship—"

"We'll win it."

"You can't guarantee that, Stark."

"No. But you can."

A new note in the man's voice, a poised withdrawal. "How?"

"You must have some planet-hoppers aboard."

The voice loosened somewhat. "I've got four."

"Armed?"

"Considering the places I get into, they have to be."

"That's what I thought. Do they have, or can you rig, loud-hailers?"

"Yes."

"Then all I need is four good pilots. How many passengers can you take?"

"Not above twenty this trip. My pressurized cargo space is pretty full, and cabins I have none."

"What about your colleagues? Would any of them be interested?"

"I'll ask."

The transceiver clicked and was silent.

Sanghalain had been looking at Stark. Bars of color burned on her cheekbones, and her eyes had gone all wintry, stormy gray with no sunlight. Morn loomed over her, the massive trident cradled in his hands.

"What of me, Stark? What of my people?"

He could see why she was angry with him; his action must have appeared both high-handed and ungrateful.

"Go with Ashton and the others," he said. "Plead your case at Pax. The more of you there are to ask for help, the more likely it is that the Union will grant it."

She continued to stare at him steadily. "I do not understand Pax. I do not understand the Union."

Pedrallon broke in, his voice vibrant with excitement. "There is much we cannot understand. But I propose to go, and I—"

Morn shook his head and motioned Pedrallon to silence. *My way is best for Sanghalain,* he said in Stark's mind. *Think.*

Sanghalain gave Morn a little startled glance, and then stood quietly, in an attitude of listening.

Stark thought.

He thought of Pax, the city that had swallowed up a planet: high, deep, broad, complex, teeming with its billions from all across the galaxy, frightening, beautiful, without compare.

He thought of Power, which was another name for Union. He thought of far-ranging law. He thought of freedom and peace and prosperity. He thought of ships that flashed between the suns.

As well as a man could, he thought of the Galaxy.

Infinitely swifter and more powerful than words, these thoughts passed from his mind to Sanghalain's, with Morn acting as the bridge, and he saw her expression change.

Morn said, *Enough.*

Sanghalain, wide-eyed, whispered, "Indeed, I did not understand."

"Ashton has some importance in that society. He will do all he can to help your people."

She nodded uncertainly and became immersed in her own thoughts.

The transceiver crackled. Penkawr-Che's voice came on again.

"No takers. Most of them have refugees aboard." Apparently Penkawr-Che did not. "Some have full cargoes or won't risk an open landing. You'll have to be satisfied with me. Where do we rendezvous?"

The arrangements were made.

"Keep them out from under, Stark, when I come down. They don't seem to understand things very well." Noises in the background told of another ship lifting off. "Really my turn now. Gods, you're missing something, though. A burning city is a lovely sight. I hope some of Gelmar's little Farers roast their arses in it."

A click, and silence.

Stark said, "How well do you know this man, Pedrallon? Can he be trusted?"

"No more than any off-worlder."

Pedrallon faced Stark squarely, and Stark realized that he was older than he had seemed at first glance, the smooth unlined skin masking maturity and power.

"No one of you has come here out of any love for Skaith. You come for your own reasons, which are selfish. And you above all have done incalculable injury to the only system of stable government my sad world possesses. You have endeavored to wrench the foundation from under an ancient building to make it topple, not for the good of Skaith, but for the good of yourself and Ashton. The good of Irnan and Tregad and Iubar is merely an accidental factor that you use for your own advantage. For this I hate you, Stark. Also, I must admit that I cannot gracefully accept the fact that men do live on other planets. I feel in my soul that we of Skaith are the only trueborn men, and all others must be less than human. But my world is ill, and like any physician I must use whatever physic is at hand fo heal the patient, and so I work with you and with Penkawr-Che and his kind, who are here only to pick Skaith's bones. Be satisfied that I work with you. Do not ask for more."

He turned his back on Stark and spoke to Llandric.

"We have much to do."

Most of that "much" concerned notifying Pedrallon's network, which seemed to reach into some surprising places in spite of its thinness. Pedrallon was not disposed to give Stark any details. The

Dark Man was taken to an adjoining reed house, out of earshot. Sanghalain and Morn went to another. Food was brought to Stark by one of the men, who refused to answer any of Stark's questions except to say that he was not a Wandsman. Without knowing it, he answered one question; Pedrallon was a charismatic leader who held his people as much by the force of his personality as by his clear-thinking mind. He would be valuable at Pax.

It was warm and still on the island, as Old Sun rose and made his daily journey across the sky. There was a feeling of immense peace and isolation. It was difficult for Stark to realize that he was almost at the end of his long journey, almost at the fulfillment of both his goals.

Almost.

Speculation at this point was futile. Events would bring their own solutions or lack of them. Deliberately he cleared his mind and slept, with the small sounds of the swamp in his ears, until he was called to join the others.

In the golden afternoon the dark little men led them through the watery ways, under the pale branches. They were seven when they started. Two of Pedrallon's men had already left on their separate journeys. At intervals the other two, and then Llandric, diverged and vanished among the ghostly trees, leaving troubled wakes to lap against upthrust roots. Llandric would take Sanghalain's instructions to her escort and drivers and then slip back into Ged Darod. Morn would go with Sanghalain. The bond between the sea-dwelling Ssussminh and the ruling house of Iubar was apparently both ancient and very strong.

They reached the place where they were to wait, and Pedrallon bade good-bye to his swamp-dwellers with much touching of foreheads and clasping of wrists. The little men took the beasts and melted quietly back into their private wilderness.

Morn thrust the tines of his trident into the mud, stripped off the leather garment and immersed himself in a shallow pool, lying with his eyes half covered by filmy membranes.

His voice groaned in Stark's mind like waves among hollow rocks. *I long for the cold sea.*

"At Pax you may have any environment you wish," Stark told him. A large part of the city was devoted to the comfort of nonhumans of all descriptions, some so alien that the quarters had to be sealed in with air locks and all communication done in glass-walled isolation rooms.

They settled themselves on dry ground at the edge of the pool, in a screen of rank vegetation. Beyond them was the plain, empty and peaceful in the sunlight. They were farther from Ged Darod than they had been when they entered the swamp the night before, and there was no sight of anything living.

For a long while no one spoke. Each was oppressed with his own thoughts. Pedrallon still wore his native garment, a robe of patterned silk, but he had a red Wandsman's tunic with him in a bundle, and he carried his wand of office. Sanghalain's misty draperies were somewhat limp, her face pale and drawn. She was afraid, Stark thought, and small wonder. She was taking a tremendous step into the unknown.

"You can still change your mind," he said.

She glanced at him and shook her head. "No."

The fairy lady of the Pleasure Garden was gone. A woman was left, still beautiful, vulnerably human. Stark smiled.

"I wish you well."

"Wish us all well," said Pedrallon with unexpected vehemence.

"Doubts?" said Stark. "Surely not."

"Doubts every step of the road. I live with doubts. If this could have been done in any other way . . . I said I hated you, Stark. Can you understand me when I say that I hate myself even more?"

"I think so."

"I could not make them listen! Yet it's all there for them to see. North and south, the cold closing in, driving the outlying peoples ahead of it. The land shrinking, with ever more people to be fed from what is left. They know what must come, if they persist in forbidding any part of the population to leave."

"They stay with what they know. They can bear the slaughter. They'll still rule at the end of it, as they did after the Wandering."

"We did much good then," said Pedrallon fiercely. "We were the stabilizing force. We kept sanity alive."

Stark did not dispute him.

"My own people," Pedrallon said, "also do not understand. They think Old Sun will never desert them as he has the others. They think their temples and their sacred groves and their ivory cities will stand forever, unchanged. They think the wolves will never come down on them, sharp-toothed and starving. I am angry with them. But I love them, too."

A sound came into the quiet air.

Sanghalain looked upward, her hand over her mouth, her eyes wide.

The sunset sky roared and thundered and bloomed pale fire. The ground trembled. The limber trees were shaken by a sudden wind.

Penkawr-Che's ship came down onto the plain.

When the first of the Three Ladies rose, Stark was in a throaty-voiced planet-hopper on his way to pick up Tuchvar and the hounds.

26

There was something to be said for modern technology. Stark was glad enough to sit and watch the miles roll away far below him in the cluster light. He had toiled over a sufficient number of those miles in less comfortable ways.

The hopper was far from new, and apparently Penkawr-Che did not go in for spit and polish; nothing shone, not even the laser cannon on its forward mount. But the engines made a healthy rumble, and the rotors chewed a workmanlike path through old Skaith's relatively virgin sky. Hoppers had been banned by the Wandsmen almost from the first, partly to keep the off-worlders from spreading too wide, partly because two or three parties had been lost through unlucky landings. The Little Sisters of the Sun had caught one group on their mountain and sacrificed the lot, singing the Hymn of Life. Wild bands had eaten another group, and a third, going down to investigate some promising ruins on an island sixty miles southwest of Skeg, had been shared by the Children of the Sea. Most off-worlders were content to do their trafficking at Skeg.

The pilot was a tough-looking, stringy-muscled man with the blue-tinted skin and elongated features of a star-race with which Stark was not familiar. He wore a gold stud shaped like an insect in his right nostril. He was a good pilot. He spoke Universal, the lingua franca, very badly and very little, which was all right. Stark was never in a chatty mood. The fellow kept glancing at him now and again, as though he thought that Stark, unshaven and still wearing the rumpled tunic he had borrowed at Tregad, was a pretty poor sort of hero.

Stark thought the blue man's skipper was a pretty poor sort of merchant captain. He had not fallen in love at first sight with Penkawr-Che, who had too much the capable look of a shark, especially when he smiled, which was too often and with his teeth only. He would not have chosen Penkawr-Che to bear shield beside him in any fight where the odds were doubtful. The man's motives were plainly mercenary, and that Stark did not hold against him as long as he kept faith. But Penkawr—the Che part only meant Captain—gave him the impression of a man whose first and only consideration would always be himself.

From these things and from his ship, the *Arkeshti*, and some of her arrangements, Stark guessed that Penkawr was one of those traders whose ventures are often indistinguishable from piracy. Still, he was Pedrallon's contact and the best there was. Like Pedrallon, Stark would have to make do.

The hopper covered the distance in a surprisingly short time. Stark saw the pilgrim roads, almost deserted this night, and the glow of Ged Darod far off in the midst of the plain. He pointed, and the pilot swung away to make a long curve over the wooded hills to the west, dropping down almost to treetop level.

There were tracks through the woods. Some led to the mountain passes, and Stark could make out straggling bands of Farers still on them, heading for Irnan. They were going to be late for the battle. Whenever the hopper went over, they rushed frantically for the imagined shelter of the trees.

The hopper swept out over an edge of low cliff and turned to hover, dancing like a dragonfly.

The blue man said, "Where?"

Stark studied the cliff, turning repeatedly to look off toward Ged Darod and the roads. The shining of the Three Ladies was soft and beautiful, and deceptive.

"Farther on."

The blue man nudged the craft on a quarter of a mile.

"Farther."

The pilgrims on the nearest road, tiny scattered figures, were stopping, drawn by the unfamiliar sound of thrumming motors.

Stark said, "There."

The hopper settled down.

"Take it up again," said Stark. "Keep the area clear any way you have to."

He pushed the hatch open and jumped, running through a pounding downwash as the craft rose above him.

It was a few minutes before he located the path by which he had come down the cliff. He went up along it, reckoning that the hollow where he had left Tuchvar was a couple of hundred yards off to his right. The insistent sound of the motors stayed with him, an intrusion on the silence. At the top of the cliff the dappled shadows lay thick under the trees.

Gerd's voice shouted in Stark's mind. *Danger, N'Chaka!*

Under the motor noise he heard a sound, felt movement, quick and purposeful. He gave a great leap sideways.

The screaming began almost at once. But the dagger had already flown.

Stark felt the blow and the numbing pain in his right shoulder. So much he had accomplished, that it struck there instead of at his heart or his throat. He saw the jeweled haft glinting dully, grasped it and pulled it free. Blood came welling after it, a hot wetness under his sleeve. There was a great amount of noise, bodies thrashing, sobs, cries, crashings in the undergrowth, the baying of hounds. He went back onto the path, holding the dagger in his left hand.

There were two men, groveling in the extremity of terror. They wore black cloaks, and when Stark pulled the hoods back, the white unhuman faces of Fenn and Ferdic stared up at him, their night-seeing eyes stretched and agonized with fear.

Not kill! said Stark to the hounds. And aloud, "You will die if you move."

The proud white courtiers lay in the dust. They did not move except to breathe.

The hounds came crashing out into the path. Tuchvar followed, a long way behind.

"Take their weapons," Stark said. Blood dripped slowly from his fingers onto the ground. Gerd sniffed at it and growled, and the hair went up stiffly along his spine.

"The flying thing frightened the hounds," Tuchvar said, bending over the two. "Then they said you were there, and we started, and then—" He looked at Gerd, and then up at Stark, and forgot what he was doing.

"Take their weapons!"

He took them.

"Get up," Stark said.

Fenn and Ferdic rose, still trembling, staring at the thronging houndshapes in the gloom.

"Were you alone?"

"No. We had hired six assassins to help us, when we had made certain you were not among the men taken at Ged Darod. It was said that you would be found at Irnan or on the way there. We left Ged Darod, in the hope—" Fenn's breath caught raggedly in his throat. "When the flying thing went over the woods, our men fled, but we stayed to see. It is an off-world thing—yet we were told that all the ships had gone from Skaith."

"Not quite all," Stark said. He was in a fever to be rid of them. "Tell Kell à Marg that I gave you two your lives to pay for the two I was forced to take at the north gate. Tell her I will not do it another time. Now go, before I set the hounds on you."

They turned and rushed away. The dark wood swallowed them quickly.

Tuchvar said uncertainly, "Stark . . ."

Grith thrust her shoulder against the boy, forcing him back. The hounds padded restlessly, forming a fluid circle, whining in a curiously savage way. Gerd's growling rose and fell and never stopped. His eyes burned in the patches of light from the Three Ladies.

Without looking away from Gerd, Stark said to Tuchvar, "Go down to the plain."

"But I can help—"

"No one can help me. Go."

Tuchvar knew that that was true, and he went, his feet dragging.

Stark stood with his weight forward over his bent knees, his feet wide apart, the dagger in his left hand. He cared no more than a tiger which paw he used. The blood dripped steadily from his fingers. He did not dare to try and staunch it; Gerd would not give him time.

His eyes had become fully adjusted to the dim light, eyes almost as good as those of the Children. He could see the circling hounds, their jaws open, hot and eager, ready to tear him as the wounded Flay had been torn on the Plain of Worldheart. "Your flesh is vulnerable," Gelmar had said. "One day it will bleed. . . ."

It was bleeding now. The hounds had accepted him as one of

themselves, not as an overlord like the Houndmaster, and he must face the inevitable consequence of his position. The pack followed the strongest, and according to law and custom, when a leader showed weakness, the next in line would try to pull him down. Stark had known from the beginning that this day would come, and he bore the hounds no ill-will because of it. It was their nature.

He could see Gerd in the pathway, huge and pale, and he thought an alien wind blew across him, bringing the chill breath of snow.

He spoke a warning. *N'Chaka still the strongest.* But that would not be true for very long.

Gerd's thoughts were incoherent. The smell of blood had roused an immense and blind excitement in him. Whatever dim affection he might have conceived for Stark was drowned in that hot redness. He ripped at the ground with his claws, shifting his hindquarters back and forth with dainty movements, going through the whole ritual of challenge.

Stark, feeling weakness beginning to creep along his veins, said, *All the hounds of Yurunna not kill N'Chaka. How can Gerd?*

The bolt of fear hit Stark. The charge would follow.

Stark threw the dagger.

The blade pierced Gerd's nigh forepaw. It went on into the ground, pinning it.

The hound screamed. He tried to wrench the blade loose and screamed the more.

Stark managed to unsheathe his sword. Wild sendings of terror battered him. He forced himself to think of nothing but Gerd; Gerd's head tossing, Gerd's mouth agape, horrible with fangs. He forced himself to go forward with all the strength and quickness he could muster and touch the swordpoint to Gerd's throat, where it swelled with corded muscle above his breast.

He thrust the sharp point in, through tough hide into yielding flesh, and Gerd stiffened and looked up at him. The hound stood very still.

Stark held the blade rigid. And now Gerd's blood ran and puddled the dry dust, mingling with Stark's.

The hellhound gaze wavered, slid aside. The huge head dropped. The hindquarters sank in submission.

N'Chaka . . . strongest.

Stark withdrew the sword and sheathed it. Leaning down, he plucked the dagger from Gerd's paw. Gerd cried.

A wave of giddiness went over Stark. He put his hand on Gerd's shoulder to steady himself.

Come on, old dog, he said. *We both want our hurts tended.*

He went along the path, and Gerd came on three legs beside him. The rest of the pack slunk after.

Tuchvar, who had not gone all the way, ran to meet them, busily tearing strips from his smock.

The blue man had had no trouble keeping the area clear. He had made one lazy circle toward the road and the pilgrims had fled. When he saw Stark and the boy and the pack of hounds coming down the path, he landed to take them aboard.

He did not enjoy the flight from that point on.

27

THE VALLEY of Irnan was a desolation in what should have been the fullness of approaching harvest. Besieging armies had ruined and devoured, trampled and destroyed. Not one blade of grass remained. The fields were dust, the orchards long vanished into the smoke of campfires. Only the city remained outwardly unchanged, gray and old upon its height, the walls battered by siege engines but still unbreached. Above the gate the mythic beast still reared its time-worn head, jaws open to bite the world.

Inside the walls the people of Irnan were starving. Each day voices grew more insistent, calling for surrender. Jerann and his council of elders knew that they could not hold out much longer against those voices. People died. There was no more room to bury them within the walls. There was no more wood wherewith to burn them. The bodies were thrown over the walls now for the carrion birds, and Jerann was afraid of pestilence.

On a dark still morning, between the setting of the Three Ladies and the rising of Old Sun, a wind came out of the east. It struck the encampments of the besiegers with sudden violence, scattering the bivouac fires, tearing down tents. Flames sprang up. A herd of cattle stampeded through the outlying rabble of Farers. Dust whirled in choking clouds.

Behind their stone walls the people of Irnan watched and wondered. It was a strange wind, and there was no other sign of storm under the clear stars.

For three hours the wind screamed and battered, striking now here, now there. At times it subsided entirely, as though it rested and gathered strength to strike again. When Old Sun rose, the encampments were a shambles of wrecked tents, of clothing and equipment tossed about and trampled. Men coughed and shielded their eyes from the dust. And then those in the farthest lines, looking toward the sunrise, cried out and reached for the war-horns.

A legion was there, poised and ready. They saw the leather-clad troops with their heavy spears, and the banner of Tregad leading them. They saw a company of villagers armed with bills and reaping hooks. They saw hooded men in cloaks of dusty purple, red and brown, green and white and yellow, with their lances and their many-colored pennants, and their strange long-legged beasts. They saw, off to one side, an assembly of small dark winged folk all glittering with glints of gold, their wings outstretched. All about them, standing guard, were ranks of unhuman shapes striped in green and gold and armed with tall four-handed swords.

The hollow-eyed watchers on the wall saw all this, too, though they did not at first believe it.

The small folk folded their wings, and a sound they had made, as of chanting, stopped.

The wind fell. The dust cleared. War-horns sounded, deep and snarling.

The legion charged.

The Farers, always disorganized, ran away. The mercenaries, taken as they were by surprise, were not so easily overrun. Horns and shrill-voiced pipes mustered them. Officers shouted them into line. They caught up what weapons they could find and ran through the rubbish of their encampments to meet the attackers.

Foremost among the mercenaries was a company of Izvandians, tall lint-haired warriors from the Inner Barrens with the faces of wolves. They had been quartered at Irnan at the time of the revolt, in the service of the Wandsmen, and their leader was the same Kazimni who had taken Stark and his party north.

Kazimni recognized the two who rode at the forefront of the

Tregadians, beside the fierce old man who captained them, and he laughed. The man, what was his name, something short and aggressive . . . Halk. Halk was shouting the war cry that had been born that day at Irnan.

"Yarrod! Yarrod! Yarrod!"

The watchers on the city walls heard it. They too recognized the big man with the long sword. They knew the woman who rode by him armed for battle, her hair falling loose from under her cap, the color of bronze new from the forges.

"Gerrith! The wise woman has returned! Gerrith and Halk!"

Jerann, not alone, wondered about the Dark Man.

Men and women took up that war cry. Irnan became, in a matter of moments, a city of the hopeful instead of the doomed. "Yarrod! Yarrod!" they cried, and the mustering horns began to call.

The two forces joined battle.

The first charge bore the mercenaries back and scattered them. But they greatly outnumbered their attackers; and they were tough, seasoned fighting men. They rallied. A force of them drove against the left of the Tregadian line, to put a wedge between it and the tribesmen. The Fallarin, idling in reserve, shot a whirlwind against them, and in its wake the century of Tarf loosed a storm of arrows and followed that with swinging steel. The mercenaries were thrown back.

They formed again. This time they went against the Tregadians, feeling that the alien troops would desert the battle if they were beaten. The men from Tregad reeled and gave back. Old Delvor roared at them, cursing them in a voice like a trumpet. They fought furiously, but still they were borne back by superior numbers.

Sabak rallied the tribesmen and came down at a run on the Izvandian flank. The Izvandians wheeled to meet them, forming a square bristling with lancepoints, archers in the rear ranks firing steadily. The charge of the Hooded Men faltered in a tumbling of men and mounts like a wave shattered on a sudden reef.

For the first time in months, the gates of Irnan opened and every man and woman who could still bear arms issued out to fall upon the mercenaries' rear.

To the south and east, a ragged multitude had come swarming out of the passes from the direction of Ged Darod. Old Sun knew how many thousand had left the temple city to pour across the mountains. Probably no more than half of those had finished the journey, driven by an all-consuming fever of holiness to accomplish the downfall of Irnan and the traitors who had come to her assistance. The Wandsmen who were scattered throughout the mass judged that twenty thousand would hardly tell their sum.

When Stark saw them from the air, they looked like one of the moving carpets one sees when an ant colony is on the move. Disorganized, untrained, slatternly, they were still a formidable weight of flesh to be dumped on the wrong side of the balance.

He nodded to the blue man and spoke into the microphone, to the pilots of the three hoppers flying with him.

"Let's build them a fence."

Out of the naked sky, four shapes came rushing toward the mob of Farers. Swift as dragonflies, they roared back and forth across the astounded and terrified front of the mob, striking the ground with lightnings that blinded the eye and deafened the ear, and each crack shattered rocks and trees and made the ground smoke.

A god's voice spoke from the leading shape.

"Turn back! Turn back or you will all die!"

The flying shapes began to quarter across the depth and width of the mob. God-voices spoke from all of them in huge tones. "Turn back. Turn back." At the edges of the mob the ground was tortured by more lightnings.

A frenzy of cries went up. Farers knelt and lay on the ground. They milled and swirled. Even the Wandsmen did not know what to say to them in the face of this stunning power.

The flying things drew off and hung motionless in the sky, in a line across the Farer front, where the smoke and dust still rose. They waited for a time. Then they began to move slowly forward, and the licking tongues of fire cracked over the heads of the mob.

"Turn back!"

The Farers turned and streamed away in panic toward the mountains, leaving behind scores of dead, trampled underfoot.

The hoppers flew on to Irnan, where the battle swayed back and forth in dust and blood and weariness.

They flew in formation, a diamond pattern with Stark's craft at the leading point. They flew slowly and not very high because there was no weapon on the ground that could harm them. They flew over the knots and clots and ranks of struggling men, and faces turned upward to stare at them, petrified. Stark could pick out the colored cloaks of the tribesmen and the distinctive dress of some of the mercenary bands, but most of them were clad in indistinguishable leather, and in any case they were too closely engaged to pick out friend from foe.

"Anywhere you can, hit the ground," he said, "without hitting anything else. No good killing our own people."

The hoppers peeled off, each pilot pleasing himself. Laser bolts cracked and smoked around the broad perimeters of the battle, and in the open places where there were only the dead, beyond hurt. It was strange to watch how the fighting quieted and men stood still with their weapons half raised, looking upward. No one of them had ever seen a machine that flew in the air, nor any weapon that made lightning brighter than that of the sky god, and more deadly.

The four craft took up formation again, and Stark spoke into the pickup of the loud-hailer. His voice, magnified, echoing, tremendous, rang out across the field of battle.

"I am the Dark Man. I have come back from the Citadel and the prophecy of Irnan is fulfilled. You who fight against us, lay down your arms, or the lightning will strike you dead."

And he began to give orders, the hopper now darting swiftly here and there as he pointed. Orders to the captains of Irnan and Tregad and the leaders of the tribesmen to disengage and draw back.

This they did, leaving the enemy isolated.

Once more in formation, the hoppers quartered the field and voices said, "Lay down your arms or die."

On the ground Kazimni shrugged and said to his Izvandians: "We were paid to fight men, and we have done that." He sheathed his sword and tossed away his spear.

All over the field men were doing the same.

To the three pilots Stark said, "Bring them together and hold them. If any try to break out, stop them." He turned to the blue man. "Set down there by those hooded riders. Then join the others."

The hopper settled down.

Tuchvar and the hounds scrambled out. Stark followed. The blue man had given him first aid, and his wound had been cared for by *Arkeshti's* surgeon, while he waited for the three hoppers to be rigged and serviced. Penkawr-Che had given him a tunic of foreign cut that showed the color of spilled blood in the sunlight.

With Tuchvar and the hounds behind him, Stark walked toward the tribesmen, and Sabak brought him one of the tall desert beasts. He mounted.

The troop formed into line: purple Hann, brown Marag, yellow Qard, green Thorn, white Thuran, red Kref.

Fallarin and trotting Tarf fell in in their accustomed place, but this time Alderyk remained with them, leaving Stark alone with his hounds at the head of the line. Ashton was with the Fallarin, where he had been throughout the battle; he, too, stayed.

They passed the ranks of the Tregadians, who were forming raggedly, and old Delvor shouted, "Let them go first, they've marched a long way for it!"

Halk and Gerrith left the standard of Tregad and rode beside Stark.

They rode toward the city, and the Irnanese in the field lifted weapons and cried out their names, hailing them.

Stark passed through the massive gate, beneath the dim heraldic beast. The tunnelway through the thickness of the wall was as he remembered it, dark and close. Beyond was the wide square with the gray stone buildings around it, and in the center was the platform where he had stood bound and awaiting death those months ago. Then he remembered the voice of the mob, remembered the spear that pierced Yarrod's heart, remembered Gerrith stripped of the Robe and Crown, standing naked in the sunlight. He remembered how the arrows had flighted from the windows around the square, a shining rain of death that struck down the Wandsman and signaled the beginning of the revolt.

Jerann and the elders, in threadbare gowns, their starveling faces overfilled with joy, stood waiting, and all about them crowds of tattered scarecrows wept and cheered.

So the Dark Man came back to Irnan.

28

STARK STILL HAD work to do. He left Jerann and the elders, with Gerrith and Ashton, in the council hall. He had told them about Pen-kawr-Che and the ship, Ashton and the wise woman could tell them all what had happened in the north. He returned to the field.

Halk rode beside him, through the filthy streets where scarecrows danced and cried and caught at them as they passed.

"I see that I must still stay my hand, Dark Man," Halk said. "If I were to kill you after this, my own people would tear me to pieces. And so I lose my revenge."

"You ought to have tried taking it before."

"The Fallarin would not have given *me* windfavor," he said bitterly. "The tribesmen would not have followed *me* after Yurunna. Because of Irnan I let you live. But I tell you this, Dark Man. I will be glad to see you gone."

And he spurred away to join the Irnanese warriors.

Pensive, Stark rode out to where the mercenary bands waited under the watchful hoppers.

He had seen the distinctive dress and the lint-white hair of the Izvandians from the air, and he was not surprised to find Kazimni leading them. He had come to like that man on the cold journey across the Barrens. And he bore him no grudge for having sold the little party from Irnan into captivity with the trader Amnir, in the hope of sharing a great profit when they were delivered to the Lords Protector. Kazimni had not taken any oath of loyalty to them, and Stark had known perfectly well what he was doing. Force of circumstance, not Kazimni, had entrapped them.

"You had poor return on your trading venture," he said, "and here you are again, leaving Irnan empty-handed. The place seems unlucky for you."

Kazimni smiled. He had slanting yellow-gray eyes and pointed cheekbones, and he wore the torque and armband of a chieftain.

"Perhaps the third time will be better, Dark Man."

"There will be a third time?"

"As certainly as there will be winter. The Wandsmen are not so easily beaten. They'll gather new forces, stronger and better organized. They have learned now that their precious Farers are of little use. There will be war, Stark."

"If things go well out there among the stars, power will pass from the hands of the Wandsmen."

"There will still be war."

"Perhaps." Stark thought that Kazimni was right. But he said, "For the present, go in peace."

They struck hands, and the Izvandians marched away. One by one the other bands of mercenaries followed. The hoppers escorted them out of the valley.

Stark rode the battlefield.

The Irnanese troops and the men of Tregad were working together, carrying supplies into the starving city from the abandoned stores, gathering the dead and wounded, rounding up livestock. The tribesmen had come out to look after their fallen and to loot the ravaged encampments. Stark did not begrudge them what they found. There were enough dusty cloaks strewn about the field, a long way from home.

When he was satisfied, Stark returned to the city in search of Ashton.

He found him in one of the chambers in the great stone pile that contained the council hall. Ashton, thin and windburned but still fit, looked at him a moment and then said:

"You've decided to stay, haven't you?"

"Until the ships come. Kazimni believes there will be war again as soon as the Wandsmen can gather up new forces. I think he's right, and I don't like leaving a job half done."

"Well," said Ashton, "I won't argue with you, Eric; and I suppose you might as well be risking your neck here for a while longer as on some other godforsaken planet."

Then he added, "I don't suppose you knew it, but Jerann asked Gerrith to go with the delegation to Pax, and she refused."

"I didn't know it," Stark said, "but I won't pretend I'm not glad to hear it."

He went to the hall to speak with Jerann and the elders. There was great activity, people coming and going, tending to the needs of the city. Jerann, in the midst of it, seemed to have shed ten years since Stark saw him in the square.

"I am grateful," the old man said, when Stark had told him his decision. "We shall all feel safer with you here at Irnan."

"Very well, then," Stark said. "I can handle one of the flying things. When you bargain with Penkawr-Che for the price of your passage, bargain for that also. Then Irnan will have a powerful weapon, and far-seeing eyes, and a radio to speak with the ships when they come."

The council agreed. Only Halk was not pleased, looking at Stark in a certain way, so that limping Gerd began to growl.

Stark's thoughts were elsewhere. "Where is the wise woman?"

No one knew.

The tribesmen and the Fallarin, not wishing to be housed in the noisome city, had made their separate encampments away from it. Stark visited them.

The tribesmen were well satisfied. They had considerable loot left by the mercenaries, and the elders had promised them much besides. They were content to remain with Stark.

The Fallarin would not commit themselves. Only Alderyk said:

"I will stay with you, Dark Man. Two of my people will go to this world you call Pax to see and observe and bring back news to me. We shall make our decisions when it pleases us. For the moment, at least we are secure in the north. As for Irnan, we shall see. I promise nothing, and my folk are free to return to the Place of Winds at any time they wish."

"But you yourself will stay."

Alderyk smiled his edged and mocking smile.

"I told you, Stark. Mine to control the whirlwind."

Three of the hoppers flew off to Tregad with Delvor and his aides. They would carry the news of the victory and fetch back with them such of the leaders of Tregad as wished to make the trip to Pax. The fourth hopper was maintaining radio contact with Penkawr-Che's *Arkeshti*, orbiting just outside the atmosphere. Not he to risk his ship until the area chosen for landing was completely cleared.

It was night when *Arkeshti* came in, dropping down through the glow of the Three Ladies, and all of Irnan was on the walls to watch.

Penkawr-Che, a long lean Antarean with skin like burnished gold and a crest of stiff-curling hair, came to the hall with Pedrallon and did his talking with Ashton and the elders. He made no difficulty about the hopper, and the spare power pack Stark requested.

Stark still did not like him.

Next day Stark went aboard the ship with Ashton to inspect the quarters the crew had been busy jury-rigging in an empty hold.

"This will do," said Ashton. "Anything will do that gets me away from Skaith." He took Stark's hand. They had already held their post mortems on all that had happened and said their farewells in the privacy of Ashton's room, sitting very late over a jug of captured wine. Now all Ashton said was, "We'll be as fast as we can. Have you seen Gerrith?"

"No. But I think I know where she is."

"Go find her, Eric."

The others were coming aboard. Stark spoke briefly to Sanghalain and Morn, and Pedrallon, and left the ship. He sent Ashton's mount back to the city with Tuchvar and Sabak, who had ridden out with them to stare wide-eyed at the ship. Then he rode away up the valley.

He had come this way only once before, at the start of the long journey, but it was not difficult to follow the road or to note the place where he must leave it to find the grotto. The wanton armies had ravaged even here, stripping the land for forage and firewood. He left his mount below the grotto and climbed the steep path.

Inside it was dark and cool, with the tomb-smell of places that never see the sun. The grotto had served generations of Gerriths, wise women of Irnan. When Stark had seen it before, there had been rugs and hangings, lamps, braziers, furniture, the great bowl that held the Water of Vision. Now the place was empty, naked, gutted.

He called her name. It echoed in the vaulted rooms.

She came from an inner chamber where one candle burned.

"Why did you run away?"

"I did not wish to see you go. And I did not wish in any way to persuade you not to go."

She waited, and he told her his decision.

"Then you see, I was right to come here." She came close and touched him. "I'm glad."

"So am I. But why did you decide not to go to Pax, when Jerann asked you?"

"I don't really know. Except that when I saw myself walking toward the ship, a barrier came between and I could not pass it. My trip will be made another time. There is something more I must do here, first."

She smiled, but he could not see her eyes in the shadowed cave.

"What is this thing you must do?"

"I don't know that, either. And I'm not going to think about it now."

He took her into his arms, and then in a little while they went out into the light of Old Sun and heard the thunder and watched the distant flame as *Arkeshti* lifted off, outward bound for Pax.

"We must send word north," Stark said, "to Hargoth and the People of the Towers, to tell them that the star-roads will soon be open."

The Reavers of Skaith

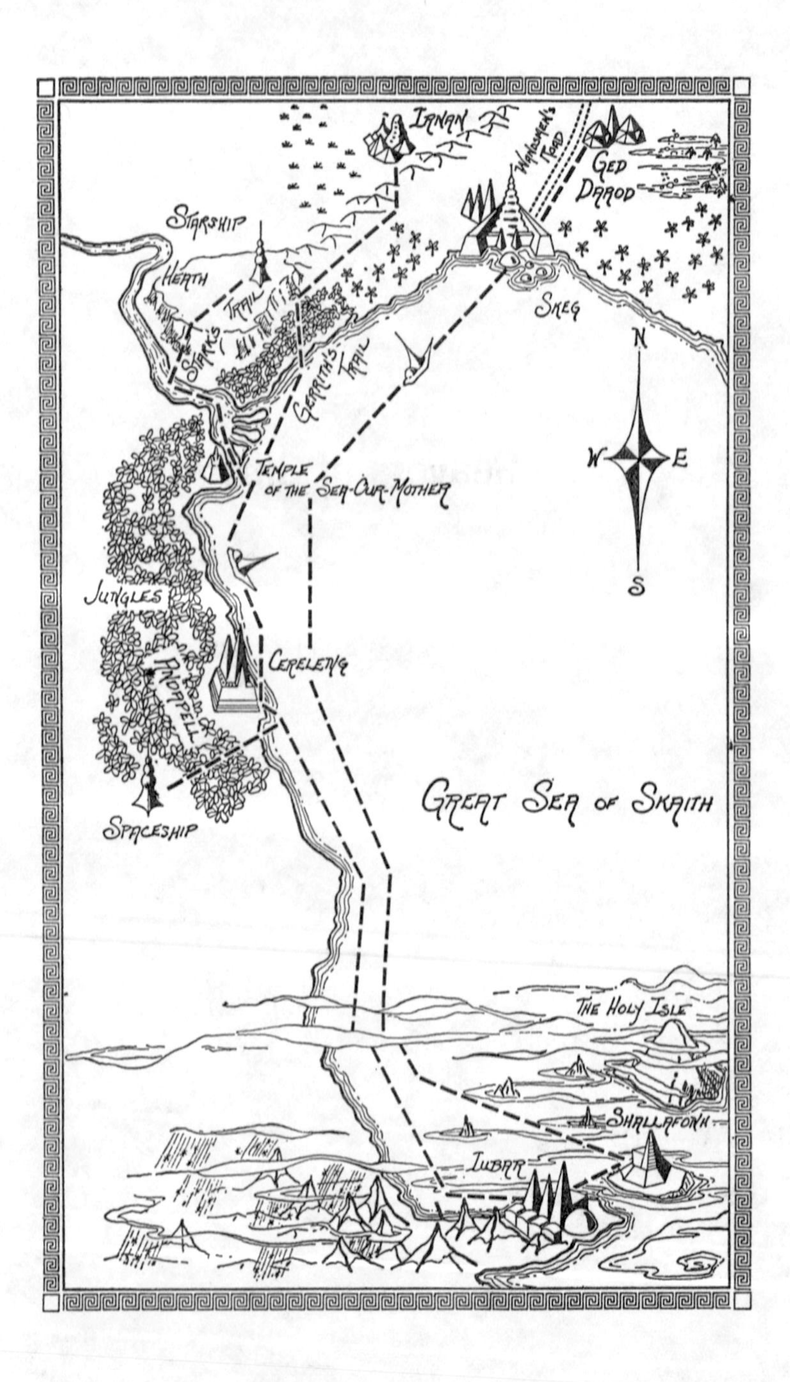
IRNAN
WANDSMEN'S ROAD
GED DAROD
STARSHIP
HEATH
STARK'S TRAIL
GERRITH'S TRAIL
SKEG
N
W
E
S
TEMPLE OF THE SEA-OUR-MOTHER
JUNGLES
CERELENG
SPACESHIP
GREAT SEA OF SKAITH
THE HOLY ISLE
SHALLAFONH
IUBAR

1

STRONG BINDINGS held N'Chaka fast to the flat, hard surface whereon he lay.

There was too much light above him. He could barely make out the face that leaned and looked down into his own. It moved and pulsed and swam with the movement of his blood, a handsome face cut from burnished gold, with a crest of hair like curled wires. There were other faces, dim in the shadows at the sides, but only that one mattered. He could not remember whose face it was. Only that it mattered.

There was pain again, the hollow jab of a needle.

N'Chaka snarled, and fought the straps.

The golden face asked a question.

N'Chaka heard. He did not wish to answer, but he had no choice. The poison running in him forced him to answer.

He spoke, in the clicks and grunts of a language so primitive that it was only a little more complex than the speech of apes.

Penkawr-Che, the golden man, said, "He reverts to that every time. Interesting. Bring Ashton."

Ashton was brought.

The question was repeated, and the answer.

"You're his foster-father. Do you know what language he is speaking?"

"The aboriginals of Sol One speak that tongue. He was reared by them after his own parents were killed. Until he came into my care—at fourteen, or thereabouts—that was the only speech he knew."

"Can you translate?"

"I was one of the administrators of Sol One. Part of my duty was to protect the abos from the miners. I wasn't always successful. But I knew them well." He translated meticulously, and smiled. "There are no words in that vocabulary for the things you want to know about."

"Ah," said Penkawr-Che. "Well, then. Let me think."

2

THE MILLION little bells of Ged Darod chimed softly from the roofs and spires of the Lower City, where the warm wind rocked them. It was a cheerful sound, speaking of love and kindness. But in the packed streets—among the temples to Old Sun, to Skaith-Mother and Sea-Mother, and to my lord Darkness and his lady Cold and their daughter Hunger, the deadly trinity who already possessed almost half the planet—the people were silent and dismayed.

The temples held many suppliants, asking the gods to protect their own; but the larger portion of the crowd looked elsewhere. Farers in the thousands filled the parks and the pleasure gardens; made up of all the races of the Fertile Belt, dressed, painted, and adorned in every conceivable manner, these free, careless, and perpetually itinerant children of the Lords Protector—who saw, through their servants, the Wandsmen, that the hungry were always fed and the needy succored—turned their faces to the Upper City. The Wandsmen had never failed them. Surely they would somehow manage to turn aside the alien menace that still threatened them from out the sky, even after the burning of the starport.

One ship had gone from Skaith carrying traitors who wished to overturn the rule of the Wandsmen and replace it with that of a foreign power. If this should be accomplished, the Farers knew that they, and the way of life that sustained them, would be swept away.

They milled in the vast square below the Wandsmen's Gate and waited in the hope of salvation.

High in the Upper City, which housed the heart and center of the Wandsmen's power, the Lord Protector Ferdias stood at a window in the Palace of the Twelve, looking down at the splendor of flashing domes and glittering peacock tiles. Ferdias was an old man, but age had not bowed his unyielding back nor dimmed the harsh fire of his eye. He wore the white robes of his rank, and no slightest shadow of humility betrayed the fact that Ferdias had come back to Ged Darod as a fugitive.

Yet he was keenly aware of that fact. Very keenly. Especially upon this day.

A massive door opened somewhere behind him. Voices sounded, subdued and distant in the cavernous room. Ferdias remained as he was. There was no longer any urgency.

He had begun his life of service as a gray apprentice within these mighty walls. He had not known then that Old Sun, the ginger star that ruled his heaven, had been recorded as a number on the galactic charts of a civilization he had never heard of. He had not known that he dwelt, along with his sun and his planet, in a remote sector of something these people had named the Orion Spur. He had not known that the galaxy, out beyond his lonely little sky, contained a vast and busy complex of worlds and men known as the Galactic Union.

How happy he had been without that knowledge! How happy he would have remained had it never been vouchsafed him. But knowledge had dropped unbidden, in flame and thunder, out of the clouds, and innocence was forever lost.

In a little more than a dozen years, the starships had brought many benefits to the sad old world of Ferdias' birth, starved for the metals and minerals it no longer possessed. So the foreign men had been allowed to come and go, carefully watched and supervised, from the single starport at Skeg. But the ships had brought less welcome things: heresies, treasons, rebellions, war—and, at the end, a mad stranger out of the stars, who had set the all-powerful Lords Protector fleeing down the roads of Skaith away from their burning rooftree, homeless as any Farers.

Ferdias set his hands on the massive stone of the windowsill and felt the solidity of it. He smiled. He saw the light of Old Sun shining upon the streets below, upon the mass of humanity that waited there, and his heart opened with a physical pang, sending a flooding warmth throughout his body so that he caught his breath and his sight became blurred with tears. These were his people, to whose welfare he had devoted his life—the poor, the weak, the homeless, the hungry. His children, his beloved children.

Because of my error, he said to them in the silence of his mind, *you were almost destroyed. But the gods of Skaith have not forsaken you.* And, he added humbly, *Nor me.*

In the room behind him, someone coughed. It was neither a hastening nor an impatient cough.

Ferdias sighed and turned.

"My lord Gorrel," he said, "get you back to your bed. You have no business here."

"No," said Gorrel, and shook his gaunt old head. "I shall remain."

He sat in a large chair that was a cocoon of wrappings and cushions; he had not yet recovered from the journey south. Ferdias thought that Gorrel was not likely to recover, and that it was less the hardships of travel than the shattering shock of what had happened at the Citadel that had broken Gorrel's health.

"Well, then," he said gently, "perhaps you may find fresh strength in what I have to tell you."

Besides Gorrel, in the room now stood five other old men in the same white robes that Ferdias wore, making up the seven Lords Protector. Behind them were the Twelve, the council of senior Wandsmen in tunics of somber red, with gold-tipped wands of office in their hands. Standing a little apart from the Twelve was another red-clad Wandsman, on whose proud and bitter face Ferdias' gaze rested for a long moment.

"This has been a cruel time," Ferdias began, "a time of tribulation, when it seemed as if the very fabric of our society was being rent. Tregad joined the revolt against us, and we suffered a crushing defeat at Irnan. We were betrayed, here at Ged Darod, by one of our own, the Wandsman Pedrallon, who caused a starship to land in defiance of our decree and take on passengers—men and women, including Pedrallon himself, who wished to deliver Holy Mother Skaith to the Galactic Union as a member planet, thus putting an end to our rule. It has been a time when we could foresee the destruction of twenty centuries of work and devotion in the service of mankind, a service which has endured since the Wandering."

He paused, aware of their intent faces all turned toward him. He smiled again, with a kind of ferocious benevolence.

"I have called you together here," he said, "to tell you that that time has ended."

Out of the sudden shocked confusion of voices, one rose strong and clear, the voice of an orator. It was Jal Bartha, who would not be chosen from among the Twelve to take old Gorrel's place among the Lords Protector when it fell vacant, though Ferdias knew that he hoped to be. Jal Bartha's lack of judgment might have been borne, but his conceit never.

"How can that be, my lord?" Jal Bartha demanded. "These traitors you speak of are well on their way to Pax, the man Stark moves among the city-states preaching the gospel of starflight, our Wandsmen are driven out or slain—"

"If your silver tongue can be stilled for a moment," said Ferdias quietly, "I shall make all things clear."

Jal Bartha flushed, and inclined his head stiffly.

Ferdias glanced once again at the thirteenth Wandsman, and clapped his hands.

A small door opened at the side of the great chamber. Two men in green tunics entered, with a third between them. He wore blue, marking his lesser rank, and he was young and utterly distressed.

"This man's name is Llandric," said Ferdias. "One of Pedrallon's creatures, a small serpent in our midst. He has something to say to you."

Llandric stammered.

Ferdias commanded, on a note of chilled steel, "Say it, Llandric, as you said it to me."

"Yes," he began, "I—I serve Pedrallon." He seemed to find his courage, facing their hostility with a sort of quiet defiance. "I believe that the peoples of Skaith must be free to emigrate, if only for one reason—that the planet's livable areas grow smaller each year and room must be made."

"We do not require a lecture on Pedrallon's heresies," said Jal Bartha. "We understand them well enough."

"I don't think you understand them at all," said Llandric, "but that's beside the point. After Pedrallon went away, we have continued to monitor the transceiver which he secured from the Antarean, Penkawr-Che, and which was Pedrallon's secret means of communication with the off-worlders. Because of that monitoring, I am able to tell you what has happened, and that is why I am here. I myself have heard the talking of the starships."

The thirteenth Wandsman stepped forward. "What starships? I drove them all from Skeg, with the flames of the burning behind them. What starships?"

"There are three," said Llandric. "One is the ship of Penkawr-Che, the off-worlder who agreed with Pedrallon and the man Stark to take our delegations to Galactic Center, at Pax. Penkawr-Che has betrayed us. He has not gone to Pax. He has returned to Skaith with the two other ships in company, and all his passengers."

Ferdias quelled the outburst that followed. "My lords, please! Let him continue."

"I first knew of this," Llandric said, "when word was brought to me that three ships had met in orbit above Skaith. I went at once to the hidden place where the transceiver is kept and listened, myself. Penkawr-Che had transferred three of his passengers—Pedrallon into one ship, Lady Sanghalain of Iubar and the person Morn into the other. This latter ship was to land at Iubar in the far south and demand payment for the Lady. The other ship was to go to Andapell, Pedrallon's country, where he is a prince and would bring a high ransom. Penkawr-Che himself was to land at Tregad and sell them back their elders, and then at Irnan for the same purpose. That has been done."

There was a silence in the room—the silence of men digesting unlooked-for news, sucking the juices from it, tasting to see if it be truth.

The thirteenth Wandsman spoke in a strange dry voice. "Irnan, you said."

"Yes."

"The man Stark was at Irnan. What of him?"

"Tell them," said Ferdias. "They are much interested in the man Stark."

"Penkawr-Che demanded Stark as part of the ransom. He has knowledge of some treasure in the High North that Penkawr-Che wants. The Antarean also took back the flying thing that he had left with Stark."

The thirteenth Wandsman reached out and grasped Llandric's tunic at the throat. "Speak plainly," he said. "To demand is not necessarily to receive. What of the man Stark?"

"He is taken. He is Penkawr-Che's prisoner."

"Taken!"

The Lords Protector savored that word. Lord Gorrel repeated it several times, rolling it between his skeletal jaws.

"Taken," said the thirteenth Wandsman, "but not dead."

"The last talk I heard between the ships was last night. Iubar had paid Sanghalain's ransom; Pedrallon had been redeemed in Andapell. They spoke about the temples and other places they would loot. Penkawr-Che had landed at a place the other captains knew of, and would begin to plunder the *tlun* villages in the jungles between the uplands and the sea. He was questioning Stark, he said, and hoped for results soon. Then he said he would kill both the Earthmen, though there was small chance they could ever testify about what the star-captains had done."

Llandric shook his head angrily. "Stark is neither here nor there. These outlaw captains have come to rob and kill our people. That is why I made the decision to give myself up to you, so that you would know all this while there was yet time to stop them. And they must be stopped!"

His voice had risen until he was all but shouting.

"I know where some of them are," Llandric continued. "Where some of them intend to strike. They don't know that they were overheard. I didn't speak to them. It would have been useless, and I was afraid they might send one of the flying things to destroy the transceiver. But the ships are at rest now, while the flying things do the raiding, and if you move swiftly . . ."

Ferdias said, "Enough, Llandric. My lords, you see how matters have turned out for us, how well Mother Skaith guards her own. The traitors have been made to pay for their folly. The man Stark is a prisoner and will soon die, along with Ashton. All the dangers that threatened us are swept away at a single stroke by one man's action. Shall we grudge that man his just reward?"

There was noise enough in the room then, voices raised all at cross purposes like the sharp waves in a riptide.

Llandric stared at Ferdias, not believing. "I thought perhaps Pedrallon was mistaken about you. I thought perhaps you honestly did not see where your policies were leading. But this is not a matter of opinion, this is fact. This is murder. And you speak of reward?"

"My young fool," said Ferdias, not unkindly, "*your* people brought this scourge about, not *we*. Do not expect us to relieve you of your guilt." He held up his hands. "Please, my lords! Let us be tranquil and apply our minds."

He moved back to the window, where he could see the flash of Old Sun's light on the golden domes and hear the chiming of the bells.

"Because of us, our world was able to survive the chaos of the Wandering and reshape itself into a new and stable order that has endured for centuries, and that will continue to endure as long as we control the forces of disruption. With the passing of the opportunity to escape by starship, those forces would seem to be controlled, since the disaffected no longer have any hope of evading their responsibilities.

"But can we be sure that the threat will not come again? Other starships may seek us out as the earlier ones did. Other folk may be tempted as the people of Irnan were tempted."

He paused, and the others waited: his six white-robed colleagues; the Twelve in red, with their gold-tipped wands; the thirteenth Wandsman with the bitter face; Llandric between his guards.

Ferdias said, "I wish this lesson to be so well learned that it will never be forgotten. I wish the name of *foreigner* to be anathema. I wish the people of Skaith to learn, in pain and terror, to hate everything that may come to them from beyond the sky. I wish no one ever again to desire foreign rule."

He looked down upon the crowded streets of the Lower City. "A few innocents will suffer, and that is to be regretted. But it is for the good of all. My lords, are we in agreement that no steps shall be taken against these star-captains?"

Only Jal Bartha raised a question.

"The depredations may not be so harsh or so widespread as to cause such a feeling among the people."

"Great trees need only little seeds to spring from. We shall see to it that the news travels." Ferdias went and stood in front of Llandric. "Do you understand now?"

"I understand that I've offered up my life for nothing." Llandric's young face had taken on a totally unfamiliar sternness. It seemed to have aged ten years. "This is how you do good. You allow your children—the children you claim to love so dearly—to be slaughtered out-of-hand as a cold matter of policy."

"That is why you could never be a Lord Protector," said Ferdias. "You have not the long view." He shrugged. "Not many will be slaughtered, after all. And in any case, how could we hope to stand against the weapons of these foreigners?"

Llandric said cruelly, "You are an old man, Ferdias, and your long view is all of the past. When the starving hordes close in on you from north and south, and there is no escape for anyone, remember who it was that barred the roads of space."

The guards took him out.

Ferdias spoke to the thirteenth Wandsman.

"A day of triumph, Gelmar, after long adversity. I wished you to share it."

Gelmar, Chief Wandsman of Skeg, looked at him with a dark glitter in his eye. "I am grateful, my lord. I shall make thank-offerings to all the gods that the man Stark is taken." He paused, and then added with savage anger, "It does not change the fact that it was my task to take him, and I failed."

"We all failed, Gelmar. Remember that it was by my order that Simon Ashton was made captive and brought to me at the Citadel. But for that, Stark would never have come to Skaith to find him; there would have been no prophecy of Irnan; there probably would have been no revolt; and the Citadel would not have been destroyed." Ferdias dropped a hand on Gelmar's arm. "It is over now. Even these last ships will soon be gone. Nothing has occurred that cannot be undone. We must begin to think now of rebuilding."

Gelmar nodded. "True, my lord. But I will not be satisfied until I know that Stark is dead."

3

N'Chaka was in a cage.

Cliffs rose up on either side of the narrow valley, stretching into black pinnacles that pierced the sky. The green place where the water bubbled was close by. His mouth was parched and his tongue a dry twig.

He could see the dark bodies on the green. The fresh red brightness of blood was turning black and ugly. Old One was dead, with all his tribe. The hammering echoes of killing still rang in N'Chaka's ears.

He howled and tore at the bars in rage and grief.

Someone spoke. "N'Chaka."

Man-Without-a-Tribe. His name. He had had another one, he thought, but that was his true name.

"N'Chaka."

Father voice. Not Old One father. Simon father.

N'Chaka held the bars and remained still. His eyes were open, but darkness still poured across them, flickering with terrible pictures that were of a glaring brilliance. Heat and hairy corpses, the smell of blood on furnace air, snouted muzzles hideously smiling. He thought, But my people never smiled.

"Eric," said the father voice. "Eric John Stark. Look at me."

He tried. He could see nothing but the flickering of dark-bright images.

"Eric. N'Chaka. See."

Slowly, far away at the end of a long, hollow blackness, something took form. It began to come closer. It rushed toward N'Chaka, or perhaps he fell toward it, with a cold tearing sound that was felt rather than heard, or heard with the raw nerves rather than the ears. The darkness fell away, hissing like baffled surf, and Simon Ashton was there on the other side of the bars.

N'Chaka shivered. The images had gone. He no longer saw the valley, the bubbling spring, the scattered bodies of his foster-folk. The men with the sharp things had gone, too; they were no longer tormenting him. But the bars had not gone.

"Take them," he said.

Simon Ashton shook his head. "I can't, Eric. I did before, but that was a long time ago. You've been drugged. Be patient. Wait till it clears."

N'Chaka fought the bars for a little while. Then he was quiet. And gradually he saw that Simon Ashton was bound, hand and foot, to a simple metal framework in the shape of an X, suspended by a rope from the limb of a tall tree, and that he was quite naked. So was the tree, devoid of leaves and bark, the exposed wood smooth and white as bone. The end of the rope was belayed around the trunk.

Stark did not understand, but he sensed that understanding would come if he waited. Ashton's framework swung slowly in the breeze, so that sometimes he was facing Stark and sometimes he was not.

Beyond the tree stretched a great emptiness, a blasted heath set with clumps of twisted thorn and here and there a flayed trunk with skeletal branches, and in between them a coarse growth of stunted grass starred with little flowers. The flowers were white with round, dark centers. They resembled watching eyes, countless thousands of eyes, peering restlessly from side to side as the breeze moved them.

It was late. Old Sun hung low in the west and the shadows were long.

Stark turned and looked the other way.

A ship stood on the level plain, a tall needle shape raking the sky. Stark knew that ship.

Arkeshti.

Penkawr-Che.

The last of the drug-mist lifted from Stark's mind.

Just so had *Arkeshti* stood before Irnan.

The blow had fallen so swiftly out of the dim sky. One moment all was well; and in the next moment—a shattering thunderbolt of sound and flame and fountaining dust—*Arkeshti* landed and the full extent of Penkawr-Che's betrayal became known.

Stark had remained at Irnan, of his own choice, to help protect the city against any threats from the Wandsmen that might arise before the Galactic Union representatives came. Faced with *Arkeshti* and her three armed hoppers, there had been nothing he could do. His own planet-hopper, obtained from Penkawr-Che when they were allies at the rescue of Irnan, and identical with the other three, possessed a laser cannon, powerful armament against the primitive weaponry of a planet long lost to the uses of advanced technology but worthless against adversaries such as these. *Arkeshti*'s impervious skin would shed the beam of the light cannon as it shed dust, and he could not hope to shoot down three skilled pilots before he himself was downed.

Even if he had wished to try, he had the hostages to think of.

There was Ashton. There was Jerann and the rest of Irnan's council of elders, and two of Alderyk's winged Fallarin, who had chosen to go to Pax as observers, all in Penkawr-Che's hands.

Only the radio in Stark's hopper had been used, to relay messages back and forth between the ship and the acting council of Irnan. For most of the time, the hostages had been held in full view of the city, in the open, under threat of death. Ashton had been with them, to ensure Stark's cooperation; Penkawr-Che had learned all he needed to know about that relationship.

Penkawr-Che also knew the exact sum that remained in Irnan's coffers.

Irnan paid. And part of the ransom demanded was Stark himself.

He had done his best to bargain for Ashton's freedom, but to no avail. Irnan's mood of savage anger and despair had given him no help.

He did not blame them. The Irnanese had endured months of siege by the mercenary troops of the Wandsmen. They had endured starvation and pestilence and the destruction of their rich valley. They had endured because they had hope—hope that all the suffering would lead to a better life on a new world, free of the oppressive rule of the Wandsmen and the burden of their army of Farer dependents, which grew larger with each generation. Now that hope was gone, shattered in a few brief moments by the treachery of an off-worlder. It would not come again in their lifetime. Perhaps it would never come again.

Meglin, who had headed the acting council in Jerann's absence, had looked at Stark bleakly and said, "The Wandsmen will come back now, and the Farers, and we shall be punished. Whether or not it was a crime, we were foolish indeed to put our trust in off-world men and foreign ways. We will have no more of them here." She had nodded toward the ship. "They are your people. Go."

He went. There was nothing else to do. Penkawr-Che had made it clear to him what would happen if he attempted to escape. Since not only Ashton but the elders were involved, the people of Irnan were making sure that he did not.

He had walked out alone to the starship. The Northhounds were of no use to him now. His comrades were of no use. He left them behind, all those who had come south with him to help raise the siege of Irnan: the boy Tuchvar, with the hounds; the company of Hooded Men from the northern deserts; the dark-winged, dark-furred Fallarin, brothers to the wind, who had stripped themselves of their golden torques and girdles to pay the ransom for their fellows.

He left Irnan behind. It was like walking away from the corpse of someone who has been for a time vitally important in one's life, and who has suddenly died.

He also left behind the wise woman Gerrith, and that was like leaving a part of himself.

They had had so little time to talk.

"You must not be here when the Wandsmen come," he had told her, because that thought was most urgent in his mind. "They'll do to you as they did to your mother."

Halk, the tall swordsman who had fought beside them both across half of Skaith, said cruelly, "We can all find safety somewhere, Dark Man, so don't concern yourself with us. Worry about yourself. You know your people better than I do, but I think Penkawr-Che means you no good."

Gerrith touched him, once, with the tips of her fingers. "I'm sorry, Stark. I did not foresee. If I had only been able to give you warning—"

"It would have made no difference," Stark said. "He has Ashton."

And they had parted, without even a moment alone to say goodbye.

Stark had passed the hostage elders, who looked at him with cold, stunned hatred—not because he himself had committed any wrong, but because they had built such hopes upon him, the Dark Man of the prophecy, who would bring them freedom. Only old Jerann spoke to him.

"We set our feet on this road together," he said. "It has been an ill road for both of us."

Stark had not answered him. He walked on to where Ashton stood between his guards, and they entered the ship together.

That had been . . . when? He could not remember.

He looked again at Ashton, hanged man on a dangling frame.

"How long?"

"You were taken yesterday."

"Where are we? How far from Irnan?"

"Very far. West and south. Too far to think of going back, even if you were free. Your friends will all be gone from there before another sun."

"Yes," said Stark, and wondered if the chance would ever come to him to kill Penkawr-Che.

The cage was not tall enough to allow Stark to stand up. He went round it on all fours, as naked as Ashton. He had nothing he could use as a weapon, not so much as a pebble. The cage had no door. He had been put into it drugged, and the remaining bars had been welded in place afterward. He tested each bar in turn. They seemed stout enough to hold him.

He fought down a surge of claustrophobia and spoke once more to Ashton.

"I remember Penkawr-Che questioning me, and I remember the needles. Did I tell him what he wanted to know?"

"You told him. But you told him in your natal tongue. He made me translate for him—only the hairy abos hadn't any words to express the things he wanted to know. So he decided that drugging you was a waste of time."

"I see," said Stark. "He's going to use you, instead. Has he hurt you?"

"Not yet."

Two hoppers came drumming in on their sturdy rotors and settled down by the ship, near two others that must have come in earlier. Men got out and began unloading cylindrical packages wrapped in coarse fiber: *tlun*, a mind-expanding drug immensely valuable in foreign markets.

"They've begun raiding into the jungle," Ashton said. "The day seems to have been profitable."

Stark was thinking of other things. "At least we have another chance."

Ashton's metal frame revolved at the end of the rope. "I don't think he's going to let us live, in any case. If, by some remote and impossible chance, one of us should get back to civilization, it would mean the end of him."

"I know," said Stark. "It wasn't love of the Children of Skaith-Our-Mother that kept me from talking."

He tested the bars again.

A yellow bird had appeared, walking through the coarse grass. The eye-flowers watched it. It came and stood beneath the tree where Ashton hung. It looked up at him, moving its head back and forth as the frame moved. It was a largish bird, about two feet high, with very strong legs. It appeared to be flightless. Presently it began to climb the trunk of the tree, striking its claws into the dead wood with a clearly audible clicking.

Both men watched it. It climbed steadily to the branch from which Ashton was suspended. It walked out along the branch to a position above Ashton's head and stood peering earnestly down at him. Its beak was black, polished and shiny, and sharply curved and pointed.

Ashton's head was bent back. He stared upward, at the bird.

It gave a happy gurgling cry and dropped from the branch.

Stark and Ashton both shouted at the same instant. Ashton made a convulsive movement that set the frame swinging. The bird clutched at him, missed its grip, and continued to drop, thrashing its small wings and squawking angrily. It struck the ground with a thump and sat there.

Ashton looked at the red lines where the claws had raked him. Stark was concentrating with single-minded purpose on one of the bars, trying to force it.

The bird picked itself up, settled its feathers, and began once more to climb the trunk of the tree.

Someone threw a stone at it. It squawked again and jumped away into the grass, where it scuttled off with amazing speed.

Penkawr-Che walked up and stood, smiling, between Ashton and the cage.

4

The Antarean was tall, and he moved with a jaunty, loose-limbed stride like a lion carelessly at ease. His skin was a clear golden color, drawn smoothly over strong, high-arching bones. His eyes were a darker gold, and the pupils were slitted. His close-curled hair was like a cap, snug against his broad skull. He wore a very rich tunic of smoke-gray silken stuff over tight black trousers. In his right hand he carried a whip with a long, thin lash. At the end of the lash, jingling lightly together, were several small metallic objects like the jointed tails of scorpions.

"In spite of its unpleasant appearance," said Penkawr-Che, "this upland does support something of a population. The tenacity of life is always amazing. One wonders. What does the yellow bird live on, apart from odd finds like Ashton? Why does it want to live at all, in these surroundings? I can't tell you. But it will be back, probably with its mate. In the meantime, you two have other problems."

He looked from Stark to Ashton, and back again to Stark.

"You will answer my questions this time, unless for some reason you are more attached to the Children of Skaith, who tried to kill you, than you are to this man, who fostered you."

Almost without looking, he flicked the scorpion-tail lash of the whip at Ashton's body. There came a short sharp cry, quickly silenced.

"Ashton is more communicative than you are under drugs. I already know enough from him to find the Witchfires, since he actually saw them when he was a prisoner in the north. But he was never inside the House of the Mother and so was only able to repeat to me what you had told him. Now, is it true that this vast complex of caverns under the Witchfires is a storehouse for artifacts from the past of this planet?"

"That is true," said Stark. "The Children have a passion for history. I suppose it has kept them from going completely mad since they left the outer world behind them." He looked at Penkawr-Che through the bars, then at Ashton's bleeding body pendant from the tree. "You could fill the holds of three ships, and three again, with the things in those caverns; and each piece would be worth a fortune in the collectors' market."

"So I thought," said Penkawr-Che. "Describe to me the entrance to the caverns from the pass of the Witchfires, and the defenses there. Describe the North Gate, by which you escaped. Tell me how many men this Kell à Marg, Skaith-Daughter, can set against me, how they're armed, what kind of fighters they are."

Stark said, "Something for nothing is no bargain, Penkawr-Che. And I don't talk well in cages."

Again the lash flicked out.

"Do you wish to torture Ashton, or do you wish to get the information?" Stark asked.

Penkawr-Che considered, drawing the long, thin lash through his fingers. "Supposing I let you out of the cage. What then?"

"Ashton comes down from there."

"Then what?"

"Let us go that far," said Stark, "and then see."

Penkawr-Che laughed. He clapped his hands. Four men emerged from the litter of the semi-camp which had sprouted overnight beside the base of the ship. At Penkawr-Che's order, they tailed onto the rope and lowered Ashton to the ground, unbinding him and helping him to stand.

"There is half your bargain," said Penkawr-Che.

Each of the four men had a stunner holstered at his belt. Two of them, in addition, carried long-range weapons slung across their backs.

Old Sun slid wearily toward the horizon. Shadows flowed together across the heath.

Stark shrugged. "The northern gate opens onto the Plain of Worldheart. There is a guardroom immediately inside, and beyond that a corridor protected by slabs of stone which can be let down to form a series of barriers. The gate itself is a slab of stone which moves on pivots. You might search for a hundred years along that face of the Witchfires and never find it." He smiled at Penkawr-Che. "There is a third of your bargain."

Penkawr-Che said, "Continue."

"Not till I'm free of these bars."

The lash flicked. Ashton's eyes filled with tears, but he did not cry out.

Stark said brutally, "Flay him if you will. Until I'm free of this cage, you get nothing more."

In a stiff, flat voice Ashton said, "If you push him too far, Penkawr-Che, you will get nothing at any time. He reverts easily."

Penkawr-Che studied Stark. He saw a man, big and dark and powerful, scarred with old battles. A mercenary, with a life spent in the small primitive wars of small peoples on remote worlds. A dangerous man. This, Penkawr-Che knew and understood. But there was something about the eyes, disconcertingly light and clear. They had a kind of blaze in them, something at once innocent and deadly—a beast's eyes, startling to see in a human face.

Ashton added, "He cannot endure being caged."

Penkawr-Che spoke to one of the men, who went away and presently returned with a cutting torch. Removing one bar, he created a gap through which Stark might leave the cage but not in any swift dramatic leap. As he levered himself out, the men stood with their stunners in their hands, watching.

"Very well," said Penkawr-Che. "Now you are free."

Stark drew a long breath and shivered slightly, as an animal twitches its skin. He stood straight beside the cage.

"In the pass of the Witchfires," he said, "just below the crest, there is a rock formation called the Leaning Man. A gateway into the caverns lies close beneath him. It, too, is a pivoted slab of stone.

Inside is a large cavern where the Harsenyi nomads come to trade with the Children. A second door leads into the House of the Mother. Beyond this door is a long corridor, guarded by barriers as the North Gate is guarded, but by more of them—and stronger. No invader has ever breached those defenses."

"I have explosives."

"If you use them, the passage will be blocked by its own collapse."

"You give me small comfort," said Penkawr-Che. "What of the fighting men?"

"Both sexes bear arms." Stark was not sure of that, but no matter. "There will be four thousand at least, perhaps five or six. I can only make a guess. During most of the short time I was there, I was lost and wandering in total darkness. Much of the Mother's House has been abandoned, and there are obviously fewer of the Children than when it was constructed. But they are by no means extinct. They have no modern weapons, but they are stout fighters with what they have." Actually, he knew that they were not. "More important, they'll have the advantage of the ground. You'd have to take the chambers one by one, and you'd never come to the end of them."

"I have lasers."

"They will hide from them. The place is a maze. Even if you were able to force an entrance, they could keep you surrounded, attack unseen from every direction, pick you off one at a time. You would not have enough replacements."

Penkawr-Che frowned, drawing the lash again and again through his fingers.

Rusty twilight crept over the heath. Lights began to come on in the camp.

Penkawr-Che flicked the lash suddenly to draw blood from Stark's shoulder. "Your knowledge has proven to be of no value after all. We've both wasted our time." He turned, impatiently, to speak to his men.

"Wait," said Stark.

Penkawr-Che looked at him, squinting in the dusk. "Why should I wait?"

"Because I know a way into the House of Skaith-Mother that even her Children have forgotten."

"Ah!" said Penkawr-Che. "And how would you have happened to find that on your one brief visit, during most of which you wandered in the dark?"

"In the midst of darkness," Stark said, "I saw light. I will sell you this information."

"At what price?"

"Freedom."

Penkawr-Che's face was a mask, dim and obscure. After a while, so that he would not seem to be too eager, he nodded. "You're worth nothing to me dead. If I'm satisfied with your information, I'll take you and Ashton to wherever you wish, within reason—on Skaith, of course—and release you there."

"No," said Stark. "Release us here and now."

"It has to be my way."

"You'll get what you want *my* way or not at all. Think, Penkawr-Che! All those caverns crammed with treasures, and nothing to stop you—not a single barrier, not a single warrior with a spear. If you intend to let us go, what difference does it make to you where or how?"

"The heath is not a friendly-seeming place."

Stark laughed.

"All right," Penkawr-Che said impatiently. "If I'm satisfied, you may go free here and now."

"Good. I want clothing and weapons, and something for Ashton's wounds."

Penkawr-Che glowered, but he moved apart with one of his men, who presently hurried away.

The man returned quickly with a battery-powered lamp that he set on a packing case. Stark blessed it silently but tried not to look at it. The heath was quite dark now and would remain so until the first of the Three Ladies rose, perhaps a space of thirty minutes.

Ashton stood quietly. The harsh glare accentuated the leanness of his body, his bones seeming more prominent, his corded muscles more like wire ropes. Blood trickled in dark streams on the whiteness of his skin. He, too, had averted his face from the lamp. But he watched Stark.

Presently other men came with clothing. One of them treated Ashton with rough efficiency from a first-aid kit and then dabbed at the cut on Stark's shoulder. The two men dressed themselves in trousers and tunics and soft boots; the tunics were pale in color, and Stark was sorry for that.

"The weapons?"

Penkawr-Che shook his head. "Later, when I've heard what you have to say."

Stark had expected this. "All right," he said, "but Ashton goes now."

Penkawr-Che stared at him. "Why?"

"Why not, unless you're lying to me? Let's just call it a token of your good faith."

Penkawr-Che swore, but he nodded his head at Ashton. "Go, then."

He was confident. He held all the winning cards. He felt that he could afford to humor Stark. Besides, Ashton could not go far.

Ashton hesitated, then went away, out onto the dark heath.

Penkawr-Che said, "Talk."

Stark never lost sight of Ashton's faintly glimmering tunic.

"As I said, the Children are not as numerous as they were in the beginning. They are a controlled mutation, with no choice but to interbreed. Much of the Great House has been abandoned for generations, and I wandered in the black dark there for days, trying to find a way out."

"And then you saw the light."

"Yes. It came through an opening in the rock. There was a balcony at the opening, high up on the cliff. A lookout post, I imagine. Probably there are others. I was not able to climb down from it, so it did not help me to escape. But it's a doorway into the catacombs, unguarded, forgotten—"

"Inaccessible?"

"To any enemy that the Children were aware of when they built it. Not to you. Hoppers could ferry men up there. You could put an army inside with not a single blow struck. You might even manage to fill all your holds before the Children even knew what you were about."

Penkawr-Che looked at Stark narrow-eyed, as if he were trying to pierce his brain and pick out the truth.

"How would I find this balcony?"

"Bring me something to draw on. I'll make you a map."

Out on the heath, Ashton had reached a clump of thorn. He paused, looking back.

A sheet of thin plastic and a stylus were brought to Stark. He put the plastic on the packing case, beside the lamp. Penkawr-Che leaned over to watch. The four men stood around at a little distance, their stunners ready. Ashton meanwhile blended imperceptibly into the shadows of the thorn-trees and disappeared.

"See here," said Stark. "Here is the north face of the Witchfires, here the Plain of Worldheart, here the range of the Bleak Mountains, the Thermal Pits, the Citadel—what's left of it. Over here, to the west, the Harsenyi road that led to their camp. That is what I saw from the balcony. I took rough bearings."

"Which you were able to do without instruments."

"I'm a mercenary by trade, you know that. I have a trained eye." He held the stylus, rolling it between his fingers. "I can pinpoint the area for you so that your search will not take you more than half a day, using the hoppers."

"But," said Penkawr-Che, "at the moment you do not intend to do so."

"No. And if I do not give you the bearings, your search will take much more time. Longer, I think, than you will care to spend."

"You're a hard man to deal with, Stark. What is it you want now?"

"Tell your men to take their weapons and go away."

"That is quite impossible."

"I don't trust you. I don't want those men where they can drop me the moment I finish the map."

"You have my word that they won't." Penkawr-Che smiled. "But I don't trust *you* either, and I think if I sent my men away you'd be gone in an instant, without finishing the map. So I'll tell you what we'll do. In exactly one minute, I shall send men after Ashton; the stunners will put you down, here and now, and we'll begin this whole weary business over again." He pointed to a small array of weapons that had been placed on the ground at a safe distance. "You won't live long without those. Finish the map, pick them up, and walk away free."

Stark's fingers closed on the stylus until it seemed that it must snap. His head dropped forward and his eyes narrowed.

Penkawr-Che said, "It's Ashton who will suffer. Shall I give the order?"

Stark let out a harsh breath and bent over the map.

Penkawr-Che smiled again, briefly. Imperceptibly, the men relaxed. They knew now what they were going to do.

"All right, damn you," Stark said, in a low and furious voice. "Look." Penkawr-Che looked, where Stark was pointing with the stylus. "The Citadel is a burned-out ruin, but you can find it behind the mists of the Thermal Pits. From the Citadel, so . . ."

The stylus began a straight, sure line.

Stark's left hand struck the heavy lamp and knocked it straight into Penkawr-Che's startled grasp. The golden man cried out with pain and dropped it from his seared hands.

Stark was already moving, so swiftly that the eye could scarcely follow him. Instead of going for the weapons, he flung himself directly at the man who stood nearest him. The man, watching Stark, had perforce been staring into the light, which was now on the ground, still shining though partly hidden by the case. During the split second in which his vision was attempting to deal with the sudden change, Stark slammed into him low across the body. The man went over, loosing off his stunner at the sky. Stark rushed off, a large animal running low in erratic leaps and swerves, into the coarse grass with the flower-eyes.

An ordinary man, even a skillful one, could hardly have found cover there. But this was N'Chaka, who had found cover on naked rock when the four-pawed death came snuffling after him. Like the four-pawed death, he moved, as he had done so many times before when he played at the game of survival, aping the pursuer-quarry sliding flat and hugging the ground.

The glare behind him wavered and flashed as the lamp was set up again, worse for the marksmen than no light at all. They were firing wild, in any case, having lost sight of him almost at once; they had placed too much confidence in their numbers and in the futility of any attempt to escape, basing their estimate on human reflexes as they knew them. Stark had gambled his reflexes against theirs, and for the moment he had won. He was quickly out of range of the stunners.

The long-range weapons now began to crack. Dirt spurted up in little fountains, some so close that he was pelted, others so distant that he knew the men were aiming systematically to cover a given area rather than to hit a specific target. Some of the fire went into the clump of thorn where Ashton had last been seen, but Stark knew that Ashton would not be there now.

In the shelter of a hollow, he stripped off the pale-colored tunic, rolled it small and stuck it in his belt. The light had steadied behind him. High up, the illumination was clear. At ground level, it was streaked and patched with the shadows thrown by each small inequality in the surface, so that the marksmen were firing into a distracting pattern of dark and bright. Stark kept as much as possible to the dark.

More weapons had joined the original two. In the intervals of firing he could hear a great deal of shouting. Then this faded and became distant, like the light, though the firing still kept up. When Stark was well past the clump of thorns and into honest night, he began to make a low, hissing sound that was like the voice of the four-pawed death but cadenced as a recognition signal. He continued to make it until Ashton's voice spoke to him from the lip of a small gully.

Stark slid down into it.

Ashton had removed his own tunic and rubbed his pale skin with handsful of soil. He had not forgotten the lessons of his active youth.

"That was the most beautiful sound I ever heard," he said, and put his hand briefly on Stark's shoulder. "Now what?"

"Go to ground," Stark said, and glanced at the sky. "We're about out of darkness."

They scrambled along the gully to where it opened onto more of the coarse grass and pallid, staring flowers. A thick clump of thorn stood at the mouth of the gully, but Stark kept on past it.

Ashton stopped abruptly. "Listen!"

From behind them, where the tall ship was, came the muffled throb and thump of motors waked to sudden life.

"Yes," said Stark. "The hoppers."

He ran on, as the first of the Three Ladies thrust the edge of her shining countenance gently above the horizon.

5

The Three Ladies are Skaith's crowning beauty, in fact her only one —three magnificent star-clusters that grace the moonless sky, shedding a light more sweet and silvery than Old Sun's rusty glare, but almost as bright. Darkness is hard to come by on Skaith, even at night.

It did not much matter now. Darkness would not save them from the hoppers.

They found more clumps of twisted thorn, shadowed and tempting. Stark ignored them. A low ridge rose to the right, silhouetted against the distant glow around *Arkeshti*. Stark ignored that, too. He stayed on the open, exposed slope. Not much of a slope, but enough to have carried off superficial drainage in the rainy season.

The throb of the motors changed. The hoppers were airborne.

"Here," Stark said, thrusting Ashton down into a barely perceptible wrinkle in the ground.

He tore up clods of grass and flowers and strewed them over Ashton, enough to break up the visual aspect of a human body. He spoke a single word to Ashton, a click-cough sound that meant *freeze*. Then he slid away up to the ridge.

From there he observed a great deal of activity around the ship. Men with lights were already on the heath, beating back and forth; and others were coming to join them, searching for dead or wounded bodies.

Up above them, the four hoppers had switched on their powerful landing beams. They swept out into a long line, rushing ahead of the men. Their loud-hailers boomed and belled, an unnatural baying like the voices of some strange breed of mechanized hound hot on the scent. Bolts from their laser cannon struck downward and clumps of thorn erupted into dust and flame.

Stark left the ridge in haste. He found another shallow fold in the slope, not enough to conceal a rabbit, but he dug himself in with his fingers as best he could and lay still among the grass and flowers.

The roar of the hoppers filled the sky, sweeping back and forth, pounding the coverts flat. One of the hoppers paused over the gully, shining down its white glare, pulverizing the shadows with flaring lightning bolts. The loud-hailer shouted Stark's name, then laughed. Stark thought the voice was Penkawr-Che's, but the metallic distortion was such that he could not be sure. The thorn thickets which had seemed to offer such tempting concealment went up, one after the other, in a rage of flame.

The fires and the edges of the landing beams lit up the slope clearly enough even without the Lady's cluster light. Stark lay and listened to the pounding of his own heart, and prayed that Ashton could lie as still as he, and as long; the hunters would be alert for movement. Habitually, Stark knew from the experience of a lifetime, they looked for two things: cover where the quarry may be hiding, or the quarry itself, caught in the open, running. They seldom looked too closely where there is neither cover nor movement, no place to hide, nothing to see. That was why Stark had chosen to remain in the open.

But the price of invisibility is complete lack of motion. Once the quarry stirs, it is lost.

A pair of yellow birds forgot that axiom. Panicked by the noise and flames, they broke and rushed diagonally upward across the slope. The loud-hailer hallooed, and a laser bolt—in massive overkill —crisped them to cinders.

The hopper hung, swinging about, questing. Apparently Ashton did not stir, for nothing else caught its attention and it roared on to devour fresh ground.

Stark continued to lie without moving. Loose dirt trickled from the clods with which he had camouflaged himself. Small disturbed things crawled on him. Some of them bit. The dark-eyed flowers peered this way and that in wild disarray; perhaps the air currents generated by the hopper were responsible. There was a smell of smoke in the air. Fire was spreading out from the thorn thickets, and the shot that killed the birds had set the grass alight. Stark could hear the crackling, entirely too close for comfort. He tried to assess the degree of dryness of the grass, hoping the flames would not spread too quickly. The line of search was drawing away, but the hoppers were bound to come back. It was too soon to move.

The flowers looked down at him from around his face. They looked over him at the fires. They looked upward at the sky. Certainly flowers did not see, but they might have other sensors. They also had a faint sticky fragrance that became more insistent as Stark breathed it, even under the taint of smoke. He also had the unpleasant sensation that the grass crept against him like a sentient thing, touching him with its blades. He had a very great desire to be on his feet again, and away from this too-great intimacy.

Smoke began to blow across him. He forgot his other discomforts in the effort not to cough, and he believed the crackling sound was louder. Little puffs of heat touched his skin.

The hoppers, having gone well past the point where their quarry might have run, wheeled round. They went more slowly on the way back, rummaging leisurely about the ruined landscape, making sure they had left no cover where a man might live. One of them came across the slope and speared Stark in the direct glare of the landing beam.

He held his breath and shut his eyes, lest they catch the light and shine. Smoke rolled across him—and that was good in one way—but he could feel the heat of the ground now with his feet. In a few moments the flames would be all around him. The grass and the flowers knew it, too; he had no further doubt that they were in some manner aware and cringing. He grappled with the panic that rose within him and held it down; there, after a lazy eternity, the hopper droned on over the ridge, back toward *Arkeshti*.

Even so, Stark did not move until he could smell the soles of his boots smoldering. Then he had no further choice. Still in the thick smoke, he bolted out of his shallow grave and hurried along to where he had left Ashton, knowing that if another hopper chanced by they would have no hope.

The fire had not yet spread near to Ashton, who had not moved. He rose up stiffly when Stark bent over him, and was obliged to stamp about in order to loosen his muscles.

"When I used to go hunting with the abos," he said wryly, "I was somewhat younger. Otherwise, Four-Paws would have eaten me." He shivered. "That last one was too close for comfort! Thank God for the smoke."

They set off, away from the ship, threading their way between fires and over patches of scorched ground. They heard no further sound of motors in the sky. Having stamped the land flat, the hunters could assume that the quarry had perished in one or another of the flaming coverts.

Presently Stark and Ashton were beyond the perimeter of the fires. They kept on until it became apparent that Ashton, who had not had an easy day, was beginning to flag. Stark found a thicket, made sure that nothing laired in it, and sat down so the thorn-trees guarded his back. Penkawr-Che's poisons were still in his blood, so he was glad of the rest.

The flowers had marked their passage. Long ripples ran across them, streaming far away, out of sight; but there was nothing strange in this except that the ripples ran crosswise to the wind.

Ashton said, "Eric, when I was lying there pretending not to exist, with the grass and flowers close against me, I got the feeling that—"

"So did I. There's some kind of sentience there. Maybe the sort of thing that tells a Venus flytrap when to snap shut."

"Do you suppose they're carrying a message? And if so, to whom?"

The heath stretched away on all sides, tilting toward the horizon, rough and rumpled, dotted with the twisted thickets and occasional blasted trees. Stark lifted his head and quartered the wind, scenting strangeness, scenting nothing welcoming to man. The faint and somehow treacherous sweetness of the flowers—endless miles of them—caught in his throat. There was nothing in all that emptiness to catch the eye, and yet he sensed presences, things awake and knowing. Whether these were human, animal, or quite other, he could not tell.

He did not like it. "I'll be glad to leave this upland," he said, "and by the quickest way."

"That's the way we just came," said Ashton. "Penkawr-Che picked his spot because the hoppers can raid down into the jungles on about a 180-degree perimeter without having to go much more than a hundred miles in any direction. Eventually, the other two ships, which are raiding elsewhere, will rendezvous with him and they'll head north together to see if they can crack that treasure-house under the Witchfires. How much did you have to tell him?"

"Not as much as he wanted. With luck, he might find that balcony within half a year." Stark frowned. "I don't know . . . The Diviners said that I would bring more blood to the House of the Mother. That's why they tried so hard to kill me. Well, they must fight their battles. We've got one of our own to worry about." He swept his hand across the limitless horizon. "We can't go eastward because of Penkawr-Che. Otherwise, we have a free choice. Any suggestions?"

"Pedrallon."

"What about Pedrallon?"

"He's a prince in his own country. His people bought him back from Penkawr-Che. He has position and power—"

"Unless his people decide to feed him to Old Sun for his sins."

"I suppose it's possible, but he's the only person I can think of who might help us, and who is also located where we might conceivably reach him. Andapell lies along the coast somewhere southwest of here."

"How far?"

"I don't know. But we could strike for the coast and perhaps get passage on a ship. Or, failing that, steal a boat."

"The last time I saw Pedrallon," said Stark, "he had very little use for off-worlders even though he was intriguing with them for his own ends. He will have even less use for them now."

"I came to know him quite well, Eric. There was a lot of time aboard ship, while Penkawr-Che was making up his mind whether to take us to Pax and be satisfied with the payment he'd been promised, or to gamble on his heaven-sent opportunity to loot a world. I think I gave Pedrallon a better understanding of what the Galactic Union is and how it works, and I think he came rather to like me as an individual. Also, he is a dedicated man, to the point of fanaticism. He swore he would go on fighting the Wandsmen, even though his hopes of ever achieving the freedom of starflight are gone. He might even find us useful."

"A faint hope, Simon."

"Worse than faint. But do we have another?"

Stark brooded. "Irnan has nothing left to fight with. Tregad and the other city-states are an unknown quantity. They may go either way. In any case, as you say, they're out of reach." He shrugged. "It might as well be Andapell."

Stark let Ashton sleep for an hour. During that time he rattled around the thicket and, by dint of tearing his hands painfully, managed to fashion two clubs from thorn-wood, snapped to the proper length beneath his boot heel. When he could find the right kind of shattered stone, he would be able to provide hand axes or knife-blades as well. In the meantime, the clubs were a comfort.

The heath was without landmarks, a country in which a man might easily lose himself and wander until he died, unless something took him first, and unaware. Here in the outer reaches of the galaxy the starfields were thin, but Stark found enough old friends to set a course by. When he roused Ashton, they headed west and south, away from *Arkeshti*, hoping to reach the rim of the upland, where it dropped down to the jungle that lay between it and the sea. Neither one had any idea how far that rim might be.

But Stark remembered how, months before, he and Ashton had set out together from the Citadel, far in the bitter north, two men alone on a hostile planet. Then, they had had weapons and supplies, and beasts of burden—and they had had the Northhounds. Now they were destitute, and all the labors of that earlier journey had been brought to nothing by the treachery of one man.

Stark's bitterness was not alleviated by the knowledge that he himself had made the arrangements with Penkawr-Che.

With all the persuasion of his considerable wealth, the Wandsman Pedrallon had not been able to talk the Antarean into getting involved in Skaith's problems beyond providing a transceiver and keeping a speculative finger on the pulse of things. Only Stark's last-minute intervention, when the starport was already in flames and the ships in the act of departure, had tipped the scales along with his mention of Ashton's rescue and the rewards to be won by Penkawr-Che through taking him and the delegations to Galactic Center. Stark could not have known what sort of man Penkawr-Che was, and in any case the Antarean had been the only hope available. But these thoughts made Stark no happier now.

He glanced sidelong at his foster-father, who ought by now to have been almost within sight of Pax and his office at the Ministry of Planetary Affairs.

"It comes to my mind, Simon," he said, "that if all I saved you for was to walk Skaith perpetually like some landbound Flying Dutchman, I might better have left you with the Lords Protector, where at least your captivity was comfortable."

"As long as my legs hold out," said Ashton, "I'd rather walk."

The flowers watched them, rippling. The last of the Three Ladies rose, adding her silvery light to that of her sisters. The heath was flooded with gentle radiance.

Nevertheless, the night seemed very dark.

6

THE GRAY old city of Irnan crouched above the valley. The circle of her walls was unbroken, but the landing of *Arkeshti* had accomplished in a matter of hours what months of siege and suffering had failed to do. Faced with the choice of renewed fighting or surrender to the forces of the Wandsmen, which would surely come, she found that in fact she had no choice. She was exhausted, stripped, denuded. She had lost too heavily of men and wealth. Above all, she had lost hope.

Under the light of the Three Ladies, a thin stream of refugees trickled steadily from the open gate and along the road that ran between ruined orchards and obliterated fields still littered with the rubbish of the besieging armies. Most of the refugees were on foot, carrying what possessions they could on their backs. They were those who felt themselves too closely associated with the revolt against the Wandsmen to hope for mercy, or who feared a general butchery when the hordes of the Farers were loosed upon them.

Within the gate, in the main square of the city, where the buildings of weathered stone stood close around and a few torches burned, a company of men and women were clotted loosely together. More joined them from time to time, straggling from the dark mouths of narrow streets. These bore arms, all of them, for the women of the city-states were trained to battle like the men, since they faced the same hazards from the roving Wild Bands and raiders down from the Barrens. They huddled in their cloaks in the cool night, for the valley was high and it was autumn, and they talked in low, harsh voices. Some of them wept, and not the women alone.

In the Council Hall, beneath the high vault hung with ancient banners, a scant few lamps burned, husbanding precious oil. But there was tumult enough if there was a lack of light. The floor was packed with a shouting, shoving multitude; and on the dais, where the elders sat, angry men and women crowded about, with raised voices and emphatic hands. The meeting, if it could be called that, had been going on since shortly after *Arkeshti*'s departure.

The subject was surrender. The mood was fear, the language cruel, and old Jerann was finding there his penultimate martyrdom.

Beyond the walls, the encampments of the allies were in the final stages of dismantling. Tribesmen in wrapped veils and leather cloaks dyed in the dusty colors of the Six Lesser Hearths of Kheb—purple Hann, brown Marag, yellow Qard, red Kref, green Thorn, and white Thuran—moved among guttering torches, loading their tall desert beasts with provisions and plunder.

Farther away from the city, arrogantly isolated, the dark-furred Fallarin sat muttering among themselves, striking little angry puffs of wind from out their wings. The Tarf, their agile servants in stripes of green and gold, with four powerful ropey arms apiece, did the work of breaking camp.

By morning, they would all be gone.

Beyond them all, the valley lay empty and quiet. But at its upper end, where the mountains closed in and rocky walls narrowed steeply together, was the grotto from which generations of Gerriths, wise women of Irnan, had watched over the welfare of their city.

The grotto had been robbed of all its furnishings, so that it was more than ever like a tomb. Gerrith, the last of her name, had renounced her status as wise woman, saying that her tradition had ended with the destruction of the Robe and Crown at the hands of the Wandsman Mordach. Yet there were beasts tethered below the entrance, and a dim reflection of light shone from it. On the ledge by this entrance a Tarf stood sentinel, leaning on his four-handed sword and blinking horny eyelids with the timeless patience of his kind. His name was Klatlekt.

In the outer chamber of the grotto, the anteroom, eleven great white hounds couched themselves, with drooping heads and half-lidded eyes that glowed with strange fires where they caught the light of a single lamp that burned on a high shelf. From time to time they growled and stirred uneasily. They were telepaths born and bred, and the human minds they touched were far from tranquil.

Three candles lighted the naked inner chamber, throwing wild shadows on the walls of what had once been the wise woman's sanctum. Some few items of furniture had been brought in—a table, a chair, the candelabrum, and a broad, flat basin filled with shining water. Gerrith sat in the chair, a sun-colored woman with the candle flames shining on the thick bronze braid of hair that hung down her back. She had been in this place ever since Eric John Stark walked out from the gates of Irnan into Penkawr-Che's ship. Weariness had drawn shadows at her eyes and etched tight lines about her mouth.

"I have made my decision," she said. "I await yours."

"It is not an easy choice," said Sabak, the young leader of the hooded tribesmen. Only his eyes showed between hood and veil—blue, fierce, and disturbed. His father was Keeper of the Hearth of Hann, and a power in the north. "The Wandsmen will surely try to retake Yurunna and drive us back into the desert to starve. We followed Stark, and gladly, but now it seems that we must go home and fight for our own people."

"For me," said Tuchvar, "there is no choice." He looked at the two huge hounds shouldering against him, and smiled. He was young, a boy only, and he had been an apprentice Wandsman in service to the Houndmaster of Yurunna. "The Northhounds will find N'Chaka if he lives, and I go with them."

Gerd, at his right side, made a thunderous noise in his throat. Grith, at his left, opened her muzzle wide and let her tongue hang red across her sharp teeth. Both beasts turned their lambent gaze on Halk, who stood at one end of the table.

"Keep your hellhounds leashed," he said, and turned to Gerrith. "Your mother, in this room, foretold the coming of a Dark Man from the stars, who would overthrow the Lords Protector and free Irnan, so that we might find a better world to live on. So much for your mother's prophecy, so much for the Dark Man. *I* am not in love with Stark, to waste what life I have in searching for him. My people are waiting for me. We intend to go on fighting the Wandsmen, at Tregad or wherever else we can. I would advise you to come with us, or to go north with Sabak and the Fallarin. Alderyk might even give you sanctuary at the Place of Winds."

Alderyk, King of the Fallarin, whose shadow lay upon the wall like the shadow of a great bird with brooding wings half stretched, looked at Gerrith with his falcon eyes and said, "You would be safer in the north. If you go southward, you challenge the full power of the Wandsmen."

"And what of you, Alderyk?" asked Gerrith. "Which way will you go?"

He cocked his narrow head. He had a smile like a dagger. "I have not yet heard the prophecy. For there is a prophecy, is there not? You would not have called us all here to speak of Stark unless there were one."

"Yes," said Gerrith. "There is a prophecy." She rose up, standing tall in the candlelight, and the hounds whimpered. "I have seen my own path in the Water of Vision. It lies south, and then south, into a terrible whiteness stained with blood, and the end of it is hidden in the mist. But I have looked beyond the Water of Vision."

Between her two hands she held a skull, a small frail thing carved in yellowed ivory and worn with the passing of much time. Its tiny, grinning face was flecked with old blood.

"This is the last fragment of the Crown of Fate. Stark brought it to me from the gallows, on the day we slew our Wandsmen. All the Gerriths who once wore that crown now speak to me through it. Their power has come to me at last." Her voice rang, clear and strong, with a haunting melancholy, a bell heard across hills when the wind is blowing.

"Halk has said that the Prophecy of Irnan was false, and that Stark is a failed and useless man, to be discarded and forgotten. I tell you that this is not so. I tell you that Stark's fate and the fate of Irnan are bound together as heart and breath are bound, and one shall not survive without the other. Stark lives, and *his* way, too, lies southward. But he walks in a great darkness, and death lies ahead of him. His salvation depends on us. If he lives to walk that southern road, Irnan will yet be free. If he dies"—she made a gesture of finality—"the star-roads will not be open in our time, nor in any time until long after the face of Skaith has changed—and that change is coming. The Goddess moves, my lady Cold with her lord Darkness and their daughter Hunger. She has sent her spies before. This winter we shall see the first of her armies. And if the starships do not come soon, there will be no escape for any of us from the Second Wandering!"

She lowered her hands and bent her head and caught a long, unsteady breath. When she looked at them again, and spoke again, she was Gerrith the woman, human and vulnerable.

"There is great need for haste," she said. "Stark moves slowly, as a man on foot, a man with a burden, amid obstacles. Yet he is far away, and even a mounted force will have difficulty reaching the sea in time—"

"The sea?" asked Halk.

"That is where our paths converge, and where his will end if we do not meet."

She moved around the table and put her hand on Gerd's massive head.

"Come," she said to Tuchvar. "We, at least, know what we must do."

They went into the anteroom, Gerd and Grith and Tuchvar and Gerrith; the other eleven Northhounds rose and joined them. They walked out onto the ledge, into the light of the Three Ladies, past the impassive Klatlekt, and down toward the tethered riding animals.

A buffet of wind plucked at Gerrith's garments and rumpled the coarse fur of the hounds. They looked up.

"I will consult with my people," said Alderyk. He came flapping down the path with Klatlekt behind him.

Halk followed, cursing. Sabak, silent, followed him.

"In one hour," said Gerrith, "we start south, Tuchvar and the hounds and I. We will not wait."

They rode away, severally, along the valley. The dim light continued to shine from the entrance to the grotto. No one had thought to blow out the candles or extinguish the lamp, or cover over the Water of Vision. And not even the wise woman gave a backward glance.

The last prophecy of Irnan had been made.

7

STARK AWOKE instantly at the touch of Ashton's hand.

The grudging rebirth of Old Sun stained the heath with a level flood of bloody light. The birds stood in it, their plumage touched to a burning gold on one side, shadows flung darkly on the other. There were about thirty of them. They watched the two men from a distance of a hundred feet or so, the flowers nodding around them.

"They came so quietly," said Ashton, who had been on watch. "I didn't realize they were there until the sun came up."

There was something unnatural about the silence of the birds, and their patience. Stark would have expected them to be noisy with greed and excitement. He would have expected them to attack. Instead, they simply stood there, unreal in that unreal light that caused the landscape to appear tilted and foreshortened, depthless, like a tapestry with golden birds embroidered on it.

Stark took up his club. He searched for stones.

One of the birds lifted its head and sang, in a very clear and flutelike voice—the voice of a woman singing through a bird's throat. The song had no words. Yet Stark straightened, frowning.

"I think we've been forbidden to kill," he said, and clicked two stones together in his hand, measuring the distance.

"I felt the same thing," Ashton said. "Perhaps we ought to listen?"

Stark was hungry. The yellow birds represented both food and menace. He did not know what they would do if he did kill one of them, for they were numerous and powerful. If he provoked an attack, it would not be easy to fight them off. Besides, they seemed to have some purpose, and that wordless song had struck a note of strangeness which made him reluctant to do anything rash until he knew more about what was afoot.

He said irritably, "For a while, at least." And he dropped the stones.

"They're in our way," said Ashton.

The birds had ranged themselves to the southwest.

"Perhaps they'll scatter," Stark suggested.

He started walking. So did Ashton.

The birds did not scatter. They stood high on their strong legs and opened their curved beaks, clashing them together with a harsh and threatening sound.

Stark halted, and the birds were still.

"We can fight them," he said, "or we can go another way."

Ashton put his hand on his tunic, over the bandages. He said, "Their claws are very sharp, and I see thirty double sets of them. Their beaks are like knives. Let's try another way."

"Perhaps we can circle them."

They tried that. The flock raced to turn them back.

Ashton shook his head. "When the bird attacked me, it was acting according to its normal instincts. These are not acting in any normal way at all."

Stark looked about him at the heath, the twisted thorn and the skeletal trees, the peering flowers that blew as they listed with no regard for the wind.

"Someone knows we're here," he said. "Someone has sent for us."

Ashton weighed his club and sighed. "I don't think I could knock down enough of those brutes, and I'd like to keep my eyes yet a while. Perhaps the *someone* only wants to talk to us?"

"If that's so," said Stark, "it will be the first time since I came to Skaith."

The bird lifted up its head and sang again.

Perhaps, Stark thought, it was the natural voice of the creature. But the feeling that some greater intelligence was speaking through it was inescapable. *Do as I ask,* it seemed to say, *and no harm shall come to you.* Stark trusted it not at all. Alone, he might have chosen to gamble on fighting his way through, even though the odds were formidable. As it was, he shrugged and said, "Well, perhaps we'll get fed, anyway."

The birds, thirty careful herd-dogs, drove them on westerly across the heath. They moved at a good pace. Stark kept one eye and ear cocked at the sky in case Penkawr-Che might decide to send the hoppers out for a final look around. None appeared. Apparently Penkawr-Che had decided that plundering villagers of their valuable drug crop was more to the point than searching for two men who were almost certainly dead, and who, if they were not now, soon would be. In any case, the chance of their being rescued and flown back to Pax was so remote that while Penkawr-Che would have killed them out-of-hand when he had them, it was not likely that he would mount any full-scale search for them. If nothing else, he lacked the time and manpower.

Old Sun sat glaring in the middle of the sky and Simon Ashton was beginning to stumble in his walk, when Stark saw two figures silhouetted on the crest of a rise before them. One was tall, with long hair and flowing robes that blew in the wind. The other was smaller and slighter, and the taller one stood protectively with one hand on its shoulder. They stood quite alone, with something regal in their aloneness and their proud bearing.

The birds made little glad sounds and drove the men onward more quickly.

The tall figure became a woman, neither beautiful nor young. Her face was lean and brown, with an immense strength, the strength of wood seasoned to an iron toughness. The wind pressed coarse brown garments against a body that was like a tree trunk, with meager breasts and thin hips and a powerful straightness as though it had fronted many gales and withstood them. Her eyes were brown and piercing, and her hair was brown with streaks of frost.

The slighter figure was a boy of perhaps eleven years, and he was sheer beauty, bright and fresh and graceful, but with a curious calmness in his gaze that made his eyes seem far too old for his child's face.

Stark and Ashton halted below these two, so that they were looking up and the woman and the boy were looking down, a nice positioning psychologically, and the bird sang once more.

The woman answered, in the sweet identical tone, without words. Then she studied the men, with a sword-thrust glance, and said, "You are not sons of Mother Skaith."

Stark said, "No."

She nodded. "This was the strangeness my messengers sensed." She spoke to the boy, and in her manner were both love and deference. "What is your thought, my Cethlin?"

He smiled gently and said, "They are not for us, Mother. Another has set her seal upon them."

"Well, then," said the woman, turning again to Stark and Ashton, "be welcome, for a time." She beckoned to them with the stateliness of a bending tree. "I am Norverann. This is my son Cethlin, my last and youngest, who is called the Bridegroom."

"The Bridegroom?"

"Here we worship the Trinity—my lady Cold and her lord Darkness, and their daughter Hunger, who come to rule us. My son will go to the Daughter in his eighteenth year, if she does not claim him sooner."

"She will, Mother," said the calm-eyed boy. "The day is close at hand."

He moved away from her, disappearing below the crest. Norverann waited. Stark and Ashton climbed to where she stood.

They looked down into a long hollow set with tents and pavilions. Beyond the hollow, clearly visible, was the edge of the plateau, which had curved round to meet them, so that they had not actually come far out of their way. Beyond the rough and channeled edge was a soaring emptiness of air, and beneath that, distant and misty, a greenness reflecting from a sea of treetops.

The encampment itself formed a rough semi-circle round an open space, where men and women busied themselves and children played. The colors of the pavilions were brown and green and russet, with here and there a gleam of gold or white, or a touch of scarlet, and menders had been at work sewing new seams and setting patches. But each tent was adorned with garlands and sheaves of grain. Baskets of roots and other things were set before them. Tattered pennons fluttered in the wind.

"A festival?" asked Stark.

"We celebrate," said Norverann, "the Death of Summer."

Between the points of the semi-circle, beyond the open space and close to the edge of the plateau, was a structure of cut stone. It crouched close to the ground, somehow ominous in its squat windowless strength, covered like an ancient boulder with moss and lichens.

"That is the House of Winter," said Norverann. "It is almost time for us to return to the blessed darkness and the sweet sleep." She bent in her stately fashion to touch the nodding flowers, which swayed toward her. "We share the sacred months of the Goddess with the grasses and the birds and all things dwelling on the heath."

"They are your messengers?"

She nodded. "Long ago we learned the lesson of our kinship. On the heath we are all one, parts of the same body, the same life. When violence was done to the eastern extremity of our body, the message was brought to us here. Burning and destruction, the slaughter of many grasses and flowers and families of thorn. You will tell me about that." She turned her gaze toward Stark and Ashton, and it was as cold and cruel as the sharpest edge of winter. "If you were not already claimed, there would be punishment."

"It was not our doing," Stark said. "Other men were hunting us. We barely escaped with our lives. But who has claimed us, and for what?"

"You must ask Cethlin." She led them down from the ridge to a pavilion of mossy green, and she lifted aside a curtain of dull umber. "Please to enter, and make yourselves fit for the day. Water will be brought to you for washing—"

"Lady," said Stark, "we are hungry."

"You will be fed," she told him, "in good time."

She dropped the curtain and was gone.

The pavilion was furnished with no more than a few rough pallets stuffed with something dry and crackly, and a store of blankets. There was dust about, but it was clean dust and the air smelled of the same things it had smelled of outside. Small personal articles were arranged neatly by the pallets. The pavilion was apparently a summer dormitory for upward of a score of persons.

Ashton threw himself down on somebody's bed with a sigh of relief.

"The promise of food is at least hopeful. And since it seems we're promised to somebody else, I gather our lives are safe for the moment. So far, so good." He added, with a twist of his mouth, "Still and all, I don't like this place."

"Neither," said Stark, "do I."

Men came presently with ewers and basins and towels. The towels were of coarse cloth, as were the shapeless tunics and leg-wrappings of the men. The ewers and basins were of gold, beautifully shaped and chased with graceful designs worn almost invisible by the handling of centuries. The golden things glowed beautifully in the mossy gloom of the pavilion.

"We are called Nithi, the People of the Heath," said one of the men, in answer to Ashton's question.

The man, like Norverann, had the look of old wood, knotty and enduring, and there was something about his eyes, brown and secret, and his mouth, which was broad-lipped and square, with strong spade teeth, that gave an impression of kinship with unknown elemental things—soil and roots and hidden water, and the dark spaces below.

"Do you have trade with the jungle folk?" Stark asked, and the man smiled slowly.

"Trade," he said, "from which they get little gain."

"Do you eat them?" Stark asked matter-of-factly, and the man shrugged.

"They worship Old Sun. We rededicate them, to the Goddess."

"You must have a way down to the jungle, then."

"That is so," said the man. "Sleep now."

He went away with the others, taking the golden vessels. The sides of the pavilion flapped in the wind. The voices of the folk outside seemed far away and unfamiliar.

Ashton shook his head. "Old Mother Skaith is still full of surprises, and few of them pleasant. That boy, the Bridegroom, who goes to the Daughter in his eighteenth year—unless she claims him sooner— Sounds like ritual sacrifice."

"The boy seems to be looking forward to it," said Stark. "You'd better sleep, if you're not too hungry."

Ashton pulled a ragged blanket over him and lay quiet.

Stark watched the slack cloth of the roof billow under the wind, and he thought about Gerrith. He hoped she was well away from Irnan. He hoped she would be safe.

He thought about a lot of things, and felt the anger rising in him so strongly that it became a fever and a throbbing, and the mossy gloom turned reddish in his eyes. Because the anger was useless, he forced it away. Because sleep was necessary, he slept.

He woke with a snarl and a lunge; and there was a man's neck between his hands, ready for the breaking.

8

ASHTON'S VOICE said quietly, "Eric, he's unarmed."

The man's face stared at Stark, already darkening, its mouth and eyes stretched with the beginnings of fear. His body was rigid, trying to accommodate the throttling grip it had not yet considered resisting. The Nithi had a reaction time more suited to trees than to fighting animals.

Stark grunted and let go. "You were crouching over me," he said.

The man sucked air and hugged his throat. "I was curious," he whispered, "to see a man from another world. Besides, you are on my bed." He looked at Ashton. "Is he, too, from another world?"

"Yes."

"But you are not alike."

"Are all men of Skaith alike?"

He thought about that, rubbing his throat.

Stark was aware now of the sound of music from outside, sweet and melancholy, and a murmur of voices gathered and purposeful rather than scattered at random. There was also a smell of cooking.

"No," said the man, "of course they're not, but that has nothing to do with foreigners." He was young and supple, with the secret brown eyes Stark was beginning to dislike intensely. "I am Ceidrin, brother to the Bridegroom. I am to bring you to the feast."

He led the way out of the pavilion, his shoulders stiff. He did not look back to see whether he was followed.

Old Sun was going down in his customary senile fury of molten brass and varying shades of copper and red. Some two hundred men and women, and half as many children, were gathered in the open space between the pavilions and the glooming House of Winter. They faced Old Sun. Atop a pillar of eroded rock a fire burned. Cethlin stood beside it. Behind him stood Norverann, holding one of the golden ewers. The music had ceased. After a moment of intense silence it began again, small flat drums and pipes and two instruments with many strings; and this time it was neither sweet nor melancholy. It was strident, hard, clashing.

It sank into the background, and the people began to chant.

"*Old Sun goes down in darkness, may he never return. Old Sun dies, may he never live again. May the hand of the Goddess strike him, may the breath of the Goddess shrivel him. May the peace of the Goddess be upon Skaith, may it be upon us all . . .*"

Cethlin took the golden ewer from his mother's hands.

At the exact moment when the disk of the ginger star vanished below the horizon, he drowned the fire on the pillar top.

"*Old Sun is dead,*" the people chanted. "*He will not rise again. The Goddess will give us peace this night. There will not be a morning . . .*"

Water and steaming ash ran down the sides of the pillar.

When the chanting was finished, Stark asked Ceidrin, "Do you do this every night?"

"Every night aboveground."

"*Most* people pray Old Sun up in the morning, glad of another day."

"The Goddess will punish them."

Stark shivered. He had felt the breath of the Goddess, that time Hargoth the Corn-King and his sorcerer-priests had sent it upon the wagons of Amnir, the trader out of Komrey, and Amnir with all his men and beasts had been received into the peace of the Goddess with the cold rime glittering on their faces. But even Hargoth had sacrificed to Old Sun, lest the Dark Trinity conquer the land too soon. The Nithi, apparently, were possessed of a full-blown death wish.

The people were finding places on the ground now, around large squares of heavy cloth spread there. Yellow birds wandered among them unconcernedly. Cauldrons steamed over thorn-wood fires.

Ashton sniffed. "I wonder what's in those pots."

"Whatever it is," Stark warned, "eat it."

Ceidrin motioned them to sit between Cethlin and Norverann. The food was served in vessels of stone which were ground fine and thin, and in baskets of woven reeds which must have been brought up from the jungles below. Coarse unleavened bread was served, with bits of Mother Skaith still in it to grate the teeth, as well as a stew made of grain and vegetables and a minute amount of meat, which was white and stringy and came on small brittle bones. Stark glanced from the portion he held to the companionable birds.

"We ask their pardon," said Norverann, "as we ask pardon of the grain when we reap it, and the growing things when we tear them from the ground. They understand. They know that they will feed on us one day." She made a circling motion with her hand. "We are all the same, each in his season."

"And your son," asked Ashton. "When his time comes, will you strike the knife into his heart yourself?"

"Of course," said Norverann, and Cethlin looked at him in mild-eyed amazement.

"Who else," he asked, "should have that honor?"

Stark ate, and the yellow birds pecked around him, eyeing him sidelong, aware of his alienage. The musicians finished their meal and picked up their instruments again. A woman rose and began to sing, her voice carrying like a flute above the gabble of voices.

"Now," said Norverann, "I wish to know what forces threaten our eastern body."

Stark explained to her as well as he could. "I think they will do no more damage, except for the landing of the other two ships when they come. Soon after that, they will be gone."

"Gone from the heath. But from Skaith?"

"Yes. The Wandsmen have driven all the ships away. There will be no more."

"That is well," said Norverann. "Mother Skaith must look to her own children now."

"You have some foreknowledge?"

"Not I. But my son has heard the Goddess speaking in the night wind. She has bidden him make ready for the wedding. This winter, or the next . . . I think we have not long to wait."

Torches had been lighted. The remains of the feast were being cleared away. The music had taken on a different sound. People were rising, moving onto the open ground between the torches, arranging themselves in the pattern of a dance.

Norverann rose and spoke graciously. "You are fed? You are rested? Good. Then it is time for you to go."

Stark said, "Lady, it would be better if we could wait until the morning."

"You will have a guide," she answered, "and the Three Ladies will light your way. Ceidrin . . ."

The young man said sulkily, "I shall miss the dancing."

"The one who waits for these two must not be kept waiting. Nor must she be cheated, Ceidrin, remember that."

Stark caught the young Bridegroom by the shoulder as he moved away toward the dancers.

"Cethlin," he said, "your mother said I must ask you. Who has claimed us, and why?"

"If I told you, you might try to evade the claimant. Is that not so?" Cethlin brushed his hand away and smiled. "Go with my brother."

Ceidrin fetched a torch and called two other men. He marched off with them toward the House of Winter. Since there was no choice, Stark and Ashton gave Norverann thanks for her hospitality and followed.

They passed by the dancing place. Cethlin had reached out and taken the hand of a girl with dazed eyes and garlands in her long hair. Languorous beguiling pipes and muttering strings lured them on. Cethlin stepped out with his partner, treading the intricate pattern of a maze dance that was both graceful and sinister. The drums beat, soft and insistent, like tiny hearts.

"How will it end?" Ashton asked Ceidrin.

"The girl with the garlands—she is Summer, you understand—the girl will be led deeper and deeper into the maze until she falls exhausted."

"Will she die?"

"Not for several nights yet," Ceidrin said. "At least I shall not miss that. It is not so easy to kill the wicked season."

"Why," asked Stark, "are you all so eager for the peace of the Goddess?"

Ceidrin gave him a glance of pure scorn. "Her rule is inevitable. We seek only to hasten the day. I hope it comes in my time. But I hope that before the Goddess takes me, I may look down from this high place and see the green jungle black and shriveled, and the worshipers of Old Sun struck dead."

"There are many of them," Stark said. "All sacrificing to Old Sun to keep him going. It will be a while before the Goddess rules all Skaith. Where exactly are you taking us?"

"Down," said Ceidrin. "To the jungle. Once there, you may go where you will."

"We need weapons."

"There are none here but kitchen knives and reaping hooks—and those we cannot part with." He added, "Even if we would."

The squat and ancient bulk of the stone house swallowed them, swallowed the sound of music and the sight of dancers treading their mazy path. Inside was a different sort of maze, full of traps and pitfalls to discourage any intruder. Ceidrin, with the single flickering torch, led the way safely past these and into a network of burrows, poor and meager in comparison with the magnificent caverns of the House of the Mother, but adequate for persons who wished only to survive the winter—though Stark doubted that winter on the plateau was all that severe. The sanctuary was probably rooted more in ritual than in necessity, though food might be a problem; the heath would be a barren enough place even in summer.

"What do you do in these dens?" he asked. "Besides the obvious."

"The flowers and the grasses rest. So do we."

In a sort of communal chamber, with a tiny fireplace and a roof so low that Stark must bend to avoid the interlaced and knotted roots that held it, Ceidrin opened one of several great stone jars that were set apart from corn bins and cisterns. The jar was packed to the top with dried flower heads. The compressed and dusty fragrance that rose from them was enough in itself to make the mind reel.

"In life they bring us comradeship, in death they bring us dreams. The winter is dark and sweet."

Reverently he replaced the lid and they passed on. The burrows were well stocked and clean. Nevertheless, Stark did not envy the Nithi their well-adapted lives.

They stooped their way along a narrow passage and finally came out abruptly into the open night, on a tiny ledge or landing like a bird's perch high above the jungle, which showed as a vast and spreading darkness far below. The first of the Three Ladies, newly risen, shed enough light so that Stark could see the way. Ashton saw it, too, and muttered something, a curse or a prayer or both.

Ceidrin put out his torch and laid it aside, because he needed both hands more than he needed light. He started down.

The cliffs were broken, pitted with erosion, gashed by falls of rotten rock. The way was sometimes a path and sometimes a stair, and sometimes no more than chipped-out foot- and handholds across a leaning face. Warm air rising from below was twisted into turbulent currents that twitched and plucked at the climbers with seemingly malicious intent. Sometimes the path was cut inside the cliff, and here the wind rushed ferociously, almost hurling them bodily upward like sparks in a flue. Certain places held ingenious arrangements of ropes and windlasses, and Stark surmised that they were used to aid in the ascent of men coming back from the lowlands laden with spoil.

The great milky cluster rose higher. Her light strengthened. In the darkness below, a glimmer showed. It spread and ran, became a silver snake winding through the black. A great river, going to the sea.

"How far . . . ?" asked Stark, shouting to be heard above the rush of wind.

Ceidrin shook his head with arrogant disdain. "We have never seen the sea."

Stark marked the direction, knowing that he would lose sight of the river later on.

The third of the Three Ladies was at her zenith and the first one had already set when they reached a hole in the rock no more than fifty feet above the treetops. Inside the hole was a landing and a narrow shaft straddled by a windlass with a mass of fiber rope wound on its drum.

"I will go first," said Ceidrin, "and open the way for you."

He lighted a torch from a ready pile and sat in the sling end of the rope. The two other Nithi men, who had spoken no word all the way, cranked him down with a creaking and a clacking of ancient pawls. The rope had been spliced in many places and did not inspire confidence. Yet it held. Ashton went down, and then Stark, fending off the smooth sides that trickled with condensation, growing green slime.

A tiny chamber was at the bottom. In the torchlight, Ceidrin moved a ponderous counterweight and a stone slab tilted open.

"Go," he said, "to whatever arms await you."

9

THEY HAD COME DOWN from Irnan, across mountains wet with autumn rain, into the foothills. They were a small company. They had traveled fast and they had avoided roads and habitations wherever that was possible, swinging wide to the west, away from Skeg. But there were watchtowers, and wandering herdsmen, and hunters. And there were places where no other way existed except that beneath the wall of a fortified town, for all to see. And as they advanced into the softer lands, the population increased.

Here were more villages and more roads, and it was the time of the seasonal migration. Long lines of traders' wagons moved southward ahead of the snows that would block the high passes. Caravans of traveling whores and parties of wandering entertainers—dancers and musicians and tumblers, jugglers and singers and dark-cloaked men who practiced magical amazements—all of them with the coin of a summer's work jingling in their pockets, were returning to their winter circuits away from the nipping frosts. Bands of Farers, too, drifted toward the fat tropics, where there was plenty of food and *tlun* for the children of the Lords Protector. The Farers did not always keep to the roads, but randomly followed tracks known only to themselves. But no group of wayfarers could remain forever unnoticed and unseen, particularly not a group containing a half-dozen winged Fallarin and twelve trotting Tarf with four-handed swords, a ten of veiled riders in colored cloaks, another ten of men and women in steel and leather, and thirteen great white hounds with evil eyes, led by a boy in a blue smock.

It was only a matter of time. And Alderyk, King of the Fallarin, was not surprised when Tuchvar, who had been scouting as usual with the hounds, came back to tell them that there were men ahead.

"How many?" asked Halk.

The company halted, with a subdued clatter of gear and a creak of leather. The beasts dropped their heads and blew, glad of the rest.

Tuchvar said, "The hounds can't count. The thought was *Many*, and close by."

Alderyk looked about him. It was an excellent place for an ambush. Far behind them was the terrain of crouching hills they had traversed that morning, lion-coated hills with autumn grass dry and golden on their flanks. From the hills the party had come into the midst of a vast field of ruins where a city had died and left its bones. Here they had followed a path like a cattle trail which showed on the weedy ground. The debris of centuries had filled the city's forgotten streets and covered some of the shattered walls; vision did not run far in any direction. Obviously someone knew the way through the tangle, but it was not the newcomers, and surely now that path could lead them only to disaster.

A spire of broken masonry lifted above the lower ruins. Alderyk said, "Perhaps from there I might see how many, and where they wait."

The spire was at least two hundred yards away, beyond his power of flight.

"Lend me Gerd," he said to Tuchvar, then motioned to one of the Tarf. "There may be pitfalls. Seek me a safe path."

The Tarf trotted ahead. Alderyk clapped his beast over the rump with the tips of his leathery wings and moved off, with Klatlekt at his left side.

Gerd ranged himself on Alderyk's right, but not happily. The Northhound was uneasy in this company. The nonhuman minds of the Tarf were immune to houndfear and their swords were very sharp and long. The Fallarin had other powers. Gerd felt a whip of air flick across him, rumpling his coat the wrong way, and he shivered.

In a few moments, the ruins had hidden the others and they were alone. The sun was hot. Small things squeaked and chittered. Beyond these tiny sounds there was nothing. Even the wind was still.

Men? asked Alderyk.

Not here. There.

Watch.

Twice the leading Tarf warned them around treacherous places. The spire rose higher, its jagged outline clear against the sky.

At length Alderyk sighed and said, "Enough." He reined in his mount and drew his small, wiry body erect, poised on the beast's back, while Klatlekt held its head.

Spreading his wings, Alderyk leapt into the air.

A clipped bird, he had said of himself, *a mockery.* The controlled mutation that was to have given its changeling children the freedom of flight had been a cruel failure. The strong wings were not strong enough, the light bodies were still too heavy. Instead of soaring like eagles, the Fallarin could only flap like barnyard fowl going to roost.

Instead of joy it was labor. Alderyk pounded the air fiercely, feeling, as he always did, the raging frustration of not being able to do what his whole being yearned to do. To ease this yearning, the Fallarin had carved the cliffs of their mountain fortress, the Place of Winds, into a thousand fantastic shapes that mimicked all the currents of the high air, so that they could at least pretend to ride the whirlwind.

Yet, even so, he always felt a moment of exhilaration, watching the ground drop away beneath, savoring that exquisite instant when the wings seemed to have achieved mastery at last and when *now,* for the first time, the sky was truly his . . .

He clung, panting, to the spire at its crumbling peak.

And he could see.

The level land sloped gently to a broad savannah. Beyond the ruins, half a mile away, was a village. He could see the walls and the warm color of thatched roofs. It was harvest time but there was no one in the fields.

Alderyk saw where the men were. He took time to see, marking several things. Then he looked on either side, across the ruins. Finally he flung himself outward and fluttered down, the air booming under his wings.

He rode back to where the others waited.

Drawing his dagger, he sketched a rough map with the point in a patch of dusty ground.

"There is only this one way through the ruins. The villagers must use it to get their herds to the hill pastures. Men wait here and here, inside the ruins, in concealment. Other men wait here, in the open, by the end of the path. And I think these men are mercenaries, for I saw steel glinting."

"Mercenaries," Halk said. "Word has gone ahead of us. How many?"

"Perhaps fifteen here, and fifteen here, either side of the path. And thirty more in the open."

"We've fought worse odds, even without the hounds."

"There are more. Here, in reserve, are the village men—forty or fifty. And in addition there are Farers, a score or more, scattered about. There may be still others that I could not see, but these I am sure of."

Halk frowned. "And only this one way through. You're certain of that."

"From up there it was plain. Away from this path, we would have to abandon the animals. Whether we could get through afoot I don't know, but it would take time. And they would still be on the other side of the ruins, watching for us."

"We could return to the hills and find another way entirely," Sabak suggested.

"No," said Gerrith. Her face had become stern, the bones more prominent, the eyes almost bleak, except that they were not the color for bleakness. "There is no time. Stark has reached the river."

"What river?"

She shook her head. "I don't know. But he is moving more swiftly now, much more swiftly, to the sea. We must go straight ahead."

Tuchvar leaned in the saddle to stroke Gerd's head. "The hounds will take us through."

Gerd half closed his eyes. Memory stirred, of days long gone, of another hand, another voice. A hand and voice that he had helped to still forever in the streets of Yurunna. The guilt was with him yet. He whimpered and thrust his head against Tuchvar's knee.

Houndmaster.

Good hound, said Tuchvar, and smiled. He looked at Halk. "Let us go, then."

They knew their battle order, all but the Irnanese among them, having fought their way together all the way from the northern deserts to the Fertile Belt: hounds first, then the Fallarin, and then the tribesmen.

The Irnanese objected to being fourth in line. "We are accustomed to lead," they said, and looked to Halk.

"If you wish to stand in the way of the Northhounds when they're about their business, you are free to do so," he told them, and nodded to Tuchvar.

Teach them, Gerd.

Gerd laughed, as a hound laughs, touching the Irnanese with a cold lash of fear.

"Are you content?" asked Halk.

They said they were.

"Then lead on, Tuchvar. And no one stops now—except for death."

Thirteen white hounds fled away along the path, baying. Their deep voices sounded in the ruins, rich and beautiful.

The waiting mercenaries, thick red-bearded men from some hill town along the edges of the Barrens, took sword and spear into their calloused hands. They set lozenge-shaped shields on their strong left arms.

Out beyond the ruins, on the clear ground, the second company of men readied their bows, nocking arrows to the strings. They listened to the belling of the hounds. They did not know that sound. They were brave men, yet some knot within them loosened and they trembled.

Kill? asked Tuchvar, galloping behind the hounds.

Too far. Soon.

The Fallarin rode high and forward, their wings half spread, so that they seemed to fly above their mounts. The Tarf paced them easily, carrying their huge swords like batons. The dusty cloaks of the Hann streamed out behind their striding beasts. The Irnanese rode more heavily, with a solid sound of iron.

Kill? asked Tuchvar.

Now.

Good. Send fear.

The eyes of the running hounds burned like lamps in the light of Old Sun. And the baying ceased.

In the sudden quiet the mercenaries waited, in their ambush of ruined walls. They waited one hard-held breath, hearing how close their quarry came.

Terror took them. A thunderbolt of fear, a tearing agony that turned the bowels to water and the bones to brittle ice. Fear that drove the heart to beat itself within the rib cage like a frantic bird.

Some of the men dropped where they stood. Others hurled their spears blindly and tried to run. On either side of the path, then, great white bodies leaped among them, and those who still had breath screamed—once.

The Fallarin swept by, along the path.

The second company of mercenaries, with their ready bows, began to run toward the ruins.

A wind sprang up, a whirlwind, rushing toward them. Dust and dry grass and fallen leaves flew up from the ground and spun wildly. Through the spinning, the mercenaries saw six small dark men with leathery wings. The wings moved all together, and beneath the skirling of the wind they thought they heard a singing like the very voice of storm.

They loosed their arrows at the winged men. Wind caught the shafts and flung them all away. Wind buffeted and blinded and confused, and when it had passed, the mercenaries saw the white hounds and the great swords of the Tarf and the companies of armed men.

"Throw down your arms!" Halk shouted. "Throw them down if you wish to live!"

The village men were streaming back through their own gate, trampling each other and the Farers in their haste. The mercenaries were outnumbered, and their noses twitched to the smell of sorcery. They had heard their comrades screaming among the ruins, and they saw how the jaws of the hounds were red and how they licked the redness from their muzzles, eager for more, and they saw how the eyes of the hounds glowed like coals in the sunlight. They calculated how much they had been paid, and decided that in losing half their company they had lost enough. They threw down their arms.

Gerrith rode forward. "Which one among you can guide us to the sea?"

No one spoke. But Gerd said, *There.*

Touch.

One of the men cried out and went to his knees.

"Come here," said Halk.

The man came.

"The rest of you, get gone."

The hounds struck them for sport and they went, running. When they had gone far enough, Halk moved his company on, keeping out of bowshot of the village wall.

"You have strong magic," said the mercenary trotting by his stirrup. "But from now on you are hunted men."

"You shall tell us," said Halk, "about that hunting."

10

STARK AND ASHTON had reached the river when the morning mists were rising. They saw nothing but a muddy bank and a broad swirl of brown water gliding, and the sounds of a world awakening. There was not even anything with which two men lacking knives or axes might cobble together a raft.

Stark listened, and sniffed the heavy air. "We'll rest awhile."

They had rested along the way, but not enough. And Ashton's face was gray.

"If something comes to eat me," he said, "don't wake me until just before the jaws close."

He lay between the buttressing roots of a huge tree and slept. Stark leaned his back against the tree and slept also, but lightly. A warm, sluggish breeze stroked his skin with uncleanness, and the taste of it in his mouth had the deceitful sweetness of poison.

Something rustled.

He was awake in an instant. Some creature moved in the undergrowth. It was neither large nor menacing, and it was perhaps thirty feet away, upwind.

Stark moved toward it, delicate as a stalking cat.

He did not know what it was, except that it was furry and fat and had a warm smell. It bustled down to the river to drink and he pounced and caught it and broke it between his hands. The flesh was not very appetizing but he ate it, saving the best bits for Ashton.

"Field rations," he said, when Ashton woke. "I'm sorry there's no fire."

He might have made one, but apart from the time it would have taken to search for the materials, it did not seem the best part of wisdom. People are apt to be curious about strange smokes.

Ashton muttered something about getting old and soft, but he choked the raw meat down as Stark buried the debris. They drank—as little as possible, for the water had a foul taste—and then they continued on downstream, sweating in the unaccustomed heat, fighting the undergrowth, and keeping an eye out for things that might be unpleasant to tread upon.

After an hour or two they came to the trail.

It was old and well-used, worn deep in the jungle floor and beaten to a glassy smoothness. It came from somewhere to the northeast to meet the river bank and follow it south. Stark and Ashton took to it, grateful for the easy going but wary nonetheless.

Several more trails came into it from the east, and it widened with each one until it became almost a road. Stark scouted ahead at each bend, distrusting what might lie beyond.

Even so, he smelled the clearing long before he saw it.

"Carrion," he said. "A lot of it. And ripe."

Ashton grunted. "It would ripen quickly in this climate."

They went along the green-shadowed tunnel under the trees, stepping softly. Stark could hear voices clashing and quarreling. The voices of scavengers. When they came to the end of the road and saw the temple and the sacred grove, the carrion-eaters were the only things that moved there.

The temple was small and exquisite, built of wood wonderfully carved and gilded, but the ceremonies depicted in those carvings that were still whole were unpleasant in the extreme. The temple had been seared with fire and its ivory doors were shattered. The bodies of priests and servants, or the rags of them, were strewn across the steps and the ground below as if they had stood there together in a posture of defense. The tongue of fire had licked them, too.

"Penkawr-Che's work."

"Off-world work, anyway. Since we're not looking for treasure, perhaps they've left something we can use."

The scavengers flapped and growled, undisturbed.

The sacred grove—many small trees grown together in a tangle, or a single tree monstrously multiplied—drooped languidly in the heat. The trunks were smooth and pale, lovely shapes of alabaster trailing graceful branches with feathery leaves.

The temple and grove appeared desolate, peaceful with the peace of death. And yet Stark did not move out of the shelter of the jungle.

"Something?"

"I don't know." He smiled briefly. "I've grown too dependent on the hounds. Stay close."

He moved out across the compound, past the sacred grove. Sunlight struck across the alabaster trunks, showing veins of a darker shade. In the shadows between them he glimpsed pale forms that were not trees, held spiderlike in a webbed embrace of branches. He saw a girl's long dark hair. But nothing within the grove stirred or spoke.

"It's true, then," he said.

"What is?"

"The tale I heard in the north, that in this country the trees eat men." He looked at the scattered human carrion by the temple, amid singed shreds of priestly robes. "I don't feel quite so much pity for them as I did."

"'And every tree holy with human blood,'" said Ashton, and held his nose. "Let's get on with it."

They skirted the grove, keeping well out of reach of the branches. Beyond it they came into the open space before the temple, where the scavengers fed and marks were on the ground to show where a hopper had landed. The ivory doors of the temple hung open onto darkness.

The scavengers hopped and scuttered away, protesting. Then, suddenly, in the midst of that raucous screeching came another voice, wilder, higher, more demented. A man ran out of the temple door and down the steps. He came in a headlong rush, naked, smeared with ashes, streaked with his own blood where he had gashed his flesh, and he held in his hands a great, heavy sword with a butcher's blade.

"Murderers!" he screamed. "Demons!" And he raised the sword high.

Stark thrust Ashton aside. He caught up a morsel of carrion from the littered ground, a gnawed skull, and he hurled it fair in the man's face so that he had to bring his arms down to shield himself. He broke stride and Stark ran at him. The man slashed out with the blade. Stark twisted in mid-leap and came in at him from the side, swinging a deadly hand that took the man under the ear. There was a dry, sharp, snapping sound and the man went down and did not move again. Stark pulled the sword out from under his body.

No one else was in the temple, nor in the living quarters behind it. They found clothing, light loose things more suited to the climate than the off-world garments they wore, and far less conspicuous. Among these were wide hats of woven fiber, and sandals. In the kitchens they found food and took of it as much as they could carry, as well as knives and a flint-and-steel. They had no trouble finding a weapon for Ashton.

A path led from the temple compound toward the river. Following it, they came to a landing where one fine boat with a high, carved prow was moored in the place of honor and two battered old dugouts were drawn up on the bank. They left the fine boat to wait for the priests who would never come and pushed one of the dugouts into the brown water. It took them—a broad, strong current without haste.

They passed a few fishing villages, keeping always to the far side of the river. The villages were poor things and the fishermen seemed content to ignore them. Later in the afternoon, when they were in the middle of a wide reach, Stark heard a faraway faint sound and stiffened.

"Hoppers coming."

"What do we do, just carry on?"

"No. They would wonder why we weren't scared. Paddle like hell for the bank and don't lose your hat."

They paddled, churning a clumsy wake across the current.

The hoppers appeared from the west, high enough for the men in them to spot the villages and temple clearings they were looking for. They came over the river and then dropped suddenly, one behind the other, until they were almost on top of the dugout.

The downdraft hit. Stark and Ashton tumbled into the water, desperately holding the dugout to keep it from turning over and dumping everything they had.

Stark thought, They know us, they've recognized us in spite of the clothes . . .

But the hoppers, having had their little joke, swooped upward again and went their way east.

Stark and Ashton hauled themselves back into the dugout, and Ashton said, "I thought they had us."

"So did I. I wonder if they're Penkawr-Che's, or is there another ship closer by? The one that brought back Pedrallon."

"I don't know. But it's likely that ship would stay, if there are enough temples to loot."

Stark dug his paddle in. "We'll keep to the bank."

After a while he added, "If there is a ship, and if we can get to Pedrallon while it's still here, and if he's willing to help us, there might be something constructive we could do."

Ashton said nothing. He waited.

"When the hoppers are away raiding," Stark said, "and there's only a skeleton crew aboard, a strong force might capture the ship and hold it long enough for us to use the deep-space communications center. It's the only hope I can see now of getting us off this planet."

"Then, let us try. Anything at all."

They sent the dugout flying.

The hoppers crossed the river again at sunset, high and heading west.

Under the shadow of the bank, Stark smiled and said, "They're not Penkawr-Che's."

Hope took them down the river faster than the current.

11

In the House of the Mother, deep under the icy sparkle of the Witchfires in the far north, Kell à Marg, Skaith-Daughter, sat on the knees of the Mother and heard what her chief Diviner had seen in the great crystal Eye.

"Blood, yes," he said. "Blood, as we have seen before. Because of the off-worlder Stark, the House will be violated and some few will die. But that is not the worst."

Kell à Marg's body was slim and proud. Her white fur gleamed against the brown stone of the Mother's breast. Her eyes were large and dark, shining in the pearly light of the lamps.

"Let us hear the worst, then."

"The Mother's heartbeat slows," said the Diviner, "and the Dark Goddess moves. She is shod with ice and her mouth breathes silence. My lord Darkness walks at her right hand, and at her left is their daughter Hunger, and where they walk all is desolation."

"They have always shared this realm with the Mother," said Kell à Marg, "since the time of the Wandering. But Mother Skaith will live as long as Old Sun lives."

"Her life draws in, as his does. Has Skaith-Daughter looked out from her high windows across the Plain of Worldheart?"

"Not since the burning of the Citadel. I hate the wind."

"It would be wiser if you did so, nevertheless."

Kell à Marg looked at her chief Diviner, but he did not waver nor turn aside; and so she shrugged and rose from her high seat, stepping from between the Mother's arms. She called one of her sleek tiring-women to come and bring a cloak. No one else was in the hall. The Diviner had wished to give her his heavy news in private.

They walked, Kell à Marg and the Diviner and the tiring-woman, through the long corridors and winding ways of the House of the Mother, past a hundred doorways into a hundred chambers filled with the relics of vanished cities and dead races. The quiet air smelled of dust and the sweet oil of the lamps, and it smelled of time also. The labyrinth extended upward and downward and on all sides through the mountain heart, the life work of this mutant race that had turned its back deliberately to the sky. Now there were so few of the Children left that a large part of the labyrinth was abandoned, with all its treasures, to the eternal dark.

A small coldness touched Skaith-Daughter, the veriest fingertip of fear.

At length they came into a corridor where there was nothing but bare stone and a bitter draft that bent the lamp flames, and at the far end an arch of light. Kell à Marg took the cloak about her shoulders and went ahead alone.

The arch gave onto a narrow balcony, a falcon's perch far below the peaks of the Witchfires that glittered against the sky, but high above the Plain of Worldheart. Kell à Marg's body flinched from the cruelty of the wind. Hugging the cloak about her, she leaned against the rock by the high parapet and looked out across the plain.

At first, she could see nothing but the glare of Old Sun and the blinding pallor of snow, shaping a dreadful emptiness. But as she forced herself to endure this ordeal, she was able to make out details. She could see where the Harsenyi road used to run, safe from the guardian Northhounds. She could see where the permanent camp of the Harsenyi had been, from which they had served the Lords Protector and such Wandsmen as had need of them on their comings and goings to the Citadel and among the dark settlements of the High North. She could see the vast, white emptiness of the plain and the wall of the Bleak Mountains beyond it; there the Northhounds had once ranged, before the man Stark had managed somehow to subdue them to his alien will.

She could not detect that anything had greatly changed. Seasons meant nothing to her, safe in the gentle womb of the Mother, but she knew that summer was a brief and stunted interval between one winter and the next, and that even in summer there was always snow. Summer, plainly, had come and gone; nevertheless, this winter that she looked upon seemed no different than any other. The cold might be more intense, the snow deeper, but she could not be sure. The wind skirled snow-devils across the plain, mingled with plumes of steam that spurted from the Thermal Pits, so that it was difficult to tell which was snow and which was steam. Beyond the pits, on the flank of the Bleak Mountains and invisible behind its eternal curtain of mist, would be the ruins of the Citadel. Because of that mist she had never seen the Citadel—only the smoke and flame of its burning.

But she saw it now.

She saw the ruins, black and broken, through the new thinness of the mist.

It frightened her. She pressed against the parapet, studying with a new intensity the action of the fumaroles. And it seemed to her that all across the thermal field the plumes of steam were scanter than she remembered, their spurting less frequent. That same thermal field underlay the House of the Mother. The food supply depended upon its warmth and moisture. If it should grow cold, all those who dwelt within the House must perish.

Great black clouds moved over the face of Old Sun. The light dimmed. The first veils of snow began to fall on the distant peaks.

Kell à Marg shivered and left the balcony.

She did not speak until they had gone from that corridor to another place that was free from draft and where the lamp flames were burning upright, and even then she kept the cloak about her.

She sent the tiring-woman away and said to the Diviner, "How long?"

"I cannot tell you, Skaith-Daughter. Only that the end is there, and that the Mother has given you a choice."

Kell à Marg knew what that choice was, but she made him put it into words, nonetheless, in case his wisdom might be greater than hers.

"We must go back into the world and seek another place, or else stay here and prepare to die. That may take some generations, but the decision cannot wait. When the Dark Goddess establishes her rule, there will be no second choice."

Kell à Marg drew the cloak still more closely about her, and still she was cold.

On the other side of the Witchfires, below the pass of the Leaning Man, the Ironmaster of Thyra cast his own auguries. He did this in private, with only his First Apprentice to assist him, in the forge that was sacred to Strayer of the Forges. This forge was set well into the towering flank of the ruin-mound where the men of Thyra burrowed and labored and brought forth iron pigs.

From the small furnace he took a little crucible of molten metal, and while the apprentice chanted the proper words he tipped the contents of the crucible into an iron basin filled with fine sand and cold water. A tremendous steam arose, and a wild bubbling, and when all that had gone the apprentice dipped away what water was left and the Ironmaster looked at the pattern that had formed on the sand.

Looked, and crossed his hands upon the great iron pectoral he wore that was wrought in the shape of Strayer's Hammer, and bowed his head. "It is the same. There is no health in the metal. The divine strength of Strayer is gone from us."

"Will you try again, Ironmaster?"

"There is no use. We have the word of Strayer, he will not alter it. Look you. These small bright rills pointing south. Always south. But here to the north, again, the metal is twisted and dark."

The apprentice whispered, "Must we then leave Thyra?"

"*We* may stay," said the Ironmaster. "That choice is ours. But Strayer has gone before us. His quality is heat, the fire of the forges. He has fled before my lady Cold."

Southward from Thyra, on the edge of the Darklands, the People of the Towers prepared themselves for winter.

The summer, always a blighted season, had been abnormally short and chill, so that the lichen-gatherers had been driven in early with a scant harvest and the hardy grasses had never come to seed. The People had faced bad winters before in their fortress-camp, where the broken towers stood around a wide circle with a faceless monument at its center. But never, they thought, had a winter come so soon as this one—with such terrible winds—and never had their beasts and their larders been so lean.

Hargoth the Corn-King and his sorcerer-priests, all narrow gray men with gray masks to cover their narrow faces from the cold, took up their ritual position. Hargoth, who worshiped the Dark Goddess but also fed Old Sun, maintaining a precarious balance between the two, spoke with his Lady. When this was done, he was silent for a long while.

Then he said, "I will cast the finger-bones of the Spring Child."

He cast them, three times, and three times, and three times.

Only Hargoth's eyes and mouth were visible behind his mask, which was marked with the stylized symbols of corn ears in a place where no corn had grown for a thousand years. Hargoth's eyes glittered and were bright with a light of madness that comes from the winter dark. His mouth spoke in jets of white vapor that blew away on the wind.

"They point south," he said. "Three times, and three times, and yet three times again. That way lies life and Old Sun. Here lies death and the rule of the Goddess. We must decide now which of them we shall choose."

He lifted his gaze to the remote and mocking sky and cried out, "Where is our Deliverer, the star-born one who was to lead us to a better world?"

"He was a false prophet," said one of the priests who had followed Stark and Hargoth to Thyra, and survived. "The ships are gone from Skaith. The star-roads are closed to us, as they have always been."

Hargoth walked toward the Towers, where his people dwelt. Beside the monument he paused and said, "For us they are closed, but perhaps they may open for our children, or for their children. And any life is better than death."

Again he cast the finger-bones. And again they pointed south.

12

ALDERYK the Fallarin perched on a rock, looking at the view and disliking it intensely.

Accustomed as he was, for a lifetime, to the cold clean northern desert, he found the steamy air of these lowlands difficult to breathe, the over-active vegetation both wasteful and repulsive. Things grew on each other's backs, so that a plant was forced under and beginning to rot almost before it ripened. A sticky, green stench always filled his nostrils, and what time his fine dark fur was not being drenched by sudden rains it was dripping disgustingly with his own sweat.

Now, stretched out before him and running away over the rim of the world, was a heaving unpleasantness called the sea.

Beside him, his friend Vaybars said, "I think perhaps we made a mistake when we decided to follow the wise woman."

Alderyk grunted, and fingered the place at his neck where his gold torque had been before he gave it to Penkawr-Che as part of Vaybar's ransom.

"At least," he said, "we're doing one thing we set out to do when we came south. We're learning a lot about this wretched world we live on."

The mercenary had led them well, after one mistake. He had attempted to betray them by leading them to a town where there was a force sufficient to overwhelm them. Gerd had stopped that, and the hounds had given the man a lesson in the folly of trying to outsmart a pack of telepaths. He had not tried again.

He had brought them by rough and relatively untraveled ways, where the only people they met were vagabonds, or armed peasants who shut themselves up in their villages and watched them pass but did nothing to hinder them, except to charge enormous prices for food, which they bartered over their walls.

Even so, the party could not have got through without the hounds. Bands of mercenaries were quartering the country, searching for them. More than once they had hidden in a wood to watch a mounted troop go jingling by, or turned aside from their chosen direction to take a roundabout way because the hounds warned them of men ahead. All of one long night they had played cat-and-mouse with a mounted band in the defiles of some jungle hills—men they never saw and only managed to avoid because of the hounds.

Now, at last, they had reached the sea; and had discovered a particularly nasty village plastered to the cliffs below the place where the Fallarin perched. Tiny round houses, whitened with the droppings of a million flying things until they looked like lumps of guano, clung to the naked rock on both sides of a narrow cleft, climbing up from a little harbor on a series of shallow steps. At the foot of the steps, on the harbor side, was a minute inn that looked villainous even though Alderyk could see nothing of it but its peaked roof. He was not versed in the lore of harbors, but this one seemed adequately deep and was sheltered by a curving mole. Only one thing was visibly wrong with it: it had no boats.

Alderyk spread his wings wider. A damp and sluggish breeze was moving inward from the sea. He caught it in his wings and it pressed against him, ruffling his fur. It smelled of salt and fishy things. It was a lazy breeze, and stupid, but it could talk. He stroked it, and listened.

Vaybars, beside him, was doing the same thing. So were the four other Fallarin, strung out along the cliff wherever their fancy took them. The breeze talked to them all, glad of the company; small, soft, indolent talk, in which they could hear the lapping of water against hollow hulls, the slatting of idle sails and slack cordage.

From a little distance, Halk watched them and waited with scant patience.

The rest of the party, concealed in the fringes of the jungle that grew almost to the cliff edge, lay and eased their weary bones—all but Tuchvar, who fussed with the hounds.

The tropic heat made the Northhounds miserable, and there had been a lack of proper food. Tuchvar caressed their staring coats and told them how all would be well as soon as they were at sea aboard the boat. *Boat* was an entirely strange concept to them. *Sea* they had looked at and sniffed at from the edge of the cliff, and they had not liked it.

Gerrith sat beside Halk, her eyes closed, her hands lax. Perhaps she slept. Perhaps she saw things behind or beyond the closed lids.

Halk had been reared, in the ancient tradition of his city-state, to regard the wise woman of Irnan as an infallible oracle, or at least one to be taken very seriously. He had done so in regard to the prophecy of the Dark Man made by Gerrith's mother, and in spite of his doubts and bitter despair the Citadel of the Lords Protector had fallen, the siege of Irnan had been lifted, and the gates of the stars had been opened—almost. Almost. Which was worse than not at all, so that the prophecy had at last been proved false, a waste of labor and bloodshed and dying. Now *this* Gerrith had prophesied, and he could neither quite deny that prophecy nor quite believe in it. If the mantle of truth had descended upon Gerrith's shoulders, and there was still a chance that Irnan might be freed from the tyranny of Mother Skaith and her Lords Protector, then he must do all within his power to bring about that end.

On the other hand, Gerrith was a woman in love with a man, and who could say how much that love might color her visions?

Holding his sword across his knees, Halk polished the long blade with a bit of silk and thought about his shield-mate Breca, and how she had died with Thyra's cold iron in her belly, and how the Thyrans had tossed her to the Outdwellers as one tosses offal to hungry dogs.

Stark had led them to Thyra. Another man might have found a better way to the Citadel. He, Halk, might have found a better way, if the prophecy had named him as the savior of Irnan—and why not he, rather than a stranger, an alien outsider from the gods-knew-where among the stars? This had rankled in him from the beginning, so that he was torn between a desire for Stark to succeed because of Irnan, and a desire for Stark to be defeated because he had no right to be what he was. He blamed Stark for Breca's death. He had wanted a hundred times to kill him, and each time had been forced to stay his hand for the sake of Irnan.

This time, if the prophecy was false and Stark should fail again, nothing but the death of one of them would save Stark from the weight of this blade.

Gerd lifted his head and growled, taking the thought from Halk's mind, and Halk glared back into the demon eyes and said, *Not even you, hellhound. If Stark can withstand you, so can I.* And he ran his thumb along the cutting edge.

Alderyk came in from the cliff.

"There are boats," he said. "Mostly small, but one is big enough for us."

"Where is this boat?"

Alderyk gestured vaguely. "Out, with the small ones. It leads them. They're on some kind of hunt."

"Fishing."

"Very well, fishing. They will not return to the harbor before nightfall."

Gerrith said, "Ours must return now." She opened her eyes and looked at Alderyk and said again, "Now."

"We are too few to call great tempests," Alderyk said. "But we will do what we may."

He returned to the cliff. The six Fallarin went apart and gathered themselves into a close group, with the Tarf standing guard about them. They spread their wings, gleaming red-brown in the sunlight, and began to sing to the little breeze that blew so soft and sluggish from the sea.

Halk could barely hear the song, but it had a quality of command, a compelling insistence that stirred deep wellsprings somewhere within his unimaginative soul. He disliked the Fallarin, as he disliked most things that forced him to stretch his mind a little wider. His passionate attachment to the cause of emigration had been purely pragmatic, based upon hatred of the slave's life his people led under the Wandsmen and the belief that life somewhere else would be better. His desire for the star-roads had held nothing of wonder. When he thought of the actual physical business of taking himself bodily to another world, he was filled with loathing.

Now he could not repress a slight shudder as the breeze began to strengthen.

Out at sea, beyond a jutting headland to the south, the fishing fleet felt a change. It was slight at first. The folk in the small boats, spread out with weighted nets dragging between them, did not notice it at all.

On the large boat, pride and protector of the fleet, the rowers snored on their benches and the master and his mate played languidly at dice beneath an awning.

The boat was designed for a twofold use—as a fighting ship to defend the fleet from marauders, human and otherwise, and as a transport ship to move the catch to market. Like most compromises, she left much to be desired in both departments. Still, she floated. She carried her own little skiff, and she had a splendid figurehead in the shape of a guardian spirit, who fronted the waves so defiantly that she appeared to have a rudder at both ends.

The big lugsail, which had been flapping listless as a bedsheet in the light breeze, began to fill. The yard swung. Cordage snapped taut, rattling through the blocks.

The master took a long pull at a stone bottle and considered whether he ought to rouse the crew and go through the tiresome business of lowering the sail—which would mean that it must then be raised again later on, an even more tiresome business. He decided to wait. The breeze might drop again. If it did not, he could simply slack off on the tackle.

The breeze did not drop. It became a wind.

The boat began to move.

The master shouted. The crew roused up. The rowers woke.

The wind was like a great peremptory hand, pushing. They could see the mark of it across the water, a cat's-paw a mile long and straight as an arrow, riffled with whitecaps. They looked at it and were terrified, because it was aimed solely at them and now did not so much as brush even one of the small craft.

The boat quickened. Her thick mast creaked with strain. White water began to break beneath her heavy forefoot.

Master and crew cried out upon the Sea-Our-Mother and rushed to get the sail down.

The wind split itself into whips and clubs and drove them off the deck, to cower in the fishy stink below. Rowers struggled with their sweeps and were knocked from the benches. Like a demented thing the boat galloped through the water, flinging up spray and burying the guardian figurehead above his pride.

The fisher folk sat in their small craft with their nets, in a calm sea, watching their flagship rush away in the grip of the eerie wind. They watched the long, wild cat's-paw follow on behind, so that all the sea was still again after it had passed. They cried out very loudly to the Sea-Our-Mother, and at each other. Then they hauled in their nets, dumping what catch they had as an offering, and began to row quickly for the nearest shore.

On the cliff above the harbor, Halk and Gerrith looked out to sea. The wind whipped their clothing and tossed their hair. Away to their left the Fallarin continued to sing their hypnotic, commanding song, beating their wings to the cadence.

The boat came in sight around the headland, with its pregnant sail and its wake of whitecaps.

It set straight in for the harbor, and Halk warned furiously, "If they're not careful, they'll pile her onto the mole."

Below, in the village, someone shouted. People ran from the houses, an ill-favored folk, and dirty, for all they wore ornaments of sea-pearls. They stood on the harbor steps and stared, their voices rising shrill like the clatter of seabirds disturbed in their nesting place.

The wind quirked and shifted, sending the boat staggering safely into harbor.

The Fallarin ceased from their singing. Their wings closed. The wind dropped. The boat drifted peacefully. A straggle of oars began to splash, working her into the mooring place by the mole.

The villagers began to stream down the steps. Men ran out along the mole to catch the mooring lines. The boat was made fast.

"Now," said Halk, and the company went down the steps into the cleft, leaving the riding animals behind. The Northhounds led the way. They came to the topmost of the wide steps that made the village street, and went down between the ugly little houses that stank of guano and old fish and less fragrant things.

Some time before they reached the mole, the villagers forgot the ship and the strangeness of the wind, and made a great confusion of screaming and scattering, of rushing and hiding, away from the terrible hounds and the winged men and the not-men and the cloaked men and the men with bright swords.

No one hindered these from boarding the boat.

They cast off and worked her—painfully, for none of them had ever handled oars before—into open water, while the master and the crew watched open-mouthed from the mole or splashed in the water where they had taken refuge overside.

Gerrith spoke to the Fallarin. "Take us south, my lords, as swiftly as your winds can blow," she said, and her face was white as bone. "They have almost reached the sea."

13

The river had widened, spreading itself into a number of channels running between muddy islands. There were more villages and more traffic. Stark and Ashton had managed to stay with the main channel by watching where the bulk of the traffic went and following it. They kept as far away as possible from other craft, and no one had paid them much attention, but by midday the river had become busy enough that they decided to haul out on one of the islands and wait for quieter times.

"There should be a town ahead somewhere," Ashton said. "Probably at the mouth of the river. We need a proper boat. This hollow log will never get us down the coast."

When Old Sun had gone to his rest, they set out again, in the brief darkness before the rising of the first cluster. The brown water, black now with a glimmer of stars in it, carried them smoothly. Here and there were boats with lanterns in their bows, where men caught whatever moved by night. Villages were scattered along the bank and on some of the larger islands. The smoke of cooking fires lay in bands across the water, and the sounds of voices came to them, and the evening cries of animals.

The dugout rounded a bend and suddenly there was nothing—no fishermen, no villages, no lights, no sounds. The men drifted in the silence, wondering.

The smell of salt water mingled with the river smell, and presently Stark could see an opening-out of the darkness ahead, marked by a spreading fan of turbulence where the rush of the river was blocked by the immovable mass of the sea.

At the very end of the jungle bank, a black bulk loomed very strangely against the stars.

"There's no town," said Ashton. "Nothing."

"That looks like a temple," Stark said. "Perhaps this is all sacred ground."

Ashton swore. "I counted on a town. We must have a boat, Eric!"

"There may be boats at the temple. And Simon, keep a sharp eye ahead."

"Something wrong?"

"There is always something wrong on Skaith."

Stark laid the heavy sword ready to hand and made sure the knife at his belt was free. The thick, wet smells of jungle and water imparted nothing to him but their presence, and yet behind them, under them, through them, subliminally, he sensed a faint rankness that stirred his memory and set the hairs prickling at the back of his neck.

The current slowed as it met the sea, but turbulence tossed the dugout roughly. They paddled in toward the bank.

"Lights," said Ashton.

The jungle had thinned. They could see the whole of the huge structure at the land's end. Low down in it were openings where pale lights glimmered. High above, shadowy pinnacles leaned crazily like the masts of a stranded ship, and Stark realized that part of the temple had sunk down and broken away, tilting toward the sea, toward the white water that quarreled and foamed.

He looked at that white water because he could see now that things moved in it, dark bodies leaping, rolling, frolicking. And he knew why this final stretch of the river was deserted.

Ashton was searching the bank. "I see a landing, Eric, and boats—two boats."

"Never mind," said Stark. "Get ashore."

He dug his paddle deep, fairly lifting the dugout with each stroke.

Ashton did not question. He bent his shoulders to it. Spray broke over them, soaked them to the skin, filled the bottom of the dugout. The bank was low and bare above the temple landing, but the jungle offered cover not too far away.

If they could just get ashore, if they could run for it—

The dugout went over as suddenly as if it had struck a rock.

It was pitch black under the water, which was filled with a great boiling and thrusting of powerful bodies. Stark fought his way to the surface and saw Ashton's face not ten feet away. He lunged toward it, drawing the knife from his belt.

Ashton vanished with a strangled cry.

Other heads appeared in a bobbing circle. They were earless and smooth as the heads of seals, with vestigial noses and the mouths of predators. They looked at Stark with eyes like pearls and they laughed, these bestial Children of the Sea-Our-Mother, with a dreadful echo of lost humanity.

Stark dived and swam, blindly, furiously, searching for Ashton and knowing that he was not going to find him. The creatures played with him. He was a strong swimmer, but they were better, and there were many of them. And he could not reach them with the knife. They let him up to breathe three times, and they let him see Ashton again, flung up bodily out of the water, still alive. Then he saw nothing more. Webbed and taloned fingers pulled him under. He lost the knife.

He had once killed a Child of the Sea with his bare hands. Now he tried to do it again, in the roiling dark, grasping at slick-furred bodies that slipped effortlessly away, until his lungs were bursting and the darkness had turned red behind his eyes. This time they did not let him up to breathe.

He came to, lying on hard stone, vomiting water.

For a while all he could think of was the need to get air into his lungs. When he finished strangling and could think again, he saw that he was on the temple landing and that Ashton was retching in a puddle a few feet away while a man in a blue robe pounded on his back. The mutant Children of the Sea-Our-Mother, to the number of a dozen, crouched along the landing, their fur streaming.

More men in blue robes came from the temple; some of them bore torches. The first of the Three Ladies had risen, so that it was light enough to see by. There was something peculiar about the blue-robes —priests or monks as they might be—something brutish. They shambled in their gait, and their shaven heads showed curious shapes.

Ashton was breathing again and the man ceased to pound on him, turning to Stark. His eyes were like the eyes of the Children, milky pearls, and his hands had webs between the taloned fingers.

"You are off-worlders," he said. "You robbed our temple."

"Not we," Stark insisted. "Other men." His limbs felt heavy and his body was a hollow shell. Nevertheless, he gathered himself, looking at Ashton. "Why did the Children not kill us?"

"All who come this way belong to the Mother and must be shared with her. As you will be shared."

His speech was thick because of the shape of his lips and teeth. He smiled, and it was not a pleasant smile, with the dog teeth sharp and shining.

"You wish to run, off-worlder? Try. You have two choices—the water, or the land. Which will it be?"

The Children dripped laughing, on the stones between Stark and the river. Several of the monks had produced long, thin tubes of carved ivory from beneath their gowns, and the tubes were pointed at Stark. Ivory, wood, or metal, and ornamented or not, a blowgun was a blowgun wherever you found it, and blowguns shot ugly little darts, generally poisoned.

"It is a safe drug," said the blue-robe. "You will be alive and conscious when the Children share you—for the greater pleasure of the Mother."

Stark measured his chances of breaking through forty monks unscathed, and decided they were thin. In any case, he could not take Ashton. If he did escape, he might or might not be able to come back and rescue his foster-father. But if he got himself knocked out by a drugged dart, there would be no possibility of escape for either of them.

He remained where he was, and did not protest when a monk with a human face and no ears came to bind his hands.

"What are you?" he asked the blue-robe. "Hybrids? Throwbacks? The Children's blood is in you."

With a proud humility the man answered, "We are the few whom the Mother chooses to be her special servants. We are the sea-born who must live on land, to keep the Mother's temple."

In other words, Stark thought, the odd births where the mutation did not quite breed true.

"Your temple was robbed?"

"By men like you, who are not of Skaith. They came from the sky with much noise and terrible lightnings. We could not fight them."

"You could have died trying. I know of priests who did."

"What would have been the point of that?" asked the blue-robe. "We lived, to pray for revenge." He looked from Stark to Ashton, who was on his feet now, and bound. "Only two of you. But perhaps you are a token, a sign from the Mother that there will be more."

Stark said, "Those men are *our* enemies, too. They tried to kill us. If you will help us to get south to Andapell, we can find means to punish them, perhaps even get back for you what they stole."

The blue-robe gave him a flat stare of utter contempt. Then he glanced at the sky, judging the time that was left until morning, and said to his fellows, "Let us begin the preparation now. We will hold the feast at dawn."

The path to the temple was broad and easy of ascent, even to bound men. The vastness of the building became apparent, its crushing bulk looming in the cluster light, rising to fantastic pinnacles all carved with the twisting shapes of sea-things.

It had many wings below. Stark and Ashton were taken into one of these, into a stone chamber where candles burned; and there the monks drugged them, anyway, by means of sharp slivers dipped in some pale liquid and driven beneath the skin.

Stark's battle was quickly over. He went from there fully conscious, seeing, hearing, and gentle as a lamb.

The night was not unpleasant. It had nothing in it of threat or danger to rouse alarm. The odd-looking men in the blue robes treated them kindly, even royally, though some of the praying was over-long and Stark slept. Otherwise, he was interested in what went on.

He and Simon were bathed in great sunken tanks of seawater, both hot and cold. The tanks were beautifully carved around their sides, and a great deal of ceremony was connected with the bathing. When it was finished, the men were dried with silken towels and their bodies were rubbed with various oils and essences, some of which smelled rather strange. Then they were wrapped in silken robes and brought to a chamber with many candles, where there was a place to sit down among soft cushions. Here they were fed a meal, a most peculiar meal of little separate dishes, each one with a different spice or savor.

In some dim, remote corner of his mind Stark felt that a few of the dishes ought to have been revolting to him, but they were not. From time to time Ashton would look at him and smile.

The remarkable thing about that whole period was that it had no edges or corners. All was rounded and smooth and easy. The night flowed sweetly, and just when the bathing and the feeding and the praying and the sleeping had begun to pall, the blue-robed men raised them and brought them by long corridors into the body of the temple.

They entered from the landward side, and it was like standing in the hold of some mighty ship that had broken its back on a reef, leaving the stern half untouched while the forward half tilted toward destruction. Looking upward into the shadowy dimness where the torch- and candlelight did not reach, Stark saw a great gash of open sky beyond a ragged edge where the vault ended.

The sky held the first faint hint of dawn.

The blue-robed men led them on, to where the blocks of the floor had drawn apart, one side level, the other raised at an angle. A way had been made across that gap, a kind of bridge, and they walked under the sky into the forward part of the temple.

Here they saw a blaze of candles, which showed the lower parts of reliefs on the walls, cracked and stained with dampness. The floor was much disarrayed, with blocks at all heights, and all running downhill to the front, where the entire wall had fallen and let in the sea. Wavelets lapped softly there with the candlelight shimmering on them. At one side, a platform built of the fallen stones projected into the water.

Centrally in this half-sunken hall, tilted crazily on her massive base, the Sea-Our-Mother rose up in whitest marble, twenty feet or more to the top of her crowned head, from a surging of marble waves about her waist. She had two faces. One was the bountiful mother who gives life and plenty, the other the destroying goddess who ravages and kills. Her right hand held fish and garlands and a tiny ship. Her left held wrecked hulls and sea wrack and the bodies of drowned men.

She had no other ornaments. Wrists and throat and the whiteness above her breasts were scarred with cruel pits; and her eyes, which had been jewels, were blind.

Stark and Ashton were made to stand before her. Their silken robes were removed. Monks brought garlands of sea-flowers and shells and twining weeds to hang about their necks. They were chill and wet against Stark's naked skin, and the smell of them was strong.

For the first time, a small worm of alarm began to eat away at his mild content.

A huge deep drum boomed in the temple, three times. Iron cymbals clashed. The monks began to chant, in growling basses that sounded against the vault as though great dogs barked in a cave, groaning out their most profound rage and misery.

Stark looked up at the vandalized faces of the goddess leaning above him. Fear shot through him, a cold spear stabbing him awake. But he could not quite remember what it was that he feared.

The monks had gathered round. They began to move, with Stark and Ashton in their midst, toward the water, and Stark could see that one of the blue-robes had come out onto the platform that jutted into the sea. He held a horn much greater than his own height in length, so that its curved end rested on the stone.

Drum and cymbals broke the growling chant with a blow of fierce emphasis, and the voices all together held one long, grinding note that was like the dragging of a boulder over rock.

It ended and the horn spoke, shouting a wild, hoarse, moaning cry out across the sea.

Ashton walked slowly beside Stark. He smiled vaguely and his eyes were untroubled.

They walked on the submerged floor, the water rising around their ankles, toward the place where the blue-robe stood with his sounding horn. They walked to the measured cadence of the chant and to the drumbeat and the cymbal clash, toward steps that rose out of trailing weed and the encrusting shells of small things that live in shallows. The sky had grown brighter and the candles turned pale.

The horn called, hoarsely, yearning, and the surface of the sea, which stretched like satin beneath the sunrise, was broken by the splashing of many swimmers.

Stark remembered what it was that he feared.

A cauldron of molten brass tipped out of the east. The burning light ran across the surface of the water. It caught in the sail of a boat going heavily before a wind that seemed to blow only for her, since all around her was a flat calm. It turned the sail to gold and the clumsy hull to a thing of loveliness.

It caught in the eyes of a white hound standing in the bows, and these flamed with a sudden brilliance.

N'Chaka, said Gerd. *N'Chaka! There! Danger. Things come.*

Kill? asked Tuchvar.

The canted spires of the temple burned in the distance. The voice of the horn came faintly across the sea.

Too far, said Gerd. *Too far.*

14

Stark was halfway up the steps. Blue-robes were in front of him, and on either side, and behind. They were absorbed in their chanting. Victims customarily went smiling to their deaths. Only at the very end, when they had been cast into the sea and the Children had begun to share them, were there cries amid the blood and the floating garlands; and both cries and blood were pleasing to the Mother. The monks sang in their growling voices and did not notice that Stark had ceased to smile.

He was still beyond any rational thought. He only knew that death was coming swiftly through the silken water to claim him. The life within him stirred—a simple, uncomplicated force that rose of itself to fight against extinction.

Ashton was at his right hand. At his left was a monk, and then a second monk, and then the unguarded edge of the steps.

Stark swung his left arm viciously. The blow took the nearer monk across the throat and swept him back into those who climbed behind him. In falling, he clutched at the second monk and cost him his balance. Blue-robes tumbled and fell, splashing into the shallow water. Stark rushed up out of the space he had opened, clearing more space ahead of him by knocking other monks into the water. Hands caught at him, tearing away the garlands but slipping on his naked, oiled body. Some of the fingers had talons that drew blood, but they could not stop him. He gained the platform with a wild bull's rush.

The blue-robe with the horn turned about, startled. He had an especially brutish face. Stark took the horn from him. With it, he broke the face and sent the blue-robe flying out into the water on the far side of the platform. Then Stark swung the long horn like a ten-foot club to clear the upper steps.

He shouted, "Simon!"

Then he heard a faint voice calling his name, *N'Chaka, Man-Without-a-Tribe,* and he wondered who on this death-bitten god-haunted planet knew that name to call him. And suddenly he realized that the voice was in his mind, and he knew it and cried out, "Gerd!"

He said it aloud, and Simon Ashton looked up at him, vacant-eyed and smiling.

Gerd, kill!

Too far. Fight, N'Chaka.

Stark lashed about him with the long horn. It was made of metal, bound and bossed, and it was heavy. He roared for Simon Ashton to come to him, roared in English and in clicks and grunts.

The chanting had become chaotic. Some of the monks in the farther ranks still kept at it as the drum boomed and the cymbals clashed, but the monks up front were in confusion. Most had not yet realized what had happened. The long horn beat among them like the flail of the Lord, and Ashton, frowning in puzzlement, began to pick his way through the floundering bodies toward Stark.

The rear ranks of blue-robes put aside their chanting. They voiced a mingled cry of outrage and fury, and charged forward up the steps, trampling their fellows.

Stark caught Ashton's hand and dragged him up onto the platform.

Gerd, kill!

Too far, N'Chaka. Fight.

Stark fought, swinging his flail until it bent and broke and he flung it away. He took hold of Ashton and leaped with him into the water, on the seaward side of the platform, where the Children were coming to share their sacrificial meal with the Goddess.

The water was unexpectedly deep. The first monk he had thrust over was drowning in it.

Now that the horn had stopped its calling, the Children seemed to have paused. He could see their dark heads bobbing some fifty feet away. They hooted plaintively as though wondering what had happened to upset the ritual. There were a lot of them. Stark did not stop to count. Pulling Ashton, he swam out around the broken wall, heading toward the nearest land. Behind him, monks tore off their robes and sprang in after him.

As soon as he was clear of the temple, Stark saw the boat. It shot toward him, parallel to the shore, blown by a narrow gale that seemed in a fair way to drive it under.

The monks swam almost as agilely as their full-mutant brothers. The Children called in their subhuman voices, and the monks answered them. The Children came on again, swerving like a school of fish, heading straight for the escaping sacrifice.

Ashton was inclined to be querulous, as one might be when shaken roughly from a pleasant nap. He slowed Stark down considerably. When they scrambled out onto the muddy beach, the monks were so close behind that one had sunk his talons into Ashton's leg and was pulling him back.

Ashton came out of his tranquil dream.

He screamed and turned to fight. Stark got both hands under the monk's thick jaw and pulled sharply upward. There came a snapping sound and the monk let go of Ashton, who crawled away from him on all fours, trailing blood. Then he got up and ran.

Stark turned to run with him, but brutish bodies were hauling out all around him. Hands gripped his ankles. He bent to free them and other hands caught at him. Things leaped upon him and he fell, amid a great squattering and splashing, to roll in the tepid shallows with a weight of rancid fishy bodies on him.

Ashton picked up a stone and came back to crack heads with it.

Stark broke free. But they brought him down again by sheer weight, and Ashton with him. A purely animal sound came from Stark's throat, once. After that he fought in silence. A leathery paw came clawing for his face and he sank his teeth into it until they grated on bone. Blood was in his mouth, strange-tasting blood. The monk wrenched his hand away, shrieking. Then, suddenly, all the monks were shrieking. The blows stopped coming. The weight of bodies lessened. Those that remained became inert.

Stark pushed them off and got to his hands and knees.

Monks lay about on the mud, their dead faces contorted with terror. The boat was riding in flat calm now, off the shore. He could see the white heads of hounds along the rail.

We kill, N'Chaka. You come.

The Children of the Sea were not coming any closer. Some of them floated facedown in the water. Those who still could were thrashing away in a frenzy of speed.

Stark got up and helped Ashton to his feet, pointing to the boat. Neither man had any idea how it had come there. Neither man stopped to question. They walked into the sea until it deepened, and then they swam. Ropes were let down and powerful arms helped them aboard.

Stark was aware of faces, aware of voices shouting, aware of the hounds clustered round him, but the only thing that was really clear to him was the face of Gerrith. She came to him and he held her, and neither minded the blood and seawater that wetted them both.

"You live," she whispered. "Now the way is open." And he tasted salt on her lips that was sharper than all the salt of the sea.

The Fallarin perched on the deck, falcons in moult with their fur awry and their sullen eyes half mad with exhaustion.

"If *more* haste is needed," said Alderyk, looking at the tribesmen and the Irnanese, "get you to the rowing benches. We are foredone." He bared his white teeth at Stark. "Show us wonders now, Dark Man. We have earned them."

Stark said, "I don't understand."

Gerrith stepped back. "Presently, the whole story. But you must have orders for us now. What are they?"

Stark put an arm around Gerd's neck, and the other around Grith's, and his mind touched the minds of all the hounds. He smiled at Tuchvar, and at Sabak and the tribesmen, who had shed their dusty cloaks but not their veils. The Irnanese he did not know, but he smiled at them. He even smiled at Halk.

"We go south to Andapell," he said. "We break our backs for Andapell, if the winds won't blow. Alderyk, loan us your Tarf. They can pull twice as well as we can."

He let go of the hounds and jumped down to the rowing benches. He was not tired now. His many wounds were slight and of no account. He looked at Halk and laughed.

"Surely you'll not stand by while the Dark Man rows? Come on, comrade. Bend your back for Irnan."

He thrust out the clumsy sweep and felt it bite. "Yarrod!" he shouted. "Yarrod! Yarrod!"

The Irnanese laid aside their arms and tumbled down to the benches, picking up the old battle-cry. "Yarrod! Yarrod!" They ran more oars out.

Halk put down his great longsword and sat on the bench beside Stark so that they worked one oar together. "Yarrod!"

The tribesmen, proud dainty riders of the cold desert, put their feet into the slopping bilges and rowed, side by side with the four-armed Tarf.

The oars dipped raggedly. They fouled each other and men cursed as the looms thumped them painfully. Gradually the stroke steadied, as the battle-cry became a chant; and they began to feel the rhythm, bending their backs in time.

The boat began to move forward.

The sea was unbroken, except for the turbulence where the river flowed into it. And nothing stirred there but the wavelets. The temple of the Sea-Our-Mother leaned wearily toward the water. In the full light of Old Sun its spires seemed very ancient, the carvings rubbed flat by the passing of centuries. No sound of drum or horn or cymbal came from the shadowed interior, nor was there any sound of voices.

The boat gathered speed, dropping south along the coast to Andapell.

15

CERELENG, chief seaport and capital of Andapell, sprawled across a circle of hills and down along the slopes to the harbor. The palace complex stood highest of all, gleaming white in the light of the Three Ladies, a gossamer fantasy of domes and arches and soaring pillars wrought in ivory and fretted marble.

The sailors' quarter stood lowest, a maze of lanes and streets, warehouses and shops and marketplaces, stretching in a wide crescent by the water's edge. The harbor was crowded with shipping, from the big roundships of the deep-sea traders to little scuttling craft that shot like beetles among moored fishing boats and floating colonies of houseboats. Riding lights were a small galaxy of stars caught in the placid water.

Ashore, the streets were crowded with folk of all kinds. Seamen from half of Skaith mingled with the local inhabitants—smooth amber-skinned people wrapped in bright silks—and with darker, knottier little men from the interior, come down to trade with bark bundles of *tlun* and precious bits of worked ivory and wood and colored stone.

Others were here as well. The tropics were comfortable in winter, and the seasonal migration of Farers was well along. Since food was come by with less effort here than in the north, there was less resentment among the people who produced it. Nevertheless, Wandsmen were present to see that the laws of the Lords Protector were kept. The Farers, in their infinite variety of hair, garments, paint, and nudity, strolled or lounged where they would, helping themselves from food stalls, chewing *tlun*, celebrating the end of their world with love and music and some really startling stenches.

Stark kept as wide of them as he could. He was clad as a wandering sailor, with his black hair clubbed at the back of his neck. He wore a loincloth with a knife stuck in it, and he carried a folded scrap of canvas over his shoulder to serve as cloak or bedding. His feet were bare and his expression stupid. He padded the dirty streets of the bazaars. He loitered around food stalls and drinking places. He bought nothing because he had no money. He listened, and avoided the Wandsmen.

Men carried on with their everyday lives and their bargaining and chaffering, but it was as though a heavy cloud hung over the quarter, so that even the flourishing sin shops were subdued and folk spoke in low voices over their wine.

Their talk was of two matters.

When he had heard enough, Stark returned to the beach where he had left the little skiff. Then he sculled out to where the boat had dropped her anchor stone in an open mooring, as far away from other craft as she could get. Cloud, with a flicker of lightning in it, had obscured the lowest of the Three Ladies. The air was oppressive, so that Stark sweated at his sculling.

The company waited under a jury-rigged awning that somewhat concealed them from curious eyes. Now that they had reached their goal, they were becoming peevish with confinement, and the hounds growled continually.

Ashton did not wait for Stark to get aboard. "The starship," he asked, leaning over the rail, "is it still here?"

"It is, somewhere." Stark made his painter fast to the rail and climbed over. "The town is all a-mutter with it, like a henroost with a fox about. They don't fear attack here, Cereleng is too large and well-defensed. But every day fresh word comes in of temples plundered, villages robbed, people killed. The Wandsmen are busy spreading tales, so probably half of them are lies. But the ship is still here."

"Thank God for that," said Ashton. "We'll have to hurry. Where is Pedrallon?"

"That is the other thing they talk about. Pedrallon, and the ransom. They're not angry about the ransom. Honor required them to redeem their prince from the hands of the ungodly so that they can punish him properly themselves. They blame Pedrallon for intriguing with off-worlders. They say he ought to be fed to Old Sun."

"He has not been?"

"Not yet. But he's out of power, a prisoner in his own palace. His brother is now Prince of Andapell, and it's only a matter of time. And not very much of it!"

Ashton shook his head. "That's hard news. I had counted on Pedrallon's help."

"Must we worry about this Pedrallon?" Halk demanded. "If the starship is still here, and is necessary to us, let us go to it."

"I'd like to do that," Stark said, "but I don't know where it is."

"Couldn't you hear? Did no one say—?"

"Everyone said. Everyone knew. I saw men come to blows about it. No two places are the same. Some one of them is right, of course, but there's no way to tell which one that is, nor how to get there."

The clouds had reached higher, covering the second of the Three Ladies. It was much darker and thunder sounded in the west. The hounds grumbled, shifting uneasily in their places.

"Pedrallon would know," Stark said.

Halk made an angry gesture. "A pox on Pedrallon! Forget the ship. The wise woman says that our road leads south."

Stark said, "I can't forget the ship."

"What, then?" asked Ashton. "There are not enough of us to storm the palace."

Lightning flickered and flared, lacing the horizon. Stark said, "We won't leave harbor anyway, until that's past. I'll go up with Gerd and Grith. Perhaps we may arrange something. Be ready to move when you see us coming."

He let himself over the rail and called the hounds, not waiting for further argument. Making Gerd and Grith lie down in the bottom of the skiff, he sculled back to the shore, and thunderheads swallowed the last of the Three Ladies.

He beached the skiff at a place where unlighted warehouses clustered about a pier where there was no one to see him. Hiding the skiff underneath the pier, he set off through furtive lanes toward the upper town, moving fast with the two hounds at his heels.

The houses here were mostly dwellings, shouldering together up the slope, redolent of sweat and spices. Only a few mean shops were open. What folk were abroad stared at the white hounds, but no one attempted to interfere.

By the time Stark had reached broader avenues, the first drops of rain were falling, great fat things that stung like hail, striking the paving stones far apart with a sharp splatting sound.

The rain ceased, and it became very dark in between the lightning. Thunder cracked the sky and made the ground tremble underfoot. Then rain came again, this time in torrents that swept the streets clean of all idle strollers.

The houses, which became larger and grander as Stark climbed, were set back in walled gardens. Heavy fragrances of unfamiliar flowers mingled with the smell of rain. Water rushed in the gutters.

The wall of the palace complex was high and white. At the main gate stood a gatehouse of marble, lovely as a jewel box, with lights in the windows and no sentries visible outside. The gate itself was barred shut. Stark passed it by. The wall was very long, girdling the hilltop in a huge irregular circle. He trotted beside it in the hammering downpour, the wet hounds flinching and groaning every time the sky split open.

Half a mile or so around, Stark came to a small gate, heavily barred. He guessed that it served the kitchen quarters. Inside it was a sentry box with a porch where a huge gong was hung, presumably for the sounding of alarms. A lantern burned inside the open door.

Men, said Gerd. *There.*

Wait.

Stark drew back a little and then ran at the wall, leaping to catch the top with his fingers. He pulled himself up and over, dropping lightly on the other side. A flare of lightning showed him gardens, drenched and deserted, with white buildings beyond. The sentry box was at his left, about twenty feet away.

Kill, N'Chaka?

Not unless I tell you.

He went toward the small stone structure, not worrying too much about stealth. The storm would cover any sound he might make. Coming under the shelter of the porch, he found two men in scarlet —the palace color—kneeling on a mat in the small room, absorbed in a game that was played with dice and ivory counters. Perhaps they felt that there was no need to keep watch in this storm. Perhaps the present prince did not want too close a watch to be kept at all, in case a mob should roll up and relieve him of the embarrassment of his brother.

The men started up, seeing Stark. They cried out with one voice that was lost in a crash of thunder, and they reached for the weapons they had leaned against the wall.

Stark kicked the wind out of one of them, knocked the other hard against the stone, and then made sure they were both unconscious. He bound them carefully and gagged them with strips of scarlet silk.

Then he went and lifted the bars of the gate. The hounds rushed in.

Find Wandsman.

He put Pedrallon into their minds, not the name but the look of him. *Wandsman who came with N'Chaka.*

He put into their minds the time and place.

Remember Wandsman, they answered. They were conditioned to remember Wandsmen.

Hurry. And watch.

They ran across dark lawns ankle-deep in water, beneath bending trees turned silver by the lightning. The palace buildings were enormous in extent, with colonnades and domed pavilions lovely as pale dreams.

Too many minds there, N'Chaka.

Try.

The palace windows were dark, as though most of its people slept. Only the guards' stations were lighted. Stark kept away from those. The hounds would warn him of patrols. But if there were any, they must have been indoors somewhere, sheltering from the storm.

Too many minds. Sleep. Gray.

Try.

They passed long, marble wings that wandered among fragrant gardens. They passed sunken courtyards and pools. They found nothing.

Stark began to believe that it was a hopeless quest, and not too bright a thought in the first place. He did not care to be caught in the palace grounds when the storm had passed. He was on the point of going back when Gerd spoke suddenly.

Wandsman there!

Lead.

"There" was a small pavilion set apart from the main mass of the palace. It was round, with graceful arches and a spired roof, and no walls. Candles burned in tall stands, the flames going straight up because in spite of the storm there was little wind. In the center of the marble floor a man knelt, his head bowed in an attitude of contemplation. There was a stillness about the kneeling figure, surrounded by brightness and seen through a curtain of falling rain, which suggested that the person who dwelt within it was far away.

Stark recognized Pedrallon.

Four men stood around him with their backs to the rain. They stood quite still, leaning on their spears, watching him. No one else was nearby. The sleeping palace was quiet and remote.

Stark gave the hounds their orders.

The storm muffled sound, swallowed up the thin screaming of men in mortal terror. Stark and the hounds gained the platform of the pavilion and the men groveled on it. Stark moved swiftly among them, clubbing with the butt of a spear until they were all silent. Afterward, he bound them, working very fast.

Pedrallon had not risen from his knees. He wore only a white waistcloth, and his slender body might have been carved from amber, so motionless he held it. Only his head had lifted so that he might see Stark.

"Why do you disturb me?" he asked. "I am preparing for death."

"I have friends, and a boat in the harbor. You have no need to die."

"Because of my dealings with Penkawr-Che, I am responsible for what has happened," Pedrallon said. "I will not live with shame."

"Do you know where this ship is that preys on your people?"

"Yes."

"Could you lead us to it?"

"Yes."

"Then there is still hope. Come with me, Pedrallon."

The rain poured down, sheeting from the roof edges, though the candles burned steadily.

The hounds nosed and prowled among the fallen guards. *Hurry, N'Chaka.*

"*What* hope?" asked Pedrallon.

"Of bringing help, bringing ships and punishing Penkawr-Che—saving the people who want to be saved. All the things you risked your life for." He looked down at Pedrallon. "Where is the man who was going to go on fighting the Wandsmen, no matter what?"

"Words. I am a captive under my own roof. I have no followers. My people scream for my blood, and my brother is in haste to satisfy them. Deeds, I have found, are more difficult than words."

His face was as Stark remembered it, a fine construction of aristocratic bones and smooth flesh, but the tremendous force that once had blazed in it was absent. The dark eyes that had burned with so much vitality were now cold and dull.

"You speak of things that concerned me yesterday, in another life. That time is gone."

Pedrallon bent his head again.

Stark said, "You will come with me now. If you do not, the hounds will touch you. Do you understand?"

Pedrallon did not stir.

The hounds touched him. They flogged him to his feet with little whips of terror. They drove him beside Stark out across the dark and streaming lawns.

"How long before someone comes to the pavilion?"

"No one comes," Pedrallon answered, sobbing, "until the guard is changed. I spend my nights and days there, fasting—"

"When is the guard changed?"

"When Old Sun rises."

Does he lie, Gerd?

No.

Does anyone follow?

They went the shortest way to the gate. The sentries were still quiet. Stark closed the gate behind them and set off down the hill. Pedrallon was beside him, heavy and stumbling, as though hunger had weakened him. Stark steadied him, his own ears stretched for any sound of alarm or pursuit behind them.

None came, nor did the hounds give any warning.

The storm rolled away slowly over the jungle. The rain slackened. It was very late now, and the few folk who prowled the swimming streets saw no more than a pair of sailors hurrying back to their ship.

Stark found the skiff where he had left it. Pedrallon sat in it with a hound front and back. Stark sculled out to the mooring.

Ready hands pulled them aboard, hoisted up the skiff to its place on the deck. Rowers jumped to the benches. The sweeps ran out.

The anchor stone came thumping up over the stern and the boat moved through glassy water, toward the open sea. Overhead, the clouds had broken, letting through rifts of silver light.

Pedrallon sat dazed and exhausted. Tuchvar brought wine and he drank it. It seemed to bring a little life back into him. He looked at the hounds and shuddered. He looked round at his shipmates, and made a gesture to Ashton, recognizing him. Then he turned to Stark.

"Is there truly hope?" he asked.

"I think so, if you lead us very quickly to that ship."

"Well, then," Pedrallon said, "I will break my fast."

16

Old Sun was newly risen, but already it was hot. Lying in the fringe of the jungle, Stark could feel the runnels of sweat trickling on his naked back.

He was looking out from under a noisy canopy of trees where innumerable nameless creatures shouted and quarreled, going about the business of a new day.

He was looking at the starship.

Pedrallon had led them well since he woke from the drugged apathy of despair. The faint hope that he might yet defeat the Lords Protector and set his world free had been enough to kindle something of the old fire in him again. The sheer, vicious desire to strike a punishing blow against Penkawr-Che had done the rest.

By his direction, the Fallarin had given them a hurrying wind south, to a tiny inlet, where the boat was worked in under oars and concealed from passing ships and over-flying hoppers. The Fallarin remained, with the Tarf, to guard her and to gather strength. Pedrallon's enemies were not likely to accept his disappearance with equanimity, and once the pursuit was under way the fugitives would have to move fast to keep ahead of it.

In the breathless heat of noon, Pedrallon had brought the rest of the troop to a village. He had hunted these jungles many times, he said, and the man who had served him as guide and tracker knew every trail in this part of Andapell. He could take them directly to the ship.

"But will he serve you now?" asked Halk.

Stark glanced at the hounds, but Pedrallon shook his head. "You will not need them."

And they did not. Pedrallon entered the village and came back with a small, wiry man named Larg, who said that Pedrallon was his lord and his friend and that whatever Pedrallon wanted, he would do.

So they followed Larg, all that day and through the night, toward the place where Pedrallon had told him to go. They halted only to rest briefly and eat the hard rations they had brought with them. And all the way Stark was haunted by the fear that they were too late, that the ship had already gone to rendezvous with Penkawr-Che on the heath and that they were straining their hearts out for nothing.

It was not necessary to say this to Ashton. His anxious face mirrored the same fear.

They came at last, in the moonless morning time before Old Sun was up, to the edge of the jungle, and they saw the great towering shape gleaming faintly in the starshine and knew they were not too late.

The ship sat on a triangular plain of gravel laid down by the flooding of two small rivers, or by two branches of the same river, that came down over a rock wall in two separate waterfalls a quarter-mile apart to join again some distance below. This was not the flood season and the water was no more than ankle deep. It made a pleasant chuckling sound going over its stony bed. But Stark was not pleased by it. He saw the stream as an obstacle; not a large one, to be sure, but one he could have done without.

The ship was small by interstellar standards. Like *Arkeshti,* she was designed for use on the out-worlds, where port facilities were primitive or nonexistent. Small as she was, she bulked impressively on the plain, propped level on massive landing legs, her outer skin scored and pitted by alien atmospheres and the dust that drifts between the stars.

When Old Sun came up, Stark was able to see more detail than he had at first, and none of it was reassuring. Three hoppers squatted in a line close to the ship. They were inside a perimeter guarded by three laser cannon on portable mounts. The cannons had their own power cells, and they were emplaced to cover all approaches to the open hatch of the ship. The two-man crews walked about or lounged beneath the canvas awnings that sheltered each emplacement.

"They run a tight ship," said Ashton, lying at Stark's left. "Without the hounds, I shouldn't care to face those cannons."

"My brother has not cared to, either," Pedrallon said. He was at Stark's right. "The Wandsmen impressed upon him the futility of an attack and he was only too eager to agree. The Wandsmen are pleased with the depredations because of the hatred they rouse against foreigners. They do not wish to have them stopped." He stared hungrily at the ship. "We must take her, Stark. If possible, we must destroy her."

Six men emerged from the ship. They spoke to the six men of the gun crews, who went up the ramp and inside—to get their breakfasts, Stark supposed, and then some sleep. The six newcomers took their places by the cannons.

Halk came up, from the place some distance away where the troop was resting, under orders to make no sound. He crouched down, glowering at the hoppers.

"Will they never take those damned things off?" he said.

"It's early yet."

"They must be near the end of their looting," Pedrallon said. "My brother has kept me supplied with each day's report of temples robbed and villages plundered. Even allowing for lies, Andapell must be nearly stripped, as well as the principalities that neighbor us."

"Let's hope the hoppers have one more day's work," Stark said. "If they open that cargo hatch to load the hoppers in, we'll have to hit them with all hands present, something I don't want to do."

"Surely," said Halk, "your Northhounds can carry all before them."

"The Northhounds are not immortal, and those are powerful weapons. A tramp like this one draws hands from all over the galaxy, and some of them may be like the Tarf, immune to the hounds. If there are too many immunes, or if there's just one and he happens to be in charge of a cannon, we won't have such an easy time of it."

"Look," said Pedrallon.

More men were coming out of the ship. They walked toward the hoppers and began to check them out.

Ashton gave a sigh of relief. "They're leaving, then."

The men completed their ground inspection. Four climbed into each of the hoppers. The rest sauntered back toward the ship. Motors woke to life. One by one the hoppers lifted, droning into the sky.

"Good," said Stark. "Now we wait a while."

"Wait?" said Halk. "What for?"

"For the hoppers to get so far away that they can't come whipping back in five minutes when somebody yells to them on the radio."

"Radio!" Halk growled. "These off-world toys are a pest."

"No doubt," said Stark, "but think how many times, on our journey north and back again, you would have given all you possessed to know what was going on at Irnan."

Stark settled himself for the wait, drowsing like a cat in the growing heat.

Pedrallon and Simon Ashton discussed between them what radio message would be sent to Galactic Center if they did actually gain their objective. The discussion was not entirely amicable.

Finally Ashton got the official steel in his voice and eye, and said, "The message must be brief and readily understood. I can't give the history of Skaith in ten words. There is no guarantee that any message is going to be received at Pax in time to do any of us any good; but I can tell you that if they receive a request for an armada to interfere in a civil war on a non-member planet, they'll pretend they never heard it. I will identify myself and ask for a rescue ship. I will also state that Penkawr-Che and two other captains are up to no good here—and they can do what they want to about that. For us, one ship is enough and all we can hope for. You'll still have to go to Pax to plead your case."

Pedrallon gave in, without enthusiasm. "Where will you rendezvous? If the ship comes at all."

Ashton scowled. That point had been a major problem between himself and Stark. The fact was that they could not guarantee to be in any particular place for any length of time. They could not even guarantee to be alive.

Ashton answered, "There must be a portable transceiver aboard the ship."

"And if there isn't?"

"We'll make an alternative arrangement." And hope, Ashton thought, remembering the inhospitable vastness of the planet.

Old Sun rose higher. The heat became a physical thing, a weight that dragged down drooping branches and pressed on the bodies of men so that breathing became a conscious labor and hardly worth the effort. The gravel plain shimmered. The starship seemed to float above it. The gun crews dozed under their awnings.

All but one man.

He was short and round and his skin was grayish-green like the skin of a lizard. His head was naked and quite broad, with a ridiculously small face set in the middle of it. His birthworld circled a lusty young primary, so he was used to heat. He had not even bothered to open the collar of his tunic. He walked toward the stream, thinking of home and friends and calculating how much his share of the loot would come to.

The jungle stood like a green wall across the stream. It was very still. All the morning noises had died under the weight of approaching noon. The lizardy man picked up a flat pebble and sent it skipping across the shallow water.

Inside the hatch, in the ship, it was cooler. Ventilators sucked and roared. The two men sitting in the open airlock were enjoying the breeze. They were relaxed and somnolent, eyes half closed against the swimming glare outside. They heard nothing but the ventilators; they did not expect to hear anything. They had heard nothing on any of the other days when they had been on guard here in this remote place. In any case, they were not worried. The people of Skaith had nothing with which to fight them.

Each of the two men had beside him a heavy automatic weapon. The hatch control was on the wall beside the opening. Their duty was to defend the hatch, activating the control if that should become necessary. They did not expect it to become necessary, and in fact they considered the duty superfluous, though they did not say so. At least it was comfortable. They could see the emplacements outside, baking in the sun, and were glad they were not in them.

They could see, also, that one of the men had gone down to the stream to skip stones. They thought he was crazy. But they did not understand it when he began suddenly to scream.

They saw him fall down, writhing in the water. Great white animals burst from the edge of the jungle and hurtled across the stream, jetting bright drops from under their paws.

Men came after them, running.

17

WATER SPLASHED on Stark's bare skin, hot from the sun. The rocks were warm and slippery beneath his feet. He watched the cannons through the flying spray, waiting for a lightning bolt that would sear them all into lumps of blackened flesh like the priests of the temple by the sacred grove.

Kill! he shouted to the hounds. *Kill!*

They were already doing that. The gun crews died very quickly in their pits, without touching the firing studs.

The hounds ran fast toward the open hatch.

A man fell outward from it, onto the ramp. He lay there, curled in a fetal ball with his arms over his head.

Other man, N'Chaka. Think harm.

Kill!

Not easy like others . . .

Stark ran across hot, dry gravel. He had forgotten the cannon. His gaze was fixed now on the open hatch. If it should be closed against them, they would have to try and blast it open with the cannon, but even if that were possible it would take too much time. If the remaining man in the lock should be an immune—

Kill!

The sound of a man screaming mingled with the sudden hammering of shots from the lock. Gravel flew in little spurts. Two of the hounds went awkwardly over their own heads and did not get up again.

The hatch remained open and there was no more sound.

Eleven hounds dashed up the ramp, spurning the dead man with their cat-clawed feet.

Kill!

Hound-minds sought through steel bulkheads, through strange distances reeking with the unfamiliar stinks of oil and metal. They sought man-minds. They sent fear.

Stark ran, and his breath was harsh in his throat. The sun beat down and the two white hounds lay bloody on the ground. Behind him, Halk and the tribesmen and the Irnanese were busy with the cannon. Gerrith, Pedrallon, and Simon Ashton followed Stark. Tuchvar had stopped by the dead hounds.

Stark ran up the ramp.

Inside the lock he heard no sound except the panting of the hounds. The second man, who had not been as easy to kill as the others—an alien with butter-colored skin and a very massive skull—lay contorted in death. He was still holding his weapon in short-fingered hands that looked more like paws. Stark took it from him.

The inner hatch was open. The short corridor beyond it was empty.

Men?

Yes. Gerd growled and the metal walls echoed menace.

Not kill?

Like Tarf. Not hear us.

Many?

One and one.

Where?

There.

"There" was up.

Gerd's mind pictured gray, hard, not friendly, not understand, dark things, bright things; the place where the men were, the place he could see through their eyes.

Men think harm, N'Chaka.

Watch.

Ashton came up the ramp, breathing hard. He paused to pick up the other automatic weapon. Gerrith came behind him. Her face gleamed with moisture. Pedrallon, at her side, was barely sweated. His eyes were bright, almost as savage as the hounds'.

"Two men are still living," Stark said. "The hounds can't touch them."

"Only two men?" Pedrallon said.

"Armed." Stark lifted the automatic. "There's no need for you to come."

Pedrallon shook his head. "I must come. This is my world."

Stark shrugged. He looked at Gerrith. "Stay here."

"As you wish," she said. "But this is not my death day, nor yours."

Outside, one of the cannons had been disabled by shearing the cable from its power cell with a battle ax. The tribesmen were struggling back across the stream with a second one. They would set it up under cover at the edge of the jungle, where they could rake the landing area in case the hoppers returned. The Irnanese were bringing the third one, to set it up inside the airlock. Both Halk and Sabak had learned the rudiments of handling a laser cannon during the time Stark had had the armed hopper at Irnan. Stark left them to it, and sent nine of the hounds back out to Tuchvar, keeping Gerd and Grith with him. He nodded to Ashton and Pedrallon, then they proceeded into the short corridor.

It was no use taking any more troops with them. They had only the two automatic weapons. Swordsmen in the narrow passages of the ship would be an encumbrance rather than a help. Stark wished that Pedrallon had stayed behind, but he could not deny the man's right to accompany them.

At the end of the corridor a round hatch gave onto the central well of the ship.

A small ship, as starships went. Yet from this angle it seemed enormous. Stark looked up and still up, past the various levels that contained the drive rooms, both conventional and hyperdrive; the heavy reactors that powered them; the cargo holds and life-support systems and storage rooms. The cylindrical walls tapered toward the nose, to living quarters and the bridge.

Up there, at the very top—along with the control systems, the computers, and the navigation tank—was the communications room.

The ventilators roared. The ringing walls were like a trap. The hounds held their heads low, rumbling.

In flight, in null gravity, this well would be the fore-and-aft axis of the ship. A metal pole, shiny with use, stretched up the center, affording handholds for men to pull themselves along in free fall, graceful as darting fish. Now, in the vertical position, with the solid pull of a planet underfoot, there were lifts to transport men and supplies to platforms that jutted out beside access hatches at each level.

Stark had no desire to commit himself to one of those lifts, but he could see no other way. He climbed onto the nearest one, with Ashton and Pedrallon and the two hounds. The platform was wide and it had a rail around it. Gerd and Grith crowded close against Stark and trembled; and when he pressed the button on the panel and the platform shot up smoothly on its steel channels, their minds were filled with the fear of unknown things and the emptiness that yawned beneath their feet.

Watch!

We watch, N'Chaka.

The lift went up swiftly, past the lower levels.

N'Chaka! There!

"There" was an access hatch on the opposite side of the well. It was open. The platform it served was above the lift, which was rising toward it. It was below the next platform on the near side of the well, so that the lift would have to pass it in order for the occupants to gain access to the top levels. An old Earth saying flashed across Stark's mind, not a comforting one. Something about shooting fish in a barrel. "I heard," Ashton said.

"Fire!"

They fired together at the opening. Harsh thunder crashed in the well. The metal surrounding the hatch became pocked and scarred.

The opening was a black throat swallowing death. The lift drew level, rose above it. No face appeared in the hatch. No shots came out of it.

Stark and Ashton stopped firing.

Dead?

No. Run. Think harm later.

Two men, unhurt, armed, were waiting to try again.

Stark punched a red button on the control panel. The lift came up to the platform and stopped.

Beyond the access hatch, in the crew's quarters, they found bodies. Two were in a corridor, where they had tried to run. Three others were inside a small wardroom, where death had interrupted them at lunch.

Stark located a vertical hatchway with a ladder fixed to the wall. The hounds would not be able to climb it, but that seemed to be the only way up.

Where men?

Close.

Stark pulled himself up the ladder.

He emerged on the flight deck. The primary control banks took up most of the central portion of this level, with computer linkages and the navigation tank. At his left, on the far side of the bridge, was the communications center. Two more bodies were huddled there. One of them had fallen from the radioman's chair.

N'Chaka! Danger! There!

"There" was behind him.

He dropped, rolling. The first burst went over him. He heard shattering noises and thought, Oh God, if they've wrecked the radio . . . !

Ashton had come up the ladder behind Stark. He fired from the level of the deck. Something blew up with a tremendous bang. Then Stark was firing from where he lay, at two figures indistinct in the sudden smoke.

Suddenly it was quiet. The smoke dissipated. Two men lay on the deck and Gerd was saying, *Dead.*

Stark got up and went over to the radio.

Ashton climbed the rest of the way up the ladder and joined him. "It's all right? They didn't hit it?"

"They didn't hit it." Stark dragged the radioman's body away from the chair.

Simon Ashton sat down. He switched power into the hyperbeam transmitter and turned on the recorder. He began to send. Pedrallon came in and stood beside him. The Skaithian watched intently, though Ashton was speaking Universal and he could not understand what was said.

Ashton had chosen his words carefully. He kept the message short, accenting the urgency of his request for a rescue ship. He mentioned Penkawr-Che and his reavers. "I am sending from one of their transmitters, which we shall have to abandon. We will try to make radio contact with any incoming ship. Failing that, the ship will please make a landing on the high heath southwest of Skeg and wait there as long as it reasonably can." He used a code signal for "Top Priority," making it mandatory that anyone receiving the message should relay it immediately to Pax. Then he set the switch on AUTOMATIC SEND and left the recorder on at REPEAT. The message would continue to be transmitted until someone came to shut it off.

"That's all we can do," he said. "That, and pray that somebody hears it."

Pedrallon pictured the terrible black emptiness of space, and was not cheered.

Stark fired a sustained burst into the control banks, making a satisfying mess. A disabled ship and a message sent would give the looters something to think about. Penkawr-Che might even abandon his planned foray against the House of the Mother.

He went over and looked at the bodies of the two men who had not "heard" the Northhounds. They did not in any way resemble each other. Stark nudged one of them with his foot.

"He was in the pit by the middle cannon this morning. If he hadn't been relieved . . ."

He turned to Ashton, thinking of the hoppers that must be well on their way back to the ship by now, unless the radioman had died before he could send off a call, and thinking also that there might be more like these two aboard them.

"Ten minutes to search for a portable radio. Then we go."

They found it in five, in a stores room on the level below, where the men apparently outfitted themselves for shoregoing expeditions. They also found arms racks, empty because the weapons were all in use, oxygen packs and protective clothing for climates not quite unfriendly enough to require full-dress armor, and several different types of portable communicators. Stark chose two powerful miniaturized radios in high-impact cases, easily carried and suitable for ground-to-ground or ground-to-orbit use. They also took as much ammunition as they could carry for the automatic weapons.

Going down on the lift, the silent ship was an iron tomb around them. Gerrith touched Stark's arm and smiled, then accompanied him out into the sunshine.

There was still no sound of motors in the sky.

Halk disabled the cannon. He and the Irnanese hurried with Stark and the others across the gravel plain. The dead hounds were gone; Tuchvar had carried them into the jungle for burial. In the fringe of trees beyond the stream the tribesmen stood by their cannon, waiting.

Sabak said longingly, "Can't we take it with us?"

Stark shook his head. "Too heavy, and we're in a hurry."

Somebody hacked the cable. Tuchvar came up with red eyes and his surviving hounds. The line formed, and Larg led the party swiftly away into the jungle.

The journey back to the sea took them longer than the journey inland, because they must needs spend hours motionless under the trees, lest the furiously questing hoppers find them. At length they no longer heard the snarling of motors overhead, and Stark concluded that the search had been dropped in favor of more pressing work, such as repairing the ship or making arrangements to shift their loot to one of the other craft.

Larg went quietly back to his village, and the rest of the party returned to the inlet very late in the second night. The Tarf were on guard, undisturbed. Stark and the others clambered aboard the boat.

The Fallarin, their dark fur patched with sweat, listened to the news, and Alderyk said impatiently, "So, then, it was worth the effort. Now let us be gone from this place. The jungle winds are slow and stupid, and they bring us no comfort."

He spread his wings and gave the sluggish air a spiteful slap.

Under oars, the boat crept out into open water, and when the sail went up the winged men filled it with a whistling breeze.

They headed southward, partly because of Gerrith's vision and partly because there was no other place to go. Northward were only enemies. In the south, Gerrith told them, were help and hope, though the white mists still clung heavily about the shape of them, so that she could not discern them clearly, and in that whiteness there was still the spreading stain of blood.

Stark said, "We'll make for Iubar. The Lady Sanghalain can give us news of the White South, if nothing else."

It was in his mind that the Lady Sanghalain might not be overjoyed to receive him, since it was by his urging that she had taken passage in *Arkeshti* and so the treasure of Iubar had found its way into Penkawr-Che's pocket. Still, it was the only place to start.

So they moved into strange waters, under strange skies, as foreign to these northern folk of Skaith as to the off-worlders.

They moved as Old Sun moved, with the winter at their backs, toward the austral spring.

But there was no spring.

18

At first they had threatening sails behind them out of Cereleng, sweeping the sea in search of the lost prince. Whenever the sails came too close, the Fallarin sent adverse winds, sudden gusts to split canvas and snap spars. After a time, they saw no more sails except those of fishermen; and sometimes, far out on the horizon, the topsails of a deep-sea trader that seemed to stand still, like a tiny patch of cloud caught between sea and sky.

They were seldom out of sight of land. Avoiding cities, or towns of any size, they ran in to fishing villages for fresh water and supplies. They had nothing with which to barter and so were reduced to stealing, with the aid of the hounds, but they took no more than was necessary to keep them alive. And the country was fat, so that a modest theft of fish and fruit wrought no hardship even on the poor.

But as they went farther down the curve of Mother Skaith's last green girdle, the Fertile Belt, this richness began to wither. The air, which had been soft and indolent, turned sharper. The milky sea grew dark. Along the shore, plantations of trees that ought to have been in blossom, or bearing fruit, were blackened by unprecedented frost. There began to be abandoned farmsteads beside blasted orchards and cold fields where seed had died in the ground. Forest as well as orchard had suffered heavily. They passed miles of skeletal trees, and where these gave way to scrub hills and open savannah, they began to come upon plundered villages, often with squattering tracks on the foreshore where the Children of the Sea had been. Farther inland they could see smoke and knew that other villages were burning.

They were careful where they landed now. Old Sun's face was hidden more and more behind dark clouds, and the Northhounds roused and snuffed the wind that blew against them out of the White South.

Snow, N'Chaka! Snow!

They began to encounter the elements of a vast army, advancing northward.

Some came by land, entire villages marching with their women and children, or bands of stragglers wandering wild along the shore. Others came by sea, in single sails or in squadrons that dotted the gray water with bright-painted hulls. All shared one thing in common.

Hunger.

"My lady Cold has been beforehand here," said Gerrith. "See how her daughter walks with these folk, like a faithful sister. The winter has been long, and it shows no sign of leaving. All their stock is used up and they are driven north toward the green lands." She smiled, without joy. "I told you the Goddess would move this wintertime. I had forgotten that the seasons are upside down in this underside of Skaith, and she has been at work through all these long months while we were lulled by summer."

"The whole south seems to be on the move," said Stark. "The people of Iubar may be among them."

Gerrith shook her head. "No. This is only the first wave of the Second Wandering. Iubar has not yet stirred."

"Well," said Stark, "if they migrate, it will be by sea and not by land. We can keep watch for them."

"It will not be necessary," Gerrith said.

And it was not.

Meanwhile, by radio, Ashton kept track as well as he could of Penkawr-Che and his ships.

He heard much talk back and forth between *Arkeshti* and the other two. The second ship, which had found leaner pickings on its way back from Iubar, joined *Arkeshti* on the heath at about the same time that Stark's party attacked the third ship in Andapell. Stark and Ashton listened to some furious conversations. Ashton's call for help, and his message about Penkawr-Che and his captains, had caused panic in some quarters.

Penkawr-Che held it down. There was no certainty, he said, that the transmission had been picked up, or that it would be forwarded if it had been. And one man's statement was no proof of anything, even if that man *were* Simon Ashton. Assuming the worst, it would still take time for any GU ship to reach Skaith.

It was decided to finish up and get out well before the earliest possible deadline, calculated on the dispatch of a ship from the nearest GU base. But the big problem facing Penkawr-Che was the Andapell ship, which Stark had severely disabled. The owner-skipper insisted on repairs, and demanded help.

Prudence dictated abandonment, since repairs would cause more delay than they could reasonably afford. Greed considered the loss of a fat cargo, which could not be easily transshipped because of the logistics involved, and also because there would not be room for it in the two remaining ships unless the attempt to loot the House of the Mother should be dropped. Nobody wanted to drop that, especially not the skipper of the second ship, who felt disadvantaged.

Greed won. From the three ships, technicians and spare parts were mustered to patch up the control system. The third ship finally lifted off and went into a stationary orbit above the heath. *Arkeshti* and the second ship joined it there. Then they shifted orbit together and dropped down over the curve of the world, and Ashton lost them.

The three ships landed on the Plain of Worldheart, under the wall of the Witchfires, where the aurora danced on glittering peaks.

The triple shock of that landing was felt in the deep levels where the Children of Skaith-Our-Mother tended their gardens and fretted at the change of temperature that had lately become apparent. Only a matter of two or three degrees; but in a closed environment, where there had been not the slightest change for centuries, the rich crops seemed suddenly frail and vulnerable.

Word of the shock was carried upward through the maze of carven halls, to the ears of Kell à Marg, Skaith-Daughter. And presently she looked down once again from her high window above the plain.

She saw the hoppers rise and bumble along the mountain wall, a droning swarm of inquisitive bees searching for the doorway to the honeypot.

Kell à Marg set watchers where there had been no need of watchers since the last of the Wandering. She spoke to her captains. Then she went with her chief Diviner through long, dim corridors past monastic quarters where young Diviners were trained—so few of them now, she thought, so very few, with how many deserted chambers on all sides—to the place where the Eye of the Mother was kept, in the great Hall of the Diviners.

The hall was circular, with a high vault from which a lamp of pierced silver depended. The lamp was unlit. Small lamps flickered round the circumference of the walls, which had once been hung with an ancient and holy tapestry known as the Veil, from which the face of the Mother, many times repeated, had looked benignly upon her children. Nothing was left of the Veil now but blackened tatters, and the walls themselves were scorched. This sacrilege had been done by a creature from the Outside, by the sun-haired woman who came with Stark, and both of them prisoners of the Wandsman Gelmar. As always, a small spasm of rage caught at Skaith-Daughter's heart when she looked upon the destruction.

Acolytes brought down the silver lamp on its chain and lighted it. The Diviners gathered round that which was beneath it, a thing waist high and some three feet across, covered with a finely worked cloth.

The cloth was withdrawn, and the Eye of the Mother caught the gleaming of the pierced lamp that swung above. The huge crystal, pellucid as a raindrop, seemed rather to absorb the light than to reflect it, so that the golden rays went glimmering down, and back and forth—now deep, now shallow, ever shifting—and the Diviners bent their heads, gazing with their souls into the depths of the crystal.

Kell à Marg, suppliant, stood waiting.

The Eye of the Mother darkened. The clear shining became curdled and ugly as if it were suffused with blood.

The chief Diviner straightened, sighing. "The end is always the same. And this time is now upon us."

"What comes after it?"

The Diviner bent his head again obediently, though he knew the answer well enough.

Slowly the crystal cleared to the placid blankness of a summer pond.

"Peace," said the Diviner, "though the Mother does not tell us of what sort."

The Eye was covered again, the silver lamp extinguished. Kell à Marg stood in the dim hall, pale-furred, large-eyed, a royal ermine graceful in bands of gold and jewels that made a rich, soft shining even in that half-light. She stood for a long time, and the Diviners stood also.

"If we fled from this place," she said at length, and she was speaking not to the Diviners nor even to herself, but to Someone beyond them all, "what would there be for us in the bitter world? We have given ourselves to the Mother. We cannot go back. Nor can we ever build again as we built here under the Witchfires. We ourselves are dying. Better to die where we are loved, in the arms of the Mother, than on the cold spears of the wind Outside."

The Diviners sighed, with infinite relief.

"Nevertheless," said Kell à Marg, "if there are those who wish to go, I shall not stop them."

She went from the Hall of the Diviners back to her own place on the knees of the Mother, and she called together her counselors and the Clan-Mothers and the heads of all the guilds—as well as the foremost of the scholars, those who were not too far lost in the vast labyrinthine House that contained the history of a planet, where generations of scholars had studied and catalogued and recreated, deciphering ancient literatures, surmising ancient musics, enjoying learning for its pure and only sake, their minds free, their bodies safe from want.

Surely, thought Kell à Marg, there is no place under the sky for such as these.

She spoke to her people, naming the choices.

"I, myself, will stay," she said, "with those who wish to join me in defending the Mother's House from these off-worlders. Those who wish to face the future elsewhere are free to go by the western gate and the pass that leads to Thyra."

No one chose to leave.

Kell à Marg rose. "Good. We shall die well—now, if we must, by the hand of the invader, or later, by the hand of time. In either case, we remain true to ourselves and to the choice we made long ago. It would not become us to outlive the Mother."

She turned to her chamberlain. "There is armor somewhere, I believe. Find it."

The Children of Skaith-Our-Mother made ready.

The attack did not come.

The hoppers bumbled up and down along the mountain wall, searching. The high windows of the Mother's House were not easily distinguished among the million rough, ice-coated crevices of the rock. The hoppers were plagued by winds, and by blizzards that hid the Witchfires in blinding snow. The Children began to hope that the off-worlders would go away.

They stayed.

Twice, hoppers swept in over the pass and battered the blank stone under the Leaning Man, and the Children slid the great blocks of their inner defenses into place. The second time, explosive charges burst in the outer gate. The Leaning Man fell down and sealed the opening with more tons of shattered rock than the off-worlders cared to move. They returned to the plain and continued their stubborn search. Though Kell à Marg could not know it, their time was growing very short.

In the end, it was the carelessness, or the over-eagerness, of a watcher that betrayed the Children: he allowed himself to be seen on one of the balconies, and the invasion began.

The winds were calm that day, with Old Sun blinking a dim eye above the peaks. The craft were able to maneuver close to the cliffs. Lightning bolts struck through the opening, licking along the corridor within. The watcher had given warning, and the Children were not there, so that the laser beams struck only unoffending rock.

After the laser beams came men. They entered the House of the Mother.

The invaders entered into darkness, for the Children had taken away the lamps; but they brought lights of their own, harsh white beams that slashed the blackness without really illuminating it. They took up positions in the corridor, with automatic weapons at the ready, covering the arrival of more men, winched down on swaying cables like the first.

The corridors and lightless chambers all around remained silent. The air smelled of dust and sweet oil and something else the off-worlders could not quite define—time, perhaps, or the subtle breath of decay exhaled from the millions of stored, separate things gathered in the uncounted rooms cut from the heart of the mountain.

They heard sounds. Whisperings. Breathings. Soft, hurried footfalls. But the stone vaults distorted sound so that they could not be sure whether what they heard was the echoes of their own movements, or something more sinister.

They found the weight of their heavy weapons comforting, knowing that there was nothing in these catacombs that could stand against them.

The Children knew that, too.

"Wait," said Kell à Marg in her beautiful, useless armor. "If they believe that we will not attack them, they may become careless."

"But they have already begun to plunder our treasures," said one of the younger captains. "Is it not our place to die well, defending them?"

"There is always time for that," said Kell à Marg, "and opportunity will not be lacking. Meantime, prepare more poisoned shafts for the crossbows."

The Children had not been forced to fight since the turbulent days of the Wandering, and that was long ago. They were not skilled with weapons, and their swords were wrought more for beauty than for use. The small, light crossbows they carried were not built to throw their bolts for long distances, because in these catacombs all distances were short; and they had little power of penetration. But once dipped in the paste made from a certain fungus grown in the lower levels, the slender bolts did not need to penetrate. A scratch was sufficient.

The Children, with their flitting lamps, kept out of sight of the intruders, moving in side corridors and through the maze of adjacent rooms. When the captains came, they knew it. When the men, growing bolder as nothing appeared to threaten them, spread out through the rock-cut chambers, the Children knew that, too, spying secretly from carved doorways.

The invaders were choosy. They wanted small things, easily portable: statuary, jewelry, fine weapons, paintings, books, any objects sufficiently alien and strange to attract connoisseurs of the *outré*. They became engrossed in their search, pawing among large and heavy things for the little pearls. Load after load went to the hoppers. Men began to pick up what they could to hide on their persons. The weather held calm, and each room led to another, and still another.

Suddenly, in one of the high windows above the plain, a watcher saw black clouds blot out the Bleak Mountains with trailing skirts of snow. He sent word to Kell à Marg.

The invaders got the same news, and began a move toward the hoppers, which would soon be forced to land and wait out the blizzard. Strung out in twos and threes among the treasure rooms, the men grabbed what they could carry.

The Children struck.

They struck from dark chambers as the bright lights left. They struck from shadowy doorways. The invaders were professionals; they retreated in good order. But the Children were ahead of them and all around them. The aliens caught glimpses of white-furred bodies in glittering mail. They saw the mad eyes of night-dwelling creatures glowing at them, swiftly vanishing in the all-encompassing labyrinth. They heard the click and whir of the crossbows, such feeble little things against the bursts of their automatics that filled the stony spaces with chattering thunder. The automatics killed; they killed quite a number of the Children. But there were always more, and their little sharp bolts went whispering into flesh and it mattered not how quickly they were pulled out.

The star-captains and the last of their remaining crews were hauled up into the hoppers.

After the sound of the rotors had died away, Kell à Marg and her captains, such as were left of them, came out into the main corridor. She looked at the scattered loot, and the scattered bodies.

"Let the bodies of the off-worlders be cast from the balcony, and let those things which are ours be replaced. Then give orders to the Guild of Masons. Every window that looks upon the world is to be blocked up forever. The gates are already sealed. We will use whatever time is left to us to further our knowledge and leave what records we may of the life-tale of Mother Skaith, here in her eternal House."

It mattered not to Kell à Marg, nor to any of the Children, that those reports would never be read.

Those whose duty it was lifted the fallen Children and bore them down through the labyrinth to the Hall of Joyful Rest, where they were united with the Mother.

Skaith-Daughter returned to her place upon the knees of the Mother. She leaned her head back, into the polished hollow between the Mother's breasts. She thought of the off-worlders and the ships and the rending of the barriers that had made this unique and holy planet only one of millions of planets, common as grains of dust across the galaxy. She was sorry that she had lived to see this. She was sorry that, in search of knowledge, she had brought the strangers into the House. She was sorry that she had not killed the man Stark. She hoped that he was dead, or soon would be.

Her tiring-women removed her armor and smoothed her fur with golden combs. She could not hear the picks and hammers of the masons at work, but she knew that in a short time the last of the hateful Outside would be walled away forever. She felt all around her the great, warm, protecting House, the unchanging womb. She set her hands on the hands of Skaith-Mother, and smiled.

In the bitter winds below the pass, where the huge ruin-mound of Thyra bulked, the hearths were cold and no smoke rose from the forges. The Ironmaster and his folk, clanking in their iron gear, burdened with beasts and impedimenta, marched southward under the sign of Strayer's Hammer.

Some days ahead of them, the People of the Towers marched behind the Corn-King and his priests, down across the Darklands.

Southward of both nations, in the Barrens, the Sea of Skorva froze six weeks before its normal time, and the people of Izvand looked with dismay at the drying and salting sheds, which ought to have been filled with the autumn's heavy catch, and which were empty. Izvand supplied mercenaries for the Wandsmen; and now the wolf-eyed fighting men began, in their turn, to wonder about the winter that lay ahead, thinking of fatter fields they knew below the Border, in the Fertile Belt.

In the high passes of the mountains, early snows caught traders and travelers by surprise. Herdsmen moved their flocks from summer pastures struck by freezing rains. In the rich valleys of the city-states, harvests withered before blackening frost, and the tithe-gatherers of the Wandsmen found scant tribute.

In the cold deserts northeast of the Bleak Mountains, at the Place of Winds, the Fallarin listened to the voices of the high air, which brought them word of the world, and they took urgent counsel among themselves.

South along the Wandsmen's Road, the fortress city of Yurunna crouched on its rock above the oasis. The women of the Six Lesser Hearths of Kheb, whose duty it was to tend the fields, saved what they could while the irrigation ditches sheeted over with ice and roots froze in the ground. The men, whose business was war, turned their veiled faces toward Ged Darod.

And at Ged Darod, the annual tide of Farers flowed in along the many roads that crossed the plain. They filled the streets of the city. They filled the squares and the pleasure gardens. They filled the hostels, and they ate of the food that was always forthcoming from the Wandsmen's bounty. And still more of them came, too early and too many, while behind them in the temperate zone the harvests failed.

The million bells of Ged Darod made joyful music in a breeze that was not as warm as it might have been. In the Palace of the Twelve, Ferdias listened to reports that were in no way joyful, and the first small worm of doubt crept in behind his triumphant serenity.

19

Below the Fertile Belt, it had become more difficult to evade the bands of refugees who plundered wherever they could in the hope of finding food. Stark steered away, out of sight of land, venturing in only when water became a pressing need.

Upon the sea, food was no longer a problem. Everything was moving north. Aquatic creatures followed shoals of the lesser creatures they fed upon. Winged things, fierce-eyed and whistling, swooped over the surface. Dark, bobbing heads showed where whole colonies of the Children of the Sea-Our-Mother migrated, feeding as they went. The hounds watched constantly, even when they slept, and the men's hands were never far from their weapons.

The boat was under oars much of the time, beating against southerly winds that the Fallarin had not yet learned to tame, though they spent hours in the forepeak with their wings spread, listening, talking.

"They're different from our desert winds," Alderyk said. "They speak of bergs and sea-ice, and they smell of water instead of dust. They have had no one to talk to, and they're proud and wild. They do not learn easily."

Snow came in whirling flakes, and the Northhounds snapped at it like puppies, rolling in the delicious chill where it collected on the deck. The first outriders of the southern ice slipped by, floating mountains glittering and silent amid flat, white pans of drift that thickened imperceptibly across the solemn ocean.

The winds died, through no effort of the Fallarin. Ahead now was a spreading whiteness that swallowed sea and sky together.

Gerrith looked at it and said, "That is where our road leads."

Stark felt the breath of the Goddess upon his cheek and shivered. "She has taken the south for her domain."

"Someone else is there. A woman with strange eyes, who waits for us."

"Sanghalain."

Gerrith repeated, "Sanghalain." And the name sounded like a call to some secret, deadly battle.

The Fallarin found wind enough to fill the sail, but they lacked vigor. Frost clung in their dark fur and rimed the stiff ridges of their wings. It was a chill that nothing could keep out. Men and women huddled together beneath their cloaks, around the galley fire, and Pedrallon shuddered constantly in his blankets. Ashton kept his small radio inside his shirt, lest his fingers freeze to it when he monitored the unchanging silence from the sky. Only the Northhounds throve.

The boat passed into that waiting whiteness. Tendrils of snow-fog wrapped it. It swam englobed in blind mist, with the pan ice rattling and racking along its sides. The men stood at battle stations with their weapons ready, and they saw nothing. The hounds bristled and growled, and gave no warning. Stark held the steering oar, seeing nothing ahead, and behind him the wake vanished as quickly as it was made. He was inured to cold and did not suffer as the others did. But the primitive N'Chaka growled and whimpered within him, as uneasy as the hounds.

Ice finally closed about the boat on all sides and held it fast. Men and hounds stood silent in the silent fog and listened to ghostly voices, the squeaking and grinding and muttering of the floes.

Then another voice spoke in Stark's mind, a deep groaning like a winter tide among rocks.

I am Morn, Dark Man. You are in my waters. My army is beneath your keel.

We come in peace, said Stark.

Then bid those beasts with the black and burning minds be still whilst I come aboard.

They will be still.

Stark spoke to the hounds, and they were shamed because they had not been aware of Morn and his people.

Minds shut, N'Chaka. We cannot hear.

Trust them.

Friends?

No. But not enemies.

Not like. Cannot hear.

Trust them.

The hounds' eyes glowed yellow and their tiger claws scored the deck. But they crouched and were still.

Astern of the boat—where there was open water in perilous cracks between ice pans—round, shining, hairless heads appeared, heads with great eyes used to seeing in the ocean depths. And presently Morn hauled himself huge and dripping over the rail and stood looking at Stark and the hounds, at the Fallarin wrapped in their dark wings and the Imanese in their leather and the tribesmen in their faded cloaks, and at the Tarf, who regarded him with mild indifference from under horny lids.

He looked at Gerrith and bent his head briefly.

Yours is the far-seeing mind. The Lady Sanghalain has awaited your coming.

Gerrith bent her head in acknowledgment, but if she made any answer it was made in mind-talk and Stark could not hear it. They could all hear Morn when he wished it, and he could hear them, but the nontelepaths were deaf to each other except in normal speech.

When Stark had first seen Morn—that time when Morn and the Lady Sanghalain saved him from the mob in the pleasure gardens at Ged Darod—Morn had been clad in ceremonial landgoing gear, a fine garment of worked and polished leather, and he had carried his badge of office, a massive trident set with pearls. Now he wore sea-harness, a scant webbing that served only to hold his weapons.

He did not need a badge of office to make him impressive. He stood a head taller than Stark, a natural amphibian evolved from some mammalian ancestor, in contrast to the deliberately mutated Children of the Sea. Unlike the Children, Morn's people were not furred, but had smooth skin, dark on the back and light on the belly, camouflage against deep-swimming predators. Also, they were intelligent and highly organized, with a complex social order of their own. The Children of the Sea hunted them for food, and they hunted the Children of the Sea as vicious brutes, despising them.

Morn's people were called Ssussminh, a name that sounded like rolling surf when it was properly pronounced. They were telepaths because mind-talk was easier than mouth-talk in their watery world; and they had an ancient, mystic, and very powerful connection with the ruling house of Iubar—a connection Stark was sure he would never completely understand. Probably it had begun as a symbiotic partnership, with the Iubarians, who had always been fisher-folk and traders, providing land-based goods and services in exchange for pearls and sea-ivory and such other unique offerings as the Ssussminh might make. Now both members of this ancient partnership were being forced from their homeland by the Dark Goddess.

In any case, Morn was the Lady Sanghalain's other voice. And when he spoke, he spoke to all of them.

At Iubar we are in a trap. Will you enter it? Or will you turn back?

"We cannot turn back," said Gerrith.

Then let us have lines. My people will take you through the pack.

Lines were paid out. The Ssussminh grasped them, many strong swimmers. They towed the boat astern and then ahead again, finding narrow leads which were hidden from a steersman by the fog.

Let your hellhounds watch, douse your fire, and let you all be silent. We must pass through an army.

"Whose?" Stark spoke aloud so that his comrades could follow his end of the conversations. They could all hear Morn.

The Kings of the White Islands have come north, all four tribes, with their belongings and their hunting packs and their sacred island. They besiege Iubar, in force.

"Why?"

The Goddess has told them that it is time for them to go and claim their ancient lands beyond the sea. They need our ships.

"What is their strength?"

Four thousand, more or less, and all fighters, except for those still in the cradle-skins. The women are as fierce as the men, and even the children fight well. Their small javelins fly for the throat.

The boat glided on black water between tumbled plains of ice. Great bergs embedded in the pack showed cliffs and caves where the mist moved vagrant about them, thinning now and then but never lifting. The Ssussminh swam tirelessly. The company stood to arms, making no sound. The hounds watched.

Men, N'Chaka. Men and things, there.

"There" was somewhere ahead.

The bowmen warmed their bows against their bodies, for the cold made them brittle. The strings were inside their shirts to keep them dry. Stark let them stand to, in case they were needed, but he and Simon took the automatics from their place of safety and loaded them. Ammunition was irreplaceable, but this was no time for parsimony. They took up positions on either side of the boat. Morn took the steering oar.

They began to hear voices in the mist, and saw lights, the faint glimmerings of blubber stoves. These were at first before, and then beside, and then behind and all around the boat, which moved with no sound but a gentle purling, creeping through the heart of an army.

N'Chaka! Things come!

The Ssussminh splashed and were gone. The lines fell slack.

The hunting packs have found us. Let your hounds kill now. And let the Fallarin give us way. Hurry!

Alderyk cracked the air with his wings. His fellows joined him. In a moment the sail filled and the boat was moving. The fighting men made ready. In the forepeak, the eyes of the Northhounds brightened and their jaws hung open, panting white smoke.

There came a boiling and moiling in the water. Beasts, shaped like giant otters and furred like snow-leopards, shot up screaming and rolled over to float like dead fish. Then voices shouted alarms off in the fog. Conchs boomed and brayed. Shadows moved on either side, where folk came running in the freezing mist. They ran faster than the boat could swim. Bone-barbed throwing spears rattled inboard.

Stark raised his hand and brought it sharply down. "Now!"

The automatics made bursts of stuttering thunder. Fur-clad forms skittered and fell across the ice. A sort of insane howling rose, and then dropped behind as the boat picked up speed and slid out into open water, leaving the floes astern.

Some trick of the currents, which ran swiftly here along the coast, kept this stretch of water clear of all but broken ice. A fleet of skin boats darted out like beetles from the edges of the floes.

Kill, said Stark, still holding the automatic in case of need.

The hounds growled.

The folk in the boats faltered and lost the paddle stroke, but few of them died, and those not quickly.

Minds fight fear. Strong. Not easy, like most.

Morn said, *The White Islanders are without fear. They are madmen. They have broken themselves by the hundreds against our walls. Now they wait, knowing that we starve. Look there.*

Iubar took form, a dim peninsula ridge-backed with mountains, snow-covered from the peaks to the sea's edge.

Those fields, said Morn, *should be green, and all this sea clear of ice. But the Goddess holds us fast, pens our ships in the harbor. Even if we could somehow free our ships and try to pass through the floes as we have just done with you, the Islanders would overwhelm us, taking each craft as it came.* He pointed. *There is your anchorage.*

Stark made out a walled town and a harbor. A gray guardian castle bestrode the walls, mailed from its foot with the ice of frozen spray. The single high tower, rising sheer from the rock, bore no battlements. There was no need for defenses atop that unscalable height.

Offshore from the castle, an island reared frosty cliffs above the water. Yet they had not quite the look of cliffs.

Shallafonh, said Morn. *Our city. Looted, like Iubar, and soon to die . . . like Iubar.*

The castle held one side of the harbor mouth in its arm, with a frowning tower for a fist. A second tower faced it across the gap, at the end of a fortified mole. Both towers were armed and manned, and a boom could be drawn to close the narrow entrance. The still water within was choked with ice, but a way had been cleared for Stark's boat to the end of the royal quay.

Let be, said Morn to the Fallarin, and they were glad to stop because the Goddess sapped their strength. Some of Morn's people caught the trailing lines again. The boat was brought into harbor, with film ice already forming behind it, and was moored beside what Stark was sure must be Sanghalain's own ship. Everywhere at the quays, white-shrouded ships lay motionless and all the normal voices of the harbor were mute.

And so, said Morn, *you are safely within the trap, though for what reason I do not yet know.*

Stark looked toward Gerrith, but she had gone apart from them.

The sail folded down like a tired wing. Men and women sat stiffly, unable to comprehend that they had reached the end of the voyage.

The great portal of the castle tower opened. A woman clad in brown appeared, and Stark knew that it must be Sanghalain and that there were people with her. But he could only watch Gerrith.

A change had come over her. She seemed to have grown taller, to have shed all the weariness and uncertainty of the voyage. She walked to the gunwale and mounted it and stepped onto the quay, and no one dreamed of offering her a hand. Stark moved to follow her, and then stopped. On the tower steps, Sanghalain and her ladies and her courtiers stood still.

Gerrith looked about her, at the shrouding mist and the dead sky. A sort of glory seemed to touch her. She shook back the hood that covered her head and her hair shone with its own light. Sun-colored woman, shining in this place of death. And Stark's heart turned in him like a sword blade.

Gerrith spoke, and her voice rang like a sweet, strong bell against the bitter stones.

"I know now why my way has led me to this place."

Sanghalain came down the steps. The courtiers remained where they were, but a double file of women followed her, all in habits of brown wool, all with faces hidden behind brown veils. They marched along the quay and halted before Gerrith, who had turned to meet them. All the brown habits bent and swayed in a kind of genuflection. Sanghalain stretched out her hands.

Gerrith took them. The two women looked at each other, motionless, their hands clasped together. Then they turned, and the file turned with them, somber skirts whipping in the wind, moving back toward the steps.

And once again Stark stood, in memory, in the House of the Iron-master at Thyra, when Hargoth the Corn-King turned in his rage upon Gerrith, whom he himself had wished to sacrifice. "You prophesied for me, Sun Woman," he had said. "Now I prophesy for you. Your body will yet feed Old Sun, though not as a parting gift."

Stark sprang onto the quay. He started after Gerrith, and Morn stood before him.

She goes of her own free will, Dark Man.

"For a sacrifice? Is that why Sanghalain was waiting for her?"

The hounds were beside Stark now. But others of the Ssussminh had gathered, barring his way. They were armed, and the hounds were of no use against them. Stark saw archers in Sanghalain's livery standing with ready bows on the lower defenses of the castle.

We will slay you all, if we must, Morn said. *It will not change this matter.*

Gerrith walked with the Lady of Iubar, up the steps and into the cold, gray tower.

20

THEY WERE in a cold stone room with faded tapestries on the walls and a tiny fire of sea-coals on the hearth. Sanghalain and the brown-veiled women of the Sisterhood of which she was High Priestess had been with Gerrith all night. They had withdrawn now, so that the wise woman of Irnan might have time alone with her companions.

She was clothed in a gown the color of her hair, which hung loose over her shoulders, glowing brighter than the firelight. She sat at a table, her head bent above a basin filled with pellucid water, provided for her by the Sisterhood.

Halk, Alderyk, Pedrallon, and Sabak stood near the table, waiting for her to speak. Simon Ashton stood by himself, a little way apart. Stark remained at the far end of the room, as distant from Gerrith as he could be, looking as if he might kill her himself if she were within his reach.

When she spoke, with the voice of the prophetess, he listened as the others did. But there was that in his face that made Ashton glance at him uneasily.

"The folk of the north have begun their Second Wandering," she said. "The Fallarin have abandoned the Place of Winds."

The sudden clap of Alderyk's wings made the candles gutter.

"They go south to Yurunna," she continued, "and such as are left of the Ochar move that way also. At Yurunna, many of the tribesmen make ready to move, for they have not enough from the ruined crops to carry them through the winter."

Sabak's blue eyes were intense above the tribal veil.

Gerrith went on. "Across the Bleak Mountains, the Witchfires are sealed. Skaith-Daughter and her people have made their choice. Penkawr-Che's ships—and I think they got little for their pains—have left the planet. The Harsenyi were scattered long since, down the southern roads.

"The forges of Thyra are cold and the people march. Hargoth the Corn-King leads his narrow folk south from the Towers. At Izvand, the wolf-eyed men look toward the Border. Other folk, whose names I do not know, are leaving their starving places. There will be much fighting, but the city-states will hold behind their walls. Irnan alone will be abandoned, for lack of food, and I see smoke above the rooftops. Her people will find refuge among the other city-states."

Halk bit his lip, but did not speak.

"The southern wave of the Wandering will die out as the survivors find better lands. Pedrallon's country and others like it can absorb most of the refugees, though their way of life will be greatly changed. But there is no help there for our cause. It is from here, from the White South, as I foretold, that our armies will come. Sanghalain, by her arts, knows that there is no longer any place on Skaith for her people or for the Ssussminh. Their only hope lies in the starships."

Stark spoke abruptly, and his words were like daggers. "I will not serve Sanghalain."

"There is no need to. When that has happened which will happen, make alliance with the Kings of the White Islands. They will be your spearhead. You shall lead them."

"Why?"

She recognized the twofold nature of his question.

"Because you are the Dark Man of the prophecy, fated whether you will or no, and the threads of your fate are knotted together in one place—Ged Darod, where you will fight your last battle with Ferdias and the Wandsmen. A battle you must win." She held up her hand to stop him speaking. "You care nothing for the prophecy, I know. You came here for one purpose, to rescue Simon Ashton. The ship you called for will come, but the Lords Protector now have the power to interfere with it. The off-world thing that Pedrallon left behind is in their hands."

"The transceiver," Pedrallon said.

Gerrith nodded. "You must make haste with your army, Stark. If you do not, the Lords Protector will send the ship away, or destroy it, and there will be no escape for you, forever."

"We also have transceivers," Ashton reminded her.

She shook her head. "I see you marching mute to Ged Darod, with nothing of the off-worlds in your hands."

"Not even the automatics?"

"Not even those."

Ashton glanced at Stark, but his eyes were on Gerrith, seeing nothing else.

"Will the Kings of the White Islands fight?" asked Halk. "Why should they help us?"

"Because they wish to regain their ancient lands."

"And where are these lands?"

"Where Ged Darod now stands."

A long silence followed. Gerrith continued to look into the clear water. Then she sighed and leaned back.

"I see no more." She looked at them, smiling gravely. "You have been good comrades. We have fought well together. You will see to the end of that fighting. Go now, and remember that the respite will be a short one. The Goddess has set her hand on Iubar."

They bent their heads, all but Alderyk, who gave her a king's salute. They left, and Simon Ashton went with them.

Stark remained.

He went no closer to Gerrith, as though he did not trust himself. "Will nothing turn you aside from this obscenity?" he said, and his voice was a cry of pain.

Gerrith looked at him with love, with tenderness. She looked at him from faraway, from some place he did not know and could not enter, but which he hated with every fiber of his being.

"This is my destiny," she said gently. "My duty, my high honor. This was the thing I had yet to do, so that I could not go with the others on the starship. This was why my path led me southward into the white mist, though I could see nothing there but blood. *My* blood, I know now."

"And Sanghalain will hold the knife?"

"That is her task. Through the sacrifice of my body to Old Sun, many lives will be saved, and my world set free. Do not betray me, Stark. Do not let what I do be wasted because of your anger. Lead, as you were fated to lead, for my sake."

Little flames hissed among the coals. Sleet tapped against the windowpanes. Stark could bear her gaze no longer. He bent his head and Gerrith smiled with a remote tenderness.

"Remember all the long way we had together and be glad for it, as I am."

Stark's heart was frozen in him and he could not speak. He turned and left her, walking softly, as one leaves a house of death.

In the drafty hall Sanghalain waited, with her veiled women robed all in brown, and her honor guard, and Morn. The Lady of Iubar wore the same brown habit. Her body was full and gracious, a very woman's body, small in the waist, rounded of breast and hip. Her hair was black, one shining loop of it showing above her forehead where her veil was thrown back. She wore no jewels—all those were now in Penkawr-Che's coffers—and her face showed the pinched lines of care. Her eyes were like the winter sea where the sun strikes it, gray with depths and darknesses and sudden tides of light. Eyes in which, Stark had felt, a man might lose himself and drown. Once he had thought her beautiful. Now, as he moved closer to her, Morn set his hand upon his knife.

Sanghalain met Stark's gaze calmly and without concern. "This is our world," she said. "You have no part in it, nor in its customs."

"That is true," said Stark. "Nevertheless, do not let me look upon you again."

He went away, along the cold corridor.

Sanghalain and her brown-veiled women entered Gerrith's room. "It is time," said Sanghalain.

And Gerrith answered, "I am ready."

She walked with the Lady of Iubar and her women through the echoing ways of the tower. Morn and the honor guard followed with torches. A winding stair led upward to the tower top. They mounted it and came out upon the wide, flat, icy stones that stretched away to the sheer edges and the drop beyond. In the center of the round space a kind of bier had been erected and draped with rich fabrics to hide the faggots of wood piled beneath. It was still dark. The dead-white mist of the Goddess enfolded the tower, so that the torches burned only feebly.

Gerrith stood silent, facing the east.

At length, in the dark and the frost-fog, low on the horizon there crept a faint smudge of coppery light.

Sanghalain held out her hand to Morn. "The knife."

He gave it to her, across his two hands, bowing low. The women began to chant, very softly. Sanghalain veiled her face.

Gerrith walked to the bier, a sacrifice going proudly, consenting.

She lay down, and saw the knife blade shining above her in the white air, striking swiftly downward.

When Old Sun rose, a dull ghost behind the shrouding mist, the folk of the White Islands saw a great blaze of flame on the tower top, and wondered.

Eric John Stark went alone with his grief and anger into the barren hills, and no one—not even Simon Ashton—tried to find him. But the Northhounds howled without ceasing for three days, a terrible requiem for the wise woman of Irnan.

21

THE HELLISH PART of the ritual was that it worked.

After that burst of flame on the tower top, the mist began almost imperceptibly to thin. At noon, the face of Old Sun was clearly seen for the first time in unremembered months, and folk ran out to stand in the snow and feel his touch upon them. Then a wind blew warm from the north. By that afternoon the thaw had begun.

It continued. As torrents rushed down the slopes and the ice began to go from the harbor, the people of Iubar, reborn, revitalized, flung themselves into the task of clearing and refitting their ships.

The people of the White Islands, with their floes beginning to rot away beneath them, attacked Iubar in successive waves of desperation. But the boom had closed the harbor mouth to boats, and the land walls held.

On the fourth day, Stark came back from his wandering, gaunt and strange-eyed. He would not enter the tower. He went directly to the boat and sent a messenger to bring his people out on deck.

They came, and no one ventured to speak to him except Halk, who faced him squarely and said, "She had a better death than Breca."

Stark inclined his head and turned away to speak to Ashton.

"Have you heard anything on the radio?"

"Nothing yet."

Stark nodded. "You'd better wait here, Simon. I'm going to parley with the Kings, and they may not give us a chance to talk."

Simon shrugged and sat down in his accustomed place, taking charge of the two automatics.

Stark ordered the oars out. But at the last minute, Morn came padding down the quay.

I will go with you, Dark Man.

Stark looked at him with utter hatred. Why?

Because you do not know the Kings, you do not even know their names. You know nothing of their customs or their history. You will never arrange a parley without me.

Stark hesitated, then nodded curtly. Morn stepped aboard. The Northhounds growled, and Stark bade them be quiet. The rowers dipped their blades in the water and the boat moved out toward the harbor mouth, where the boom was swung aside enough to let them through.

While they rowed across the open water, Morn talked. And because Simon Ashton had taught him well, Stark listened.

When the first of the skin boats came out to challenge them, Stark shouted, "We claim the Peace of Gengan and the Holy Isle of Kings! Who denies us this is cursed."

Reluctantly the people in the skin boats put their weapons aside and formed into a sort of ragged escort, while four of the boats darted off among the rotting, jostling floes.

Stark could see that numbers of the White Islanders had been forced to move their skin tents onto the shore, wherever they could find high ground. The people in the boats had stripped their outer furs in the glow of the ginger star, which had been bought at such price, and their heads were bare. They seemed to run to every shade of color in their hair, which was clubbed, warrior-fashion, to give no grip to a foe. Their faces were uniformly windburned, a paler streak rimming each face where the tight fur hoods normally covered them. Their faces were also uniformly savage, with powerful jaws and cheek ridges, and deep-sunk eyes that carried an expression of single-minded ferocity. Stark wondered if these people would ever be found relaxed and smiling.

One of the skin boats took the lead, and Stark steered after it until they reached a solid line of ice so old and thick that it had barely begun to wear away in the sunlight.

The rest of the journey must be done on foot, said Morn. *See there.*

Stark saw the crest of a giant berg glittering in the sun.

That is the Holy Isle. Leave your hounds and your weapons. You will have no need of them. Bring an escort, but no more than four besides ourselves.

Ashton came, and Alderyk, and Halk, and Pedrallon. Sabak was left in charge of the boat, Tuchvar of the hounds. He had difficulty controlling them. The smell of violence and the red thought of killing were all around.

The Islanders hauled their skin boats onto the ice and followed. Afoot, they moved with a kind of controlled ferocity, setting their feet as a hunting animal does before the spring. But their weapons remained untouched.

They are fighters, Morn said, catching Stark's thought. *Killing machines. They are bred to nothing else. Any child that shows fear or weakness is thrown to the hunting packs.*

Some of the leopard-spotted beasts had come onto the ice, moving agilely enough on their short powerful legs, with broad paws that could disembowel a man in one swift stroke. The Islanders kept an eye on them, and from time to time beat back those which became too much interested in the foreign-smelling flesh.

The shining peak of the berg came closer. Stark could see its foot, broad and massive, a veritable island of ice. The clear slopes rose above, and they were marked with curious dark blots, set in regular ranks one above the other.

Morn said, *That is where they bury their kings.*

Four men stood before a standard set on a high pole of sea-ivory cunningly joined and bound. The standard flashed in the sun with the untarnished brilliance that only gold can show. Its top was in the shape of a man's head, somewhat larger than life, and the expression of the face was one of gentle and sorrowful dignity.

Beneath it the four Kings of the White Islands regarded the foreigners with the eyes of wolverines.

Delbane and Darik, Astrane and Aud, the Sons of Gengan.

Four separate small knots of people stood near the Kings, presumably their honor guards. And all up and down and across the slopes of the berg, the dead kings watched, upright in their burial niches, sealed in the ice and preserved without change by the perpetual cold. Stark could not count them, and presumably the ranks extended around the berg where he could not see.

Trickles of water were beginning to run down those cliffs, and Stark wondered what would happen to the Holy Isle as the tribes moved northward.

They will leave it here, said Morn, *under the care of the Goddess. They will take with them only the Head of Gengan.*

A herald came forward. He was dressed no differently from the other Islanders, but he carried a staff of sea-ivory topped with a small copy of the Head, which was also wrought in gold.

"Who are you, who would speak with the Four Kings? This one we know, his people are our old enemies." He gestured with his staff at Morn. "But you are strangers. You came from the north, with his help, and killed many of our people with unknown weapons. Why should the Four Kings grant you audience?"

"Because," said Stark, "they wish to regain the lands from which their forefathers were driven. We can help them."

The herald returned to the standard. He spoke with the Kings. Then he marched back.

"Come," he said. And when they had advanced, he said, "Stand here."

The four killer faces fronted them, under circlets of ivory set with great pearls brought out of the sea. The glance of their small, bright eyes was a stabbing rather than a seeing. Like their people, they had had all the softer places of the soul cut ruthlessly away, leaving nothing of love or laughter or mercy or kindness. The hairs rose at the back of Stark's neck, and N'Chaka repressed a challenging snarl.

The four pairs of eyes roved over Ashton; over Alderyk, pausing curiously; over Pedrallon, hunched in his furs; over Halk's tall bulk. They settled at last on Stark, and stayed there. Something in his dark face and cold, light eyes spoke to them.

"We march northward to the sun," said Delbane, the oldest of the Kings, and Stark recognized something in the man that he had seen before in the High North: the madness of a too-long prisoning in cold and darkness. "We have waited for generations, preparing ourselves. Now the Goddess has told us it is time. We are fated. How can such as you give us help?"

"You have lost the ships of Iubar," Stark said, and the warmth of Old Sun on his face was like the warmth of shed blood. "Your people must do their marching on land, at least for the time being, since your skin boats won't live in the open sea. You know nothing of the world, and the north is full of hostile people. If you march alone, you will never see those lands you covet."

Aud, the youngest of the Kings, leaped forward as though to sink his powerful teeth in Stark's throat. Instead, he began to orate, stamping his feet and flinging his arms wide.

"For generations! You heard him say it, my brother-enemy. Countless years of waiting, until we were ready. You see there, the golden head? That is the head of Gengan, who was our lord and king at the time of the Wandering. He was a philosopher, a peaceable man. We were a peaceable people, we bore no arms, we kept no army, we were proud of our pious and lofty peacefulness.

"But when the strong hands of well-armed countries, under which we had sheltered, let go, and the wolves they had held in check were loosed upon us with their weapons, we could do nothing but run.

"We ran, all down the curve of Mother Skaith. And at last, the remnant of us were driven far into the White South, into a place so cruel and barren that no one else wanted us; and there we halted, and survived.

"We taught ourselves new skills. The four grandsons of Gengan became each one a king over a fourth of our people, and each fourth has been at perpetual war with the other three. Only the fierce and the able live, and if they live too long they are sent to the Goddess. Now we are ready. Now we go to take back what was ours, to live again under the sun."

Aud ceased his orating and looked contemptuously at the strangers. "If a child cries in the cold we slay it, so that weak seed will not be passed on. How can soft creatures like you be of use to us?"

"These soft creatures managed to kill quite a number of your people," said Stark, showing the edges of his teeth.

A dull flush came across Aud's cheekbones and his eyes burned. Stark stepped past him and spoke to the elder Kings.

"Do you know where to find your lost lands?"

Each King drew from among his furs a golden plaque, pierced at the top to hang about the neck on a leather cord. Each plaque showed an identical map, deeply incised; and though the scale was all wrong, Stark was able to recognize the general contours of sea and land, the place where Skeg now stood, and the plain of Ged Darod to the northeast.

He placed a finger on Delbane's plaque. "Here," he said, and they were astonished, catching their breath sharply.

"How can you know?" demanded Aud. "You, a stranger?"

"Strangers often possess some scraps of knowledge. For instance, I can tell you that a great and powerful city stands there, the city of the Wandsmen, which you will be forced to take before you can occupy your land again."

He turned and swept his hand in a wide gesture across the floes. "You are fighters and know no fear. But you could not break the walls of Iubar. Ged Darod is a hundred times stronger. How can you, with your bone-barbed spears, hope to batter down its defenses?"

The Kings glared at him with their little stabbing eyes, sunk behind slabs of hard fat against eternities of wind.

Darik said, "How do we know this city exists?"

"Morn has been there. Let him show you."

Now they glared at Morn. But Astrane said, "Show us."

Morn nodded, summoning up the memories. Presently Stark could see again, in his own mind, the temples of Ged Darod with their shining roofs, the masses of people crowding the streets, the high bastion of the Upper City, which was the seat of the Wandsmen's power.

The Kings made grunting sounds and shook their heads. They would not show dismay.

"We are strong," they said. "We are fighters."

"You are savages," said Stark. "You have not seen the world for centuries. You could not fight it with nothing more than your courage, even if your numbers were great—and they are small. How many have you lost here, gaining nothing?"

He looked again at the wretched encampments of skin tents. And the Four Kings glared and said nothing, until Delbane spoke.

"We move north, regardless. But there may be truth in what you say."

"You need allies. Numbers. Weapons. As the spearhead of an army, you would be formidable. Iubar, too, moves north. You need her, she needs you. Make alliance. You will be serving only yourselves."

The warm wind blew. Streams of water blurred the faces of the ice-eyed kings who kept their long vigil in the cliffs of the berg. No one spoke.

Aud began suddenly to rant again, pounding his fists on his chest.

Delbane silenced him and asked Stark, "Do you promise us ships?"

"Somewhere along the way, surely."

Delbane nodded. "We will take counsel, the four of us."

22

As Gerrith had prophesied, Irnan was a dead city. Because of the siege, her fields had yielded no crops that year but corpses, and her people were dispersed among the other city-states to wait out the winter. The great gate hung open, and there was no one to oppose the Farers when they came.

These numbered fewer than a hundred, mostly stragglers from the great rout of the Farer army, and who because of fear or injuries had hidden in the hills instead of returning to Ged Darod with the bulk of the mob after the alien lightnings had barred their way to Irnan. There had been more of them. These were the survivors.

The cold had come upon them like a furtive enemy, long before its time. They suffered from hunger and the attacks of the Wild Bands. They shivered in their nakedness, in their faded body paint, in their inventive rags and tatters. The chill wind urged them south.

They paused at Irnan only to see what pickings might be left there.

They passed along the tunnel through the thickness of the wall and came into the great square beyond. And they found that the city was not quite deserted.

A girl sat cross-legged on the platform that rose above the center of the square. It had been used for public executions, as was the custom, but the posts where once the victims were bound had been chopped away. The girl's dark hair covered her like a cloak, except where the wind lifted it to show her body painted in half-obliterated whorls of pink and silver, marred by time and rain and bramble scratches. Her eyes were closed, as if she slept.

A thin trickle of smoke rose from one of the buildings.

A man came out into the square, a muscular fellow clad in some burgher's cast-off robe. He had an indolent mouth and clever, mocking eyes, and he carried a drinking cup in his hand.

"Never mind her," he said to the newcomers. "She got kicked in the head at Tregad and she's daft ever since. My name is Wendor. Welcome to our city, and get your arses in out of the cold."

But the girl on the platform opened her eyes.

"It began here in Irnan," she said, and her voice echoed eerily from the walls. "They were the first traitors, these Irnanese. They wanted the ships to take them away. Because of them, it all happened. Their wise woman made the prophecy about the Dark Man from the stars who would destroy the Lords Protector."

Her voice strengthened, ringing away along the narrow streets that opened into the square.

"I was here," she cried. "Here in this square. I saw the Dark Man bound on this platform, with the traitor Yarrod and the traitor Halk. I saw Yarrod die. How we tore his flesh when they threw him to us! I saw Gerrith, the daughter of Gerrith, stripped and bound in his place. I saw the elders of Irnan in chains. And then the arrows flew."

She stood up, flinging wide her arms. Wendor leaned himself in the doorway and sipped from his cup. The Farers shivered together but could not quite tear themselves away.

"From those windows the arrows flew. There, and there! They struck the Wandsman Mordach. Wandsmen and soldiers they slaughtered, and Farers—Farers! Us, the children of the Lords Protector. The arrows sang, and the cobbles were slippery with blood. They killed us and set the Dark Man free, to bring down the Citadel."

Her voice had risen to a harsh screaming, like the cries of a predatory bird.

From among the Farers, as she paused for breath, another voice spoke. "The Irnanese are beaten and the Dark Man most likely dead. Let us all go inside, girl, away from this wind."

She looked at them with mad eyes. "The Dark Man routed us at Tregad—"

"He had some help," Wendor said cynically, "from Delvor's army." He turned to the Farers. "Baya has this special feeling for the Dark Man, you see. At Skeg she betrayed him to the Wandsmen, but he survived. She tried to betray him again, but he caught her and carried her, a prisoner, almost to Irnan." He laughed. "I think she's in love with him."

"Give me a stone," screamed Baya. "Just one stone, that I may kill that vermin!"

"Come away in," said Wendor. "She'll be quiet when there's no one to listen."

The Farers flapped and shuffled across the square and through the doorway.

Wendor shouted at Baya. "Vermin, you call me, when I kept you alive all that time after Tregad, and you wandering in a daze? Vermin yourself! I don't care what you do. Burn the bloody city and yourself with it, if you want to, I've sat here long enough. I leave tomorrow."

He went inside.

Baya looked at the city and smiled, and said aloud, "Of course, burn it. That's why I came here."

She climbed down the steps from the platform, hugging herself. She felt the wind now.

It was warmer in the hall, where Wendor had made a fire of broken furniture. A cask of wine sat with its top stove in and Farers fighting to dip into it. Others were pulling down hangings wherewith to wrap themselves.

"The pigs left everything they couldn't carry," Wendor said. "All their old clothes, and the wine. Make yourselves free." He moved abruptly to haul Baya away from the fire, where she was setting an improvised torch alight. "Leave it! We're not quite finished with the city yet."

He cuffed her until he was sure she understood.

Baya wandered off. She found odds and ends of clothing and put them on, taking pleasure in the chill emptiness of rooms and passages, desolate places that had once been homes. She shouted defiant obscenities to the hollow spaces, in which Stark's name was prominently echoed. "Beaten, beaten, beaten!" she cried. "And where is your strength now, Dark Man? Mother Skaith was too strong for you. *We* were too strong for you!"

She ran out of breath at last, and began to search for food. The Irnanese had left little enough of that behind them. Still, she found a smoked joint forgotten in a cupboard, and only partly gnawed by the small creatures who had found it first; and after that a cheese. She filled her mouth and went on her way, munching, carrying the food in her looped-up skirt.

In one kitchen she found a flint-and-steel, and, in a dark stores room, lamp oil. Smiling, she gathered together a heap of debris, of hangings and furniture, and splashed oil over it; then she set herself industriously to make sparks.

For a while Baya warmed herself, watching the flames lick up and catch in the wooden ceiling. When hot ash began to fall on her, she went away into the narrow street. Back in the square, she climbed up on the platform again and sat herself down. She ate some more while the smoke rose above the roofs, thinly at first, then more sturdily until it was a black and ever-widening pillar against the sky.

The wind helped.

When night came on, she could see the flames. She was still sitting there, watching, when Wendor and the others, roused from wine-heavy sleep by each other's coughing, staggered out of the smoky hall. By now the square was illumined by a red glare. Flames danced, roaring, over the rooftops.

Wendor climbed the platform. He picked up what was left of the joint and the cheese and threw them to the others, then he picked up Baya and carried her down the steps and through the gate. He beat her all the way, but she only watched the flames and smiled.

Irnan burned for seven days.

It made a great smoke; but Kazimni of Izvand, riding at the head of a troop of two hundred warriors, was too far away to see it, though it would have brought him pleasure. He and his mercenaries had twice suffered defeat there, first as garrison at the time of the revolt, and then as assault troops at the siege, all in the service of the Wandsmen. He knew Stark well. He had given the off-worlder safe-conduct as far as Izvand and then sold him to Amnir of Komrey for a good sum, to be resold to the Lords Protector. He had been amazed and respectful when Stark turned up alive to raise the siege of Irnan. Now surely the Dark Man was dead, and more pressing matters occupied Kazimni. Matters such as starvation and survival.

They had come east from Izvand across the Barrens, plundering where they could, with scant profit. They crossed the Border in frost and hail and came down on Tregad. But Tregad's walls were thick and her home bands well-trained. Kazimni poked and prodded, hoping for a weak spot. He found none and took his men off toward Ged Darod.

"In these times," he said, "the Wandsmen will likely have need of us. And in any case, we won't go hungry."

Folk would go hungry in Izvand that winter. He thought of his beloved city beside the frozen Sea of Skorva, and his hard jaw tightened. If what the wise men said was true, and the Goddess had set her hand on Izvand, then that city's day was done. He remembered Stark and his talk of better worlds beyond the sky, and he remembered his own answer. "The land shapes us. If we were in another place, we would be another people." The Izvandians had chosen, at the time of the Wandering, to remain on the edge of winter, in a climate similar to that of their original home farther north. Now it seemed that they might well be forced to move again, and the thought was a black one to Kazimni.

Yet he did not shirk it. If it were so, other folk would likewise be forced south, and much blood was bound to flow as they fought each other for land. It was better to be in the vanguard, to take first and hold on.

He thought of Ged Darod and its temples crammed with treasure, and he wondered secretly if the Wandsmen had not outlived their usefulness.

To the north, other men moved down along the Wandsmen's Road. There had been a drawing of lots at Yurunna, based upon the amount of food available. Those who drew the black pebbles were now upon their way, with their families and possessions, hooded tribesmen in dusty cloaks of the six colors, fierce blue eyes showing above their veils and weapons at their belts. Behind them came the

Tarf, enclosing within their green-gold ranks the hundreds of the Fallarin with folded wings, perched on tall desert beasts and looking forward savagely to a future in an unknown land.

Far behind, ignored in their orange cloaks, came the remnants of the once-proud Ochar, First-Come of Kheb, who had broken their might upon their own ambition.

The army marched on its way. In the low desert, frost had dimmed the reptilian colors of sand and rock, and in the debatable lands beyond the trees were hung with funeral draperies of dead leaves, which dropped steadily before a keening wind. Every pond was frozen.

Foraging parties found no food. Packs of starving wanderers attacked them for their own flesh. Wild Bands, subhuman creatures who knew no law but hunger, leaped at their throats from ambush. The men from the north pulled their girdles tighter and hastened south, keeping to the road because it was easy and well-marked.

The stations of the Keepers of the Middle Road were abandoned. Since the fall of Yurunna, the Wandsmen had had no occasion to travel this far. Their boundaries were drawing in, around the warm plain of Ged Darod.

23

THE KINGS of the White Islands found their ships at last, and not a day too soon.

Progress had been rapid enough earlier, but not easy. The Islanders, tireless on their ice floes, were unused to hill-climbing. They became sore-footed and irritable. There were quarrels and killings, and only the cruel hands of the Four Kings held them from tribal warfare.

Several hundred of the people of Iubar had been forced to march by land as well, because there was not room for them in their ships. They, too, were sore-footed and irritable, and they suffered from the steady diet of fish, which they insisted on cooking. Nothing was available from the land, and scurvy plagued them, as did the dysentery common to camps. Daily halts were made for burial parties. The Islanders ate everything raw, and throve. They became increasingly impatient with the Iubarians, threatening to go on alone and leave them to their misery.

Stark and Halk spent much time trying to hold the ill-mated force together. Stark was a grim and silent man these days, and even Halk walked wide of him. Gerd and Grith were ever at his heels, and the whole pack followed when he went among the ranks.

Morn was Stark's liaison with the ships of Iubar, and the situation there was worsening with each rising of Old Sun. Over-crowded and deep-laden as they were, the ships could still outdistance the marchers on land, and must needs heave to and wait, lest they lose touch entirely.

There is sickness aboard, said Morn one day. *It costs my people much effort to find food for so many. Water becomes a problem. There is fear, and much discontent. The Lady Sanghalain is told by her advisers to forget the promise of starships and sail on to seek new land for her people, abandoning those on shore. They care nothing for the Islanders.*

They will, said Stark, *when they need them to fight. And what about the Iubarians here, Sanghalain's own folk?*

There are those who say that they must be sacrificed fror the good of the rest. One day, she will have to listen.

Stark did not need to be told how near this shaky alliance was to breaking up. He could feel it, as a man feels quicksand beneath his feet.

So, when Morn brought word of a fortified town ahead, and a harbor filled with ships, he took the news at once to the Four Kings where they marched beneath the gold-bright Head of Gengan.

Aud showed his large, strong teeth. "Now," he said, "we shall see how the Dark Man fights."

It was a simple operation, swiftly done.

The Irnanese had chosen to march by land, with Halk. All the rest were in the boat, which did not sail in company with the ships of Iubar but stayed closer inshore, in constant touch with Stark. Now the tribesmen and the Fallarin and Tarf, except those necessary to crew the boat, joined the land forces, glad of something to do.

Leaving Halk in charge, Stark and Tuchvar ranged ahead with the hounds in two separate parties, to locate any landward guardposts.

The Northhounds found and silenced them before the watchers were aware of any force approaching through the thick woods with their curtain of frost-blighted leaves.

From a ridge of high ground, Stark looked down at the town.

It seemed cramped within a ditch and palisade. Probably it had grown too rapidly, as lost and landless people accreted around the strong leader whose crude banner hung above the gate—a tanned hide with a splash of color on it, indistinguishable at this distance. Some of the buildings were old. Others were new or still in the making, and many were rough shelters of boughs and skins.

In the small, crowded harbor were craft much like the one Stark's people used, designed alike for fishing and for battle. A number of these had been stripped and supplied with mechanisms that had nothing to do with fishing. Most of the half-dozen coasting traders moored along the outer quay at the far side of the harbor were probably prizes captured by the refitted boats. The quay itself, like the houses of the original village, was old, a rough construction of logs and stones.

People moved in the streets of the town. There was a market. The hammers of builders rang. Along the harbor front fishermen mended nets and among the boats a scattering of men repaired rigging or banged away at carpentry.

On a small island, little more than a hump of rock beside the harbor mouth stood a tumbledown tower with a mangonel on top and some armed men lounging about. A narrow causeway led from the tower to the end of the quay, and people were fishing from it with hand lines. Some sort of ordered life had found a footing here and was resuming its normal patterns. It seemed a pity to break them up again, but there was no help for it and the damage ought not to be irreparable, no more than a severe shaking-up.

Stark looked at the sky. Then he went back down from the ridge to where the army waited. By the sea's edge he conferred with the Four Kings and with his own leaders, and with Morn, and presently Morn slipped into the tideless water and disappeared, heading for Sanghalain's ships, which lay out of sight beyond a headland.

Stark said to the Four Kings, "Pick your men." He turned to Aud. "You and I will march together."

Aud smiled. "Where are your very powerful weapons, Dark Man?"

"They're not needed here," Stark said. "Unless you would feel safer?"

Aud snarled, and went to collect his force.

They set off through the woods, making a long circle around the town. The hounds ran ahead as before, to clear the way. They were excited, impatient for battle. They growled and whimpered, and their minds were filled with sparks of fire.

Stark's mind, like his heart, was filled with blackness. He needed the release of battle even more than the hounds, before that which was inside him should overwhelm him. He led the long line of Islanders—Aud's and Astrane's—among the blighted trees, going fast, with a morose and savage face that made Aud think better of his taunts.

Old Sun dropped over the edge of the world before they had completed their circuit.

In darkness, Stark led the way down toward the harbor side. They waited among the trees, where scrub woods covered a slope above the water. Gerd and Grith pressed close to Stark, panting, and he laid his hands on them as the first of the Three Ladies rose in the northern sky. Stark's eyes caught the light and shone like ice, whereas the eyes of the hounds were hot and yellow.

The palisade gate was shut. The town was remarkably quiet, showing few lights. The sentries the hounds had slain must have been found by now. Stark wondered what the leaders had made of them, being dead with no mark on them except the look of fear, and whether they knew about the army so close at hand. Certainly they would be alert and on guard. The only surprises would be in the method of attack and the size of the forces involved—which would not include the Iubarian marchers, who were far behind.

The second of the Three Ladies rose. The harbor water gleamed pure silver, the dark hulls and masts in sharp silhouette against it. The only lamps were in the island tower at the end of the quay, a few vagrant yellow rays showing through arrow-slits and cracks in the masonry.

The Islanders were as still as couching beasts. Stark could hear their breathing, and the rough panting of the hounds. He listened beyond these sounds, stretching his hearing against the outer silence, and all at once he heard a small splashing, as though a fish had jumped, close by the tower.

Dark shapes broke the quiet silver. They were all around the tower, on the causeway, rushing the inner defenses. A man screamed, and the night shattered into barbs of sound.

Stark said, "Be ready."

The Islanders gathered themselves, a faint rustling among the trees.

Voices shouted in the town. A flat-toned drum pounded and a horn blew.

More dark shapes appeared on the quay. Their wet hides glistened as they busied themselves among the mooring lines.

"Now," said Stark. And Astrane's men went, with a crackling of leaves, straight for the quay, where they would guard the Ssussminh.

The town gates burst open. Armed men rushed out, heading for the harbor.

"Now!" Stark shouted to Aud, and ran from the woods with the Northhounds baying before him.

The townsmen turned to fight. Stark saw a jostling of hard, leathery faces in the gentle light, and a brandishing of weapons. He heard screaming as the hounds killed. Then he was in the midst of it.

He was only dimly aware of Aud fighting beside him, silent and deadly. The Islanders never made a sound, either of challenge or pain, and he felt something eerie in that voiceless ferocity that contrasted with the shouts and cries of the townsmen, who outnumbered the Islanders but who quickly became uncertain whether they were fighting men or trolls.

Nevertheless, the townsmen fought fiercely, until the other part of the army came pouring down the cliffs and took them in flank. Then they retreated, running in panic for the gate until a powerfully built man with a mane of yellow hair roared and rallied them and beat the Islanders back. Stark crossed blades with him briefly, and then the fighting swept them apart. A few minutes later, the townsmen were shut inside their palisade again and Stark stood shivering and sweating while the hounds fed around him. Aud looked at him once, then turned away.

The small army leaned on its spears and waited until the coasting ships and a sufficient number of smaller craft had been towed or worked out of the harbor, with the aid of the Ssussminh, the Fallarin putting a breath of wind in the sails. Sanghalain's larger ships now stood off the harbor mouth to discourage pursuit by sea. The Islanders withdrew, making their way back to the shore, and the gates of the town remained closed.

The lengthy process of embarkation began.

When the last of the Islanders and Iubarians were safely crammed away somehow in the captured craft, Stark returned to his own boat and slept for a long time. When he awoke, the strange look was gone from him, and Ashton was at pains to hide his relief.

The ships sailed in company, in two separate wings that did not intermix. They made good speed with a following wind. Old Sun's rusty fires burned hotter with each day. At night the Three Ladies mounted higher overhead, their brilliance echoed in the phosphorescent wakes. It was necessary to put in to shore for water, and often there was fighting. At sea, predatory sails showed from time to time, and then sheered off when both the size and poverty of the fleet became evident.

Pedrallon put off his furs and ceased to shiver.

Neither the Iubarians nor the Ssussminh had any use for the rotting tropics, and in any case these were already beleaguered, crowded with refugees from both north and south and violently disinclined to welcome any more. It seemed that Sanghalain had no choice but to go on to Ged Darod, in hopes of the starship that Gerrith had promised.

But all that way north across the Great Sea to Skeg, the radio gave not even the faintest whisper of a human voice. They heard only the far-off hiss and crackle of star-talk, where the great suns spoke among themselves of things unknowable to man.

Stark could not imagine that Gerrith would have lied to him, but in her state of exalted self-deception she might have believed anything. Prophecies were slippery things, blades to turn in the believer's hand and pierce him. Stark looked at Old Sun and knew that the ginger star was like to be the only sun that he and Simon Ashton would ever see.

And then that happened which made him think that, after all, Gerrith might have seen true things in her Water of Vision.

A sudden tropic storm struck the fleet. Its brief violence did for several of the smaller craft, and Stark's was among them. Her mast went by the board and her sprung seams took water so rapidly that there was no time to save anything but their lives. Transceivers and automatics went to the bottom, leaving them as Gerrith had said—mute, and with nothing of the off-worlds left in their hands.

The need to reach Ged Darod quickly became like a fever that ran through all ranks. Ferdias now possessed the only voice on Skaith that could be heard beyond the sky.

24

THE HIGHEST VANTAGE POINT of the Upper City of Ged Darod was a marble kiosk atop the Palace of the Twelve, where members of the Council might sit, if they chose, and look out over their domain.

Ferdias and the five other Lords Protector—old Gorrel was on his deathbed—stood here with the wind stirring their white hair and snowy robes. They stared out over the Lower City to the gray-green plain, laced with the ribbons of the pilgrim roads which came from every direction to converge upon Ged Darod. Each northerly road spawned its own dustcloud, perpetually rising.

"Is there no end to them?" asked Ferdias.

It was too far to distinguish individual characteristics, but Ferdias had seen the pilgrims at closer range than this, and he knew that too few of them were in fact pilgrims—visitors who would make their offerings in the temples and then go away again. Too many were refugees, bringing carts piled high with belongings and old people and children, victims of the Goddess seeking help from the Wandsmen. Ferdias would not have believed that the hills and valleys of the North Temperate Zone contained so large a population, or that one season's crop failure could create such widespread destitution. Of course, the Wandsmen's tithes took a fair portion of the surplus, so that little was left for hoarding. But even so . . .

The streets and hostels of the Lower City were full. Camps had sprung up outside the walls, and they grew larger by the day.

"We must have more supplies," said Ferdias.

"The north has no more to give, my lord," said one of the red-robed Wandsmen who stood behind with their wands of office.

"I am aware of that. But the south has suffered no killing frosts. There are fish in the sea—"

"There is great disruption in the south," said another red-clad Wandsman. "The whole pattern of distribution has changed. There are many refugees, twice as many people to be fed, either by trade or rapine. Our requests are refused, or evaded. Wandsmen have been attacked. The southern princes tell us that the needs of their own people must be met before any other."

"Our fisheries," said a third Wandsman, "have been much disturbed by the movements of the Children of the Sea, who demand their own tribute."

"Yet these people here at Ged Darod must be fed," said Ferdias, with an edge of iron in his voice. "I have before me now a full inventory of the contents of our storehouses in both the upper and the lower cities. Even with the strictest rationing, which is not practical, a month would see the end of our supplies." He swept his hand wide in a gesture that took in the city, the plain, and all living things therein. "How will it be, do you think, when they come to our table and find it bare?"

The red Wandsmen, members of the Twelve with their pride and their gold-tipped wands, looked everywhere but at Ferdias. And he thought that he could see fear peeping out of their eyes.

"They will go elsewhere," one of them said.

"They will not go elsewhere. For two thousand years we have taught them not to go elsewhere. We are their hope and their promise. If we fail them—"

"There are the mercenaries."

"Shall we use them against our children? And besides," Ferdias added, "who can say where their loyalties will be when their own bellies pinch?"

Softly the myriad bells tinkled on the peacock roofs of the temples below. On the other side of the thousand-windowed building that rose like a white cliff above those roofs, the inner courts and cloisters of the Wandsmen's city basked in the sunlight. Ferdias thought of the Citadel, and of Yurunna, and the withering-away of great power; and it was almost as though the man Stark had somehow induced the Dark Goddess to favor him, so that they moved hand in hand across the planet to destroy everything the Wandsmen had labored so long to build.

"Do you not see?" said Ferdias to the twelve Wandsmen. "These people must be fed!"

Kazimni of Izvand was thinking along much the same lines.

A portion of the pleasure gardens in the Lower City had been set aside for the mercenaries to make their camps. And other troops besides the Izvandians had come to Ged Darod seeking food and employment. A sea of Farers milled around them, occasionally lapping over their boundaries. The mercenaries policed their camps. The Farers did not. The stench of the once-beautiful gardens was overpowering, and it was no better in the streets.

Facilities that had been ample, over the centuries, for the normal influx of pilgrims and wintering Farers were inadequate to cope with the unprecedented numbers of people who ate and slept and performed their bodily functions wherever they could find room. The hospital and the crèche were overrun. Even the temples were not spared. The Wandsmen and their servitors did what they could, but outbreaks of disease had begun in the city and in the refugee camps outside. Distribution of food to the multitudes was slow and difficult. There were fist-shakings and screams of complaint, and sometimes small riots in which supply carts were forcibly taken. Increasingly, the mercenaries were called in to keep order. And increasingly, the over-stretched fabric began to crack.

Walking guard with his men to protect the supply carts, or lying at night in the camp with the breathing, stirring, stinking mob around him close enough to touch, Kazimni could feel the city as a tangible weight that could easily move and crush him. He knew now that he had not been wise to come here—no wiser, in fact, than the Wandsmen had been to reject the starships. He considered what he ought to do when the bounty of the Wandsmen was used up, and his gaze turned often to the white pile of the Upper City.

Far out on the plain, a mad-eyed girl in faded body paint of pink and silver danced in the dust of the western road, on the way to Ged Darod.

In a defile of the mountains, the People of the Towers had halted in their line of march. There were not as many of them as there had been when they left the Darklands. Degenerate creatures lairing in the dead cities of the north had taken a toll. So had the long, cold journey itself, and not always of the weakest. They traveled light now, having eaten all their beasts. What they had left of supplies were easily carried. Their gaunt and narrow bodies, clad all in close-fitting gray, were narrower than ever, so that they looked like a company of ghosts moving through the snow squalls on the mountain's flanks. Now they stood still, not knowing why, weapons ready, pallid eyes alert behind the holes of their tight gray masks, most of which were unmarked by any sign of rank. They waited, children and adults alike, without question or complaint.

At the head of the line, Hargoth the Corn-King, with the stylized wheat-ears worked on his mask, stood facing a band of women.

They had appeared out of the veils of snow to bar the way, and their only garment was a kind of black bag that covered the head. Their naked bodies were scraggy and lean, and the skin of them was like the bark of old trees, roughened by many seasons of exposure.

The foremost among them cried out in a harsh, creaking voice that Old Sun was dying. The other women echoed her, wailing. They tossed their arms skyward and turned their hidden faces to the dim glow of the ginger star among the stormclouds.

"Blood," screamed the woman. "Strength. Fire. There are no men left upon the mountains, and Old Sun starves."

"What do you want of us?" asked Hargoth, though he knew very well what they wanted, and he glanced quickly upward at the steep sides of the defile, where bark-brown shapes lurked behind boulders, ready to push them down. He made a sign with his fingers, but it was not needed. His sorcerer-priests were moving quietly behind him into the ritual pattern of the Calling. Behind the priests, a man with twin lightning strokes on his mask was passing whispered orders to men who carried javelins.

Hargoth extended his arm. With his priests standing now in a half-circle at his back, he was like the point of an arrow nocked on a bowstring. The power of the linked minds joined to his began to pour through him, channeled and directed as he chose.

"Tell me what it is you want."

"Life," said the foremost woman. "Life to pour out sweetly for our lord and brother. We are the Sisters of the Sun. We serve him, keeping him strong with his proper food. Give us, that we may feed him."

"I, too, worship Old Sun," said Hargoth softly. His eyes shone through the holes of his mask, bits of winter sky, chill and colorless. "I also worship the Three, my lord Darkness and his lady Cold and their daughter Hunger. They tread close upon my heels, little sister. Can you not feel the breath of the Goddess, bringing you peace?"

The cold had become intense. A rime of frost settled on the women. Falling snow clung to it, ice to ice. The air was full of tiny sounds, cracklings and tinklings as though the air itself froze and fell.

Up on the slopes groans and cries could be heard where flying javelins found their mark. A single boulder came crashing down, missing by a hair two priests who scrambled from its path. The pattern was broken and so was the force of the linked minds that had willed the cold. But that single thrust had been enough. Tree-bark bodies lay still, or feebly tossed their scrawny limbs. Others who had not received the full gift of the Goddess crept away whimpering into the forest.

"Let us go on," said Hargoth. And the long gray line began to move again, quietly through the snow.

It came down out of the mountains at length, into a valley where abandoned plowlands glistened like dark metal with the frost. A city sat on a height of land, a burnt-out shell drifted with ash. Still, much of it could be made habitable again, and the climate was mild. There was some talk of stopping here. But there was nothing to eat, so the talk died quickly.

Hargoth cast the finger-bones of the Spring Child. Three times he cast them, and three times they pointed to the east. The People of the Towers went on, along the northern flank of a mountain range much higher than the one they had just traversed, its peaks hidden in thick cloud.

The men of Thyra marched more slowly, bearing their heavy weight of iron in solid ranks that ground relentlessly onward, with Strayer's Hammer at the fore. Within their clanking lines were the women and children and beasts of burden. They halted only when attacked, and then their iron swords and shields swung outward in a deadly defensive wall.

Because they lacked the cunning and the ghost-footed swiftness of Hargoth's people, they were attacked much more often. At Izvand they dallied, scenting food in plenty behind the walls. But the gates were too stout for their battering. They ate the last of their beasts and passed on.

Crossing the Barrens, they forced their way through the mountains, treading down the snow in the passes. When they came at last into the warm lands of the south, with green things growing on every side, they had lost above a hundred of their original number, not counting women and children. Enervated now by the heat, weakened by the long journey, sweating and chafing in their iron mail, they tramped on in search of food.

A dim path led them to a clearing where half a dozen thatched huts stood and half a dozen families were winnowing their small crop of grain. The farmers died swiftly.

The Thyrans rested and fed full. On the third day, a Wandsman in a green robe and a ten of armed mercenaries came looking for a share of the harvested grain.

They were surrounded before they knew it. They were brought to where the Ironmaster sat, with Strayer's banner beside him and Strayer's Hammer in dark metal upon his breast.

"Tell me," he said, "where I may find Gelmar of Skeg."

The Wandsman was young, and he was frightened, looking at the swords. "There is not so much iron in all the Fertile Belt," he said. "You must come from far away."

"From Thyra, close to the Citadel. We took captives for Gelmar once, a red-haired woman and some others from Irnan, and a man who was said to have come from the stars. Gelmar paid us well. Perhaps he will help us now. We seek a place where we may set up our forges again, away from the Dark Goddess who takes the strength from iron. Where may we find Gelmar?"

Gelmar was at Ged Darod, but the Wandsman lied because there were already too many folk there to be fed.

"He is at Skeg," he said, and told the Ironmaster how he might come there. "Now," he said, "I see that you have already eaten most of the grain, so I will go my way."

But he did not go anywhere, and he never knew the fruits of his lies.

25

THE SHIPS MADE landfall of Skeg. The two wings divided, Stark's wing going to the north and Sanghalain's to the south, so that Skeg could be attacked by land from two sides, with the Ssussminh coming in from the harbor. The action was badly timed, so that Stark and his force joined Morn in the wreckage of the marketplace and had the town well in hand before the first of Sanghalain's men showed up.

Fortunately there was little opposition. With the burning of the spaceport and the foreign enclave, Skeg had sunk back again to the status of a small port dealing lethargically in fish and grain. Most of the inhabitants ran for their lives and were not pursued. A brief, hot skirmish took place at the fishery, where a troop of mercenaries stood guard against raiders and protected the Wandsman who claimed most of the catch. The Wandsman was taken alive.

Stark questioned him, about Ged Darod.

"All is well there," said the Wandsman. His face was strained, and he would not meet Stark's eyes. "There are ten thousand ready fighting men, and twice that number in reserve—"

Lies, said Gerd, and lifted his lip on one side to show part of a row of fangs.

Touch him.

Gerd's eyes glowed. The Wandsman sank down to his knees, sobbing.

"I will ask you again," said Stark. "How is it in Ged Darod?"

The Wandsman was middle-aged. He had memories. He looked at Stark with black hatred and said nothing.

Touch him.

Gerd touched, flicking the whip of terror across the Wandsman's mind.

"They come," said the Wandsman, stammering. "From everywhere they come, the hungry and the homeless, and we"—he bent his head and shivered—"we cannot feed them all. When the food is gone . . . I do not know. Their faces terrify me. It is the end of us, I think."

"Are there no troops? Mercenaries? Surely the Upper City is defended."

"Defended? Oh, yes. And there are mercenaries. And many others who will fight. But once we have failed our people, once they have lost faith in us—"

"You failed them when you sent the ships away," Stark said. "And now the Goddess is bringing home the truth. I'm minded to make an offering to her when we reach Ged Darod." He turned to the captain of the Iubarians and said quietly, "I advise you to be a little more prompt next time. If the Islanders should come to believe that you're deliberately sending them in ahead to do your fighting for you, you may have some unpleasantness to deal with."

"Hold the brutes back then, if you can," said the captain. "We'll not run to catch up!"

He went away with his men to establish a defense perimeter, which was held while supplies were unloaded from the ships and the war engines brought ashore piecemeal to be prepared for the march.

No attacks came. During the delay, Stark scouted the countryside with the Islanders to keep them busy. They were tight-coiled, savagely impatient now that the promised land was just beyond the horizon. Stark knew how they felt: every laggard hour was torture to him, wondering if the rescue ship had come, and if Ferdias was in touch with it. Stark had feared that the Islanders would wilt in the heat. Instead they had bloomed, stripping away their furs, offering their pale bodies to the sun until they were as dark as teakwood. They went about near naked now, men and women both, charged with a vitality that was almost frightening. The Four Kings fingered the gold plaques around their necks, their eyes turned always to the northeast.

The Ssussminh did not fare so well. They hid their bodies from the drying sun that cracked their skin. They moved heavily on land, and the heat seemed to sap their strength, though they were still formidable enough. Nevertheless, they did not complain. But whenever Stark was near them his mind was aware of sadness, and he "saw" things that he had never seen with his own eyes: the halls and chambers of a city beneath the sea, beautiful with pearls and coral and ivory and many-colored shells. He walked in the streets of that city, and he watched it die as the dark seawater flooded in; and he felt the terrible regret, the yearning after things forever lost.

In what was really a very short time, though it seemed like an eternity, the army took the Wandsmen's Road and went north, traveling as fast as men might travel, dragging catapults and the great war engines on wheeled carts built for them by ship's carpenters during the voyage. The women of Iubar, who did not bear arms, remained behind with their children and a strong guard in the old fortress beside Skeg harbor. No one knew what would happen at Ged Darod. Only Sanghalain went with the fighting men, surrounded by tall Ssussminh who carried her in a chair with long poles, which they set upon their shoulders.

Stark's own small company went ahead of all, even before the Head of Gengan. Alderyk, who had turned broody and ill-tempered as a falcon in moult, was as impatient as the Islanders.

"My people are somewhere on this road. It was a mad dream that made me leave them."

"You came to control the whirlwind," Stark said, "so that it should not do too great damage to your world. Remember?"

"A fool's reason. I was led by my own desire to see more of that world. The Place of Winds was a prison. Now that my people have been forced to leave it, it seems incalculably beautiful and precious."

"The Goddess has claimed it. You can never go back."

"And where shall we go, Dark Man? Where shall we find another home?"

"If a ship comes, as Gerrith promised—"

"I am weary of this talk of ships."

Alderyk's wings spread and snapped shut again with a vicious crack. Dust sprang up from the road in a whirling cloud.

Halk laughed. "We are all weary of your ships, Dark Man, and of Gerrith's prophecies. We can trust to nothing now but our own strong hands." The hilt of the great sword glittered in the sun above his left shoulder. He said softly to Stark, "I have not forgotten my pledge to you."

"Nor have I," Stark answered angrily. "How is it that a child can grow so tall?" He strode away, taking his growling, bristling hounds with him.

It was while he scouted ahead with the pack that he received Gerd's warning. *Men!* And a little later he saw the dark mass of them barring the way.

The Ironmaster's folk had gone aside from the direct path to Skeg in search of food. They found a guard station on the Wandsmen's Road and took it. Both men and beasts were there, for these stations on the Lower Road were still maintained, and the Ironmaster was well pleased.

Until the army came upon him.

At first sight of the dust, the shield-wall formed. Women hastily piled human carcasses on the beasts of burden. The Ironmaster stood beneath Strayer's wind-whipped banner, waiting.

The army halted. Stark looked at the banner. At first he did not believe what he saw. But then the glint of dark iron from the rows of shields and caps and breastplates left no doubt.

"Thyrans," he said.

Halk, who had come up with him, reached his two hands to the longsword and brought it singing out of its scabbard.

"I remember them." He lifted the sword high. He shouted to the Islanders and plunged forward.

Stark kicked Halk's feet from under him and knocked him flat with a blow across the back of the neck. *Hold him*, he said to the hounds, and picked up the sword.

The Islanders had begun to move, eager for battle. Stark shouted to the Four Kings, "Call them back!"

Delbane said, "We do not fear their swords and shields."

"There's no need for such haste. Halk has a personal quarrel with these people, who killed his shield-mate. Unless they attack us, let be until I talk to them."

Morn had come up to see what was the matter. Stark spoke to him briefly and he went back to the Iubarians. Then Stark glanced at Halk, lying fire-eyed in the dust with the pack around him, and called to Gerd and Grith. He walked forward toward the Ironmaster.

"The last time we met," said Stark, "was in your house at Thyra, when you sold me and my people to the Wandsmen."

The Ironmaster nodded. He looked at the Northhounds. "We heard that you had stolen the guardians of the Citadel. We did not quite believe." He shrugged, and the hammer symbol lifted on his thick chest. "So. You outnumber us, and you have the death hounds. Still, we can fight." The iron ranks crashed blades on shields. "Or you can let us go on our way peacefully to Skeg."

"What do you hope to find at Skeg?"

"The Wandsman Gelmar. We need a new place to build our forges, beyond reach of the Goddess. He may help us."

"Gelmar is not there. Few are there now except Iubarian women and children." He looked past the Ironmaster and the soldiers to where the laden beasts stood with the arms and legs of their burdens dangling down. "You will understand why we can't permit you to go to Skeg."

"What, then?"

"The Wandsmen's day is done. Come with us to Ged Darod and help finish it."

"We have no quarrel with the Wandsmen. We want—"

"—a place to build your forges. It will have to be on another world, then. You have more metal on your backs than has been seen in the Fertile Belt for a thousand years, and you'll find no city here like Thyra. The Wandsmen can give you nothing."

"That is only your word," said the Ironmaster. "The word of an outlander."

"It is the only word you have," Stark told him. "Join with us, or we will crush you."

The Ironmaster considered. There were many men, and not-men. Archers had moved out to the flanks. A strange machine was being trundled up. Battle now, against these odds, would mean the destruction of his people as an entity, no matter if some of them did survive. He looked up at the banner above him.

"Perhaps it is Strayer's will," he said. "So be it."

"You'll march with me," said Stark, appreciating the simplicity of one-man rule, where no time need be wasted haggling with committees. The Ironmaster spoke, and it was done. "Remember that the Northhounds can hear your thoughts. If there is treachery, you will be the first to die."

The Thyran men, in two parties, were sent out to take point on either side. The Thyran women, their children, and their laden beasts with their grisly burdens—decently covered, for neither the Iubarians nor the Islanders were man-eaters and both considered the habit gross—were placed in the center of the line.

Stark returned the longsword to Halk. Nothing more was said on either side. But Stark put two of the hounds to watch at Halk's back.

The Ironmaster's standard-bearer came with him to Stark's side. The army moved on again—a long, fat, motley-colored snake winding along the dusty road.

"How was it with Hargoth and his people?" asked Stark.

"The Gray Ones had already fled. We never saw them." The Ironmaster shrugged. "Perhaps the Goddess devoured them all."

The long miles fell behind. One by one, the stations were overwhelmed. And on a hot noonday they came to the plain of Ged Darod, where Stark pointed out the roofs of the city a-glitter in the sunlight.

The Four Kings stepped forward beneath the golden Head of Gengan. They knelt and touched the ground with their hands.

Stark looked up sidelong at the rusty blaze of Old Sun. *Your favor was bought dearly*, he said, but only the hounds heard him, and whined. *I hope the taste of her blood was sweet. Be patient, I will give you more.*

The Islanders did what he had known they would do. They broke from the line of march, disdaining orders, forgetting everything but the sight of their ancient home. Like a company of tigers, they bounded out across the plain.

Ashton shouted, "Eric!"

But he was gone, running with the Islanders and the white hounds, leaving the Thyrans and the men of Iubar to follow as they would.

26

THE SUN was hot on his face. He smelled sweat and dust; the animal smell of the Islanders; the coarse, hairy reek of the hounds. He ran, and the sword in his hand was bright.

People scattered from the pilgrim roads. The many-gated walls of Ged Darod rose above the plain, and the gates were open. They were always open. But now the heavy valves were stuttering to and fro. The army had been seen, the order given to shut the gates that had not been shut for centuries. Those within struggled to obey. But from the huddled camps without the walls came panic mobs to push the other way, lest they be barred out and left to the mercy of the foe.

Stark yelled—a high, strange cry that startled even the Islanders, a cry that belonged far away on another world where snouted half-men urged each other on to the kill. The Northhounds bayed, a deep-mouthed sinister belling.

One gate of all the gates, the nearest one, became the focal point of their rush. People were locked there in a single, swaying mass that broke and fragmented before them, shredding away at the edges, falling beneath swords and spears and the killer-minds of the hounds.

No firm resistance was met. One small band of mercenaries fought determinedly but were soon disposed of. The others—Farers, pilgrims, refugees—simply ran. The Islanders had scarcely lost momentum. With great difficulty Stark held them until Ashton and part of his own troop came up, the Thyrans clanking after them, grunting and puffing. The Fallarin had drawn aside with their Tarf to sit out the messy business; there was nothing much they could do in a battle of this kind.

Stark saw that the Iubarians were coming, for once on the double, except for the men who hauled the catapults. He detailed a force of Thyrans to secure the gate and then ran on again with the Islanders—Irnanese and tribesmen at his back and Halk's longsword swinging. The balance of the Ironmaster's force tramped heavily behind, a moving shield-wall bristling with swordpoints.

Pedrallon alone bore no weapon. Himself a Wandsman of high rank before his downfall, this had been his city, where he walked in pride and power. Stark wondered what his thoughts must be as he walked here now, seeing what had happened to Ged Darod.

For much had happened.

Buildings were in flames. Storehouses had been plundered. The temples with their peacock roofs had been sacked, even the golden Sun Temple, where bodies were scattered on the steps. Dead priests and Wandsmen floated in the sacred tank. Ragtag mobs ran this way and that, disorganized gobbets of fear and fury. They did not present much of a threat, but Stark knew that mercenary troops were in Ged Darod, and he wondered why they did not appear.

The stench of the streets rose about them in the heat. Delbane spat and said, "Our land has been defiled."

Darik answered, "It shall be cleansed."

Gerd growled. *Death, N'Chaka. Men fight. Kill.*

Stark nodded. He had already heard the distant voice of war.

Again he restrained the Four Kings, all but beating them back to give the Thyrans time to close up. He felt nervous in the narrow streets, which compressed and diminished his effective force.

He led on toward the roar of the mob, because that was where they had to go.

They came out into the vast square below the Upper City. It was packed with people, a surging multitude that beat like surf against the white cliff that reared above with its rows of small, secret windows. The outer portions of the mob were Farers and refugees, armed with whatever makeshift weapons they could lay their hands on. Up front, and leading the assault, were the mercenaries; and now Stark understood why they had not bothered to defend the city. They were clustered on and around the dais from which the Wandsmen had used to speak to their people, and there were more of them in the tunneled gate above, where ceremonial steps ran upward, out of sight. From deep within this tunnel came the muffled booming of a ram.

"What are these people doing?" asked Delbane.

"That is the sacred enclave of the city. They want to take it."

The mob had begun to turn and face the new threat. The mercenaries, from their higher vantage point, had also become aware of them. Stark saw a sudden flurry of activity around the tunnel mouth. Tough, well-disciplined ranks began to form.

"But we must have it for ourselves," said Delbane. "Is that not so?"

"That is so," Stark answered, looking at the overwhelming mob and the monolithic wall beyond it.

"Well, then . . ." said Delbane. He turned to his brother Kings. "Let us sweep this scum away!"

It was Pedrallon who said, "Wait!"

Something in his voice carried enough conviction to make the Islanders listen. They despised him for his physical weakness, but he was still a red Wandsman and a prince, and the old authority was there. He gestured toward the tunnel.

"No one will gain entrance through that gate. Because of the angle of the steps, a ram is almost useless. They may pound till they drop, but the gate will stand. It would be the same for us. I know another way. The way I used when I had occasion to leave the city unseen."

Stark could hear the Iubarians coming up. Between them and the Thyrans, the besieging force could be contained, and possibly defeated. He gave quick orders to the Ironmaster and then spoke to the Kings.

"We follow Pedrallon."

The Islanders snarled. The mob was upon them and they wanted to fight now. In a moment more they would have no choice, and Stark grasped Delbane by the thong of the golden plaque at his throat.

"Do you want this city, or don't you?"

The fierce eyes stabbed at him. The bone knife in the powerful knotted hand lifted. The hounds clamored warning. Stark silenced them. He twisted the thong tighter.

"Do you want this city?"

The knifepoint lowered. "Yes."

Stark turned and motioned on his troop. They began to run—away from the square.

The mob swayed forward, hurling stones, swinging makeshift weapons. They enveloped the Thyrans, who formed square to protect their flanks and rear and began to crunch forward with their shield-wall. The first Iubarian contingent came up, with some of the tall Ssussminh. Within seconds, the square was a floundering confusion as the disciplined ranks began to push the mob back against the pressure of the advancing mercenaries.

Pedrallon led the way swiftly, by streets that were almost deserted now, toward the Refuge, where the Farer girls came to have their babies and give them to the Wandsmen to rear. The windows of the Refuge were full of anxious faces, and there was a great crying and wailing and clashing of shutters as the troop swept by.

Behind the Refuge, and behind the high hostel where Farers who were past their faring could idle out their last years, the wall of the Inner City bent itself around a shoulder of rock. Storage sheds were built against the rock, and at the back of one of them, hidden from any but the knowing eye, was a narrow door.

Pedrallon took them through it into a night-black passage, a rathole where they must tread in single file, Stark and the tall Irnanese doubled forward under a low roof.

"This is madness," Delbane objected, thinking of his men strung out in a long and useless line. "Will the other end be guarded?"

"The hounds will let us know," said Stark. "Just hurry!" And he asked Pedrallon, "Are there more secret ways like this one?"

"Several. Palace intrigues are not unknown among Wandsmen. Also, there are times when the monastic life becomes too boring, and some things are better done unobserved."

There were no side passages, no fear of losing the way. They shuffled forward at a rapid pace, and then came to steps, steep and winding, that slowed them down. The steps went on until all were breathing hard, and it was a relief to find a level stretch again.

"Softly now," Pedrallon warned, and the long line jarred slowly to a halt, all the way back down the stairs and into the lower passage.

Gerd?

Wandsmen. There. Waiting.

Kill!

Somewhere a man screamed.

Pedrallon fumbled quickly in the dark. A strip of light showed, widened, and became an oblong through which Stark ran with his hounds into a huge chamber filled with dusty boxes, dead furniture, and dying Wandsmen with futile weapons in their hands. The chamber contained no more than a dozen of them, more than enough to hold the narrow doorway against any ordinary force. In any case, they could hardly have believed that anyone would come.

The hounds finished their work quickly. Men poured into the chamber in a steady stream.

"We need room," Halk said. "If they come at us now in any force . . ."

Beyond the chamber was a corridor, stretching away on either hand between rows of doorways. They saw a flickering of robes—blue, green, apprentice gray—where men and boys ran from the intruders or stopped to fight them. But there was only token resistance.

Some of Stark's men were deployed to hold the corridor while the rest of the Islanders caught up. Then the head of his line moved on to a wide doorway, and through that into a cloistered quadrangle where there was more than enough room in which to form their ranks. Wandsmen shouted from the high windows on three sides, and Stark could hear the sounds of the Upper City all around him, stirring and crying like a disturbed aviary.

The cat-footed Islanders formed their companies quickly, rallying to the golden Head. Then they set off again, across the quadrangle and through an arch into a place where three streets came together. All three were narrow, cramped between massive walls. One was short, ending almost at once at the ornate portico of some administrative building. One led steeply downward to the square behind the gate. The third became a flight of steps that swept upward to the Palace of the Twelve.

The square was crowded with Wandsmen, mostly young ones in the lower ranks. A company of mercenaries stood within the gate. From their appearance and accoutrements, they had come from several different troops. Stark could not see how many there were. On the steps of the palace more mercenaries stood on guard, with ranks of Wandsmen behind them.

Stark said to the Four Kings, "There is the gateway to your city. Take it and hold it."

Aud said scornfully, "There is not honor enough there for all of us. What will *you* do?"

"Take the palace."

"Good," said Aud. "Let us go forward."

The mercenaries on the palace steps included a company of bowmen. They commanded the street up which the attackers must move. Aud was for rushing them at once, but Stark restrained him. Delbane, Darik, and Astrane were already pelting down the way to the square. The sharp, clear sounds of strife from beyond the gate were drowned by sharper, clearer sounds from within.

Stark said to Aud, "We'll parley first."

He borrowed a shield from one of the Irnanese and went up the step, his right arm upheld, weaponless.

Halfway up, he stopped and shouted, "There is an army in the Lower City. There is another one here. You fight for a lost cause. Lay down your arms."

The captain of the mercenaries answered, "We have taken gold. We will not betray it."

"You are honorable men," Stark said, "but foolish. Think."

"We have thought," said the captain, and the arrows flew.

Stark crouched behind the shield. Barbed heads thumped on the hard leather. Shafts whistled past him. No sound came from the Islanders, but one of the hounds screamed and cries rang out from among the tribesmen and the Irnanese.

Kill! said Stark to the hounds, and they killed, and the human wolves behind Aud came up the steps with such ferocity that they almost overran Stark, who had taken time to draw his sword.

Another flight of arrows cut into his front ranks, but those behind simply hurdled the bodies without pausing. There was no third flight. The hounds were angry and their eyes blazed like evil moons. The mercenaries fell, and then the Wandsmen; and those who could do so fled back into the palace.

Stark and the Islanders burst in after them. The bone-barbed spears rose and fell. Beautiful carpets and marble walls were stained with blood.

A magnificent staircase rose from the vaulted hall to the upper floors.

Stark found Pedrallon, and asked, "Where is Ferdias?"

Pedrallon pointed to the staircase. "The apartments of the Lords Protector are above, on the next floor."

"Lead!"

Stark half carried Pedrallon up the stair. The hounds raced ahead and he did not care who followed. But Ashton came, and Halk with his handful from Irnan, and Sabak with his Hann tribesmen, and those of the Islanders who were not still busy.

They found halls of many-colored stone, marvelously fretted and carved; windows of pierced work; doors of carved wood with splendid lintels.

Wandsmen of all ranks tried to defend the halls against these wild, bloody, wayworn men and their terrible hounds. But they had lived so long in an ambience of power—unassailable, unthreatened, adored as demigods by their children—that when the unthinkable happened and these same children came howling at their gates, hungry and betrayed, they had no defenses. They had depended always on mercenaries to do for them what disciplinary work was needed among the providers to keep peace and order. Now even the mercenaries, knowing their power was gone, had turned against them. They were as helpless before the wrath of the lawless as monastic communities have always been, and the proud Wandsmen of the palace died like seals under the spears of the barbarian.

Pedrallon pointed to a massive doorway at the end of a long, painted hall and said, "There."

But Gerd said, *N'Chaka. Wandsman. There!*

"There" was a side corridor, and the likeness of the Wandsman Stark received from Gerd's mind was the likeness of Gelmar, who had once been Chief Wandsman of Skeg.

Think he kill.

Who?

Not person. Thing. Strange thing. Not understand. His mind think: voice that speak, kill.

Stark said to Aud, "I want the Lords Protector alive, you understand that?" Then he was off at a flat run, along the hall, into the branching corridor.

He saw the swirl of a red robe as it vanished through a doorway.

There! said Gerd. *Kill?*

Wait . . .

The door was of dark wood, polished and blackened by the passage of centuries. The metal of the latch was cool and smooth, worn by the touching of countless hands. It worked easily. The door swung inward, into a small room with beautiful linen-fold paneling. A table stood against one wall. On it was an ugly, incongruous black box, defiling with its mass-produced dials and verniers the loving handwork of the wood below and behind it.

Gelmar stood before the box, smashing at the perspex dial covers with the iron pommel of a sword.

"They won't break," Stark told him.

Gelmar dealt the plastic one last vicious blow. "May the gods curse all such matters! And all the men who make them!" He turned the sword on Stark.

Let be, said Stark to the angry hounds.

There was little fencing room in the small chamber, but not much was needed. Gelmar was no skilled swordsman; he only wanted with all his heart to kill. Stark parried his first savage rush, surprised at the man's strength. A sharp clash of blades sounded, and then Stark struck the weapon from Gelmar's hand.

"I will not hold the hounds another time," said Stark.

The dark blood that had been in Gelmar's face drained away, leaving it pale and set, the face of a man who has reached the end of his way and knows it. Yet his voice was perfectly steady when he spoke. "The transceiver is of no use to you, in any case. Ferdias has already spoken to the ship. It has left us, and will not return."

27

GERD GROWLED, muttering of lies. But Stark was already reaching for the black box.

"Then why were you so anxious to destroy it?"

Gelmar did not answer.

Aud's Islanders had gone on, but Stark's people had followed him. Now Ashton joined him by the transceiver, as the troop stayed in the hallway, shuffling nervously, awaiting some attack. Soon there began to be terrible sounds not far away. The Northhounds whined, bristling and uneasy.

Wandsmen, N'Chaka.

They did not distinguish individual names, but they knew one Wandsman from another well enough, and they knew Ferdias and the Lords Protector as they knew themselves. Stark understood that these were somewhere close at hand.

There.

"There" was beyond a paneled wall, which showed the outlines of a door.

Stark pointed to it. "Halk. Tuchvar. Take the hounds. I don't trust the Islanders."

"Why so tender of the Lords Protector?" asked Halk.

"They're old men. Besides, Ashton has a use for them."

Halk shrugged and went off through the small door, which revealed a connecting passage. The Irnanese went with him. Tuchvar followed with the hounds, leaving Gerd and Grith, who watched Gelmar with baleful eyes.

The room became very quiet, except for the sounds from the black box, which seemed very loud—and very empty. Only the eternal cross-talk of the universe, having in it nothing of human comfort. Ashton's voice was a monotonous counterpoint as he moved the needle carefully across the shipbands, repeating his name and the emergency code letters, requesting an answer.

There was none.

Gelmar smiled.

Stark asked, "How long ago did you speak to this ship?"

"Three days."

Lies, said Gerd.

"Try again."

Ashton tried again.

The plain of Ged Darod, beyond the walls, held a milling chaos. Where folk had been pouring into the city for weeks, now they poured out of it all at once, dragging wounded, dragging the sick and the old and the very young, dragging burdens of loot. The plain became littered with people and things dropped by the wayside. Streams of folk still incoming along the pilgrim roads collided with the refugees, adding to the chaos as it became apparent that Ged Darod no longer offered any hope.

By the one gate that was solidly held, Sanghalain of Iubar waited with Morn and a guard of Ssussminh. Nearby, the Fallarin also waited, surrounded by the Tarf with their four-handed swords. Alderyk's thin nostrils quivered with disgust at the mingled reeks of unwashed humanity and unlimited filth that the warm breeze brought to him along with the dust and the noise. From time to time he clapped his wings against the breeze, ordering it aside. But the smells did not lessen, nor did the incessant shrieking.

Klatlekt blinked his horny eyelids with the expression of indifference common to his race. His banded torso glistened in the sun. So did the long, broad blade of his sword, which a strong man could not have lifted. He watched the scurryings and cryings on the plain with the incurious contempt he felt for all beings who were not Fallarin.

At length, he saw something in the distance which caused him to raise his round and hairless head even higher. He turned to Alderyk and said, "Lord . . ."

Alderyk looked and saw a great cloud of dust rising on the Wandsmen's Road, coming from the north.

He called Morn and pointed out the cloud. "Get word to Stark, if you can, and warn the Ironmaster and your own captains."

Are these enemies, or are they the allies the wise woman told of?

Alderyk's wings made a small thunderclap. "We'll soon know."

A voice spoke in the room. It was thin against the cracklings and hissings, but it was there.

"Ashton? Simon Ashton? But they told us you were dead."

"Not quite."

"And the other man. Stark."

"Here. They told you I was dead, too."

"Yes. Not more than an hour ago."

Stark glanced at Gelmar, whose face showed nothing. "Ferdias told you that. The Lord Protector."

"Yes. We were forbidden to land, and knowing how touchy the situation is on Skaith . . . Well, with you two gone, we thought we had no reason. We were shifting orbit, preparing to jump. Another twenty minutes and we'd have been gone."

"Hold orbit above Ged Darod," said Ashton, and the sweat was running down his cheeks like tears. He wiped it away. "We're securing the area now. We'll let you know when it's safe to land. Keep open for transmission."

"Understood," the voice said, and was silent.

Ashton turned to his foster-son. They looked at each other, but said nothing. There were no words for what they wanted to say, and in any case they did not need them.

The dustcloud on the Wandsmen's Road halted its forward motion. It bunched up and remained stationary while the dust settled and the leaders took stock of what was happening at Ged Darod. In a little while, Alderyk's falcon gaze was able to distinguish the blocks of color—dull purple, red, white, green, yellow, and brown—all in the faded leather of the Hooded Men, and beyond them a larger mass of green-gold enclosing dark shapes that perched on tall desert beasts like birds poised for flight.

And now the wings of the Fallarin set up a wild whirlwind that rose high above the plain in dusty greeting.

The six old men in white—Gorrel was dead at last and there had not been time to fill his place—sat in the lofty chamber where the casements opened onto the beauty of the temple roofs and the chiming of the bells. Sounds of bitter strife now marred the sweetness of that chiming, and a pall of smoke had dimmed the brightness of Old Sun.

Five red Wandsmen stood by the Lords Protector. The remainder of the Twelve had died defending their lords, and some of the five were wounded. The room and its antechamber were choked with bodies, chiefly in the red robes of high office, but with many others in green and blue and even one in apprentice gray, a boy not yet bearded. It was here that the Wandsmen had made their final stand. Now the naked Islanders kicked the bodies aside to make standing room, and stared with their small, fierce eyes at the men and hounds who held them from further killing.

The hounds grumbled and whined and drooped their great, rough heads. They remembered the mists and snows of Worldheart, where they had served these six old men with their lives.

Pedrallon asked, "Where is Llandric?"

"It was necessary to find your transceiver," said Ferdias. "He did not survive the questioning."

His back was as rigid as ever, his iron composure unshaken, at least on the surface. He regarded the Islanders with disgust. For the others, his bitter loathing was more complex, and for Stark he had a look that was quite indescribable. Nevertheless, he betrayed neither weakness nor fear.

Pedrallon's anger was obvious. "You murdered him. You allowed hundreds of your people to die. And even with your last citadel besieged by your starving children, you sent away the ship that might have brought them help."

"This is a time of change," said Ferdias. "A Second Wandering. Without traitors, we would have survived it. Without traitors, this last citadel of ours would not have fallen. We would have brought peace and order to the world as we did before. A smaller world, it is true, but *our* world, Mother Skaith, untainted by the ways of strangers."

He turned to Stark. "For some reason which is obscure to me, we seem to have lost the favor of her we tried to protect." He paused, and then added simply, "We are ready to die."

"That was in my mind," Stark said, "but Ashton is wiser than I."

Ferdias turned with frosty courtesy to Simon Ashton, who had been his prisoner for months in the Citadel in the High North.

"The Lords Protector will come with us, in the ship," said Ashton. "Nothing else can better prove to the people that a new time has come to Skaith."

"They will know that we have been forced. They will hate the off-worlders even more."

"Not when food and medical supplies begin to arrive. You can plead your cause before the Council at Pax, of course, but I hardly think that the idea of condemning half your population to death rather than letting them emigrate, simply to perpetuate your own rule, will gain you much applause. You can still help your people, by using your special knowledge to help us in organizing the distribution of food and the mass transportation of those peoples who wish to leave Skaith."

Ferdias was amazed. "Surely you do not expect our help!"

"Damn it!" Ashton roared, in sudden fury. "Somebody has got to feed these infants you've created. More than enough of them are going to die anyway, thanks to you."

Unperturbed, Ferdias said, "Suppose that we refuse to go. Will you turn us over to *them?*" He nodded at the sweating Islanders.

"Oh, no," said Stark, smiling. "Not to them. To your own people, Ferdias. To your starving children."

Ferdias inclined his head.

"I take it you're requesting asylum," Ashton said.

Ferdias looked away. And now at last the rigid line of his shoulders had crumpled, just a little. "Our own storehouses are empty," he said. "We gave them all we had. But they would not believe."

28

With the coming of the army from the north, the battle for Ged Darod was soon over. The Islanders held the Upper City, and presently the surviving Wandsmen were joining the fugitive masses on the plain, stripping off their robes and casting away their wands of office, not wishing to be known.

Much of the crowded Lower City was burning, and nothing much could be done about that. Patrols went through the streets that were still passable, rounding up, mopping up. They were assisted in this by the mercenary troops, who had decided to change sides as a simple matter of common sense. Kazimni of Izvand, for once, had more than wounds to show for his trouble, having been among the first with his men at the sacking of the temples.

The patrols overlooked a narrow cul-de-sac beside the Temple of the Dark Goddess, which had been set ablaze by a long-haired girl who sat contemplative in the hot wind of her own creating. The faint traces of body paint were gone from her skin. The bones showed through it, and her hair was matted. Her eyes, like her soul, were now completely empty. Wendor had abandoned her, but that did not greatly disturb her. It was the custom among Farers. She had lost her faith in the immutable power of the Lords Protector. She was unable to imagine a world without them, and she had no wish to live in one.

The Dark Man had destroyed her. She could still see his face, strange and wonderful and frightening. She could still feel his touch. Perhaps Wendor had been right, and she did love him. She did not know. She was very tired. Much too tired to move, even when the flames of the burning temple swept around her.

Within twenty-four hours, the situation on the plain had been stabilized. Most of the able-bodied had fled south, where they had at least a chance of finding food. Those who could not run were gathered into camps under Sanghalain's care. Large bodies of Iubarians and Ssussminh started back for Skeg. Eventually all would return there, to hold the fisheries and control what would once again become a star-port.

The tribesmen and the Fallarin proposed to follow, but Alderyk himself would now lead his delegation to Pax. Morn and the Lady of Iubar would go, as before, with Pedrallon and Sabak and other leaders of the Hooded Men, including one of the last of the Ochar. The Ironmaster, having touched and felt and tasted of the soil of Ged Darod, which was barren of ore, announced that he, too, would look for a new forge-place among the stars.

Reluctantly, Kazimni also volunteered for the ship. Somewhere there might be another Sea of Skorva, where his people could build another Izvand in the clean coldness that kept a man strong.

Tuchvar stroked his hounds. He had grown older and leaner since Stark first found him in the kennels at Yurunna, but he could still weep, and he wept now. "I would go with you, Stark. But I am Houndmaster now. I can't leave them. I'll find a place somewhere, an island, where they can do no harm to anyone, and where they can live out their lives in peace. Perhaps then I can follow you to the stars."

"Of course," said Stark, and knew that he would not. Gerd and Grith pressed close against him. "These two I will take with me, Tuchvar. They would not consent to stay behind." He paused. "Only keep them for me now. I have one more thing to do."

And he left them, protesting, to join Ashton in the Palace of the Twelve, which was now the Palace of the Four Kings.

Ashton was speaking again to the captain of the starship. "You may land at your convenience."

"You're on the dark side now. We'll land at dawn."

"We'd appreciate any rations you can spare."

"I've already checked on that. It won't be much, but it may help. Oh, by the way . . . I think you and Stark will be pleased to know that Penkawr-Che and his raiders were intercepted by GU cruisers off the Hercules Cluster. They put up quite a running fight, but the cruisers had the weight. Penkawr-Che was among the casualties."

"Thank you," said Ashton.

Stark was glad, but in a remote way. The weariness of all the long months on Skaith were superimposed now on the briefer but more acute weariness of battle and sleepless hours. The joy of victory was shadowed by the pain which had left him since the flames on Iubar's tower top rose up to warm Old Sun.

He turned to one of the Irnanese who stood guard over the transceiver.

"Find Halk," he said. "I will wait for him in the quadrangle."

Lamps burned in the cloisters and the Three Ladies shone above. There was light enough. The night was warm. The city was quiet, the air tainted heavily with smoke from the fires that smoldered below the wall.

Halk came. The hilt of the great sword stood up over his left shoulder, gleaming.

"I don't see your guardians, Dark Man."

"They're with Tuchvar. They've been ordered not to harm you, if you kill me."

Halk reached up and stroked the smooth, worn metal of the hilt. "But what if *you* kill *me*, Dark Man? Who will gather the people of Irnan together to wait for the ships?" He brought the blade up out of the sheath, then thrust it back again with a ringing clash. "I have much to do. Too much to be risked for the pleasure of cleaving your head from your body. Besides, I think you have taken a deeper wound than any I could give you. I leave you with it."

He turned and strode away across the quadrangle, into the dark.

The last of the Three Ladies sank in the west. It was the moonless time when sleep came heaviest, but Hargoth the Corn-King could not sleep. His people were camped in the hills above a wide plain whereon a city was burning. He did not wish to go near the city, having a distaste for that kind of violence. But when he cast the finger-bones, the Spring Child pointed inexorably toward the smoke.

Hargoth felt at once afraid and excited. The blood quivered within his meager flesh. He stood quite still, waiting, without knowing what he was waiting for, knowing only that when it came, much would be changed forever.

The dark time passed. Old Sun poured forth his libation of molten brass over the eastern horizon. The folk of the Towers began to stir, and Hargoth motioned them to silence. His eyes were fixed upon the sky, pale and bright behind his mask.

There was first a sound, terrifying, heart-stopping, magnificent. The brazen sky was torn apart with sound, and a great shape came dropping down, riding a pillar of fire with majestic ease. Hammers beat against Hargoth's ears and the ground shook beneath his feet. Then flame and thunder died and the ship stood tall upon the plain of Ged Darod, looking even in that moment of rest as though it merely gathered itself to leap again toward the stars.

"Up," said Hargoth to his people. "Up and march. The long wait is over, and the star-roads lie before us."

He led his people down from the hills, singing the Hymn of Deliverance.

Stark heard the chanting. He looked toward the long gray line, and sent word swiftly that there was to be no attack. While stores were unloaded from the ship and the passengers began to embark—the willing and the unwilling, with Gelmar among the red robes that went to serve the white—Stark went with his two hounds to meet the Corn-King.

"You see?" he said. "I was the true Deliverer, after all. Will you come into the ship?"

"No," said Hargoth. "Until all my people can go, I stay with them. But I will send two of my priests to speak for us." He gestured, and two of the lean, gray men stepped forward. Then he glanced again at Stark. "What of the sun-haired woman?"

"The prophecy you made at Thyra was a true one," Stark said.

He walked back to the ship with the priests beside him and the two hounds at his heels.

Ashton was waiting for him in the airlock. They went together into the ship and the outer hatch clanged shut. In a little while, the flame and thunder shook the air again and set the ground a-tremble. The shining hull sprang upward into the sky.

Old Sun watched it with a dull, uncomprehending eye until it disappeared.

GUIDE TO CHARACTERS AND LOCALE

THE BACKGROUND

SKAITH, dying planet of a dying star far out in the Orion Spur. Knowledge of the inevitable demise of their world has colored every facet of life for the people of Skaith, giving rise to many strange religions and customs. Over the centuries, different groups have sought salvation in different ways.

Some preferred, through controlled genetic mutation—a science now long lost—to worship a chosen deity with their whole being, as:

THE CHILDREN of the SEA-OUR-MOTHER, who have returned to the primal womb whence all life sprang, losing their humanity in the process, and with it their understanding of the coming doom;

THE CHILDREN of SKAITH-OUR-MOTHER, who worship their equivalent of the Earth-Mother, dwelling deep within her warm, protective body, safe from the creeping death Outside;

THE FALLARIN, who wanted wings, the better to adore their dying lord, the Sun. In them, however, the mutation was imperfect—they have wings but cannot really fly. In compensation, they have become brothers to the winds, with power to call upon the currents of the air to do their bidding. They are served by

THE TARF, who are genetic mutations from nonhuman stock;

THE NORTHHOUNDS, genetically mutated animals bred as guardians of the Citadel. They are telepaths, and kill by destroying human minds with fear. Stark became their leader at the Citadel.

The above are relatively small groups. Most of the other survivors of the Wandering—that time of chaos when the great cities of the

north were abandoned to the cold—have adapted to existing conditions and lead not-uncomfortable lives in the Fertile Belt, though strange survivals still exist in the Barrens and in the Darklands of the north (such as the Harsenyi, a tribe of northern nomads, message-bearers between various groups, and the Outdwellers, a strange far-northern people given to cannibalism). The productive section of the population has been harnessed to the support of the largest body of doom-worshipers,

THE FARERS, who, feeling that all effort is useless because there is no future for Skaith, spend their lives in faring from place to place as the mood takes them, filling their hours with the gratifications of the moment, secure in the knowledge that they will be fed, housed, clothed, and cared for by the authority of

THE WANDSMEN, whose rule brought stability out of chaos after the Wandering, but who, after two thousand years or so, have become onerous to many, as their original plan, which was to protect the weak from the strong, to feed the hungry, and to shelter the homeless, has become warped by time and the necessities of power into a serfdom under which the providers labor. The Wandsmen enforce their laws by the use of mercenary troops. The Wandsmen's superiors, or "officers," are

THE LORDS PROTECTOR, a council of seven old men drawn from the highest ranks of the Wandsmen, chosen for their wisdom and ability. These are regarded almost as deities by the Farers, and since their rule has been unbroken and their individual personalities always hidden from the vulgar gaze, they are thought to be immortal.

Skaith, in her heyday, despite advanced technology, scientific knowledge, and industrial might, never developed space-flight, so that when she began her long dying, depleted of resources and her people slipping back into barbarism, there was no chance of escape for anyone—until the starships came. Then the poison of hope began to work, and the lines of battle were drawn between the entrenched power of the Wandsmen and the rebels who have demanded freedom to emigrate to a better world.

THE PLACES

THE CITADEL, a half-legendary retreat of the Lords Protector, in the High North. Destroyed by the off-worlder Stark.

GED DAROD, holy city of the Wandsmen, a place of pilgrimage, seat of their temporal power.

IRNAN, a city-state in the north temperate zone. Here Gerrith, the wise woman, made her prophecy of the Dark Man from the stars who would destroy the Lords Protector and set her people free. For this she was slain by the Wandsmen. The Irnanese were prime movers in the fight for emigration.

TREGAD, a similar city-state, sometime ally of Irnan.

SKEG, a seaport and formerly the location of the one and only starport, until that was burned by order of the Wandsmen and the starships banished forever from Skaith.

YURUNNA, a northern base of the Wandsmen, where the Northhounds were bred. Captured by Stark with a coalition of desert tribesmen and Fallarin.

THYRA, a place south of and near the Witchfires, where a race of smiths reclaim iron from the rusting bones of a great ruined city.

THE TOWERS, another ruin, where the People of the Towers dwell in the northern cold and darkness, awaiting the coming of the starships.

IZVAND, a city by the Sea of Skorva in the Barrens. It is inhabited by a hardy people: fisherfolk and mercenary soldiers.

ANDAPELL, a principality in the tropic zone of the Fertile Belt.

IUBAR, a principality in the White South, with a close bond to the sea and sea-faring, and to the neighboring Ssussminh.

THE WHITE ISLANDS, the half-legendary abode of the Kings of the White Islands, deep in the frozen wilderness of the far south.

PAX, the hopefully named administrative center of the Galactic Union, a vast and far-flung confederation of worlds totally unknown to Skaith before the starships came. Pax is both a world and a city—a city so vast that it covers an entire planet. Pax contains closed-environment quarters to suit the needs of delegates, human and otherwise, from all the federated worlds; and it is to Pax that delegates must come from those *un*federated worlds, such as Skaith, which seek to join the Union.

THE PLACE of WINDS, home of the Fallarin, isolated in the northern desert.

THE WITCHFIRES, a mountain range in the north, beneath which the Children of Skaith dwell in the House of the Mother.

THE THERMAL PITS, spoutings of underground hot water, south of the Bleak Mountains.

THE BLEAK MOUNTAINS, in the High North, location of the Wandsmen's Citadel.

THE PLAIN of WORLDHEART, flat region south of the Thermal Pits and north of the Witchfires.

THE DARKLANDS, a forested, danger-filled area north of Izvand and the Sea of Skorva and south of the Witchfires.

THE PEOPLE

ERIC JOHN STARK, called also N'Chaka, Man-Without-a-Tribe. A feral child reared by half-human aborigines in a cruel environment on the planet Mercury; in his mature years, a wanderer and mercenary specializing in the small wars of remote peoples fighting for survival against stronger opponents.

SIMON ASHTON, Stark's foster-father and friend, an official in the Ministry of Planetary Affairs at Pax. When Ashton disappeared on Skaith, Stark came to search for him.

YARROD, a martyr of Irnan, slain by the Wandsmen.

GERRITH, daughter of the slain Gerrith, who succeeded her as wise woman of Irnan.

HALK, Yarrod's companion-in-arms, an unwilling ally of Stark.

BRECA, Halk's shield-mate, slain at Thyra.

ALDERYK, King of the Fallarin, companion of Stark.

KLATLEKT, a Tarf, loyal servant-in-arms to Alderyk.

SABAK, leader of the desert tribesmen who followed Stark south.

TUCHVAR, former apprentice to the Houndmaster of Yurunna, follower of Stark, devoted to his hounds.

BAYA, a Farer girl who betrayed Stark and then was captured by him. Freed by the Wandsmen, she again sought to destroy Stark at Tregad.

FERDIAS, chief of the Lords Protector, Stark's bitter enemy.

GELMAR, Chief Wandsman of Skeg, a bitter enemy also.

PEDRALLON, a Wandsman of high rank and prince of Andapell, in the tropics. A champion of emigration, he was punished as a traitor by his peers.

KELL à MARG, Skaith-Daughter, ruler of the Children of Skaith-Our-Mother.

THE IRONMASTER, ruler of the smiths of Thyra.

HARGOTH the CORN-KING, ruler, with his sorcerer-priests, of the People of the Towers.

SANGHALAIN, Lady of Iubar, a principality in the White South.

MORN, leader of the Ssussminh, an amphibian race closely allied to the House of Iubar.

KAZIMNI of IZVAND, a mercenary captain.

PENKAWR-CHE, a star-captain who made arrangements with Pedrallon and Stark to transport a delegation from Skaith to Pax in order to plead for membership in the Galactic Union. Penkawr-Che then betrayed his trust, held his passengers to ransom, and in company with two other ships has seized the opportunity to loot Skaith.

NORVERANN, matriarch of the People of the Heath, a folk adapted to a seasonal life-cycle like the flora and fauna of the wilderness area they inhabit; so much so that they have become a part of the mystic body of the heath, sensitive to every change in the environment. Norverann's son,

THE BRIDEGROOM, will be sacrificed in due course to his Bride, the daughter of the Dark Goddess whom they worship.

DELBANE
DARIK
ASTRANE
AUD, kings of the White Islands, descended from the four Sons of Gengan.

GENGAN, the leader who, after the Wandering, brought his defeated and dispossessed people to the cruel haven of the southern ice.